ALSO BY LINDSEY HUTCHINSON

The Workhouse Children
The Lost Sisters
The Orphan Girl

The Wives' Revenge

LINDSEY LIVES in Shropshire with her husband and dog. She loves to read and has recently discovered photography. Lindsey is the daughter of million-copy bestselling author Meg Hutchinson.

Lindsey HUTCHINSON

The Wives' Revenge

An Aria Book

This is an Aria book, first published as an ebook in 2017 by Head of Zeus

This edition first published in the UK in 2018 by Head of Zeus

9 7 5 3 1 2 4 6 8

A CIP catalogue record for this book is available from
the British Library.

ISBN (HB): 9781788542005
ISBN (E): 9781786692528

Typeset by Divaddict Publishing Solutions Ltd

Printed and bound in Germany by CPI Books GmbH

Head of Zeus Ltd
5–8 Hardwick Street
London ECIR 4RG

WWW.HEADOFZEUS.COM

I think women are foolish to pretend they are equal to men,
They are far superior and always have been!
William Golding

The Wives' Revenge

One

On 20th June 1887 all children had been given a day off school in order to mark Queen Victoria's Golden Jubilee, celebrating the fiftieth year of her accession to the throne.

Primrose Berry from up the street, the girl Violet Clancy hated with a vengeance, had come to play in Violet's yard and had cornered the cat from next door in the backyard. The yard was a dumping ground for anything Violet's mother, Kath, couldn't find a home for but now Primrose was using it as her own arena. Primrose had the cat by the scruff of the neck and Violet knew its suffering was imminent. Picking up a small stick that lay nearby, Primrose stabbed it into the cat's eye. With an ungodly screech, the cat took off with the stick poking from its eye socket.

Violet's mother appeared on the back doorstep shouting, 'What's going on out here?'

Giving Violet a quick vindictive smile and before Violet could speak Primrose burst into tears and sobbed, 'Violet hurt the cat!'

'Bloody hell, Violet, what you done now?' Kath Sligo was

interrupted by a banging on the front door. Kath turned to answer the door. Primrose had a vindictive glint in her eye as she looked at the shocked girl in front of her.

Violet heard the neighbour's voice, 'Your bloody daughter has maimed my cat! I'll have the coppers on you; you see if I don't!'

The front door slammed and Kath reappeared on the back step. 'Primrose, you get yourself off home now, wench.'

With an evil grin, Primrose tossed her golden ponytail in Violet's direction, her blue eyes flashing a warning as she left via the side gate. Violet's heart sank knowing she would be getting the blame for the beastly thing Primrose had done.

Kath was on her daughter before the gate had closed, grabbing her dark plaits and dragging her into the house. 'Why? What makes you do such awful things?' Kath threw Violet into a chair and stood over her daughter, with her arms crossed across her chest.

'I didn't do it, Mum!' Violet wailed as she felt the slap sting her cheek.

'Get to bed,' Kath puffed, 'and wait 'til your father gets home!'

Defiance swelled in her as Violet slammed the door. 'He's not my father!' she yelled back, taking the stairs two at a time. Lying on her bed, Violet resolved to run away if that man ever came into her room again.

Time passed as Violet lay on her bed in the tiny two-up, two-down house. Every couple of houses which lined both sides of Hobbins Street had an entry which led to a side gate at the back. The rows of houses all looked the same in the small town of Wednesbury, a layer of grime from the foundries and factories coating them all. The pall of smoke lay heavy in the air, giving the town a look and feel of being constantly in the shade. The houses had two rooms upstairs and a tiny living room and kitchen on the ground floor. Some had managed to put a lean-to scullery on the end of the kitchen. The lavatory was housed in a small brick building at the end of the yard.

Laying there on her bed, the aroma of cooking reached Violet's nose. Her stomach growled but she knew there'd be no tea for her that night.

Violet waited, knowing he would be home soon. The man her mother had married not too long after her birth father had been killed in a cave-in at the Monway Colliery. Her dad, Harry Clancy, a gentle soul who would help anyone; his soft voice never raised in anger. He taught her from his books, history, geography – all the countries of the world; all the seas and rivers. He shared stories of mythical beasts in wondrous lands.

Violet remembered the warm summer nights sitting on the back doorstep with her father pointing out the stars. The Plough, he would tell her, and, look, there's Orion's Belt. She recalled, when she was small, the time they played cowboys and Indians and her father had used her mum's rouge to paint his face. Violet smiled as she also remembered the scolding he'd received from her mother for wasting good cosmetics.

Violet's thoughts wandered freely down memory lane as a picture of her father formed in her mind. Harry was always smiling. No matter the trials and tribulations he had to face, the ever-present grin never diminished. Coming home from the coal pit covered from head to toe in coal dust, he would smile as he saw his little girl. White teeth shone from his blackened face and he would chatter away to his daughter while Kath heated pans of water for his wash down. Her dad, who she missed dreadfully. Silent tears ran down her cheeks as she wished him back with her once more.

Hearing voices downstairs, Violet knew *he* was home from the coal pit. Why couldn't he have died instead of her dad! This man was so different from her real father in every way. Heavy footfalls on the stairs heralded his arrival outside her bedroom. Without knocking, he flung the door open and stepped inside, kicking the door shut with his foot.

'Right,' he said, 'your mother tells me...'

'I didn't do it! I wouldn't!' Violet interrupted his sentence, her anger beginning to bubble up.

She watched him pace the small box room. Mr John Sligo, the man her mother tried to get her to call 'father' but in her heart she knew he would never be that to her. He stood six feet tall, with dark hair even without the coal dust that peppered it. His eyes were almost black, sinister-looking as they gazed at her on the bed. He was well-muscled given his work of digging the coal from the pits, and was renowned for having a bad temper especially when he was drunk.

The men he drank with on a Friday night disliked him, Violet knew. John Sligo never bought a drink she'd heard the women in the market say, he was always making some excuse as to why he shouldn't. Violet's family were never invited to anything going on in the town anymore because the women hated Sligo even more than the men, and it was the women, behind the scenes of course, who ran things in the town.

The town of Wednesbury stood midway between the larger towns of Birmingham and Wolverhampton on a trajectory that sliced through the Black Country, so called because of the heavy black smoke belched out from the factories and furnaces day after day. No amount of cleaning could completely erase the layer of soot from domestic chimneys in constant use, even in the summer.

Standing before Violet, John shouted, 'You callin' your mother a liar, girl?'

Girl! She had a name but he never used it.

'No!' she gasped in utter disbelief. 'But I swear I didn't hurt that cat!'

'Well who did?' John asked, a touch of sarcasm creeping into his voice. 'Oh don't tell me, it were young Primrose! Sweet kid like that? I don't bloody think so!'

John stood legs astride and hands on hips as he glared at Violet.

'Primrose did do it, I saw her!' Violet said sharply.

Half turning away from her, John said quietly, 'We'll sort this out later, I'm going to have my tea first.' With a nasty grin, not too dissimilar from Primrose's, he left her room and padded down the stairs.

Violet breathed a sigh of relief, although she knew in her heart that this wouldn't be the end of the matter; he didn't believe her, neither did her mother.

If I get a thrashing for this, I'll get you Primrose Berry!

An hour or so later, Violet heard the back door slam shut. Closing her eyes, she prayed it was Sligo who had gone out.

Her prayer went unanswered as moments later he burst into her room once more.

Violet winced as he removed his large buckled leather belt and she knew what was coming next.

'You hurt me again and I swear I'll tell Mother this time!' Violet's bravado was superficial however and it quickly turned to fear as she saw him raise his belt and sneer at her.

Panic rising Violet tried to scramble away from him. The belt caught her across the back and she screamed. Grabbing her hair, John dragged her across the bed before unbuttoning his moleskin trousers.

'I... I'll tell... I swear!' Violet said to him as she watched the evil grin spread across his face. She tried desperately to get away from him but there was nowhere to go. She was trapped.

'Who's gonna believe you?' he smirked. 'Everyone knows that you're a liar, a troublemaker.' He advanced on Violet, pinning her to the bed. Snatching her knickers down then pulling them off, he prised open her legs before pushing himself into her. Violet cried out loudly and screamed for him to get off her, but she knew he wouldn't... not yet, not until he'd finished as he had the last time. Pulling away, he spurted over her, leaving her feeling disgusted and dirty.

Violet scrambled away to the corner of the bed, and curling into a ball she snarled her hatred. She determined he would not see her cry, and her eyes shot fire as she watched him.

'Let that be a lesson to you, girl!' he said as he fastened his trousers. Swinging his belt in his hand, John Sligo left her bedroom with a smile on his face.

As soon as he was gone, Violet got up and poured water from the jug into the bowl standing on the dresser and scrubbed herself until she was sore. Sitting on the end of the bed, she sobbed her misery. She wanted so much to tell her mother what John had done, but how? What could she say? Would her mother believe her or would she think her daughter was making it up? Maybe John's words were true that everyone thought she was a liar. One thing she was sure of, she could not stay in this house much longer.

Violet cried quietly long into the night, and when at last

the tears stopped, she thought hard about what to do about her situation and... Primrose Berry.

*

The next morning, Violet trudged up Hydes Lane and out across the waste ground to Mesty Croft School, having not eaten the night before, with only a slice of bread and margarine in her hand. Munching the bread, she formulated her plan. She was going to paste Primrose Berry today!

In class, everyone stared at her and she knew little Miss Berry had relayed the story of the cat to them all... making Violet out to be the villain of the piece. Judging by the glare from the teacher, she had obviously heard the same tale.

Head held high, Violet took out her books, slamming the desk lid down, and waited for the lesson to start.

At the end of the school day, Violet followed Primrose out of the school gate and quietly stalked her down Moore Street. Primrose stopped every now and then to pick the wild flowers growing in the hedge unaware of the shadow following her, until they reached the end of the street which opened out onto the small patch of heath. They would have to cross there to get to their houses and Violet thought... now, before she gets too far!

Dropping her bag, Violet leapt on Primrose's back; grabbing the girl's hair, she yanked hard. Primrose stumbled, grazing her knees, and her pretty yellow dress gained a few grass stains. Violet pummelled Primrose with her fists as the girl cried her apology.

'I'm sorry, Violet! Stop... stop it! I said I'm sorry!'

Violet's diatribe came through clenched teeth as she punched Primrose with all her might. 'You lying little bitch!'

Violet huffed, 'You hurt that cat and blamed me! I had a hiding for something I didn't do! So... if your mother won't punish you... I will!' With that, Violet let fly a kick.

Looking at the sobbing girl at her feet, she leaned over and said acerbically, 'I warn you now, Primrose Berry... don't you ever mess with me again!'

Grabbing her bag, Violet left Primrose snivelling as she lay in the grass. Then she walked home, wondering how long it would take before Mrs Berry was knocking on their door.

A melange of feelings surrounding her, Violet guessed she would have to take what was coming to her. However, as she neared home, she thought, No, I don't have to take it anymore. Violet determined she would not take any more slaps from her mother and certainly no more abuse from John Sligo!

Two

What was wrong with Violet? Rolling out the pastry for the pie for tea, Kath Sligo's thoughts ran over themselves. She knew Violet hated John, and God knows he had no time for her daughter, but she didn't understand what got into Violet at times.

She recalled the time John had told her he'd taken his belt to Violet over something or other, which had caused a dreadful row between them. It had happened when Kath had been out at one of her friend's houses. She'd told him in no uncertain terms it was up to her to discipline her daughter, not him. She had threatened to throw him out if he ever tried it again. As far as she was aware, John had left Violet alone since then.

Lining the bowl with the pastry, her thoughts remained with her daughter. Violet missed Harry Clancy, her real father, Kath knew, but if only she'd try with John.

She recalled, as a widow, how she had worried herself sick at the possibility of having no money coming in and the threat of poverty hanging over her and her daughter. The prospect of ending up in the workhouse had terrified her. That was until the money came through from Harry's solicitor after his death. Then she'd had the opportunity to marry John Sligo. She shuddered as she thought how Violet had reacted to the marriage. Her daughter had sulked for what seemed forever. Refusing to speak or even acknowledge her new stepfather. Kath knew then in her heart Violet would never accept John Sligo, if anything they had grown further apart.

Putting meat and potato into the pastry, her mind continued its train of thought.

Violet used to be such a good girl... until the cave-in at the colliery. After the funeral of Harry, Kath had watched Violet become withdrawn; it was to be expected, of course, as they had been very close. Kath felt a pang of jealousy rise at the thought. She *was* jealous of the relationship father and daughter had shared; Harry had doted on his daughter... but not nearly so much on Kath herself.

Stopping what she was doing, she looked down at her clothes. Then walking to the small mirror hung on the wall, she gazed at her reflection. Her dark hair was scraped back into a bun at the nape of her neck; her brown eyes stared back at her, no joy held within them. She was still attractive, she thought, but she was a little thin. Her skin was smooth and held no wrinkles which she felt were the road map of life.

Striding back to the table, she put the pie in the oven then cleared the mess and again a myriad of thoughts engulfed her. John had taken them on after Harry's death. Yes, he liked a drink on a Friday night, as did the other miners, but he always ensured there was housekeeping money.

Kath's thoughts moved to the bedroom and John's roughness with her... so different to Harry. Kath felt a shudder rattle her underweight frame. Why did she put up with it? She put up with it because he had control of Harry's money which had reverted to him on their marriage.

Violet. Kath wondered how she could make life easier for her daughter. Violet never confided in her, never told her anything. She had no idea what went on in that girl's brain. She loved her daughter with all her heart, but Violet could make it so difficult for her to show it. Violet was unhappy, and Kath knew she was to blame for that. Her husband and her daughter were always at odds, and Kath was stuck in the middle, constantly refereeing their disagreements. She made up her mind to try to make Violet's life a happier one somehow.

Speak of the devil, Kath thought as Violet walked in through the kitchen door.

'Hello, love, how are you?'

'All right, what's for tea? I'm starving!'

Kath watched as Violet snatched a piece of carrot from the chopping board.

'Pie and vegetables... roast potatoes.' Kath gave her a smile. She watched her daughter as she skipped from the room, returning shortly afterward having changed out of her school clothes.

Kath tried to instigate a conversation by asking about her day at school and watched the darkness settle on the young features as Violet mumbled something then disappeared into the back yard.

So, school today had not gone well... Something had happened, but what? Kath sighed, she felt sure she'd find out soon enough.

As John, Violet and Kath sat eating their meal later that evening, the front door knocker rapped three times. John threw Kath a look as she stood to go and answer the door. Violet kept her head down.

Mrs Berry stood before Kath on the front step, holding Primrose by the hand.

'Mrs Sligo,' she began, 'look at what your daughter has done to my Primrose!'

Kath watched Mrs Berry turn the child this way and that, revealing cuts and grazes. She saw the bump on Primrose's head and her eye beginning to turn a nasty shade of blue.

'Mrs Berry…' But before Kath could continue, the woman interrupted.

'Don't you "Mrs Berry" me!' The cadence in her voice would no doubt be alerting the neighbours that a 'show' was in the offing. 'Look at the state of my Primrose and it's all your daughter's fault!'

'Mrs Berry…' Kath tried again, 'won't you step inside?'

'I'm not stepping inside that pigsty you call home,' the woman rasped, 'and my Primrose will have nothing more to do with your Violet! That girl should be ashamed of herself, and you also as her mother!' Mrs Berry turned on her heel and stalked away dragging Primrose behind her.

Kath stood and watched them walk away before closing the door quietly. Waiting a moment, she tried to gather her thoughts. *If John hears about this, he won't be happy*, she conceded. It would cause yet another row between them. Feeling sure God had deserted her, Kath walked back to the kitchen table and sat down to finish her meal, her appetite now had all but vanished.

John was not at the table when Kath returned and she raised her eyebrows in question.

'He's in the privy,' Violet tilted her head towards the back yard.

Just then he walked back into the kitchen.

'Who was that?' John asked.

Violet's eyes looked up with pleading in them. She'd heard who had been at the door… and why.

'Mrs Berry,' Kath said, looking at Violet. She saw the crushed feeling settle over Violet as the girl pushed her empty plate away.

'Oh aye? What did that stuck-up bitch want?' John asked, piling more food into his already full mouth.

'Nothing much.' Kath's mind worked fast to find an excuse to avoid John getting angry. John looked at her his fork halfway to his mouth, questions in his eyes. 'She just wondered if Violet wanted to go and play with Primrose. I said she couldn't as I wanted her to do a few chores.'

John harrumphed and continued to eat.

Violet and Kath watched each other over the table, warning showing in Kath's eyes, grateful thanks in Violet's.

Washed and changed after dinner, John took off for the Old Barrel Inn on the Holyhead Road and Kath decided now was the time to approach the subject of Primrose.

Sitting Violet at the table after the dishes were washed and put away, she said, 'You know why Mrs Berry came calling don't you?'

Violet nodded.

'Did you give Primrose a hiding today?'

Violet nodded again.

'Why?' Trying to keep her voice calm and quiet, Kath looked at her daughter across the table.

Looking back, Violet's eyes blazed their anger. 'She hurt that cat, Mum, then blamed me for it!'

'Violet…' Kath started, but Violet cut her off.

'Oh I know you don't believe me, but it's the truth! She

stabbed the cat in the eye with a stick! What a wicked, cruel thing to do!'

Kath watched Violet's eyes brim with tears and suddenly the thought struck her that Violet might actually be telling the truth.

'Why did you not tell me this before?' Kath asked.

'I did, but you and *he*,' Violet spat out the last word, 'didn't give me much of a chance!'

Kath saw the anger building in the small body of her young daughter and said, 'I'm sorry. Violet, but...'

'No, Mum!' Violet spat vehemently, 'I don't want to hear it! I always get the blame for everything that goes wrong. I've had enough of it!'

Reaching her hand across the table, Kath said, 'What do you mean, Violet?'

Anger swelling in her, Violet shouted at her mother as she stood, pushing the chair back with her legs. 'You two! The pair of you! You never believe anything I say, that's supposing you give me time to speak! Well, I've had enough of you smacking me and his...' Stopping herself, Violet looked at her mother, and clamped her hand over her mouth in an effort to prevent any more words spilling out.

'His what...?' Kath asked calmly, but her heart was beating so fast it threatened to burst from her chest.

'Nothing,' Violet sat again at the table, her eyes cast down.

'His what... Violet?' Kath's voice commanding, she asked the question again.

'Mum... please...' Violet's eyes begged her mother not to ask further.

But ask she did. 'Violet... tell me!' Kath shouted.

Tears coursed down her face as Violet shouted, 'I'm sick to death of him making me do things – horrible things!'

Shock took her breath away as she Kath saw the distress on Violet's face. What was Violet trying to say? What had John done to her daughter? Had he taken his belt to her again after he'd promised not to? Had he done something more... something terrible? A sudden dreadful thought had her holding her breath. *Please God, not that!* she thought.

Kath stammered, 'I thought maybe he'd used his belt again.'

'Yes,' Violet said, her anger still bubbling, 'he used his belt *first*!'

Violet suddenly dissolved into a flood of tears.

Staring at Violet, the awful truth hit her like a tram. Rushing to the scullery sink, Kath threw up, retching until her stomach ached. How could she have known? How could she have let a man into their house that would do such a thing to her daughter?!

Cleaning up the mess she swilled her mouth. Taking a deep breath she tried to calm herself down then she returned to the table and looked her daughter square in the eyes.

'Now then, I want to know exactly what's happened,' Kath said, feeling the bile rise at the back of her throat.

Violet shook her head, her eyes tightly shut. Kath's horror threatened to overwhelm her as she saw her daughter so troubled by her memories.

'Sweetheart, you have to tell me. If I'm to tackle John, I need to know what's gone on.' Kath's voice trembled.

'I didn't... want to,' Violet sobbed, 'he forced me, Mum – he made me do things. He... he put his thing in me and...' She burst into tears; she could say no more.

Dashing around the table, Kath wrapped Violet in her arms and hugged her tight as the long-held emotions poured from her daughter's young body. Holding Violet tightly, Kath thought about Violet being violated in the most despicable way by her husband.

'Violet, I swear to you I had no idea, may the Lord strike me dead! Oh my sweetheart, my lovely girl...! Violet, I promise you this... he will never hurt you again!' Kath's blood was up.

'Mum, I tried to stop him, I did but...' Violet sobbed, her tears rolling down her face and soaking into Kath's cardigan.

Kath whispered, 'I know, bab, you are in no way responsible. John bloody Sligo carries the blame for this, and as God's my witness he won't get away with it. Cry it out, sweetheart, cry it out, because it's the last time you'll cry in this house, I'll make damned sure of that!' Then pushing Violet to arm's length, she looked into her distraught face. Lifting Violet's chin with her finger, she said, 'Now, the next time Primrose Berry blames you for something you haven't done, you have my permission to paste her good and proper! Is that clear?'

Violet nodded and Kath could see they had reached an understanding as they watched each other. Both stood ramrod straight as Violet's tears slowly evaporated, leaving in their wake a dogged determination.

Kath continued, 'As for John Sligo... you leave him to me!'

Three

Walking down Holyhead Road to the Old Barrel Inn dressed in his Sunday best, John Sligo had to admit he cut a dashing figure.

Marrying Kath Clancy some years earlier couldn't have come at a better time. Unbeknown to her, he had, today, put in his notice at the colliery – no more coal mining for him! Harry Clancy had left Kath very well off financially and on John's marriage to Kath that money had come to him by law. He congratulated himself for the thousandth time. He had been keeping an ear open for a business up for sale. He had made up his mind to get out of the dirty coal industry; he wanted to be the boss of his own firm.

Working at the pit and not saving any money had been a foolhardy thing, but then along had come Kath. Thinking about his wife, he swung jauntily down the road. *She's not a bad-looking woman, a bit thin, but then you don't look at the mantelpiece when you poke the fire!* John chuckled to himself. Kath was a good cook, she kept the house clean, washed and ironed his clothes, did all the things a good wife should do. She warmed his bed and kept his 'old man' happy. And then there was her daughter.

John's smile spread into a grin as he thought of Violet. The brat! Always in trouble that one, but, he felt, as the head of the household, he had free rein to discipline her... now that he did enjoy! He could have mother and daughter whenever he wanted with no one to stop him. He loved the feeling of power; it was so heady.

Walking into the public bar, John Sligo saw some of the blokes he worked with and made his way across to them. Oh he knew they didn't much care for him, but that was no loss to him. His having money – being wealthy, you might say – didn't sit well with them. Jealousy is a terrible thing, John thought as he sat at the table with a few of the 'lads'.

A pint of ale appeared before him as if by magic and he clinked glasses with the man who'd bought it, the man's smile of deference obvious to all. John gloated.

'Ah hear your lass has been in trouble agen, Jack.' The voice belonged to Geordie Slater, the nickname given to him on account of his hailing from Newcastle upon Tyne in the North East of England. Strange how people always referred to those called John as 'Jack', but Sligo didn't mind, he was used to it.

'She ain't "*my* lass", as you put it, Geordie. What's she supposed to have done now?' John asked, rather miffed they obviously knew something he didn't.

John watched with disdain as the smiles appeared on the faces around the table one after the other. Geordie caught a nudge to the ribs from the man next to him, daring him to reveal all.

'Aye well, I heard summat about young Violet havin' a

set-to with Mrs Berry's kid,' the melodious cadence in his voice began to irritate John.

He watched the grins broaden. *That kid will be the death of me*, he thought but said instead, 'Oh that, you know what kids are, fighting one minute, best of friends the next. It'll all be forgotten by tomorrow, you'll see.'

A murmur of agreement ran round the table. Good, that subject was closed... for now... until he got home. The thought warmed him; Violet would get his belt... then she would get him!

Conversation moved to the coal pit, as usual, about working conditions being so bad, the money being worse, and management not being any better. The threat of closure hung over them and every day they dreaded the thought of being out of work if that should come to pass.

Sensing an opportunity to drop his bombshell, John emptied his glass as he stood to head for the privy outside. 'Won't be affecting me for much longer,' he said and strode off imperiously.

Minutes later, he returned to his place at the table and John saw his glass had been filled once more. 'Cheers lads,' he said, lifting his ale to his lips. He wallowed in the power he held over these men by the fact he never had to put his hand in his pocket for drinks.

Geordie asked, 'You gonna tell us what's occurring then?' Obviously elected spokesman for the evening, Geordie Slater was the only one amongst them with any balls.

'I'm leaving the pit!' John watched as mouths opened and glances were exchanged. He revelled in the mystery until Geordie spoke again.

'How come like?'

'Geordie, I'm one of the richest people in the town as you

know, so I've made up my mind – I don't need to work in the pit anymore.'

Nods affirmed his statement as true and Geordie said, 'Eeh man, what'll ya be doin' with your time then?'

'I'm thinking about going into business, although as yet I haven't quite decided *what* business.'

A quiet chuckle spurred him on.

'I can afford to take some time to find and buy a going concern. Then, I can build it up and eventually expand. Money begets money they say.'

The men at the table sat quietly, each in his own pool of jealousy and John watched them, a big grin spanning his face as he leaned back in his chair.

After another few pints John Sligo staggered out of the Old Barrel Inn to make his way home. Singing to himself, he felt immensely pleased he had not only stuck a craw in the throats of his work colleagues, but they had paid for that privilege by buying all the beer!

He must have superior intellect over those dunderheads, John thought as he swayed along the cobbles of Holyhead Road. He was feeling good and when he got home he knew he was going to feel a bloody sight better!

*

Kath sat in her chair knitting as usual when he walked in, and the girl was abed. Good, that was where John liked her. He felt a grin spread as Kath looked up.

'Had a good time in the pub, I see,' she said.

John tried to decide whether she was being sarcastic.

'I have indeed,' he slurred, 'told the lads the news, you

should 'ave seen their faces.' John felt the silly grin cross his face but was powerless to do anything about it.

'And what news would that be?' Kath asked, looking at him, her knitting needles seeming to have a life of their own.

'Told 'em I was leaving the pit, didn't I? Told 'em I was going into business for myself.' The silly grin remained in place as John swayed from side to side.

Kath's needles stopped their clicking as she watched him. 'Is that right?' she asked scornfully. 'And just when were you going to tell me about this?'

Feeling the anger rise in him, John yelled, 'I'm tellin' you now, ain't I?'

'Don't you yell at me, John Sligo! Don't you bloody dare!'

Kath's outburst took him a little by surprise; normally she was so acquiescent.

Leaning forward, he shouted into her face, 'I'll yell all I want woman, and don't you forget it!' Trying to straighten up, he felt himself begin to totter before falling into the chair. 'Where's my supper, woman?' he asked when he managed to sit up.

'Supper you say?' Kath asked caustically. 'Make your own bloody supper, I'm off to bed! Oh and John... you'll be sleeping on the sofa tonight!'

John felt his mouth drop open as Kath disappeared through the door to the stairs, slamming it behind her. How dare she speak to him in that manner! Who did this woman think she was?

Getting to his feet unsteadily, John carefully dragged himself up the stairs to find the bedroom door locked. Going across to Violet's room, he opened the door. John was set to have a little fun and Violet was going to provide it if her mother wouldn't.

Moving across to the bed, he discovered it was empty. 'What the...?' he muttered.

Two steps back to the other bedroom door, John hammered on it as he shouted, 'Open this door, woman, I want my congimicaal rights!' He tittered as he tottered by the door waiting for it to open.

Instead he heard Kath say, 'You'll be getting no more of *that* from me... or from Violet!'

Like a slap in the face, John felt the sting of her words. That bloody brat had told her mother then!

Christ! he thought. *I'll deny everything... she always believes me and that kid of hers is forever lying through her teeth.* Well, Violet Clancy would have no teeth left to lie through when he got hold of her. Seeing Kath was not in the best of moods he decided to let sleeping dogs lie – for now.

Trying to make his way back downstairs, John tripped and reached the bottom quicker than he had anticipated. Staggering to the sofa, groaning, he lay down and promptly fell asleep.

Waking the following morning with the hangover from hell and to no breakfast, John washed and changed into his work clothes he'd left in the scullery and set off to work his last week at the Monway Colliery. The thought lightened his mood until a grumble in his stomach reminded him he was hungry. No breakfast ready, no lunch tin provided... it was going to be a long day.

Kath and her brat of a daughter were going to suffer for this – even more so if his tea wasn't on the table when he got home from work!

Four

Holding her daughter while she slept, Kath had watched as dreams took the girl's mind to a nicer place.

She felt lucky John had not kicked the bedroom door down, but then the amount of ale he'd consumed had prevented that; he could barely stand up let alone kick down a door.

Thinking it through, Kath knew the time had now come to do something about that man. She and Violet could leave, but with no money except the little housekeeping he gave her, Kath knew they wouldn't survive long. The money Harry had left her after his death had, by law, reverted to John on the day of their marriage. Kath had been a fool to have married him, but love is blind, they say. Was it love though? Did she love him? Thinking back, she realised she did not. Then why did she marry him? So she wouldn't be alone when the time came for Violet to marry and leave home.

Kath had been terrified of living alone, but now she wished she hadn't been so quick to marry and taken in by Sligo, for then none of this would have happened and Violet would have been safe.

Poor girl, no man would want Violet now – soiled goods.

Her heart ached for her young daughter; Kath felt she had failed her, but she resolved to protect her only child in the future, for all her life if need be.

*

Hearing John stomp around the house getting ready for work, she'd waited for the slamming of the back door before getting up to make Violet's breakfast.

Violet stirred as Kath moved from the bed. 'Mum?'

'Mornin', love,' she said gently, 'you hungry?'

Eyes wide with fear, Violet listened and Kath assured her, 'It's all right, John's gone to work, come on we'll have a fry-up!'

Violet jumped from the bed; standing before her mother, she said, 'Oh Mum, I'm so sorry,' the tears welling in her eyes.

'Bab...' Kath used the old Black Country term of affection, 'you have nothing to be sorry for... but that pig John Sligo has! I intend to make sure he gets what's coming to him. Now, you get ready for school.'

After a hearty breakfast, Violet set off on her walk to Mesty Croft School with Kath's words ringing in her ears, 'You remember what I told you about that Primrose Berry!'

With Violet gone, Kath wrapped her shawl around her shoulders and set off herself down Hobbins Street and across the town to the marketplace. She knew the miners' wives would be shopping at the stalls there looking for cheap cuts of meat to make a meal from; they could not afford to buy at the butcher's shop in Trouse Lane like she could.

Sidling up to a tall woman dressed in a bottle green blouse and a long black skirt with a green shawl wrapped around her shoulders, Kath heard the jolly banter she was having with the man running the vegetable stall.

Looking at Kath, the woman nodded. 'Hello Kath.'

'Hello Martha,' she replied.

Martha Slater was an old friend and wife to Geordie who also worked at the pit, and Kath knew he and John drank together, along with others.

Martha looked at her and said knowingly, 'I hear there's cheap meat further along; I think you and me should have a look.'

Turning, Martha grabbed Kath's elbow and pushed her forward in order to walk down the market together, nodding their greetings to others as they went.

'Don't often see you down here no more,' Martha said as they walked, 'an' I can see you're here for a reason, Kath Sligo.'

Tears filled her eyes as Kath looked at her friend, saying, 'Just Kath, if you don't mind, Martha.'

The woman stopped and, turning to her, said, 'I see. Meeting then is it?'

Kath nodded and Martha resumed, 'Right. You get off home and I'll round 'em up. Get the kettle on, we won't be long.' Pulling her shawl around her in a business-like fashion, Martha pushed her head up to scan the market, then set off in search of the other wives of the coal miners.

Walking home, Kath reflected on her long-time friend-ships with the wives; of how she and Harry had enjoyed their company over the years. On Harry's death, they had rallied around Violet and herself, offering support as well as practical help. However, when Kath had married John, their visits to the house became less frequent until eventually they stopped altogether. Kath knew why, they hated John

Sligo. John didn't like his wife mixing with the other wives, believing he and his wife were above everyone else. Kath had never believed it for an instant and occasionally she would go surreptitiously to the marketplace to catch up with her old friends. They did not hide their dislike of Kath's husband and she respected them for it.

Now she was about to ask their help. Would they give it? Dread descended over her like a shroud as she set out mugs for tea and cut a cake she'd baked the previous day, waiting to see who, if anyone, would turn up.

*

Kath heard the chattering of the women before they entered her kitchen. No knock came, for there was never the need to knock on a friend's door, and her heart lifted at the good omen. These women were here as her friends... to help.

Around the kitchen table sat Martha Slater, Geordie's wife; Mary Forbes, married to Jim, and Annie Green, married to Charlie.

Kath looked at the women one by one. Martha, tall and straight with confidence in abundance. Always dressed in dark colours, Martha never wore any cosmetics or scent. She was outspoken to the point of being rude, caring little for what people thought of her. She was a bossy boots and had always been seen as the leader of their little group. Kath thought she would have made an excellent good witch in children's stories. Martha cared strongly about people but had difficulty showing her emotions, but to her friends, Martha was the most loyal, honest person in the world. She and Geordie had eight children and she adored them all.

Kath's eyes moved to Mary Forbes. Short and a little

overweight, Mary was not the sharpest knife in the drawer. She spoke without thinking, which had often caused raucous laughter from the others. Her blue eyes would twinkle as she constantly tried to shove her wayward mousy brown hair back into place as it escaped the confines of its pins. She and her husband Jim had decided not to have any children when they married and Mary made no secret of the fact. It wasn't that she didn't like kids, she just didn't want any of her own. She also had a strong loyal bond to her friends, one they'd shared since being children.

Then there was Annie Green. Kath's eyes settled on her friend. She was seen as the lady of the group. Her skin was smooth and fresh, even in winter, and her light brown hair shone as did her blue-green eyes. The slightest dab of rouge on her cheeks, which she wore every time she went out, gave her a healthy glow. Annie often walked on the heath in the summer collecting herbs and flowers to dry for use in her cooking and her skin creams. Her clothes, although old, were always immaculate. She took pride in her appearance at all times. Annie and Charlie had never been blessed with children which Kath knew was what her friend wanted above all else. It was a constant sadness to her which she kept well hidden.

Tea and cake served and general chat over with, Martha spoke. 'So Kath, what's up?'

Breathing deeply, Kath began with, 'Firstly, I'm sorry I haven't been able to socialise as we used to, but John...'

Mary cut the sentence in half with a sharp, 'Oh him! Don't you worry none about that, love, just tell us what's going on.'

Kath knew without doubt that these women would keep her secret when they learned of it, and drawing another deep breath, she lunged in, 'I need to be rid of John Sligo!'

The faces of the women around the table never flinched. All but Annie, whose hands were placed neatly in her lap, sat with arms crossed over chests and each nodded for her to continue.

Right, Kath thought, *so far, so good.*

'I can't leave him because he has my money, as you all know...' More nods. 'So...' she faltered.

Annie asked gently, 'Kath, what's he done to bring you to this, wench?' The women leaned forward in order not to miss a word.

With silent tears rolling down her cheeks, Kath said quietly, 'He's raped my Violet!'

Hands flew to mouths in shock as the women's eyes widened.

'Oh my God!' Martha gasped.

Kath nodded, saying, 'He beat her with a belt first and... I have to stop him!' She burst into tears, great sobs racking her thin frame.

Annie shot from her seat to envelop her friend in her arms as she cried. 'Let it go, Kath, let it go. It does no good to hold on to it,' she comforted.

The others sat quietly watching the woman, who at one time was filled with confidence, now a sobbing wreck.

This was John Sligo's doing. He had worn Kath down to leave her a shadow of her former self.

Martha stood using her stock phrase, 'Right, more tea... this needs a deal o' thinkin' on!'

All morning and most of the afternoon was spent discussing ways of dealing with John Sligo. It was decided that Kath pack Violet's things and she would go to stay with Martha and her family. They lived halfway down Hobbins Street, so it was not far, but she was away from Sligo. All the kids got along fine so that wouldn't be a problem for Violet. John was to be told Martha had invited Violet to stay over with her kids for a time, and Kath promised if he got antsy with her she would go to Annie Green's house. Kath explained she needed to remain in the house to have it out with John once and for all. Annie and Mary lived at the end of the same street, next door to each other.

It was also decided that the women would talk over Kath's problem with their men. Confidentiality assured, she reluctantly agreed.

'We'll need another meeting at the end of the week,' Martha said in her usual bossy way. The others nodded, and she continued, 'It looks like we, the Wednesbury Wives club, have quite a task ahead of us.'

*

By the time Violet arrived home from school, her things were packed and Kath told her she would be staying at Martha's house for a while for her own safety. Relief showed on the girl's face as she checked she had all the things she would need.

After an early tea to avoid seeing John, Violet and Kath walked down the street to Martha's house. Kath explained on the way that Martha was aware of what had gone on and she assured Violet that their secret would be safe. She watched as her daughter relaxed a little knowing she would be welcomed by Martha.

Violet had no problems settling right in amongst the hoard of laughing children in the Slater household.

Martha hugged Kath as she left, saying she and the others would be round on Friday morning and not to worry about Violet, she was now out of harm's way.

Walking home, tiredness overcame her as Kath thought about what would happen when John returned from work. Sitting on the sofa once she got back in, she fell asleep through pure exhaustion.

*

It was a while later when Kath woke to the sound of John slamming the door and marching into the living room. He had gone straight to the pub from work and had, by all accounts, had quite a skinful.

Standing with legs astride, he looked around and sniffed audibly.

'I don't smell anything cooking,' he said spitefully.

'That would be because nothing *is* cooking,' Kath said sarcastically, remaining on the sofa and rubbing the sleep out of her eyes.

'Oh I see! Gone on strike have we?' His accusatory tone lanced into her. Striding across the room, he raised his hand high.

'I wouldn't do that if I were you, John Sligo!'

The hand came down hard and hit Kath's face with such force she toppled sideways on the sofa as he said, 'Well you ain't me!' Stepping back to look at her, he went on, 'Now, woman, get my tea ready, and make it bloody quick!'

Kath jumped to her feet and lashed out at her husband, her hand catching him sharply on his cheek. Anger rushed through her in a torrent. 'I've had about as much of you as I can stand!' she yelled. 'First you force your filthy ways on my girl, and now you think to set about me? No Sligo! You've had the last fun you'll ever have with my family!'

Shocked at her outburst, John wavered as Kath's raging continued.

'I warned you John...'

Coming quickly to his senses again, he began to rain blows down on his wife.

With a surge of adrenaline and a screech like a banshee, Kath launched herself at him. Absolute fury fuelled her actions as she kicked out at him; her fists pummelled him at every chance she got.

'I want you out of this house!' Kath yelled. 'I don't ever want to see you again, you filthy swine!'

John tried to grab her wrists in an effort to quell the anger he saw for the first time in his wife, but Kath was too quick for him.

On and on they battled until tiredness began to take the place of anger.

With a last show of strength, the palms of her hands struck his chest, which forced him backwards. Her last-ditch attempt to get him away from her. She watched, as if in a daze, as he toppled backwards in slow motion and she heard the sickly crack as his head bounced off the corner of the stone mantelpiece. She heard his strangled cry as he landed hard on the stone hearth.

'Get up you horrible little man! Get up and get out!' Kath berated her prone husband but John had stopped moving.

Slowly her anger began to subside and as she looked at the body on the floor Kath's first thought was – had she killed him? As she stood staring down at him, she saw the blood begin to pool around his head which still lay on the hearth. Fear gripped her and she turned and fled from the house.

As Kath ran to Annie Green's house, she felt her face

swell and her eye begin to close. That would be black come morning, but all Kath could think about was John lying unmoving on the floor.

Annie looked at her as Kath walked into her kitchen, saying, 'Christ girl! Come on in, look at the state of you!' Pulling Kath inside to her glowing fire, she called, 'Charlie, pour a cuppa for Kath!'

Kath sat in front of the fire, shaking from head to foot.

Annie asked, 'What's happened, wench? Mind you, looking at your face I can see for myself!'

Kath couldn't speak, she was in shock. Taking the cup offered by Charlie, her hand shook so badly the tea slopped onto her skirt.

Annie grasped the cup and helped move it to Kath's lips. 'Come on, sip this. It will help a bit.'

Kath did as she was bid and very slowly the shaking left her limbs.

'What's caused this?' Charlie asked as he sat in his armchair.

Kath shuddered violently as she heard Annie's words. 'Sligo's raped Violet!'

'Bloody hell!' Charlie said, sitting bolt upright.

Annie nodded as she continued to help Kath drink her tea.

'Where's Violet now?' he asked as he got to his feet.

'Martha's house,' Annie answered.

Charlie sat down again, saying, 'Kath, I ain't saying nothing you don't already know... but I ain't got no time fer that man!'

Giving an understanding smile which only raised the corners of her mouth, Kath answered with a sob, 'I know, Charlie, no one has.'

'We are having a meeting on Friday mornin'... to decide what's to be done about all this,' said Annie.

'Well wench, you know yer can rely on us blokes if yer need us, and Kath...' patting her hand, Charlie went on, 'yer secret is safe with us.'

The silent tears rolled down Kath's cheeks unchecked and feeling uncomfortable at the sight of her crying, Charlie stood to say goodnight and head for his bed.

'Charlie... I think John is dead!' Kath blurted out.

Five

Martha's children jostled to sit next to Violet on the floor around a set of rough-hewn building blocks. Three sets of twins, all boys, and two girls were quite a handful, but Martha loved them all the same.

They were excited that Violet was staying with them and she was to sleep top to toe with the eldest girl Nancy. She always got on famously with the whole family and the joy of her being there raised no questions as to why, they just enjoyed being with her, and she with them.

After a hearty supper, Violet snuggled down beneath the eiderdown, her head by Nancy's feet, and sighed. Her belly was full, she was in a warm bed, and she was safe with friends. Nancy wiggled her feet when she said goodnight and they both giggled.

Violet woke in the night with terrible pains in her stomach and she got up to visit the lavatory outside. Lighting the lantern hung in the toilet building with the matches kept at its side, she saw blood in her pyjamas. She began to panic but then realised... she had started her monthlies. Back indoors, she changed quickly into clean nightwear and made her way to the sink in the scullery. As she was trying frantically to wash the blood out of her clothing, she fretted. This would have to happen now, her first time and being away from home. Then a hand touched her shoulder. Jumping out of her skin, Violet cried out, 'Please... don't!'

'It's all right, bab, it's only me. I heard you get up and I was worried.'

'Oh Martha! I'm sorry I woke you but...' Violet held up her pyjamas and Martha saw the blood stains.

'Ah right, welcome to the club, Violet, seems you have now become a woman.' With a smile, she led Violet to a cupboard where she kept all the necessities.

'The "women's cupboard"...' she whispered, 'help yourself. You know what to do?' Violet nodded and as Martha turned, she added, 'Leave those pyjamas in the scullery and I'll boil them tomorrow.' Then she returned to her bed.

As Violet lay in bed once more, she reflected. Her mother had told her all about 'becoming a woman', of pregnancy and childbirth. A shudder ran through her when she thought about John Sligo and what he'd done to her. She said a silent prayer of thanks that her periods had only just now started. God knows what might have happened had she become pregnant by the ghastly man! Closing her eyes tight, she sent up another silent prayer of thanks to the Almighty. Grateful she didn't have to remain living under the same roof as that monster, Violet still worried for her mother. She hoped with all her heart her mum would be all right.

*

Over the next few days, Violet, unaware of the drama unfolding at home, fell into the ways of the Slater household easily; going to school with the clan. She missed her mother though and ached to see her. Martha explained it was too dangerous for her to return home especially now and she gave a sly wink. Violet wasn't sure what this meant, but felt comforted nonetheless.

Violet had been assured she would return home to her mum once things had been sorted. Quite what 'sorted' meant was a mystery to her but she gleaned enough to know that when she did eventually go home – she would be safe.

Things were looking up at school too; Primrose Berry had stayed away from Violet, especially as Violet now had Nancy Slater on her side. The odd sly look from Primrose thwarted any action on her part by a raise of Violet's finger in warning and a nod towards Nancy. Having been asked by a couple of the other kids why she was staying with the Slaters, Violet had told them in no uncertain terms to mind their own business! The less said the better as far as she was concerned and she settled into working hard at her studies.

Although young, Violet had seen the amount of poverty and unemployment in the town of Wednesbury and she had made up her mind to endeavour to make something of her life. She had no intention of working herself into her grave; she was going to ensure that her education would benefit her later in life, so it was up to her to study hard now.

Violet for the most part was happy with the Slaters, but her nightmares came and went, going swiftly on the occasions when Nancy's feet collided with her head. Hearing Violet cry out in her dreams, Nancy would tap the girl's head with her toe, enough to bring Violet from sleep into wakefulness. Strange as it seemed, Nancy's feet were a real comfort to her in those dark hours of the night.

She did, however, live in dread of meeting Sligo on her way

to and from school. Violet knew it was unlikely as the miners started work very early in the mornings, but she still kept a wary eye out in case he was late getting to work. John Sligo was not above giving any child a clip round the ear, so she kept her silent vigil on her journeys.

Violet couldn't wait to return home to her mother… safely. She knew she was to stay with the Slaters for a week, but to Violet it seemed like an eternity.

Six

Charlie and Annie glanced at each other as Kath spluttered through her tears the events of the previous hours. 'I was so angry with him Annie, and when he began to attack me… we fought. I pushed him hard. He fell backwards and hit his head on the fireplace and then… then… the blood, oh my God there was so much blood!' She burst into tears again.

'Right,' Charlie said, grabbing his jacket, 'I'll go round to yours and take a look, Kath. Annie, you best fetch Geordie and Jim… just in case.'

Annie settled Kath with a cup of tea before saying, 'I won't be long. You stay there and rest.'

Returning, Annie explained that Martha and Mary would not be long in coming. Just as she finished her sentence, the back door opened and their friends rushed in.

Annie made fresh tea as the others moved to sit by the fire.

Martha sighed loudly through her nose when she saw Kath's swollen face.

'That bugger needs a hiding!' Mary said sharply.

Kath tried to tell again about the fight at her house but she faltered. Annie took up the explanation, watching mouths drop open.

'Oh God!' Kath wailed. 'I think I've killed him!' She began to shake once more.

'Now then,' Annie soothed, 'you're still in shock.'

'From what you said, it seems to me it was an accident,' Martha said in her ever-present sensible manner. 'You pushed him – right?' Kath nodded. 'He fell and banged his head on the hearth – yes?' Another nod from Kath. 'There you go then – an accident.' Martha spread her hands, justifying her words.

But Kath began to fret that the police may not reach that same conclusion as her friends.

'Well,' Mary said, 'if he is dead, we won't need that meeting at the end of the week.'

'Mary!' Annie exclaimed.

'What? I was only saying.'

*

It was past midnight when Charlie, Geordie and Jim arrived back at the house. Kath searched Charlie's face for an answer to her unasked question.

Charlie sat down next to Kath and at his nod she burst into fresh tears. 'I wanted rid of him, you all know that,' Kath said between sobs, 'but... I swear to God it was an accident!'

'We know that, wench, don't you upset yourself anymore,' Martha said, trying to console her friend.

Suddenly jumping up, Kath said, 'Oh Martha, I have to go. I have to get rid of the body! I have to find a place...'

Charlie placed a hand on her shoulder, pressing her gently back into her seat. 'It's all right, wench, he's gone.'

'I know, Charlie, but I have to move him, I need to find somewhere to dispose of...' Kath was about to stand again.

'Kath, he's gone. We "walked" him down to the cut like he was a drunken sot. We were all singing and laughing so anyone who might have seen us would be none the wiser. Everyone knows how he was whilst drunk, it would be no surprise to anyone seeing him in that condition. Anyway, when we got to the cut, he sort of... fell in! After that we went back to your house and cleaned up the mess. You don't have to worry, folk will think he fell down drunk and hit his head before falling in the canal and drowning.'

Kath let go of the breath she held and her eyes said her thanks to each of the men who had helped her that night.

Martha said, 'Kath, my girl, best get your weeds out because in the eyes of the town this time tomorrow you'll be a widow!'

*

On Saturday morning Violet returned home. She was horrified by the sight of her mother's swollen face and black eye.

'It's all right sweetheart,' Kath said, giving her daughter a hug. 'We had a fight and now John's... gone. He won't be coming back – ever.'

Violent hugged her mother before she went happily to her room while Kath made tea for herself and Martha who had brought Violet home.

'You all right girl?' Martha asked.

Kath went to her, giving her a hug and saying quietly, 'Never better, thanks to the Wives club and their husbands!'

*

The police found John Sligo floating in the canal a couple of days later. The bloated body was dragged out and hauled off. Enquiries by the police showed Sligo had been drinking heavily that night, celebrating his last day at the coal pit. For some reason they could not fathom, it seemed he'd taken the circuitous route home via the canal towing path. Unsteady on his feet due to the amount of beer he'd drunk, Sligo must have slipped and fallen in the canal. Unable to get out, he'd drowned.

The Coroner's verdict – Accidental death.

The constable had visited to give Kath the news when Violet was at school and had asked why she had not reported him missing the last few days. Kath had told him that she and John had argued heatedly and she had told her husband to leave and never come back. Looking at her injuries, the constable accepted her statement and without further ado had left her to make arrangements for the funeral. Very few would attend, it was thought.

Whatever truly happened to John Sligo would remain a mystery, Violet thought. She had her suspicions especially when she had seen Martha leave the house so late. She had wondered where her mother's friend was going at that time of night, although she realised she would probably never know. As for herself... she was glad he couldn't come back to hurt her ever again, and she determined she would keep her counsel as to what she suspected may have happened to the man she hated beyond belief.

Kath's money returned to her now she was a widow for the second time. She swore never to marry again and after her experiences Violet swore never to marry at all.

Seven

Violet grew into a beautiful young woman. She was watched over by her mother and the other Wives and all were very proud of the way she appeared to have pushed the Sligo incident behind her. They knew it would never truly be forgotten but, for the most part, Violet was happy. Only time would tell how the girl would cope if ever she had a beau.

Violet left school and searched for work, but none was to be found in the poverty-stricken town. Nevertheless she continued to look; she was determined to earn a wage and contribute to the household funds.

One day Kath called Violet in to have tea with the Wives who were settled around the kitchen table.

Martha said, 'Come on in, Violet girl, and get a cup of tea down yer.' Mary grinned at Martha taking charge as usual.

A strange feeling crept over Violet. Why was she being invited to join them? As she sat and listened to the talk around the table, all became clear.

Kath began to explain the mystery of the late John Sligo. 'You are old enough now to know the truth,' she said.

Violet nodded – she felt no remorse, although the old feeling of fear had made her shudder as she had listened to her mother's words. Drawing in a deep breath, Violet said firmly. 'That man ruined my life, spoiled any chance I have of marrying and having children of my own. His death was not your fault, Mum, and I, for one, am not sorry about what happened to him!'

The women watched Violet closely as she showed no concern over the way Sligo had died. They then went on to explain about the exclusive club of the 'Wednesbury Wives'. Martha explained the four women were there to help other women who had problems that needed solving; problems that the law couldn't or wouldn't ever find in favour of the women. It was a man's world and women were there to fetch and carry, clean and raise the children. Women had no rights. So, each time a woman came to them with a problem – they did their best to solve it.

Martha related about how it had all begun. She, Martha Slater, was a force to be reckoned with and she brooked no nonsense from anyone. She was respected by other women because of this and their men admired her confidence and tenacity. A threatened eviction had come to her ears years ago whilst chatting in the market. It was before Violet and Nancy were born, and she had intervened on behalf of the victim with her landlord. The landlord and Martha, with her reputation as a terrier, had come to an arrangement; he would allow the tenant extra time to pay rent owing and Martha would allow him extra time to continue to breathe! He had, albeit begrudgingly, admitted defeat. The woman she had helped had contacted Martha again after hearing of a friend who had a problem. This time, Martha had enlisted the help of her friends.

Mary, Kath, Annie and Martha had been friends since their first day at school. They had grown up together, played, laughed and cried together over the following years. Their problems had been shared before being resolved and even without really realising it they began to help other women solve their problems. They had formed an exclusive club, a women's version of the Masonic organisation.

The husbands had stayed in the background while they came together as an immovable force when faced with difficulty. Oh the men knew what the women were about but no questions were ever asked; no recriminations, in fact a little help was given here and there on occasions. The rest was left to their Wednesbury Wives. Kath had never mentioned this to John for fear of his trying to put a stop to them helping other women.

Every woman who had her problem solved by the Wives was sworn to secrecy and because she was free of her particular problem had no cause to speak of it to anyone else. Each case was taken on its merits and dealt with in complete confidentiality.

The Wednesbury Wives had tackled some different diffi-culties over the years, wife beaters, rapists, drunks, but none had ended with a loss of life. Although the club had been formed around a financial issue in the first place, it had grown to encompass broader problems for women and wives. Somehow they found a way round each problem, carefully avoiding contact with the law, leaving nothing to trace back to them.

Now, as Violet was of an age, they were asking her to join them.

'I... I'm not a wife... nor will I ever be!' she stammered.

'Oh,' Martha chuckled, 'that don't matter none, wench,

it's just that we was all married when we started up that's all.'

'Oh I see.' Violet wasn't sure what would be asked of her if she joined their little band.

The thought was broken when Martha said, 'Have a think on it and chat with yer mum, she'll fill in the details for you. Then you can let us know when yer ready.'

Violet gave them her thanks and sat listening but not really hearing their chatter. Her mind was going over what she'd been told about Sligo. Thinking again of the things he did to her, her anger mounted. Then she said forcefully, 'Count me in!'

With more tea and hugs from everyone, Violet had officially joined the Wives club.

*

One day a knock came to the open back door. Kath was out at the market and Violet was alone in the house. Going to the doorway, she saw a woman dressed in drab clothes with a shawl draped over her hair who said, 'I was looking for Kath Clancy.'

Kath had reverted to her previous married name after the death of John Sligo; it was a way in which she hoped she could forget him and the terrible things he had done.

'She's at the market; I'm Violet, her daughter. Won't you come in and wait?' she said, knowing in her heart this woman was in need of help. Violet's feelings were a melange of excitement and fear. This was the first woman to ask for help since she had joined the club. She felt excited at possibly being able to help, but worried about what might be asked of her.

Looking around, the woman said, 'No... thanks. I need to talk to Kath, it's urgent.'

'Please,' Violet urged, 'come in and have tea, she won't be long and... it's safe here.'

The woman stared at her long and hard before walking into the kitchen.

Sitting her at the table with a slice of cake, Violet set about making the world's best remedy for any problem... a cup of tea!

*

Kath stepped into the kitchen and she and the woman sat at the table and exchanged a glance before the woman returned her look to her teacup.

Violet raised her eyebrows at Kath as she set out another cup.

The woman watched them before she said, 'Mary Forbes said to come see you.'

Kath nodded, 'What can we do for you?'

'I'm Joyce Clews, an' I live across in Brick Kiln Street.'

Mrs Clews paused again; obviously she was finding the reason she had come here difficult to discuss. Kath and Violet waited patiently. Joyce Clews' age was hard to determine; hard work and poor living conditions took their toll on the women of the Black Country. Dark straggly hair was revealed as she pushed her shawl back to rest on thin shoulders. Her eyes, although blue, seemed lifeless, as if the holding of too many secrets had killed their sparkle. Tears lay along the dark lashes threatening their overspill. Her thin lips parted as she drew in a ragged breath.

Kath's hand covered Joyce's which lay on the table and

Violet noticed the woman's fingernails were chewed down to the quick. 'Take your time Joyce,' Kath said gently.

'Mary said...' Joyce began again, 'Mary said you might be able to help me.'

'In what way, Joyce?'

'I don't know!' The tears that had only threatened before began their downward journey. Silent tears, Violet knew all too well, harboured the worst kind of anguish.

'Why don't you tell us... from the beginning,' Kath urged when at last Joyce got her emotions under control.

Violet set to making more tea as she listened to the woman's story interspersed with heart-rending sobs. Joyce, it seemed, had thought herself unable to conceive. She and her husband Ray had been trying for some years for a family. Ray wasn't that bothered about having kids, she confided, but it was all Joyce ever wanted – babies of her own to care for. Then came the elation of finding herself pregnant. All of her friends had provided things their children had grown out of as a way of helping out. Money was very tight; Ray's wages as a pit worker barely covering their rent and food but they would get by, she would make sure of it.

Joyce was deliriously happy as she prepared for the birth of her first child. She was in her fifth month and had been busy washing and drying more baby clothes given to her by a neighbour. Ray had returned home from work and his tea wasn't ready, Joyce was so wrapped up in the ecstasy of being pregnant, all thought of preparing a meal had evaded her. In a foul mood, Ray had stomped off to the Green Dragon Hotel in the marketplace with their rent money in his pocket...

Violet watched the emotions play over the woman's thin face, her distress evident as she continued her tale.

'He's usually such a good man,' she cried, 'but when he gets drunk...'

A feeling of dread began to creep over Violet as she looked from Joyce to her mother who nodded her head. They both knew well what men were like when they'd had a few too many.

Joyce Clews continued, 'When he got home he'd spent all the rent money on ale... he had nothing left... not a penny!'

The rest of the story unfolded. Joyce had naturally become upset; how were they to pay their rent at the end of the week now he'd spent the money on beer? How would they eat? With no rent paid, the pit boss would turn them out onto the street without a care! How would they bring up a child then, with nowhere to live!

Ray's temper had flared before becoming an inferno as he had set about his wife with slaps and punches. How dare she question his actions? He was head of the household and could do whatever he pleased!

Eventually having punched Joyce to the floor, he had kicked her violently and repeatedly in the stomach – the result of which had seen her lose her baby.

Ray's reaction – one less mouth to feed!

Kath comforted a sobbing Joyce as best she could then asked, 'What do you think we can do to help?'

'I don't know...I'm feeling bereft – I only just lost my baby! The one thing in all the world I wanted! Now the pit boss said we have to be out by Friday... we have nowhere to go and no money to go with!' Tears ran down Joyce's face as she spoke.

'And what about Ray... what does he say?' Violet asked very gently.

'He doesn't care; says he's still got his job, so he'll be all right... as for me, he says I'll 'ave to go to the workhouse!' The horror of the workhouse was well known to all... once in there the only way you came out was in a box!

'My job at the nail making factory wouldn't pay enough for me to rent a place so I'll be out on the streets! I had to get back to work sharpish after... after...' Sobs racked Joyce's thin frame yet again.

'Right,' said Kath, 'Violet – you nip round and fetch the other wives while Joyce and I have another cup of tea.'

Eight

'Martha... Mum says to come! A meeting is needed!' Violet said breathlessly as she ran in through the kitchen door.

'All right, bab, you go and get Annie and Mary an' I'll see you at home.'

Violet ran out again as Martha plucked her shawl from the nail on the back of the kitchen door. Making her way up the road to Kath Clancy's house, she wondered what problem the Wives would be asked to help with this time, although she suspected it might involve, in part, a man. She reflected how lucky she was compared to a lot of other women, including Kath. Her husband, Geordie, was a diamond; hard worker, good father to their eight children who were all now in work and school. Geordie enjoyed his couple of beers on a Friday night with the lads, but never came home drunk. He along with Mary's husband Jim, and Annie's husband Charlie, had been aware of the Wednesbury Wives from the outset. They had supported them from the off, believing that all women should have rights. Harry too, in his time had been supportive, before that brute Sligo had come along.

They were way ahead of their time. Martha smiled, thinking of her good fortune in finding Geordie and the life she had with him.

Hearing quick footsteps behind her, Martha turned as Mary, Annie and Violet caught up with her. Looking at Violet as they trudged on, she asked, 'Who we seein', bab?'

'Joyce Clews from Brick Kiln Street,' she said.

'Oh that poor bugger!' Mary said. 'I told 'er to go and see Kath when she came to me in the market.'

Martha nodded her agreement with Mary's actions as they piled into Kath's kitchen.

Joyce was in no condition to relate her tale again, so Kath, holding the woman's hand, brought everyone up to date with the situation. Violet made tea and they listened sympathetically to the sad story unfolding across the scrubbed wooden table.

Kath's narration ended and Martha looked at Joyce, asking, 'Well, love, what do you want doing about this?'

'There's nowt can be done,' Joyce said resignedly as her hand covered her belly where her long wanted child had once rested.

To everyone's surprise, Violet replied, 'There's always something can be done... we just have to decide what.' The others smiled at her showing she had voiced their own beliefs that there was always a solution.

Suggestions criss-crossed the table long into the morning before Joyce eventually stopped them with, 'That bastard killed my babby even before I'd seen it! Ain't there something in the Bible that says "an eye for an eye"?'

Looking at Joyce, the understanding written all over her face, Martha said, 'Ar there is that about it. Now then, let's just say... if your Ray wasn't around anymore... just sayin'...

what would happen to you? Because the way I see it, you are in a cottage tied to the pit – with rent owing...' Martha raised her hands as Joyce drew breath to speak, then went on, 'So how do you propose to raise that rent? And once paid, the pit boss will still want you out as you'd be a lone woman an' all... if Ray wasn't around anymore. The boss would want the cottage for another family.'

Laying her hands flat on the table showed Martha had finished speaking. She listened to the quiet mutterings of her friends in the small kitchen; then seeing a look pass between Violet and Kath, Martha instinctively knew Joyce's accommodation problems could possibly be resolved.

It was Violet who spoke. 'Mum, Mrs Clews could come and stay with us... I mean, I don't mind giving up my bed...'

God love the girl! Martha thought. Violet was respectful, quick-witted, courteous, kind and thoughtful. She was going to fit in with them right well; already showing signs of leadership.

'Oh I couldn't do that... I couldn't impose on yer both like that!' said Joyce.

Kath picked up, 'Joyce, it's no imposition. I agree with Violet, so here's what I propose...'

Kath then laid out her plan; she would lend Joyce the money to pay the owed rent, to be paid back in instalments from her work as a nail maker. Joyce would then collect her belongings and move into Violet's room – board and lodging to be agreed between the three of them. Violet would sleep in with her mother.

Once all that was agreed, Martha turned again to Joyce, 'Right, now that's settled, what do we do about Ray Clews?'

'That swine killed my babby! I know it hadn't been born and wasn't breathin' yet, but he made sure it never would!'

The force of the explosion from Joyce rocked everyone. 'I don't think he should be allowed to breathe himself one minute longer than is necessary! I want that bugger dead an' I'd be happy to do the job myself!'

At a round of applause from the occupants of the table, Joyce stood and took a little bow. Nervous laughter took them all before order was called once more by Martha.

"You'd be caught Joyce, so don't even try it." The others nodded in agreement. Martha lowered her voice saying, 'This is murder we're talking about here. It's hardly the same as threatening to give the man a slapping! So I ask you, is there any way around this that doesn't involve Ray Clews' death?'

'The idea *is* very drastic,' Annie conceded.

'There must be something we can do though,' Violet added.

'Fair enough,' Joyce intervened, 'this is something I should never have asked of you, but I will say this, it was Ray's fault I lost my baby!'

'All right if that's decided, how do we go about it?' Her stomach roiled at the thought of taking a life and glancing around the table she guessed the others were feeling the same.

'He'd be in a gin pit if he were mine!' Mary muttered almost to herself, looking into her empty cup. 'He'd never be found if we pushed him down one of those besides the fall alone would kill him!' Mary's nerves jangled as she thought about what she'd suggested.

The 'gin pits' were holes left behind after coal mines had been worked out and were left scattered all over the heath. They were very deep, making walking the heath dangerous. Few walked there at night unless they were extremely well versed with the tracks. All were aware that anyone falling into one would never be found.

'It's an idea,' Annie said, 'but how do we get him out

on the heath at night? We all know the safe tracks, so that wouldn't be a problem, but Ray Clews ain't daft... he would know the heath and gin pits – he's a miner at the Monway Colliery after all!'

Kath provided a loaf of freshly baked bread and some cheese with more tea for their dinner while they hatched out a plan. She felt sick at the thought of deliberately sending someone to meet their maker, but then hadn't she done just that with John Sligo, albeit by accident?

Joyce was to tell Ray she was leaving him. She would pack her few paltry things and meet Mary at the bridge by the canal where they had met once before. Ray would fume at Joyce's decision to leave; she would tell him she was meeting someone who was going to look after her. Ray's jealousy would not allow him to *not* discover who was to be at the clandestine meeting with his wife, late at night, out on the canal towpath; he would, no doubt, follow her to the bridge.

Annie, Kath, Violet and Martha would wait in the dark shadow of the bridge for his arrival, with rope to bind his wrists and ankles and a rag to be used as a gag. When he was bound and gagged, they would throw him down the deep gin pit not far from the bridge, never to be seen again. Great care would have to be taken to ensure they did not endanger their own lives in the process.

Joyce would then go home and unpack her things again, making everything appear normal. The following day she would take Ray's lunch box to the pit office, saying he'd forgotten it and that would be when she would learn he had not turned up for work.

Naturally the office would know they were in arrears with the rent and were due for eviction by the end of the week, so it would be quickly surmised Ray Clews had disappeared into the night so as not to have to pay the owed rent. He would be seen to have done 'a moonlight flit'.

Very apt, Martha thought.

The women sat around the table and discussed their plan. Questions were raised again as to whether there was any other way of dealing with this problem. This was the first time they had considered murder and if at all possible they wanted to avoid it, but after much debate, it seemed it would be their only course of action. Joyce, they knew, would find a way of disposing of her husband on her own if it came to the put to, and in her haste would almost definitely be caught by the police.

Martha secretly prayed there would be no moonlight the following night when they would put their plan into action.

Hugs all round saw them off about the rest of the day's business. Each woman was scared witless. Their Wives club had agreed to commit murder. This was the first time a death would be the solution to a problem faced. They prayed that if their plan worked, they would not be caught, but such a lot could go awry. Not one of them wished to take the life of Ray Clews, and had done their best to dissuade Joyce from this plan, but they knew Joyce would have no other outcome. She would not settle for the Wives running him out of town, after all – he might return to give her another severe beating. No, Joyce wanted that man dead and that was all there was to it. At least this way the poor woman might be saved a jail sentence to be rid of her abusive husband – safety in numbers.

The women had given their word to help and they would keep it no matter how bad they felt about committing the act.

Violet thought it all seemed so simple as it had been discussed. However, she was extremely worried the actual act of disposing of Ray Clews could go badly wrong and see them all behind bars.

*

The following night as darkness fell, they all kept to the shadowed Portway Lane and headed for the bridge. Seeing Mary waiting for Joyce, Martha whistled softly and a gentle whistle came back in reply. Joyce was hurrying towards Mary with a bag containing a few of her belongings in her hand. They also saw, trying his best to keep from being seen, Ray Clews. Dodging from one shadow to another, he followed along behind Joyce.

'Oh my God, Mary,' Joyce whispered. 'I was so scared he'd beat me again!'

'It's all right now. Don't look round but he's followed you. I saw him a minute ago; he's trying to hide.' Mary gave Joyce a hug and felt her body shaking with fear. 'Come on, let's get moving.'

When Ray saw the two women hug then start to walk across the heath, he rushed forward, shouting, 'So, it's a woman you are meeting! You dirty cow!'

Mary and Joyce turned to face him as the barrage went on.

'Wait 'til the people of Wednesbury hear about this one! I always thought you to be a whore, Joyce Clews, but another woman...!'

'Actually it's more than one woman!' Annie said, stepping out of the darkness. 'And we'd like a word with you Ray Clews.'

'Come on then!' he challenged. 'Joyce you tell me what the hell you are doin' and you tell me right now!' Ray's blood was up as he glared at his wife through the semi-darkness.

'I've had enough of you! That's what is going on!' Joyce spat back.

Kneeling behind a nearby bush, Violet clutched the rock tightly in her hand. She was scared beyond belief and shaking. She had agreed to her part in the plan because she was the quickest and most agile, but now she wasn't so sure she could go through with it. However, her anger swiftly mounted as she saw Ray take a step towards his wife, his arm raised ready to strike her.

Violet rushed behind him. Seeing her movement in his peripheral vision, Ray began to turn her way in surprise and she swung her arm with all her might and let go of the stone. The rock caught Ray on his right temple and he faltered in his footing. Clutching his head, he turned fully to face her as the others stepped forward.

As they surrounded him, Ray began to laugh, still unsteady on his feet. 'What do you lot think you are doin'?'

'This!' Mary said quietly as she swung her rock at the back of his head. Spinning in her direction, extremely wobbly now, Ray's body faltered again. Touching his head, his fingers came away covered in blood.

'You're all mad!' he said as he turned within the circle of women bearing down on him. Raising his fists like a bare-knuckle fighter helped little as another rock caught him on his left temple... Annie's aim was true.

Ray Clews fell to his knees shaking his head as another rock came down again on the back of his head. Throwing a punch Violet's way caught her sharply in her stomach and she went down gasping for breath.

'Aha...' Ray spluttered at his small triumph, 'come on then, let's be havin' you – one at a time or all at once – makes no difference to me.'

Breathing easier, Violet dragged herself to her feet and quite suddenly everyone lunged at Ray who was trying to maintain his stance but fell again to his knees. Mary strode forward and, stamping a foot hard down on his shoulder, pressed him to a lying position. With Ray now lying face down on the ground trying in vain to punch and kick out at them, they piled onto him struggling to hold him in place.

With Annie sitting on his one arm, Martha sat on the other. Mary sat on one leg and Violet on his other, Kath sat on his back. Joyce picked up a huge rock and moved in close.

Raising his head slightly, Ray saw the look of pure hatred on Joyce's face, and with their faces so close together, she said quietly, 'Ray Clews, you will never hit another woman, nor kill another babby! I hope you rot in hell!' With that she brought the rock down full force onto the back of his head, and now filled with fury, hit her husband time and again until his struggles finally ceased.

Joyce was exhausted and dropped to sit on the heath as the others scrambled off the man. She looked at the bloodied rock in her hand then at her clothes and said breathlessly, 'Christ! That's another frock ruined!' Standing, she gave her husband a final swift kick in the ribs. 'That's for my dress!'

Surprise formed on the faces of the Wives in the darkness at Joyce's renewed anger. Then they began to drag Ray Clews to the edge of the gin pit before pushing him down into the bowels of the earth. Gathering the rocks used, they were sent in after him.

'Joyce,' Violet said, still holding her stomach from Ray's

punch, 'you must burn your clothes as soon as you get home, do you understand?'

Nodding, Joyce looked at each of them in turn and muttered, 'Thanks wenches.'

Curt nods given in return, they turned to leave, making their way back to the bridge before returning to their homes.

The plan had been executed flawlessly and Joyce took them all by surprise as she asked quietly, 'Can I join your club ladies... please?' It was surreal as a silent vote was called for out in the darkness and as hands were raised, they found themselves with another member of the Wives club.

But as the days passed, each member of the club relived the incident over and over again in their minds. They had taken a life. They were now murderers. A meeting was called and the conversation centred solely on the deed.

'I can't believe we actually did it,' Mary said. 'I feel so bad about it.'

'It was necessary,' Martha took up, 'you know as well as I that Joyce would not have had it any other way, but I have to say I feel really bad about it too. I just hope God forgives us.'

Violet shuddered. 'I hope we never have to do that again.'

'You can bet your life we may have to face this at some point in the future, but I think we should do our utmost to avoid it at all possible costs. We would have to find another way of dealing with problems.' Kath said.

'At least Ray Clews can't hurt Joyce, or any other woman or child, again,' Annie said quietly.

'Well, it's done now,' Martha said sternly, 'and there's nothing we can do to make ourselves feel better about it. We chose to take that path and we have to suffer the consequences of living with it for the rest of our lives. I just hope we don't have to endure jail time as well.'

Nine

Joyce had moved into Kath's house and rumours were rife about the disappearance of Ray Clews until eventually everyone in the town had agreed he had run off, owing rent and leaving poor Joyce to face the music alone.

Listening to her mother's breathing beside her, Violet again thought on her life over the last few years. She had become a murderer along with her mother and the Wives. She did not kill randomly like a crazy person though; she felt it was justice. The police and courts almost always found in favour of men in domestic disputes. Women could be beaten and raped within a marriage, there was no law to say otherwise... except the law of the Wednesbury Wives. This kind of treatment of women would not be tolerated by their little group but they had to be very careful in their dealings and the punishments that followed. For the women of Wednesbury to be safe, it was imperative the Wives remain anonymous to the law and authorities. God only knew what would happen were they to be discovered.

Violet felt remorse at what she had done; she felt shame also but certainly no pity for the man she had helped to dispose of. She felt strong in the belief that no man would judge her – she felt only God had that right.

*

Time slipped by in the Clancy house and in Wednesbury. The passing years had seen the Wives deal with relatively few cases. A wife beater had been threatened with a thrashing himself which had curtailed the physical abuse doled out to his wife. Another who had been accused of raping a young woman on the heath had admitted it when faced with the Wives. His crime had shown him named and shamed and fear of a jail sentence had him leave the town sharpish.

Each time justice was served, there was a risk of the Wives being discovered. But the secret grapevine of the women of the town knew that to divulge any information to the local constabulary of their identities or intentions would see many more women in peril. The women of Wednesbury would band together in a crisis and the secret was kept on pain of their own possible suffering in the future.

Once more summer gave way to autumn and the leaves began their annual cycle of turning colour. It promised to be an 'Indian summer', the good weather lasting well into the autumnal months.

Walking up Union Street after shopping in the Shambles, a small market at the centre of the town, Violet heard a horse trotting on the cobblestones behind her. Turning, she saw the rider. Black hair blowing from his face by the wind, with strong legs and arms guiding his mount, he pulled up beside her. Dark eyes sparkled as he jumped down from his horse.

Fear swept over her as he approached. Other than Geordie, Jim and Charlie, Violet had no dealings with men at all other than those the Wives doled out justice to, which merely fuelled her anxiety and her fear of them. After Sligo, she wanted nothing to do with them. She was afraid they might all be like he was. She would shy away from any man who looked as if he might speak to her.

The man's wide smile showed white even teeth. Looking around her, Violet searched for a means of escape.

'Hello there!' His voice had a deep timbre. 'How are you this fine morning?' Cultured too. Receiving no reply, he went on, 'My apologies, where are my manners?' Bowing deeply, he grinned, saying, 'My name is Spencer Gittins. My father is Joshua Gittins of Gittins' Nails in Wednesbury.'

Still receiving no word from Violet as she turned to continue her journey, he placed his hand on her arm, saying, 'Don't go, stay and talk awhile.'

Snatching her arm from his hand, Violet hissed, 'Don't you dare touch me!'

'I apologise, Miss,' he said in surprise and moved back a step, 'I meant no offence.'

'Did your father, Joshua Gittins of Gittins' Nails never teach you that you do not accost women out on the street?' Venom swam like a river through her words. This was the first time she had been touched by a man since Sligo, and it stirred all the old anger in her again.

Standing with his mouth open, he stared as Violet continued acerbically.

'Now if you'll excuse me, I'll be on my way and I'll thank you to move aside and let me pass!' Her whole body was shaking as her anger and fear suffused.

As he took another step back, Violet hurried away from him, her heart beating nineteen to the dozen. She arrived home in double quick time all of a fluster.

'Whatever is the matter?' Kath asked, moving to her daughter who was shivering despite the good weather.

Violet explained in halting words about the man in the street. 'Oh Mum, I was so frightened!'

Kath gave the girl a warm hug. 'I can see that, love. Sit down, I'll make some tea then you can tell me all about it again.' Kath began to wonder if Violet would ever get over her experience with Sligo. Would she ever be able to associate with a man in the future? Kath hoped with all her heart her daughter would someday come to the realisation that not all men were like her late husband.

Joyce on her wage as a nail maker, was unable to save enough money to rent a place of her own and so had remained living with Kath and Violet. It was a happy arrangement, and all were in agreement of it.

Joyce had arrived back from her work and hearing what was being discussed, she said, 'Oh him, that's Spencer Gittins, the gaffer's son. Nice lad, bit headstrong, but a lovely kid. Just him and his dad now, his mother died giving birth some years ago. Child died too as I recall. Shame... nice family. It's Gittins I work for, Violet.'

Violet remembered once Joyce had jogged her memory. What she couldn't remember was ever seeing Spencer Gittins before, but then they hardly moved in the same social circles.

*

Violet thought a lot over the next few days about the young man in Union Street. In her mind's eye she saw the dark hair and brown eyes that twinkled. She heard again the cultured voice that made her stare into space for minutes at a time. She found herself daydreaming about him a lot before snapping herself out of it to return to whatever task she was undertaking.

Violet was laying the table for another meeting of the Wives, all but Joyce who was still at work, and realised some considerable time had elapsed since the last gathering. Who would be coming? What would it be about? Although she knew it to be important, she prayed it would not end with someone's death. It had been some years and other cases since they had killed only one man, but the fear was always there that the next case would call on them to do something similar.

Everyone sat around Kath's kitchen table and Annie walked through the kitchen door looking like she was dressed for an evening out. A thin girl followed behind her.

The girl spoke quietly, 'Hello Violet.'

Shock took her as Violet looked into the eyes of her childhood arch-enemy. Primrose Berry.

Given tea, she sat down as Violet stared at her. Barely recognisable, she had all but wasted away. Her once bouncing blonde curls had given way to thinning hair; sparkling eyes now looked almost dead in her gaunt face. Violet couldn't believe the difference a few short years had made and found herself wondering if she still had her spiteful streak.

Primrose held her cup with both hands as if stealing the heat to warm her cadaverous frame. Violet found herself watching the bird-like movements; eyes that darted this way and that, fear wrapping itself around the girl who sat opposite her. Violet had heard that Primrose's mother had died the previous year and had felt a twinge of sorrow for the girl, although she was still wary of her.

She watched intently as Primrose bolted the bread and

cheese offered, eating as though she'd never been fed. Whatever had happened to bring her to this?

While everyone ate, they chatted about everyday things, putting Primrose at her ease somewhat, and Violet cast her mind back.

The marketplace was the fount of all knowledge, where gossip was rife, messages could be passed safely, and help could be sought and given. It was here she'd learned of Mrs Berry's death and of Primrose's marriage. The girl had been married off to a man much older than herself and Violet winced, thinking the spiteful streak obviously ran through her mother too. Primrose's marriage was an acquisitive one: no love there, only the worship of money and the prestige it brought with it. Primrose had married Francis Woolley, the owner of a nail-making business – Woolley's Nails. The making of nails in the Black Country town was big business and they were transported all over the country. The two firms had always been friendly rivals for contracts.

Bringing herself back to the present, Violet took in the now Mrs Primrose Woolley. The same age as herself, she looked older than any of the women who sat at the table. Sunken cheeks stretched into the ghost of a smile in thanks for her food. Primrose's eyes could not meet Violet's and she knew the girl's mind was also reliving the spite she had shown Violet as they were growing up.

Pouring more tea into her cup, Violet said, 'Drink up, Primrose, you're safe here with us.'

Violet saw the pride emanate from her mother which made her blush. Whatever was ailing Primrose Woolley, Violet felt sure the Wives could resolve it.

Ten

Primrose sat at the table looking at each face in turn but seeing only her life of the last year.

Her mother had come to the last of the money left to them by her father on his death: It was time for Primrose to marry, she'd said.

Francis Woolley had shown an interest in the girl and he was a self-made man. Owning Woolley's Nails, he had built up his company and was now a successful businessman, albeit known to be ruthless. He cared for no one save Francis Woolley.

Frank, as he preferred to be called, was a rough man and twenty years Primrose's senior. Her protest at being married off to a man so much older than herself had fallen on the deaf ears of her mother... he had money, and lots of it!

Frank Woolley was short in stature and fat, with a red nose, from the constant drinking of alcohol, taking centre stage on his round face. His small piggy eyes would squint at the columns of figures laid before him at the end of each day's trading. Anyone found to be short on their tally of making nails would be given the sack and found themselves out on the street with no job regardless of their circumstances. These vacancies weren't vacant for long – someone was always looking for work in Wednesbury. The 'bread line' of people out of work standing at the corner of the market grew longer each day.

The women around the table where Primrose now sat waited patiently as if they too were seeing the events that had shaped her life.

Primrose had worn her mother's wedding gown on the day of her marriage to Frank Woolley but there had been no joy in the wearing of it. The ferocity with which he took her on the wedding night compounded his rough nature. She was left bruised and bleeding. Badly wanting a son to succeed him, Frank had abused her body in an effort to make her pregnant. His efforts were thwarted however, and she had not conceived; beatings followed in the wake of his anger and frustration. He felt he had married a barren woman and now he was stuck with her. Although not practising, Frank was a Catholic, and divorce for him was not an option.

Her mind snapped to attention as she heard Violet's words again: *you're safe here with us...*

She blurted out, 'He beats me!'

Martha said, 'Well, gel, there's a lot that gets beaten hereabouts.'

Feeling her stomach sink, Primrose felt sure she was not going to find help here with these women. She remembered how she had plagued Violet mercilessly in their childhood, so why would they help her now? Standing up, she mumbled her apologies for disturbing them and walked towards the back door.

Annie Green caught her arm gently, saying, 'Sit down, girl, and tell us what the problem is.'

Resuming her seat at the table, Primrose drew in a breath like it was the last of the oxygen on the planet. 'He beats me because I can't give him a son! He says I'm barren and now he's stuck with me! Although I've begged him he won't divorce me because he's a Catholic, but he never goes to church. And...' she went on, 'I'm sure Frank Woolley killed my mother!'

A collective intake of breath stole air from the room before being released through clenched teeth. She watched the looks pass from face to face as horror turned to puzzlement.

Martha asked, 'How do you work that one out? I thought your mother died of the influenza last winter that took a lot of others along with it.'

'That's what the doctor said when Frank eventually paid his fee to visit my mother. She starved to death, Martha, she starved because Frank refused to help with food or money!'

'So,' said Mary Forbes, 'in her weakened state the influenza caught her and carried her off.' It was not a question, more a statement of fact.

The women looked at her as Primrose burst out, 'Frank Woolley deliberately starved my mother to death knowing her impecunious lifestyle! It was premeditated murder!'

'That's as maybe,' said Martha, 'but Frank Woolley is a big name in this town and it's not like an accident could befall him with no suspicion laid.'

'Martha,' Primrose said calmly, her emotions once more under control, 'you misunderstand me, I don't want Frank to have an accident.'

Kath Clancy asked, 'Then why are you here?'

'I want...' she said, placing her hands on the table and leaning forward, 'I want Frank Woolley ruined! I want to see his business go down the drain! I want to see him penniless and starving... before I leave him!'

Gasps sounded in the tiny kitchen as Violet said, 'That's a big ask, Primrose.'

'I understand that, Violet, and anything I can do to help bring about the downfall of my *husband* I will do!'

Violet looked at the girl she had once hated and she asked, 'What about you, Primrose, what will happen to you if Frank's business is ruined?'

Unable to hold back her tears any longer, Primrose let them fall freely, 'I don't know and I don't care, but I swear to you ladies here, if he tries to beat me one more time I'll knife him where he stands and hang the consequences!'

'Christ, girl, you can't do that!' Mary muttered.

'Right,' Martha began in her chairwoman's voice, 'let's see what can be done to help Primrose. But, my girl...' She paused looking directly at her, '... you utter one word of this to anyone and it won't be Frank Woolley's downfall you'll see... but the downfall of every woman in Wednesbury!'

Swearing her oath of silence and allegiance to the Wives, Primrose listened to the verbal exchanges across the kitchen table.

Agreeing a plan could be constructed, and knowing this would take time to formulate and execute in the utmost safety, she reluctantly agreed to return home and 'put up' with her husband's abuse until the time came when she would no longer have to.

The women knew time was of the essence as Primrose said the beatings were getting worse; Primrose could avoid Frank at times but there would still be occasions when he was drunk that he would be trying, yet again, for the son he so desperately sought.

Walking back to her house in Church Hill, her thoughts returned to Violet Clancy and of all the nasty situations Violet had found herself in, all of Primrose's doing. Now here she was, along with those other women, trying to help. She felt the warmth of shame colour her cheeks as she trudged wearily homeward.

Walking up Ethelfleda Terrace, past St Bartholomew's Church, Primrose continued up Church Hill. Rose Hill House, Frank's house where she too now lived, stood in its own grounds and was backed onto by the Vicarage. Three stone steps led up to the front door which was flanked by stone columns. The gardens were extensive but in need of help from a gardener: Primrose had lost interest in it. Entering the huge house, Primrose heard Frank's voice boom out, 'Where the bloody hell have you been?'

'The market,' Primrose said quietly, hanging her shawl on the coat stand in the hall.

Frank continued, 'And you ain't bought nothing?'

'No,' her answer was short and simple; the less she said to him the better she liked it.

He shot another barb with, 'Not like your mother for that, thank God! That woman could spend my money like water gushing down a drain!'

'What money?' The words were out of her mouth before Primrose could stop them. 'You never gave her any money!' Oh well, in for a penny in for a pound – the thought made her smile as she turned away from him.

'You bloody ingrate!' Storming towards her, he swung her to face him, his fingers digging into the flesh of her arm. 'I looked after your grasping mother the same as I look after you!'

Looking down at her thin body and her worn-out clothing,

Primrose shot back, 'I hope that shouldn't be for too much longer then!'

Slapping her across the face, his words intermingled with little bells in her ears. 'What do you mean by that?'

No answer was the stern reply which he took as her being timorous.

'Oh never mind,' he said nastily, 'just get up those bloody stairs… I mean to beget me a son!'

Dread filled her whole being as he dragged her up the staircase and threw her onto the bed.

'Now then, woman,' he hissed, removing his clothes before they burst their buttons of their own accord, 'get your clothes off and let's get to it!'

As Frank Woolley's body pumped on top of her thin frame and he puffed his exertion in her ear, Primrose tried to ignore the pain by turning her thoughts to the help about to be given to her by the Wednesbury Wives. She hoped it would come sooner rather than later.

Eleven

How on earth could the women bring down one of the wealthiest and well-known industrialists of Wednesbury?

They had to know more about Frank Woolley, of his business, who he dealt with, and what his business associates thought of him.

Somehow they had to shut down his operations, but this was something that would affect his workers – badly. They would find themselves out of work and having families to feed with no money coming in...

Listening to the women's banter in the tiny kitchen, Violet's mind whirled. This latest task given to the Wives seemed impossible to complete without adverse effects on the town and the people in it.

Excusing herself, she decided to go for a walk on the heath to clear her mind. She strode out along the streets of the town before they met the bridge of the canal. Suppressing a shudder as she was reminded of the last time she was there with Joyce and the others, she walked onto the heath. The sun was still warm on her back as she lazily strolled alone.

She stopped occasionally to pick the wild flowers, arranging them in a small bunch. She was admiring them when she heard the sound of hoof beats. The blood quickened in her veins as the horse stopped beside her and the rider jumped down. Her heart beat faster as she looked into the dark eyes of Spencer Gittins. Pushing his unruly black hair back, he gave a small bow.

'Miss Clancy,' he said formally as he kept his distance from her this time, 'I'm pleased to make your acquaintance once more.'

'Mr Gittins,' she said, nodding once before turning away from him to walk back towards her home. She could not deny he sparked her interest. Before she knew it he was walking beside her.

'You are not surprised I know your name?' he asked, a mischievous twinkle in his eye. Ignoring him, Violet walked on. 'Please Miss Clancy,' he intoned, 'I ask only to be your friend.'

Violet stopped and turned to face him. 'Why?' she asked. She had never expected to meet a man who would not make her feel angry or frightened, but this young man made her feel neither. She was curious that this was a new feeling for her.

A grin spread over his face showing his even white teeth. 'Because I like you.'

'You don't even know me, Mr Gittins!' She said as she stepped forward once more. A blush rose to her cheeks at the pleasure she felt at his words.

'Ah, Miss Clancy, that's where you are wrong. You see I made it my business to know everything about you.'

Not everything! Violet kept the thought to herself saying instead, 'Now why would you do that I ask myself?' Her voice maintained its hardness, but with a hint of sarcasm lacing through it. There was no point at all in encouraging this young man, she knew it could never be that a relationship between them could exist. If it should be that they became sweethearts and he found out about her being abused by Sligo, he would hate her. Then her terrible secret might become common knowledge! No, there was no way she could risk that happening, so it would be best not to encourage him.

'Miss Violet Clancy,' he went on, 'you intrigue me. I have thought of you a lot since our last meeting. You have haunted my dreams.' He gave a small sonorous laugh.

Stopping again to look at him, Violet said sternly, 'Mr Gittins, I don't know what you want from me, but whatever it is – you can't have it!'

'Miss Clancy!' he feigned shock and hurt and she couldn't prevent the corners of her mouth lifting slightly in a tiny smile. 'God forbid you should think this to be anything untoward! I should merely like to become a friend to you and your family in the first instance and then...'

'Why?' she asked again. Her mind was questioning his motives.

Lowering his eyes, Spencer Gittins fumbled with the horse's rein in his hand. 'Miss Clancy,' he said quietly, 'I would like to visit you and ask your mother's permission for us to step out at some time in the future.'

Oh Lord! Spencer Gittins wanted to court her!

'I know we don't know each other as such and I would be more than willing for you to bring along a chaperone. I would never wish to cause you any upset or fear.'

His eyes met hers once more and Violet felt the blush rise in her cheeks.

'Mr Gittins, I'm afraid that won't be possible.' Turning away from the disappointment she saw in his eyes, she walked briskly up Portway Lane and headed for home. She did not look back.

Once in the kitchen, Violet could not turn her mind from the handsome young man she'd spoken with on the heath. She had gone out to ponder Primrose's predicament and come home with one of her own.

Settled with tea before a raging fire in the hearth, Kath said, 'You want to tell me about it?' Looking up sharply, Violet's mouth dropped open. 'Violet, you're my daughter and I know when something is troubling you. Get it off your chest, wench, maybe I can help.'

Violet told her mother of the meeting on the heath, of the words spoken between Spencer Gittins and herself.

'Why,' her mother asked, 'would you not want to be courted by this young man? Don't you like him?' Seeing the flush rise to her daughter's face, Kath went on, 'Ah, I see that you do!'

'Mum... how can I after... after...'

'After John Sligo?' Kath's face screwed up as she remembered. 'Yes, I can see why now, but, Violet, someday someone will want you for who you are; they won't care a jot about your past, they will love *you*, and you need to give them a chance.'

'Mum... I couldn't... you know...' Embarrassment flooded through her.

'One day, all that will be forgotten, sweetheart. The man you love and marry will help you forget, I promise.' Kath held Violet in her arms, kissing her hair, 'Take your time, find the right man, you'll know when you do.' With that she climbed the stairs to bed, and Violet sat before the fire.

I think I have found the right man, her mind said, *and I think it's Spencer Gittins!*

*

Violet heard voices in the living room as she entered the tiny kitchen the following day.

'Oh Kath, I'm so sorry but he was at me, questions coming so fast I didn't know what to say!' Joyce simpered.

Kath replied, 'It's all right, Joyce, I don't think Violet knows he was asking you about her.'

Hearing her name, she stood and listened behind the slightly open door.

'Just tell me what he was asking, Joyce.'

'Well... he wanted to know all about your Violet, her name, where her lived, who her lived with...' Joyce pulled in a breath, '...had her got a financee?'

Kath laughed, 'Fiancé, Joyce, the word is fiancé.'

'I don't give a bugger what the word is, he wanted to know had her got one!'

'What did you tell him?'

'Well,' Joyce continued, 'I told him she hadn't. Said we three lived here together on account of you helping me with money a while back and I was paying you back. I made no mention of the Wednesbury Wives, Kath, honest! I wouldn't, you know that!'

'Rest easy, Joyce, I know you wouldn't. So tell me more about young Spencer Gittins.'

So that was who they were discussing! Joyce had been asked all about Violet. The question now was, just how much had she told him?

Determined to find out, she waited, hardly daring to breathe, in her hiding place behind the kitchen door.

'Well,' Joyce resumed, 'he said as he wanted your permission to court young Violet and I told him he had to see you about that.'

'Quite right,' Kath said.

'Ar, and then he asked why her weren't married already.'

Violet listened eagerly for the answer, moving closer to the doorway.

'And what did you say to that?' Kath asked gently.

'Well he was insistent... why weren't her married? Had anyone asked for her hand? Had her refused anybody? I was flummoxed I can tell you! I got to the state I was meeting myself coming back! Then it just sort of came out...'

'What did?' asked Kath feeling concerned.

'Well you know... about John Sligo! Oh God, Kath, I'm real sorry. I could have bit me own tongue off!'

Joyce had told him! Spencer Gittins now knew Violet had been violated and was soiled goods! A sob escaped her lips and tears rolled down her face.

Kath had heard Violet come into the kitchen but she had not entered the living room. She had kept her counsel, after all the girl had a right to hear what was being said, but as she heard the sob she knew Violet would now need the comfort of her mother more than ever.

Pushing the door open Kath rushed to her sobbing daughter.

Joyce followed close on Kath's heels and wailing sorrow at seeing Violet's distress. 'Bloody hell!' she cried, 'my mouth opens and both my clodhoppers wade in!'

Despite her misery, Violet gave a little laugh at the

expression. 'Joyce,' she said through her tears, 'it's all right, he would have found out sooner or later, I don't doubt. I know how persistent he can be.'

'Oh cocker,' Joyce wailed again, 'I ain't half sorry!'

'It was never meant to be,' Violet said, accepting the inevitable along with a cup of tea from her mother. 'I only pray he keeps the knowledge to himself!'

Twelve

Watching Violet set off for the market, Kath sat with her tea by the fire allowing her thoughts to roam.

John Sligo had died, by her hand. She felt guilt and shame at what she'd done, even though it was an accident and several years ago now. She knew it would haunt her for the rest of her life. He had ruined her daughter's chance of a husband and a normal life. He had spoiled any possibility of Kath having grandchildren. The hatred of her deceased husband swelled in her again, shutting out her previous feelings.

Lost in anger and misery, Kath wasn't sure she'd heard a knock on the door until it came again. She rose and opened the door to be faced with a very handsome young man.

'Mrs Clancy?' he asked confidently. Kath nodded her response, and he went on, 'Forgive my visit to your home. My name is Spencer Gittins. Ah, I see you have heard of me.'

Enlightenment showed on Kath's face as she saw the genuine smile cross his face.

'Come in Mr Gittins,' she said, stepping back to allow him entry. 'Please, take a seat and have some tea.'

Sitting at the table, he cast a glance around the tiny

kitchen. 'This is lovely, so warm and cosy.' There was no condescension in his tone and Kath found herself warming to the polite young man.

'So Mr Gittins, may I ask the reason for your visit?'

Replacing his cup carefully on its saucer, he looked her straight in the eye. *Good breeding*, she thought... *confident too.*

'Mrs Clancy, I came to ask your permission to court Violet...' Seeing her face harden, he rushed on, 'with a chaperone of your choice at all times of course.'

'Mr Gittins,' Kath said quietly but meeting his eyes full on, 'I am aware of the enquiries you have made regarding my family and – more importantly – my daughter. I gather you know what has happened to Violet in her past...' Kath saw him take a breath to intervene and held up her hand in prevention, 'so why would you wish to step out with her?' Placing her hand flat on the table she gave him leave to answer.

'I have met Violet twice now, as I'm sure you're aware, nothing untoward you understand, and both times she has left me confused and bewildered. I don't know if you believe in love at first sight, Mrs Clancy, but believe me when I say I do!'

Leaning back in her chair, Kath gestured for him to continue.

'I pestered the life out of Joyce Clews to tell me everything she knew about Violet; I would not let up until I knew it all. I fully intend to apologise to Mrs Clews for the harassment, I assure you.'

Kath thought to herself, *my dear young man, you don't know it all, in fact you don't know the half of it.* Keeping the thought to herself, Kath listened as he continued.

'I know what she suffered at the hands of John Sligo, and it's just as well he drowned as, forgive my saying, had he not I would have killed him myself!' Kath was shocked at the young man's outburst, but slowly the surprise turned to a warmth towards him.

Kath had heard Violet creep into the house and knew she was listening to every word said.

Kath, feeling sure she knew the answer already, asked Spencer, 'And knowing this, how does it make you feel towards Violet?'

'Oh, Mrs Clancy,' he breathed, 'I can't get her out of my mind. I want to take care of her, treat her like the lady she is, and I promise I would love her all her days. I'm sorry for the way she was treated by that blackguard Sligo, but I'm glad he got what was coming to him. I assure you it makes no difference to the way I feel about your daughter.'

'If I didn't know better, Mr Gittins,' Kath said with a smile, 'I might think that a proposal of marriage.' Watching his reaction carefully, Kath was surprised he didn't pall, instead his face flushed with unfettered excitement.

'It is! Mrs Clancy, if Violet would have me, would you give your consent? Naturally we would wait until we knew each other better, and if at any time she wished to withdraw from the engagement I would honour that. With your consent and Violet's agreement you would both make me the happiest man alive!' His excitement bubbled over at the last.

'My goodness, Mr Gittins, a proposal after only two meetings? Well, the decision would be Violet's. If she agreed to your proposal, you would *never* mistreat her in any way otherwise you would have me to deal with, and I warn you now… you *would* lose out!' Kath paused to allow her words to sink in. 'Should Violet *not* accept your proposal, you will not meet with her again intentionally or accidentally. Actions speak louder than words as I know to my cost, so this is my way of ensuring my daughter is safe and happy. Do I make myself clear?' Kath was impressed by the young man and pleased about his proposal, but her first concern was Violet.

The young man nodded until Kath thought his head would roll off his shoulders. 'As crystal, Mrs Clancy.'

'My daughter has been hurt very badly in the past, Mr Gittins, and I could not protect her then, but be very sure I can and *will* protect her now.' Kath's voice carried a warning that left him under no illusion that she would not carry out the underlying threat.

'Mrs Clancy,' Spencer said leaning forward, 'you have my word as a gentleman that I will protect Violet with my life.'

Kath nodded. She had never heard words like this before and from such a young man too. Her heart softened to him even more.

'I wish you luck, Mr Gittins; you have my blessing but... only on Violet's decision. She can be very stubborn, as I'm sure you'll find out. The decision will be made only by her, with no cajoling from you, my lad!'

Exchanging a smile, Kath set the kettle to boil once more, wondering what Violet had made of her exchange with Spencer Gittins.

*

Joyce, Violet and Kath had finished their evening meal and sat by the fire when Kath said, 'Violet, I know you heard what Spencer Gittins and I spoke of this afternoon...' without taking her eyes away from the flames dancing in the grate, she went on, 'and I'd like to hear what you have to say about it.'

Joyce jumped in, 'Spencer Gittins came? This afternoon? Why... what did he want?'

Kath stayed Joyce's tongue with a raise of her hand.

Violet blustered, 'I... I don't know. It was a bit of a shock hearing him ask for your permission to propose marriage...'

Joyce slapped her hands to her mouth to prevent her further intervention in the conversation.

'I... I never thought... I never dreamed...' Violet was all of a fluster. 'Besides, what about you? It would mean leaving you!'

'Yes,' Kath said quietly, 'that's what newlyweds do, they set up on their own. What I want to know is how you feel about marriage... how you feel about him?' Kath was not so afraid of living alone now she had Joyce with her; she just wanted to see Violet happy. After all, this was an opportunity Kath had never foreseen for her daughter.

'Oh I *do* like him!' Violet burst out. 'But I'm scared, Mum, because... you know what he'd want and... and I don't think I could!'

Tears fringed her lashes as Violet looked at her mother.

'Well,' Kath said, 'you heard what he said about honouring your withdrawal from the engagement at any time if you chose to do that...'

'Bloody hell!' Joyce could not hold her tongue any longer. 'He said that? Bloody hell!'

'He did, Joyce,' Kath said, giving Violet a warm smile.

'Take him up on it,' Joyce said. 'I bloody would!'

'Think about it, wench, you don't have to decide right away, but he will be wanting an answer at some point.'

Kath's words closed the conversation and the three of them sat silently each with their own thoughts.

*

The next meeting of the Wives was called for Sunday so Joyce could join in, not having to work on the Lord's Day.

Primrose Woolley was still having to bear the brunt of Frank's anger and frustration at her not conceiving him a son and heir. The Wives needed to come up with a foolproof plan to bring down the nail-making giant and see his business in ruins.

Kath had to admit her mind was more on Violet and the possibility of her marrying Spencer Gittins, but she listened to what was being said around the table.

Joyce had volunteered to try and find out if anyone knew who Frank Woolley dealt with. She had laughed, saying her questions probably wouldn't be out of place... everyone knew her as a busybody!

The nails were made in Frank's factory but more information on his buyers was needed. They also needed to know if he paid outworkers, people who made nails for him in their own homes, probably receiving a paltry sum for their hard labours hour after hour.

The invisible grapevine in the market would answer that question, and Mary and Annie were charged with the task of setting the grapevine to work. The answer would be back within the week. It was possible suspicions would be raised, but once aware it was information for the Wednesbury Wives, it would be given with impunity.

When everyone was satisfied with the plan of action, Martha raised the subject of the women they were helping.

'Now,' she said, 'I know most of these wenches who we help out are in an imp... impy...'

'Impecunious,' Violet aided.

'Ar, in an impeckoonius situation, that's to say they don't have much or any money...'

Nods of understanding from the others spurred Martha on, 'So it's my thinking that if they are in a position to do so, they should pay a bit for us helping them out of a predicament even if it's only a halfpenny.'

Annie drew breath to speak but Martha beat her to it. 'I know, but think about this. What if one of us was caught by the coppers? What if we went to jail? We'd need some money for feeding the kids. Somebody to look after them until we got out. So, if these women paid a bit towards the solving of their problems, we could have that money put by for when it's needed.'

'Bloody hell,' Mary said, 'you make us sound like paid-for-hire killers!'

Titters ran round the table at her words.

All smiles faded at Martha's next words. 'That's exactly what we are. The only difference now is... we ain't paid!'

Thirteen

Mary and Annie strode to the market early hoping to catch the women, from Frank Woolley's factory across The Mount in Crankhall Lane, doing their shopping before the work day began.

A few questions were whispered and promises of answers were given. No one asked why the information was needed, after all it was only for the grace of God *they* were not asking the help of the Wednesbury Wives themselves. Besides, who knew... in the future they may well find themselves in that very position.

Arriving home, Annie was pleased that the message on the grapevine had begun its surreptitious journey. As she busied herself with the baking of pies for tea, she reflected on Martha's words. They were killers, all of them, and no they had never received monetary payment for any debts owed. The women's gratitude and silence had been payment enough, but there was wisdom in Martha's words.

Annie thought of her husband Charlie, and then of Martha's children. Yes, she knew the Wives would take care of them, but money would be needed in order for that to happen. Kath had her own money, but none of the others would ever ask for her to pay for the upkeep of their family. The thought of charging a fee or asking for a donation didn't sit well with her, it felt dirty somehow. Not that doing away with someone's husband wasn't, but it appeared to shed a whole new light on things. Besides, it was only the really bad cases that would see that happen. Annie realised she was trying to rationalise this in her own mind. She couldn't; she was – they were killers and there was no getting away from the fact.

It had been agreed that Kath would hold any money given over for 'favours' done as she had a better notion of finance than the rest of them, having dealt with her own. Everyone concurred that if anything should happen to Kath, such as being arrested, God forbid, then Violet would take over the financial situation in the interim.

Pies in the oven to bake, Annie sat with a cup of tea, pondering the plight of Primrose Woolley and whether she could contribute to the coffers.

A shout from Violet reached her ears, 'Annie, it's only me.'

'Come on in, wench, I have cake fresh out of the oven and the tea is mashed.'

Watching Violet savour her slice of cake closing her eyes with the enjoyment of it, Annie waited. She had something to tell or ask and it would come in her own time.

'Annie, I want to ask you something... well tell you something first.'

'Oh ar,' Annie said, her heart swelling with love for Kath's girl, 'and what would that be then?'

'Well,' prevarication hovered on Violet's lips but then all

in a rush it came out, 'I don't know if Mum told you, but Spencer Gittins has asked mother's permission for me to marry him!'

'What? Joshua Gittins' lad?' Annie asked, taken aback. Kath had not mentioned it to her, but then this was between mother and daughter.

'Yes! The very same!' Annie saw the emotions flicker across Violet's pretty face. She had grown into a lovely young woman, why was Annie only noticing this now? Maybe the mention of marriage had triggered the observation.

'Well now,' Annie said, trying to find the words 'And...?' was all she could manage.

'I wanted to ask your advice, Annie. What do you think I should do?'

Violet and Annie had always had a good relationship and they would often chat over a cup of tea, but this was quite another thing, asking her advice about marriage.

'Well, now,' Annie began again, 'I'm not one for giving advice, as well you know, but I'd ask you these questions. Do you, or could you, love him? How would you feel about living with him rather than your mum? What about sleeping in his bed with him? And, don't get upset, love, but what will happen if he finds out about what John Sligo did to you?'

'Oh he knows already!' Violet said matter-of-fact.

Annie's eyes widened and her mouth dropped open at the words.

Popping a bit of cake into Annie's open mouth, Violet laughed as she related the conversation that had taken place between her mother and Spencer Gittins.

When she ended, Annie asked her question again, 'Do you, or could you, love him?'

'Yes,' Violet gushed. 'Oh, Annie, I think I could!'

'Then that's half the battle won!' Annie declared. Seeing the meaning of it dawn on the girl, she quickly added, 'The rest will come in time, if it is God's will.'

Giving Annie a kiss and hug Violet set off home and Annie sat with silent tears coursing down her face happy at the trust shown in her.

The good Lord had not seen fit to grant Annie and Charlie any children and over the twenty years of their marriage her husband had never laid the blame at her feet. Whatever the reason, she had tried to come to terms with the fact she would never be a mother. Never hold and suckle a baby; never watch her child grow to adulthood; never see them marry and never have any grandchildren. The fact that young Violet had come to ask her for advice about marriage had her heart bursting with happiness and pride. Annie knew Kath would have suggested it and to share her daughter in this very important thing filled Annie with exquisite pleasure.

In bed that night Annie related to Charlie about Violet's visit and as they lay wrapped in each other's arms, they both quietly wept their longing for children of their own into the darkness.

*

Within the week, as promised, the grapevine had done its work and it was reported back that Frank Woolley only employed workers in his factory; he had no outworkers. He relied on one buyer in Wolverhampton. Eggs and basket sprang to Violet's mind on hearing this.

Passing this information on in the weekly gathering, the

question was raised about how the group could interfere with the wholesaler buying his nails from Woolley.

Kath said, 'The buyer could always buy from Joshua Gittins.'

All eyes turned to Violet and she flushed to the roots of her hair. They were all, it seemed, in the 'know' regarding Violet's proposal of marriage although to her knowledge nothing further had been said or done about the matter.

Joyce said, 'Gittins' Nails are more expensive though.'

'Ar,' Martha intervened, 'that's as maybe, but what if the quality was better from Gittins'?'

'How do you mean?' Annie asked not quite understanding the meaning behind the words. She had been busy inspecting her fingernails for chips or cracks.

'Well,' Martha said, a mischievous twinkle in her eye, 'what if, say, the quality of the nails made at Frank's factory were suddenly to be inferior? In which case, the wholesaler would stop buying from Woolley's, and look for another supplier. The only other big place making nails in Wednesbury is Gittins'.' Excited realisation showed on each face as her words sunk in.

'If we could carry this off,' Annie asked, 'and we shut Woolley's place down, what would happen to the women from his factory? I mean, they'd be out of work and they wouldn't thank us for that!'

Violet smiled, adding, 'Well, if Gittins' Nails had a regular big order from a new wholesaler, the one that Frank Woolley supplies at present, then Joshua Gittins would have to take on more workers – the ones laid off by Frank Woolley!'

'Exactly!' said Martha triumphantly. 'The question now is whether the women of Woolley's factory will go for the idea. It's them, after all, who will be sabotaging the nails. I'm reliably informed Joshua Gittins pays his workers a higher wage, but it's a risk.'

'I'll get the grapevine working again,' Violet offered, 'we'll soon know if they'll take the risk in support of the Wives.'

Fourteen

Spencer Gittins and Violet Clancy walked over the heath many times in the following days, with Mary and Annie trailing behind. Knowing her history and the abuse Violet had endured at the hands of John Sligo, they were all very protective of her, for which she was grateful.

The weather was still warm and the prediction of an Indian summer was proving to be correct. Early morning mists were burned off by the sun and days seemed long and endless. The trees were slow to drop their multicoloured leaves and insects still buzzed busily in the hedgerows. The blue sky was dotted with white fluffy clouds floating lazily past.

Mary and Annie were chatting and laughing behind the couple as they strolled in the sunshine on their latest jaunt across the heath when Spencer said, 'I meant every word I said to your mother, Violet; I suppose she *did* tell you?'

'I heard,' was all she said.

Spencer had been true to his word and not pushed Violet as she appeared to be happy taking things slowly. However he had a sense of their relationship becoming ever more serious and so had plucked up the courage to ask for her hand again. His excitement was getting the better of him and he was eager to know one way or the other.

Nodding, he asked her to consider his proposal of marriage and if her answer should be a refusal, he would abide by his promise to her mother to not meet with her again, although it would break his heart to do so. Violet told him she would consider it and would not keep him waiting too long for her answer.

Slowly, as they walked and talked, Violet began to relax in his company and all too soon it was time to part. Spencer thanked Annie and Mary for taking time out of their busy lives to chaperone them, as he always did, before requesting that all the families join him for a picnic in the grounds of Gittins Manor the following weekend.

On the Sunday morning of the picnic, Kath gave her daughter a package. Opening it, Violet discovered a beautiful dress of pale lemon linen covered with lace, a lemon ribbon tying at the waist.

Kath bound her hair up pinning it securely and when she saw herself in the mirror Violet gasped with pleasure.

'Oh Violet,' Kath said with tears in her eyes, 'you look so beautiful; I'm so very proud of you.'

Joining with the other families, they all wandered down Hobbins Street, up through Meeting Street and into Trouse Lane before reaching Gittins Manor. The grand house with its pillars flanking the front door seemed huge. The windows either side of the door glittered in the sunlight as did the bedroom ones. The tiled roof spread out with two chimneys sprouting from it. Tables full of food and drinks were laid out on the expansive lawns. A sandpit had been specially dug out under a shady tree for the younger children to play in and with the huge gates closed, everyone was safe inside the high walled garden. A peg was hammered into the lawn for the men to play horseshoes, should they feel the need of a little rivalry, whilst comfortable seating was set out around the tables for the women to enjoy their conversation but enabling them to keep an eye on both their children and their men.

Spencer led Violet to a food table where an older man stood. 'Violet, this is my father Joshua Gittins. Father, meet Violet Clancy.'

The man turned, a smile plastered across his face. 'I'm pleased to meet you Violet,' he said. Then turning to Spencer, he added, 'You were right, son, she is a beauty.' He boomed his laughter and Violet immediately warmed to him.

'Mr Gittins,' she said with a smile.

'Joshua – my friends call me Joshua.' He grinned.

After a brief chat, Spencer led her away again to refresh her glass of lemonade.

Violet had been nervous about meeting Spencer's father, but the man had instantly put her at her ease. She liked him – very much. She had been in awe at first sight of Spencer's house with its servants. Then she'd thought about her feelings for the man and realised they were growing in intensity.

Everyone enjoyed their fill of food, drink and fun, and as darkness began to descend, the maids lit the candles in small jars hanging from the tree branches and on the tables, bathing the area in a fairy light glow.

Having had Spencer's undivided attention for the whole day, Violet walked home with her mother in a dreamlike state. She wondered now if what she was feeling was love. She found herself eagerly awaiting Spencer's arrival whenever they went for walks on the heath, her excitement reaching fever pitch. She took special care of her appearance on the days they were to meet. She thought about him all the time they were apart, wondering where he was and what he was doing. He had maintained his gentlemanly behaviour at all times, and Violet relaxed with him more as time went on. She revelled in the knowledge that Spencer felt the same way about her, and soon it would be time to reply to his proposal.

*

The women working at Woolley's factory sent their answer via the grapevine in the market. It was a resounding yes! They had agreed – every last one of them! A consignment of nails would reach the wholesaler but the batch would be inferior and not fit for purpose. The iron was to be heated as usual, but not quite enough so they would have tiny fractures at the junction between the shank and head; they would look normal but the heads would come loose on being used.

Frank Woolley, it was known, treated his workers with disdain and disregard. The women worked shifts and were paid next to nothing for their hard work. Woolley allowed them no time off to see to their sick children and he insisted they worked six days a week only allowing Sundays off because it was the Lord's Day of rest.

Joyce had said in the meeting that Joshua Gittins, on hearing of Woolley's rulings, had made a new ruling himself. Saying that his 'ladies' in the factory would be given Saturdays and Sundays off work should they wish to take them. The money they were paid would not be affected, and anyone wanting time off for a good reason – it would be granted. The rivalry between the two nail-making giants had been evidenced over the years and this latest episode proved no exception.

The Wives gathered once more in Kath's kitchen where everyone was still gushing over the good time had at the picnic. Kath called everyone to order and the meeting began.

Violet asked when the plan was to be put into action and was told it was already in force. It was just a case of waiting to see the reaction of the wholesaler on his consignment of inferior nails.

Violet was to ascertain as much information as possible from Primrose in the market about whether Frank's business was suffering and if their plan was working. It would not seem out of place that two women who had attended school together would stop and chat while shopping.

The talk at the meeting centred solely on Primrose's predicament until eventually it turned back to the picnic and Violet.

Annie asked, 'Violet, wench, have you decided yet on an answer for Spencer?' The love shone from her eyes as she asked and Violet saw her mother stiffen.

'I have,' she said and left it at that. Looks passed from Violet to Kath and back again.

'Well, sweetheart, what have you decided?' Kath asked nervously.

'I'm going to say yes, but...' Looking at each woman in turn, Violet went on, 'If I'm unhappy for any reason, I want to be sure I can come home to you, Mum.'

As she flung her arms around her daughter, Kath said, 'You can always come home, for a visit or for good. I pray you'll have a happy marriage, but God forbid you don't, we'll all be here to welcome you.'

Hugs and kisses later, the talk of wedding plans began.

'Before we plan a wedding,' Violet said amid the joviality, 'might it not be a good idea to tell Spencer he'll be getting married?'

Kath said, 'Oh yes, you're right! You know Spencer's father may want to be involved.'

Everyone howled at Violet's expression of horror at the thought of a man trying to organise a wedding. Annie hugged her, saying, 'Don't you worry, gel, we'll keep him in check.'

Just then a knock came on the kitchen door and Kath, answering it, came back through with Spencer trailing behind her. He was given tea and cake before Violet spoke.

'Spencer,' she said shyly, 'regarding your proposal of marriage...' He looked from Violet to Kath, then to each woman in turn. Returning his eyes to Violet, she went on, 'I have reached a decision and the answer is... yes!'

Jumping out of his seat slamming cake plate and cup and saucer on the table, he threw his arms around her waist; lifting her high, he swung her in a circle.

'Violet, may I kiss you?'

Blushing scarlet, Violet nodded and Spencer, at the smile from her mother, placed a tender kiss on Violet's cheek. Applause rang out as he took Kath's hand, and kissing the back he said, 'I promise to look after Violet, she will never suffer harm by my hand or any other's. I promise she will be safe with me and loved by me all her life.'

Poor Spencer then endured the tears, hugs and kisses from Joyce, Annie, Mary, Martha and even Kath, who whispered to him, 'I'll hold you to that, young man!'

*

Lying in bed that night with the house quiet around her, Violet thought about her forthcoming marriage. Would it turn out to be terrible like Primrose's? Or her mother's awful marriage to Sligo? Or would she be lucky and have a married life like Annie's, being loved no matter what? The saving grace for her was that she knew she could return home at any time.

Violet thought how wonderful it would have been for her beloved father, Harry, to have walked her down the aisle. A tear escaped from the corner of her eye as she thought how proud he would have been to see her marry. She still missed him dreadfully and the pain of her loss stabbed in her chest. Wiping away the tears now flowing freely, she moved her thoughts to Primrose.

Violet would no doubt see her in the market in the next few days and they might know the outcome of the first batch of inferior nails, which were to be 'of no fit purpose'.

Violet felt sure that Frank Woolley would rant and rave before having the women make another batch of nails... which would also be inferior, unbeknown to Frank Woolley. A smile crept over Violet's face before she fell into a deep sleep.

*

Primrose was smiling when Violet intercepted her in the market a couple of days later. 'Frank was raving mad...' she whispered, 'his wholesaler played hell with him; refused to pay for the last batch of nails, saying they weren't up to standard! The wholesaler had three different complaints from customers and Frank was told his workmanship was shoddy!'

'Oh blimey! But that's good,' Violet said out of the side of her mouth, 'our plan is working.'

'Yes.'

Violet touched Primrose's arm and she winced.

'Oh Primrose, did he beat you again?' Violet's heart went out to her as she remembered the sting of Sligo's belt on her own back. She searched Primrose's face for any outward signs of Frank's abuse but there were none. She wondered if the man was too sly to allow any bruises to show.

'I'm all right, it will be worth everything when I see him go under. I hope he finishes up in the workhouse!' Primrose shuddered before she went on, 'I'll know about the next batch soon, he's got the women working overtime to refill the order.'

Parting at the edge of the marketplace, they went their separate ways.

Calling on the Wives on the way home, Violet told them of the displeasure of the buyer of Woolley's inferior nails, and related it again to her mother on reaching home.

They were, once more, playing a waiting game.

Fifteen

Riding home from his latest visit to Hobbins Street, Spencer counted his blessings. Violet Clancy had consented to become his wife. Never before had he felt this way about a woman and he'd shared a bed with a lady only once before. Violet set his pulse racing, made him feverish with excitement. He counted the hours until he would see her again.

Spencer couldn't wait to share his news with his father who had been away on business for the last few days. Steering his horse off Trouse Lane leading to Gittins Manor, he made his way down the streets before taking off over the heath to his father's factory at Stone Cross at a gallop. Spencer would tell his father now... today!

Keeping his eyes on the ground before him, Spencer avoided the holes in the heath that could befall his horse and endanger them both.

Dismounting and handing the reins to a lad who tended the horses, Spencer strode into his father's office in the works, shouting, 'Hello Father, I have some good news for you.'

Leaning back in his chair, Joshua smiled at his son before saying, 'Good news is always welcome.'

'Indeed, Father, I'm getting married!'

'Well, my boy,' Joshua stood to shake his son's hand, 'it's about time!' Laughing together they sat before Joshua asked, 'Who is the lucky girl?' It never occurred to him it might be Violet. He had considered that to be a flight of his son's fancy.

'You met her at the picnic father, it's Violet Clancy.'

Joshua's face fell as he asked, 'Ain't she the stepdaughter of that fella who drowned in the canal a few years ago?'

'Yes,' Spencer said bewildered at the instant change in his father's mood.

'Hmmm, you know the rumours that surround that family I presume?'

'Yes Father, and that's all they are… rumours.'

Spencer knew the truth but could never admit that to his father; he knew Joshua would do his utmost to prevent the wedding taking place. No, he would not confirm these rumours to his father.

'Son… I'm not sure this is a good match for you…'

Spencer cut across his father's words with, 'It is the perfect match for me, Father! We are in love and she has agreed to be my wife. I'm sure in time you will see how wonderful she is. Then you will know all the rumours around her family are speculative nonsense!'

'Son, the girl has no money behind her from what I can discern, and I had hoped you would marry into a wealthy family.'

'I don't care whether she has money, Father!' Spencer was becoming irate. 'I love her, and that's all that matters.'

'I'm only thinking of you, lad, and I have to say I ain't happy about this!' Joshua went on.

'I know you are worried but please don't be. In the end it's not about whether you are happy about the wedding, but more about me being happy with it – and I am!'

'I understand that, but have you thought this through? It all seems rather sudden to me.'

'Look, Father, I'm going to marry Violet Clancy with or without your approval! Naturally I would prefer to have it, as I don't want this to always be a thorn in the relationship between you and me.'

Joshua could see he was determined and raised his hands in surrender at Spencer's outburst, saying, 'All right then lad, if that's how you feel, then I very much look forward to meeting with your intended again.' Seeing Spencer's frown turn into a smile, he added, 'Now then, shouldn't you go and buy the girl a wedding ring before she changes her mind?'

Joshua clapped his son on the shoulder then watched him leave the office. Sitting in his chair once more, Joshua mulled over his doubts about Spencer marrying Violet Clancy.

*

The next few days saw Spencer visit the marketplace, where he requested that Mr Westley of Westley's Jewellers make a wedding ring in the purest gold he had, and he dropped in on Mr Powell, his tailor, to be fitted for his morning suit. He did not intend for the grass to grow under his feet – just in case Violet *should* change her mind.

Standing now on the gravel driveway to his house after his visit to the jeweller, Spencer looked up at the building he had bought with the inheritance from his mother and had named it Gittins Manor. He could barely remember her but he knew she had died in childbirth when he was a small boy. His father had kept the money safe in the bank for him until the day came when he would need it. Until that time he had lived at Gittins Lodge with his father.

He stared at the red-brick building with its pillars standing sentinel either side of the front door. Large windows looked out onto expansive lawns, which were dotted with small topiaries. Trees grew tall and straight and encircled the property behind which stood high walls.

The house at one time had been extended and had many rooms both up and downstairs. From the hall, the parlour, drawing room and study could be reached. On the other side of the hall was the living room, sitting room and music room. Each room had had another built onto it with a door leading out onto the gardens. These rooms lay empty but could be used as extra bedrooms if ever the need arose. The kitchen and scullery lay at the back of the house and an outbuilding housed a double privy. The long staircase led to eight bedrooms. A back staircase wound their way up to the servants' quarters. Away from the house was stabling for four horses and a carriage. There was also included an old cottage down by the canal which was rather rundown and would need some renovation in the future.

Spencer had decided to have his house cleaned from top to bottom and the maid bustled about cleaning everything in sight; washing curtains and bed linen; chimneys were swept, stables and horses taken care of. The lawns were cut, topiaries trimmed and flowers tended. A flurry of excitement about the forthcoming wedding kept everyone busy day after day. The house was finally to have a new mistress.

Leaving the staff to go about their business, Spencer

attended to his own down at the factory with his father. He watched as Joshua chatted to a couple of the women on the factory floor. Joining them, Spencer accepted their congratulations on his upcoming wedding when his father said to him, 'You heard the latest?'

At once thinking he was about to release a tirade about Violet's family, Spencer snapped, 'You shouldn't listen to gossip and rumour, Father!'

'Oh this isn't a rumour, it's a fact!' Joshua's smile split his face as he pointed to the women he'd been talking to. 'These ladies here tell me Frank Woolley's last consignment of nails has been refused as substandard! He's set his workers on overtime to fill the order again!'

Looking at the women, they nodded confirmation of Joshua's words.

'How come?' Spencer asked.

Joshua said, 'No one is sure about what went wrong, but the nails were faulty! Neither use nor ornament!' A hearty laugh followed as Joshua went back to his office and the women resumed their work.

Something wasn't right about this situation, but Spencer couldn't put his finger on quite what it was. Woolley's nails were usually good – easily as good as the ones Gittins' Nails produced, so what had gone wrong with that batch? How come all the nails made by different women had been faulty? Could it have been the iron used?

It was well known Frank Woolley was a bit of a tyrant in his factory as well as at home; his poor young wife could lay testament to that. Spencer had seen Primrose Woolley many times heading for the marketplace, her shawl pulled over her head trying to hide the bruises Frank had inflicted on her.

He had been in the Green Dragon Hotel on occasion and heard Frank Woolley boast about his factory and lifestyle. Frank lived in one of the larger houses on Church Hill, an expensive area, but he had no servants; that's what his wife was for, Spencer had heard him say.

Frank Woolley was not well liked in the town but he provided jobs, not well paid, but it was work. People thereabouts found work where they could, and once acquired – they held on to it. Life was very bleak without employment and the threat of entering the workhouse had seen people take their own lives before going in there!

Spencer suppressed a shudder as he silently thanked God for his own good fortune.

'I wonder...' Spencer said as he entered Joshua's office, 'what went wrong with Woolley's nails?'

'I have no idea,' his father returned, 'but if he doesn't get it sorted, he'll lose his buyer.' Suddenly looking up at Spencer from his desk, a smile spread on the older man's face, 'If he should lose his buyer...'

Spencer finished his father's sentence, 'We could step in!' He was not normally one for wanting his rivals to suffer, but then everyone knew Frank Woolley was not a good man.

'Son,' Joshua said, 'I want you to do something for me.'

Nodding, Spencer knew what was about to be asked of him.

'I want you to keep an ear to the ground, see if you can find out what's behind this, because if Woolley's next batch is as bad, that buyer of his won't pay. That being the case we could offer our nails – step in and secure the contract – and save the buyer's day!'

'Yes, Father. Even though our nails are a higher price, he

might go for it – he'll need his regular order filled on time after all.'

Rubbing his hands together, Joshua said, 'Off you go, my son, see what you can find out!'

Riding back to town, Spencer again thought about the inferior nails and Frank Woolley's predicament. It could have been just one faulty batch, in which case the next would be up to the usual standard. However, if something had gone wrong in the iron itself, or the sizing, then the next batch could also be faulty, Woolley would not be able to sell them and would be left with useless stock and no money coming in. With no money from the buyer, he would be hard pushed to pay his workers, which would mean the women would be laid off.

The thoughts followed in a stream in his mind. If Gittins' Nails got the contract from the buyer then more nails would have to be made to fill the order; more staff would be needed – they could hire any women Frank Woolley laid off!

Spurring his horse to a gallop, Spencer determined to learn more and try to unfold the mystery of Woolley's faulty nails. However, the first call he would make would be to Violet, he needed to see her again; he needed to tell her that her wedding ring was *in* hand before he placed it *on her* hand.

Sixteen

Primrose and Violet met in the marketplace as usual. The young woman was sporting yet another black eye and Violet's concern for her grew.

Walking home together, Violet asked about her eye.

Touching it tentatively, Primrose said, 'It's nothing... just another of his rages.'

Watching Primrose as she limped alongside her, her disconsolate mood emanating like a living thing, Violet then asked why she was limping.

Stopping in her tracks, she rounded on her, 'Don't ask! Violet please,' she said more gently, 'please... just don't ask.'

Walking on in silence, Violet's heart went out to her. The child who had teased her mercilessly at school was walking beside her now, a careworn young woman.

'Primrose, I'm sorry you're having to go through this,' Violet ventured, hoping not to upset the girl, 'but hopefully it will all be worth it in the end.'

Primrose again stopped and as Violet looked at her questioningly said, 'I'm sorry for all the hurt I caused you when we were kids. I was a spoilt brat and there's no excuses – just apologies.'

Violet sighed loudly then said, 'Apology accepted. I'm sorry I gave you a pasting too.'

Primrose gave a tiny smile. 'My mother was furious about the grass stains on my dress.'

'I remember,' Violet said as they walked on again. 'Prim, it's all in the past now so why don't we forget that and concentrate on what lies ahead of us.'

'Thanks Vi,' Primrose smiled, pleased they were friends enough to shorten each other's names.

The smell of Kath's fresh baked bread hit them in a warm, tantalising wave as they stepped into the kitchen.

'Hello girls, just in time. Sit down, tea's just brewed.' Kath pushed a plate of bread and cheese to Primrose who ate gratefully.

All his money, Violet thought, *and he doesn't feed his wife!*

Primrose finished her food like she'd never been fed. Kath refilled her plate and poured the tea as the Wives trooped in bearing more food and took their usual seats.

Martha had brought some apples her boys had scrumped from a farm across the heath; Annie had baked a farmhouse cake and Mary produced a pat of freshly made butter from Spittle's Shop in the Holyhead Road – a real treat!

Everyone tucked in. Just then a knock sounded on the kitchen door, and in walked Spencer Gittins. Rounding the table, he kissed the back of each woman's hand before going to Violet. Holding both her hands, he cast a glance to her mother, and on her nod of approval, he planted a tender kiss on his sweetheart's cheek.

Laughing at the oohs and aahs from the women, he told Violet about the wedding ring he had ordered. Trying to eat, drink tea and talk at the same time, the little boy in him warmed Violet's heart. He told everyone of the work being done at his house, Gittins Manor, in readiness for Violet taking up her role as mistress.

Amid the laughing and banter, Spencer said, 'Primrose, it's nice to see you enjoying the company of these wicked women.' Spencer was unaware of the Wives club and Violet had wondered whether it wise to tell him. The laughter increased and he continued, 'I was sorry to hear of your husband's misfortune with his buyer.'

Kath and Violet exchanged a look as Primrose said quietly, 'Mr Gittins, I know nothing of business.'

'Yes of course,' Spencer returned, 'my apologies. Please give your husband my good wishes.'

Primrose gave a curt nod in response.

As the talk once again returned to the forthcoming wedding, Violet sighed with relief that the subject of Woolley's inferior nails had been dropped.

Kath assured Spencer that the wedding preparations were well under way, and with a polite refusal of his offer of financial help saw the young man happily on his way.

Primrose was the first to speak up once the women were alone, 'It's all over the town about Frank's failure to sell his nails, but that young man had me worried there for a minute. I thought he knew about our plan!'

Kath asked, 'What about the new batch? Did the wholesaler buy them?'

Primrose smiled and shook her head. Applause rang round the tiny kitchen.

'What's Frank gonna do now then?' Martha asked.

'He can't pay the workers; he relies on that money for wages. Although he's said nothing to me, I suspect he's used up his savings on wages and more iron already! I think he might be laying off some of the workforce, but…' she paused for breath, 'he still won't be able to pay the remainder. No one wants to buy from him – his reputation is sinking fast.'

More applause before Violet spoke, 'Joyce, this is where you come in. You need to get to see Joshua Gittins, ask… ask for a raise or something, but see him! Let him know that Woolley's buyer has deserted him and half the workers are being laid off. Tomorrow Joyce, get in there fast, make sure Joshua Gittins approaches the buyer before somebody else does!'

'Ar, Violet,' said Joyce, 'I'll make sure of it.'

*

After everyone had left, Kath called Violet upstairs. 'I want you to have this,' she said, showing her daughter a beautiful white lace wedding gown, 'I wore it when I got married.' Seeing the look of horror on Violet's face, Kath hurriedly added, 'No, not to John Sligo… to your dad!'

Violet's fears laid to rest, she slipped into the dress which was her exact fit. The satin gown reached to the floor and was overlaid with white lace. The veil of fine net was draped over her head, reaching to her chin at the front and hanging to her shoulder blades at the back. The headdress of tiny white silk flowers holding the veil in place, Violet looked in the mirror, then to her mother. Tears rolled down their faces as they stared at each other. Finally it dawned on her – she was to be married.

Folding the dress carefully, Violet sat on the bed beside her mother, shed tears now drying on their faces.

Holding her daughter tightly, Kath whispered, 'I know

you're scared, wench, but remember what you told me Spencer said, he would never force you to do anything you didn't want to.'

Violet nodded as she recalled his words spoken out of earshot of their chaperones one day, *if you prefer the marriage to be unconsummated… I would accept that… always.*

The conversation had taken Violet completely by surprise. She remembered her horror of his broaching the subject of the bedroom. She had blushed to the roots of her hair as he had whispered those words, but she had loved him for them. Violet had confided in her mother, which had put Kath more at ease about the situation.

'And,' Kath added, 'if you are ever unhappy for any reason, you come home to me. I will ask no questions, I promise – if you want to come home – you come home!'

Hugging her mother tightly, Violet whispered her thanks and her love and yet again they cried together.

*

The following day, Joyce acted out her part at work perfectly – according to her anyway.

'I marched up to Gittins' door and banged on it an' walked straight in, cheeky as you like. I told him, "Mr Gittins," I said, "I wants a raise." Well, he looked at me one o'clock half struck before he said no, he couldn't afford it.'

Violet loved Joyce's odd expressions and the way she could relate a tale. She had a knack of being funny without even trying.

Joyce went on, 'I sez to him, "Well you would be able to afford it if yer got yer arse in with Woolley's buyer". That's when he started to take notice. "Care to explain?" he arkses me. "Ar," I sez, "Woolley's nails aye bin no good, he cor sell them and his buyer needs a new supplier." Well, his eyes fair lit up they did!'

Joyce was enjoying relaying the exchange with her employer and had exaggerated her Black Country way of speaking to enhance the tale. She moved on swiftly.

'I watched him rub his hand over his whiskers an he said, "Joyce, my girl, if I get that contract, you get your raise." Well, I was right pleased with meself, I can tell yer! I never expected him to give me a raise either!'

'Good work, Joyce!' Violet said, pouring more tea. 'Now, we sit back and watch Frank Woolley and his factory go down the drain.'

*

Spencer and Violet had met with Joshua for dinner on one occasion, and despite her worry that Joshua had reservations about the wedding in the first place, she felt he had warmed to her now. They discussed the preparations for the wedding which were well underway. Kath and her daughter were both very excited about the prospect, and Violet's feelings towards her intended grew stronger each time they met. The church was booked and the flowers were ordered. Then all of a sudden the day finally arrived for Violet's wedding and the sun shone as if just for her. St Bartholomew's Church bells tolled, calling everyone invited in for the service, and she and Charlie, Annie's husband, walked up through the streets to Church Hill. Women and children came to their garden gates as the entourage wound their way up Trouse Lane and Wellcroft Street into Ethelfleda Terrace, calling their good wishes as they passed by on their way to the church that sat at the top of the hill.

'Thank you for giving me away, Charlie,' Violet said as they walked.

'Thank you for asking me,' he answered, 'I feel very honoured especially as I don't have a daughter of my own. Annie cried buckets when I told her – in fact I'll bet she and your mum are crying right now.'

Violet smiled, 'I wouldn't be surprised.'

As Violet entered the church, she spotted her mother who was dressed in a green brocade dress edged with darker green silk piping and hat to match sat in the front pew with Annie. Violet heard the gasps as Charlie walked her down the aisle to where Spencer stood. Turning to look at the man she was about to marry, Violet smiled as she wiped away a happy tear rolling down his cheek.

The service was conducted and Mrs Violet Gittins left the church on Spencer's arm; a new husband, a new name and a new life.

Outside the church gate stood a white horse with white ribbons plaited in its tail and mane. The carriage behind the horse had white ribbon bows on the door handles. Climbing into the carriage, Violet and Spencer were pelted with rice before they set off for Gittins Manor and all invited guests strolled along behind chattering contentedly.

The gardens had been set out much the same as they had been for the picnic, tables and chairs, food and drink, but first Violet had to meet the staff. They were lined up at the foot of the front steps of the house and a round of applause sounded as she stepped down from the carriage aided by Spencer. Walking along the row of staff, he introduced them one by one, Betty the maid, Mrs Jameson the cook, Harold the gardener, and Fred the stable boy... Her head was spinning thinking she would never remember their names but she maintained her smile. The very idea of having servants overwhelmed her somewhat, but she kept her head high and smiled graciously.

Before long, people arrived and began to mingle, having a thoroughly enjoyable day. Violet was with Kath and the Wives when Spencer approached, with his father by his side.

'Darling,' he said taking Violet's elbow, 'come and say hello to Father. Father, say hello to my wife.' She flushed at his introduction as it was the first time she had been referred to as his wife... and she liked it.

Joshua said, 'Forgive my not being able to meet with yourself and your family more often, my dear, but business has been erratic, I'm sure you understand. Welcome to our family, Violet.'

Spencer introduced everyone to his father and leaving them to talk he pulled his new wife away, saying, 'He just loves you!'

Violet said, 'Of course he does, why wouldn't he?' Laughing together, they mingled and chatted with everyone.

As night fell, people left for their homes until it was just Spencer and Violet remaining. The staff had been dismissed, retiring to their beds above the back stairs, and the pair walked up the sweeping staircase. Opening the bedroom door, Violet felt panic sweep over her. Taking her in his arms, Spencer kissed her tenderly before saying, 'Goodnight darling.' Violet was surprised to say the least as he closed the door quietly behind him. Her surprise was tinged with a little disappointment at being left alone, but she realised Spencer was giving her time. He had been so kind knowing she would need this time to come to terms with living with a new husband. Violet looked around her new bedroom and smiled. Not his and hers – just hers. Again she was surprised for it had not been discussed that she would have her own bedroom.

Seventeen

Frank Woolley had called his foreman to the house and when both were ensconced in the 'den' he had raged at the poor man. It was hard not to hear the ranting of her husband even had Primrose not tried.

The foreman, Jack Hesp, had explained that he couldn't understand why the nails were not up to their usual good standard. Nothing had changed in the process of making them, as far as he was aware.

The nailer's equipment was simple. There was a hand hammer, a small anvil, a 'bore' or hollow tool in which the partly finished nail was placed to have its head formed, and a treadle-hammer for heading. The iron rods were heated in a small hearth, similar to that used by a blacksmith but much smaller. Skills were developed by long practice and the nailer could make two brush nails, which were like large tacks, every six seconds. They were surprisingly uniform in size and shape, the more so as the nailer had no means of measuring and judged the amount of iron needed which was worked solely by eye.

Jack Hesp went through the process before Frank yelled,

'I don't bloody care, Hesp! But I tell you this, if I can't sell those nails we all go under – you an' all. Lay off half the women, I ain't got the money to pay them, and if the next batch is the same as the last lot, every last one of you gets the sack. Now get out!'

Primrose heard Jack Hesp leave the house and braced herself for the verbal onslaught she felt would surely come her way.

Frank blustered into the room, standing in front of the fire, legs astride.

'Bloody work is more trouble than it's worth,' he huffed.

'What's happened?' Primrose asked.

'Nothing to bother your head about. Women don't know about business, so keep your nose out!'

'Sorry,' she muttered.

Pacing the room, Frank spoke as if to himself. Listening keenly, Primrose feigned disinterest. 'Bloody women at the factory buggered up the nail process, I'll be bound! Now that bugger in Wolverhampton won't buy the nails, he says they're inferior... my nails inferior! Bloody cheek! Chucked them back at me he did, he said the workmanship was shoddy! He said he'd had complaints of nail heads coming off!'

Primrose watched him make a track in the rug as he marched up and down the room, his hands behind his back, making his stomach stick out even further than usual.

'I'll have to find another buyer now and bloody quick, otherwise...'

Pricking up her ears she waited.

'I've laid off half the workers, the rest will follow suit if I'm not careful, then I'll have to sell the bloody factory, as if anyone would buy it. I'll be bloody penniless!'

There it was! Just hearing him say the words was music to her ears and a discreet smile edged her mouth.

Her smile quickly disappeared as he spoke again, 'You're not much better, with your barren body, can't even give me a child! Don't know why I married you in the first place! Oh sod it – I'm going to the Green Dragon to get drunk!' With that he strode from the room slamming the door behind him and Primrose's smile grew wide again as she settled in her chair before the fire.

*

Primrose saw Violet in the market the next day. Wedding or no wedding, life pressed on relentlessly. She whispered the news and both women nodded. They rushed off together to Kath's house and after tea and cake Primrose explained Frank's rage of the previous evening.

Primrose said urgently, 'He's looking for a new buyer!' Worry was written all over her face.

'Who is?' Martha asked, walking in the back door.

'Frank,' Primrose said, 'he can't sell the nails round here so he's looking for a new buyer!'

'Don't fret yourself wench,' said Martha, 'we can put a stop to that an' all.'

'How? How can we stop him?' Panic began to rise as Primrose saw all the hard work of the Wives slipping away.

'Time we had a word with the canal people?' Violet asked.

'Precisely,' Martha said with a wink.

The waterways of Wednesbury were linked over most of England and they joined Gas Street Basin in Birmingham and ports further afield such as Liverpool and Manchester. Barges laden with goods travelled the canals, stopping off regularly to load and unload cargo or just moor up for the night. The canal people – locally known as the 'cut-rats' – carried news up and down the waterways.

Violet said, 'We need to feed the news to the canal people so they can pass it on that people should stay away from buying nails from Frank Woolley...' she looked at Primrose, 'because they are no good. They can also say to buy from Gittins'.' Casting a look at Martha, she received a beaming smile in return.

'Oh Violet!' Primrose said with the utmost respect. 'Thank you! Thank you all!'

*

Walking home, Primrose felt better than she had in a very long time. The Wives were helping her exact her revenge on her abusive, spiteful husband. She almost felt a spring in her step as she went, thinking it wouldn't be much longer before she would see Frank Woolley down and out.

The spring she almost had in her step was lost completely as she realised she still had to go home. She still had to live with Frank a while longer. She still had to endure the verbal lashings aimed at her every day, and she still had to bear the beatings for being unable to conceive.

Primrose prayed the canal people would be kind enough to spread the message far and wide. Someone's bad luck always made for good gossip, so it was a sure bet Frank's bad luck would be known round and about in next to no time.

As she walked she had noticed, as if for the first time in her life, the difference in the housing in each street. From the small two-up two-down houses in Hobbins Street which opened directly onto the cobblestone road, where she had once lived herself, each crammed against the next with the entryway leading to the back; to the houses in Trouse Lane which boasted three or more bedrooms and stood in their own grounds; to the still larger properties where she now lived, in Church Hill. She fretted about where she would live once Frank was undone. She wouldn't be able to stay in the house so she would have to leave him, or more likely he would throw her out. How would she live? For the moment, however, her mind was still on seeing her brute of a husband brought down and as poor as a church mouse. Once that was achieved she could concentrate on herself.

Stepping up the drive to her house, Primrose thought again of the canal people relaying the message of Frank's faulty nails and allowed herself a big smile before walking in through the front door.

Eighteen

With tea finished and the dishes washed, Violet and Kath had walked along to the canal towpath towards the Basin. There were barges moored up all along the pathway and they stopped at every one under the pretext of inspecting the goods for sale.

Besides toting cargo, the canal folk, as Violet preferred to call them, made 'dolly' clothes pegs – a piece of wood with a wedge cut into one end and rounded like a head on the other end – beautifully painted roses on tin kettles and pots and pans – all manner of things which they sold to anyone who would buy.

'Cut-rats' had become a derogatory term used to describe the people of the canals. A few caught thieving or fighting while drunk had unfortunately tarred them all with the same brush. Most were just trying to eke out a living, as indeed everyone else was, and life on the canal was known to be very hard.

Passing from barge to barge, the gossip was shared about the roughshod way Frank Woolley ran his factory and the rubbish nails he tried to pass as good products. Gittins', on the other hand, took care in their work, producing good nails time after time, as well as looking after their workers. People would be well advised to buy their nails from Joshua Gittins in the future.

Having bought a little something from each barge, Violet's purchase would ensure the message would be spread – and quickly. Even as they walked back along the towpath, barges began to move away, and with a wave, their message had set out on its maiden voyage.

Back at Gittins Manor, Violet rang for the maid to bring tea then asked her to find places for her little purchases, a bucket, a pot, and a few clothes pegs. Kath listened to Violet gently humming a little tune and her heart swelled.

'So how goes married life?' Kath asked tentatively.

'Oh Mum,' she said, 'it's only been a few days!'

'I know,' Kath said, 'I was only asking.'

'So far so good,' Violet said as they exchanged smiles. 'Mum, you have to come and see my bedroom!' Getting up, Violet didn't see her mother tense. 'It's so lovely.' Casting a quick glance behind her to make sure her mother was following her out of the room, she went on, 'Spencer gave me my own bedroom.'

'I'm glad, sweetheart,' Kath said, 'so you're happy then?'

'Oh yes!' Violet gushed. 'But...'

Dread filled her as Kath watched her daughter as they walked up the staircase to her bedroom. The room was beautifully decorated with drapes around the large feather bed, a cheval mirror stood in one corner and a matching jug and bowl set adorned the mahogany dresser. Kath gasped at the beauty of it, but she felt something was wrong. Had he hurt her? Had he gone back on his word to her? Kath waited, feeling impatient.

'Mum, I need to ask you something but...'

Impatience got the better of her and Kath snapped, 'Well spit it out, wench, the answer will come quicker when I hear the question!'

Sitting together on the end of the bed, Violet said nervously, 'Well I need to know how to please Spencer... you know... in bed... when the time comes.' She tapped the eiderdown as she spoke. The blush reached Violet's hair as she hung her head. All of a fluster now she tried to hide her embarrassment.

'Oh Violet, daughter of mine, the best advice I can give you is to be yourself. Don't ever change for anyone. And, when the time comes that you and Spencer share the same bed... relax. Explain you'll need time and patience and, above all, tenderness.'

Hugging her mother, Violet said, 'Thanks Mum, you always know the answer.'

*

In the early evening, Kath passed the few houses in Hobbins Street on her way to see Annie Green. Now *she* needed someone to talk to. Telling Annie of her afternoon with Violet at the canal then their conversation at Gittins Manor, Annie smiled, saying, 'You'll be a grandma before too long, just you mark my words.'

Laughing together, Kath saw Annie's eyes cloud over wistfully.

'Funny,' said Annie suddenly, 'how young Primrose Woolley doesn't seem to be able to have kids either, you know – the same as me.'

Kath's heart tightened as she watched the emotions play on Annie's face.

'We never did know if it was me or Charlie who was at fault, but either way, it was never meant to be.'

'Annie, I never thought much about Primrose not conceiving. I know that's why Frank beats her – he wants an heir to his fortune.'

Suddenly the irony struck them both and they laughed until their sides ached, then Annie spoke again. 'Young Primrose is too thin to carry full term, it would kill her or the baby. She's far too undernourished, I bet she doesn't even get her monthlies.'

Kath nodded agreement, and they drank their tea in silence each with their own thoughts for company.

*

The following Sunday, Spencer sent the carriage to collect Kath, she had been invited to lunch and Joshua Gittins was also to be there.

Violet rushed out to meet her mother when she arrived and Spencer hugged his mother-in-law with genuine joy.

Over their Sunday dinner, the four of them chatted and before long the conversation turned to Frank Woolley and his bad luck. Violet had spent little time with her father-in-law since the marriage; he had been busy with work and lived across town from them so there had been little opportunity to socialise.

'What do you make of it all, Kath?' Joshua asked. His warm nature endeared him to Kath but she eyed him suspiciously across the table.

'Oh Joshua, I don't know anything about making nails or business come to that.'

Sipping his wine, he eyed her across the table. 'I think you have a savvy head on those pretty shoulders of yours.'

Was Joshua Gittins flirting with her, or was he fishing in her pool?

'I'm sure I don't know what you mean,' Kath replied, desperately wanting to get off the subject of the nails.

'Come on, let's take a walk in the gardens, and leave the kids to their own devices for a while.'

Giving Violet a little wink and smile, he rose from the table and, taking Kath's elbow, they walked out onto the path surrounding the extensive lawns. The weather held a chill now and she shivered.

'Now then, Kath Clancy,' he said as they strolled, 'I want to know what you know.'

Looking at him, she feigned ignorance.

'Right,' he went on, 'the way I see it is this. Frank Woolley had problems in his factory, lost his buyer who… as I'm sure you know, is now my buyer.'

Kath could barely contain herself at this unexpected good news.

'Joyce Clews works for me, but lodges with you. Joyce informs me of Frank's situation. Word of Frank's bad workmanship travels incredibly fast and it seems he can't find a new buyer. How am I doing so far?'

Continuing to stroll, Kath shook her head and raised her hands palms upward. He took this as a sign to resume.

'Frank lays off half his workforce who are now working for me…'

Kath swallowed, more good news, the end was in sight.

'Should Frank lay off the rest of the women, which I expect to happen in the next few days, I will employ them…'

Keeping her counsel, Kath was thrilled at his words.

'Then all that Frank Woolley will have left is an empty factory building. Once sold – if it sells – which I doubt, Frank Woolley will be ruined and penniless. Now what I want to know is…' Turning her to face him, he looked her straight in the eye. 'Exactly what part you'd played in bringing down Frank Woolley?'

He registered the shock on Kath's face as she said, 'Joshua! How could I possibly have anything to do with Frank Woolley's business?'

'Spencer tells me young Primrose has been spending a lot of time at your house lately,' he probed.

'She and Violet went to school together,' she responded. Kath worried that he may have got to the bottom of their plan.

'Ar well, Violet doesn't live with you anymore, so…' Letting the sentence hang, Joshua waited.

'Joshua,' Kath said, keeping her voice steady, 'it's none of your business who I associate with, but I will tell you this, Frank Woolley brought this on himself. That,' Kath said vehemently, 'is all I have to say on the matter!'

Turning away from him, she walked back into the house feeling the burn of his eyes on her back.

'Time I was away home,' Kath said to Violet and Spencer left the room to call the carriage.

Quietly she added, 'Be wary of Joshua, he's been questioning me about the Woolley affair. Don't be drawn in by him, he's wily. You don't know anything, act a bit dizzy if you have to.'

Nodding, Violet walked Kath to the waiting carriage.

'Come for tea in the week,' her mother called as the carriage moved forward.

'I will,' she heard Violet call back.

Sitting and thinking once she was home, Kath wondered whether Joshua Gittins knew more than he let on. But the real question that bothered her was, did he know about the Wednesbury Wives and that she was one of them?

Nineteen

Kath Clancy knew more than she was willing to share. Sitting at the desk in the study at his home, Gittins Lodge chosen and named by his dear departed wife, Joshua Gittins took out a pencil and paper and began to draw. In a circle, Kath Clancy – a line to her husband Sligo, deceased. Beneath Kath was Violet, her daughter. In other circles were Joyce Clews – husband missing, and Primrose Woolley, married to Frank Woolley; each with a line leading to Kath Clancy.

Studying the drawing, Joshua tried to work out the connections. He recalled meeting Kath's friends at the picnic and his son's wedding. He was in no doubt that they were friends, but there was more to it than that, he felt. Baffled, he stared at the diagram as he sipped his brandy.

Kath was a wealthy woman in her own right. Primrose Woolley stood to inherit the house if anything happened to Frank. Joyce was as poor as a church mouse. No, he didn't think money was the connection. So what held these women together so tightly? At a loss for an answer, Joshua went to bed determined that one day he would find out.

*

It was a couple of days later that Spencer charged into the office. 'Father, there's a line of women outside asking for work – they've come from Woolley's!'

So, Frank Woolley had gone under and Woolley's Nails had closed the factory doors for the last time.

'Right, lad,' Joshua said, 'get them set on, God knows we need the help, what with all the new orders coming in. They're coming out of the woodwork they are!'

The workers were taken on there and then and now all of Frank's former employees were now in Joshua's employ, including Jack Hesp, the foreman, who covered one shift with another foreman taking over at shift change.

The women, just glad to be in work and on a higher wage, were happy to do shifts to fill the quota of orders. Work was coming in thick and fast from up and down the country and Joshua had no time to wonder how it had all happened so suddenly, but he was happy to see his profits soaring.

Looking down on the factory floor from his office doorway, he watched as each new woman was set to work.

Settling to study his ledgers Joshua had to ensure there would be enough in the bank to pay the new workers. Working long into the night, he was satisfied he was still turning a good profit after all the wages and overheads were paid, but his accountant would confirm that.

Leaning back in his chair, Joshua clasped his hands behind his head and his thoughts turned again to Kath Clancy.

What was it about her that intrigued him so much? She was attractive, of that there was no doubt. She was confident too, with an air of sophistication. Twice married, she had buried both husbands, not that unusual in these times. The men worked themselves to death in the pits. Kath Clancy, however, had been alone, except for her lodger and her daughter, these past years. Why had she not married again? Maybe she preferred living alone; maybe no one worthy of remarriage had caught her eye. Maybe, and more likely, she wanted to be in sole control of her money.

Sensible woman, Joshua thought as a picture of her appeared in his mind. *Attractive sensible woman*, he thought again.

*

Days of hard work wore on with no let-up in the orders coming in. Joshua kept his ear to the ground regarding Frank Woolley but nothing was forthcoming. Frank had, it seemed, shut himself away in his house receiving no visitors and no one appeared to know anything more.

As Joshua had predicted, Frank's factory was up for sale but there had been no takers. Money was too scarce to go buying empty buildings. The thought struck a chord and Joshua whistled across the factory floor for Spencer.

As his son entered the office, Joshua said quickly, 'Find out who is selling Frank Woolley's factory for him, and then find out how much it's going for!'

'Father you can't be thinking of buying it surely!'

'Do as I ask, lad, and step to it, I need to know fast.'

Within a couple of hours, Joshua had the information on Woolley's factory.

'Two thousand pounds!' Joshua said in astonishment. 'No wonder there's been no takers!'

'It's a hell of a lot of money, Dad,' Spencer said, concern evident in his voice.

'It is an' all,' Joshua agreed, 'but here's what I want you to do. Go to the estate agent and offer him two hundred pounds to be paid immediately contracts are exchanged.' With a nod from his son, he went on, 'Now off you go and get it sorted.'

Joshua felt sure his offer would be accepted before the factory became a millstone around Frank Woolley's neck.

He was not disappointed, for within the week he saw the contract for Woolley's factory in his hands.

Joshua suggested that Spencer and Violet plus Kath Clancy and he should have dinner together in celebration. Spencer agreed it for the following evening at Gittins Manor.

*

Joshua's excitement mounted as he rode down to his son's house at the other end of Trouse Lane, the contract tucked safely in his pocket. Was it the disclosure of the acquisition of a new building that had him so on edge? Or was it the thought of seeing Kath Clancy again?

Chiding himself as he greeted everyone, it soon became evident it was Kath that was the cause of his nerves.

Before dinner was served, Joshua tapped his wine glass with his knife and stood to share his good news.

'Ladies,' he lifted his glass first to Violet then to Kath, 'my son,' his glass lifted again, 'as you may or may not know, I have recently bought Frank Woolley's factory.'

Gasps and glances passed from mother to daughter and then back to Joshua.

'Now,' Joshua went on, lifting the contract from his pocket

with a dramatic flourish, 'I give it to you, Spencer – to do with as you will.'

Applause rang out in the dining room and dinner was served as questions were asked and answered. Joshua saw the sparkle in Kath's eyes as she congratulated her son-in-law. He had known for a long time that he had fallen deeply in love with Kath Clancy, but only now as he watched her across the table would he finally admit it to himself.

Twenty

Kath had told everyone the good news of Joshua Gittins having bought Woolley's factory at the weekly meeting, and although pleased they had accomplished what they set out to do, Violet was worried.

Voicing her concern, she said, 'Has anybody seen Primrose lately?'

The joviality stopped in an instant as everyone realised they had not, in fact, seen the girl in the previous few days.

'Christ no!' Martha said, now also full of concern.

Mary asked, 'Oh God! You don't think he's done her in do you?'

Mutterings ran round the table, then Violet said, 'I'm going to visit tomorrow to see if she's all right.'

'Frank's holed up there, he won't let you in,' said Kath.

'I'll come with you,' said Annie, her worry evident, 'he knows you two are friends, he might let one of us in at least.' Violet felt happier knowing she didn't have to face Frank Woolley alone.

The following day, Violet and Annie set off for the Woolley house in Church Hill, their minds full of trepidation.

The weather had turned colder as winter set in. Their feet were cold despite the woollen stockings and leather boots as they trudged along Meeting Street. Woollen shawls were tight about their heads and their noses turned red in the icy wind.

As they turned to walk up Church Steps, Annie said quietly, 'I don't fancy this one bit.'

'Neither do I,' Violet responded, 'but we need to see Primrose, we have to make sure she's all right.'

As Annie nodded, her paisley shawl slipped from her soft shiny hair. She drew it back into place with a sharp tug.

The bells of St Bartholomew's Church began to toll.

'Sounds like practice for another wedding,' Annie mused.

Turning into Church Hill, they bent forward into the sharp wind and strode towards Rose Hill House.

Marching up to the door, Violet gave the knocker three sharp raps.

The crapulous voice of Frank Woolley boomed out, 'Bugger off!'

Annie looked at Violet. 'He's drunk!' she said.

Violet again slammed the knocker against the door.

'I told you to bugger off!' Shouted Frank.

Lifting the knocker again, Violet saw the fear in Annie's eyes. She slammed the door knocker yet again, continuing unrelenting until suddenly the door opened and Frank swayed unsteadily on his feet before them.

'What d'you two bloody want?' he asked, swinging a brandy bottle in his hand.

'We've come to visit Primrose,' Violet said, showing no signs of fear, but feeling it nonetheless.

'Oh have you indeed?' he scoffed. 'Well she ain't receiving visitors, so bugger off!'

He made to close the door but Violet wedged her foot in the doorway, saying again, louder this time, 'We've come to visit Primrose!'

Stepping back, he pulled the door wide open before staggering off with, 'Go on then, I don't bloody care!' His arm waved in the direction of the stairs.

Leaving the front door open, the women climbed the stairs quickly, calling out to Primrose as they went. They eventually found her in bed. The shock of seeing the state she was in shook Violet to her core. Black and blue from head to toe, she lay unmoving. One eye swollen shut, the other filled with tearful relief on seeing the women.

'Oh dear God! My poor wench, what's he done to you?' Annie's words came through her tears as Violet gently pulled back the covers, revealing Primrose dressed only in her underclothes. Violet's hands flew to her mouth as she saw the extent of Primrose's injuries.

Primrose's lips cracked and bled as she tried to speak, 'Oh 'hank God you're here!'

'Annie,' Violet took command immediately, 'I'll go tell mother, Martha and Mary what's happened and tell them to bring a door.'

Annie looked quizzically at her, and Violet said, 'Well, we need to get her out of here and she isn't going to walk in that state!'

Violet rushed from the house not stopping to answer any questions Frank may have had. Annie talked quietly to Primrose.

'The others are coming, wench, we're gonna take you to my house. You'll be all right with me and Charlie.'

Tears rolled down the sides of Primrose's face, just about

squeezing through the swollen lid. 'Oh Annie!' was all she could manage to say through unmoving lips.

Annie stayed by Primrose's side, listening to Frank rant and rave downstairs. Hearing smashing glass, she said, 'Sounds like he finished the brandy then!'

The poor girl couldn't smile but the twinkle in her good eye glittered. 'Carehull...' she whispered through cracked lips and broken teeth.

'Oh don't you worry, wench, I'll be ready for him if he comes.' Reaching into her shopping bag, she pulled out the poker she'd lifted from the fireplace before leaving home.

Annie saw the twinkle in Primrose's eye again in response.

The shouting and raging downstairs went on as Frank rattled in the cupboards searching for more alcohol, until at last it went quiet.

Looking at the doorway then to Annie, Primrose said, 'He's ashleeh!'

'Bloody good job an' all,' Annie answered, 'otherwise I'd have helped him to sleep with this!' Holding up the poker for Primrose to see, the twinkling eye glittered once more.

Quietly giving her the news of Joshua Gittins buying Frank's factory to give to his son, Annie felt Primrose hook a finger round hers. 'Good news eh wench?' she asked.

The girl's finger squeezed Annie's, showing her pleasure.

Poor wench, Annie thought, *she can't even talk properly.*

Suddenly there came the sound of footsteps on the stairs accompanied by puffing and panting.

Annie saw the horror on Primrose's face and said, 'It's all right, it's the others, they're here.'

Martha came into the room first and her reaction was echoed by Kath and Mary. 'Dear Lord! Oh dear God!' Kath and Mary brought an old privy door through and laid it on the bed beside Primrose, still puffing with the exertion of having carried it through the streets.

Fear showed clearly on Primrose's bruised face when Violet told her, 'We're going to have to strap you on that door, Prim, so we can carry you downstairs. You have to hurt a bit more before we can get you to safety. All right love, understand?'

Mary said, 'It's a shame our men are at work, they would have done this easier than us.'

Kath nodded, saying, 'We'll manage.'

Primrose squeezed Annie's finger once more and they saw her mentally prepare herself for the pain she knew would wrap itself around her again.

Very carefully they freed the bedclothes from the corners of the bed and in one quick movement they shifted the bedclothes and Primrose onto the door.

Wincing, the girl moaned and Violet said, 'All done now, but we're going to strap you down so you don't roll off, we can't have you breaking a leg now can we?'

Primrose's eye twinkled yet again. Even through everything she was bearing, the girl could see the funny side of the situation.

While the others stripped sheets from a bed in another room, Annie chatted quietly, trying to comfort the girl who was in so much pain.

Once the others returned with the sheets Violet said, 'Right, Primrose, brace yourself so we can get you tied on the door.' She gave the girl a reassuring smile.

With Kath and Mary at one end and Violet and Martha at the other, they lifted the door as Annie pushed a sheet beneath it. They managed between them to get Primrose strapped firmly. Now all they had to do was get her down the stairs.

Kath and Mary each took an end of the door and lifted it from the bed. Annie went down the stairs first with her weapon in hand. Finding Frank in a deep drunken sleep in the chair, she gave a low whistle as a signal for the others to bring Primrose down.

Tilting the lavatory door to manoeuvre it through the doorway, Kath and Mary descended the stairs, being careful to keep Primrose level.

The girl made no sound as she left her husband's house strapped to a privy door and covered by a blanket Violet had snatched from the bed.

They walked through the streets, ignoring the stares and mutterings of people passing by before stopping at the corner where Trouse Lane met Meeting Street and Martha took over from Kath with Violet relieving Mary of the other end. They then continued on until they reached Hobbins Street. Carrying Primrose to Annie's home, the women tried not to jostle her. For all she was as light as a feather from lack of nourishing food, it was still hard work carrying the makeshift stretcher.

As they neared the house, Annie ran on ahead. Flying up the entry at the side of her house, she ran in through the back door, through the kitchen and across the living room to open the front door. Martha and Violet gently tilted Primrose a little to one side and winced as the girl groaned. Once they were inside the room Annie closed the door on the prying eyes she knew would be watching.

Holding the stairs door open, Annie watched as the board levelled out once more and Primrose was carried to the spare bedroom.

Very carefully Violet removed the blanket and untied the restraints. Kath and Violet lifted Primrose as gently as they could while Martha and Mary slid the door from off the bed. The ailing girl moaned in pain before she opened her screwed up good eye and looked at each of them in turn; with a wink, Primrose had thanked them the only way she could.

Grabbing the door, the others left the room and Annie stayed with the injured girl. Talking quietly to her, she cut away Primrose's underclothes carefully and bathed her gently with a soft cloth and warm water. Deciding against moving her again to get her into a nightgown, Annie let her lie naked beneath the bedclothes. A cup of tea was brought in by Violet and Annie helped Primrose sip.

''hank you, Annie,' she whispered before falling into a deep exhausted sleep knowing she was safe at last.

Returning to the kitchen and a cup of hot tea, Annie looked at the women around her table.

'Primrose will stay here with me and Charlie...' she said, 'now what's to be done about Frank Woolley?'

Sat once again in a meeting but at Annie's house this time, the Wives set about contriving yet another plan. Frank Woolley needed to pay somehow for his brutality.

Twenty-One

Leaving Primrose in Annie's care, they elected to go home and think about what, if anything, should be done about Frank Woolley.

As Violet, wrapped up against the cold, sat on a bench in the garden at Gittins Manor looking over the well-kept lawns, she silently mused on what had happened since Spencer had bought the factory.

Spencer had decided that he, with help from his father, would grow the nail-making business in his new factory. The Woolley's Nails sign had been replaced by one now stating the factory belonged to Gittins' Nails. Keeping the name had been agreed between father and son, but each to be in charge of a factory. Working together, they felt, would be more lucrative than Spencer trying to set up in another trade.

Spencer had grown up around nail-making, learning from his father how to run the business as he got older. All the women who had once worked for Woolley were now at the Gittins' factories. Spencer and Joshua had met with the accountant and were assured the business could stand taking on new workers, thus bringing much-needed employment to the town. Gittins' was fast gaining a reputation for being the best nail-makers in the country.

The canal people had also played their part, having spread the message far and wide for people to buy their nails only from Gittins'. And Joshua had kept his word to Joyce, ensuring she, as well as all the other workers, got a small raise in earnings. As far as that side of things had gone, everything had worked out well. Then her thoughts turned to Primrose.

She saw the girl again in her mind's eye, lying on the bed unable to move or even speak properly. Her husband had beaten her to within an inch of her life. She was wondering what the Wives would do about the situation when a voice shattered her thoughts.

'Violet! Enjoying the weather I see!'

Joshua Gittins shivered as he strode over to where she sat on a bench in the garden. He planted a kiss on her cheek. She had been so deep in thought she had not heard him arrive. She smiled at her father-in-law and it occurred to her how much she had grown to like this man.

'Hello, Joshua, got no work to do?' she said, laughing, knowing only too well his factory was working to full capacity.

Rolling his eyes, he flapped his hands up and down before sitting beside her on the bench.

'So,' Violet added, feeling a tad uncomfortable at this unexpected visit from her father-in-law, 'what can I do for you?'

'Just thought I'd see how things are with you, my dear,' he said, not looking at her.

'Come on now, Joshua, you don't just drop in on people unannounced, it's not your style.' Violet gave him a wide smile, and kept her mind guarded, as he only now looked at her. Why had he come to visit her? What did he want? Holding tight to her patience, Violet felt sure he'd let her know before long and got up and headed indoors to the welcoming fire which was more conducive to a tête-a-tête.

After tea and cake, Violet's patience was rewarded when Joshua said, 'You know, I questioned the match at first...' Seeing her puzzled look, he went on quickly, 'Between you and Spencer, but I see now that I was wrong to do that. You make a perfect couple and I look forward to what the future will bring.'

Dread filled her as she waited for his next words so she continued to look into the flames in the grate. What was it he was alluding to? Was he asking in his own inimitable way when they would be starting a family? This was something she and Spencer had not as yet discussed. Or was it something to do with business?

'I'm sure it won't be too long until we hear the patter of tiny feet.'

There it was! Her question had been answered.

As he watched her closely, Violet said, 'Oh Joshua, there's plenty of time for that; besides, I want to support Spencer in his new venture at the factory.'

'Ar, you're right there, wench,' he said, beaming with pride.

Was that the sole reason for his visit, or was there something more? Violet waited, sipping her second cup of tea.

Clearing his throat, he spoke again, 'I heard about young Primrose Woolley being carried on a board through the streets of the town...'

So that was it!

'Indeed,' was all Violet said in answer.

'Ar well, erm...' Searching for the words to ask his questions, she decided to make him work for the answers she wasn't entirely sure she would give. 'I was wonderin' if you might know why that was.'

'Yes.' Violet deliberately kept her answers clipped. Either Joshua would cease his questioning or, more likely, he would persist.

'I was also wonderin' if you might tell me what it was all about.' Again he avoided eye contact, keeping his eyes trained on the fire, and Violet knew he was feeling uncomfortable.

'No,' Violet said flatly.

'Oh!' Joshua said as he snapped his head round to look at her, he was surprised that she had refused to divulge the information he so obviously wanted. 'And why would that be?' He looked at her expecting a favourable answer.

Violet remembered her mother's words: '...be wary of Joshua... he's wily...'

'Because I don't gossip.' Her tone took on a slight air of exasperation.

'But I heard you were one of them carrying the wench on the board!'

Looking at him, she said, 'You heard correctly.'

'Well...' he said incredulously, 'I thought you might...'

'Might what Joshua?' Violet's question hit him like a slap. 'Might tell you *my* business? Might tittle-tattle? Might pass on gossip?' The change in the tone of her voice now evident, she forged on. 'No, Joshua! Whoever you *heard* from obviously only gave you half a story. I suggest you return to them for the full account of events. Oh, and be sure to tell them my husband will hear of their touting my business all over the town!'

With open mouth, her father-in-law stared at her before throwing back his head and laughing loudly, slapping his hands on his knees he rocked his upper body back and forth.

'By God, wench,' he said at last, 'I am right proud of you. Spencer was right to choose you as his wife and I am glad you chose him as your husband.'

Despite her earlier indignation, Violet smiled, and was surprised at his next words.

'You are just like your mother. Speaking of Kath, how is she?'

Sliding a sideways glance at him, Violet said, 'Mother's fine, thank you for asking.'

'She never remarried did she? You know... after her husband drowned. I remember the gossip was all over the town,' Joshua said as he gave her a quick glance. 'I would have thought she would have, handsome woman like Kath.'

'Clearly, being married twice was enough for her,' Violet answered. 'But then if you wish to know the reason, maybe you should ask her yourself.'

'Erm...' he began again. 'I was wonderin'...'

She laughed and said, 'Stop wondering, Joshua, and go and visit her, she would be pleased to see you and... she bakes the finest bread in Wednesbury!'

'Ar well...' Flustered now, he stood to leave, 'Maybe I will, I like a bit of good home-made bread.'

With a wave he was gone. Sitting alone once more, Violet pondered their conversation, and smiling to herself she came to the conclusion that her father-in-law was carrying a candle for her mother!

*

Over their meal in the evening, Violet told Spencer of Joshua's visit. They both laughed as they speculated the scenario of his father and her mother coming together as a couple. Now that would be very strange indeed!

'So,' he asked her eventually, 'what on earth were you doing carrying Primrose on a board across the heath?'

She knew it would come and she was prepared. 'She had not visited any of us for a while, Spencer, and we were worried about her! Annie and I went to visit and found Frank drunk out of his mind. Primrose was upstairs in her bed and… Oh Spencer, he'd battered her beyond belief!'

'Oh my God!' Spencer rushed over and knelt before his wife, holding her hands as her tears welled.

'We couldn't just leave her there, so Annie stayed while I fetched the others.'

Violet's tears fell as she told her husband how they carried Primrose through the streets on a lavatory door as that was all they could think of and that she was now staying with Annie and Charlie.

'But what if Frank comes for her?' Spencer asked.

'I don't think that's likely to happen, he's wallowing so deep in self-pity he won't give another thought to his poor wife.'

'Very well, but if any of you ladies need my help, you have only to ask.' Squeezing her hand, Spencer once again took his seat at the table. 'So…' he picked up, 'my father could be interested in courting your mother?'

Smiling again, Violet said, 'If I'm reading the signs correctly, yes. There could even be a wedding!'

She rushed to her husband, patting his back gently as he choked on his food.

Twenty-Two

Geordie and Martha Slater sat in their kitchen when all the kids were in bed and Martha told her husband the story of Primrose.

'Eeh lass,' he said as she finished, 'Ah'd heard summat of it from the lads, ya nah, about you lot carryin' her over to Annie's place.'

'Ar cocker,' Martha said, 'news travels fast in this town, as well you know.'

'So, what's gonna happen now then?'

'That's the question we have to decide on.' Even Martha, usually so full of ideas, was at a loss.

'D'ya not think ya should ask the wench herself?' Wise words from a wise man.

'You know, I think that might be for the best. You are a clever man sometimes, Geordie Slater,' Martha gave him a wide grin.

Smiling back, he gave her a kiss before he said, 'Ah'm away to my bed, pet.'

Watching him go, Martha thought how lucky they all

were, even Kath now she was rid of John Sligo! Without looking at her knitting needles clacking away in the silence of the room, her thoughts returned to Primrose. How long before she could tell them how she felt? How long before they would have an answer regarding Frank Woolley? With a big sigh, Martha put her knitting aside and climbed the stairs to bed.

*

It was the following week when Annie called in to see Kath and Violet, who had ventured out in the freezing cold to visit her mother. The usual tea provided, they sat in the warm kitchen to chat.

'I think young Primrose might be ready to talk with us,' Annie said, 'although she isn't well enough to get out of bed yet.'

'Then we'll come to her,' Violet said and they set out immediately.

Taking a walk down Hobbins Street, they collected the others and made their way to Annie's house.

Gathering around Primrose's bed, Violet smiled at her, 'How are you feeling, Prim?'

'Ever so much better thanks to you all and especially to Annie for looking after me.' Her speech was still a little odd, due to the remaining swelling and one or two broken teeth but at least the bruising was going down.

'That's good to hear.' Violet pressed, 'Prim, we need to ask you something.' Nodding carefully, Primrose watched as Violet prepared herself to ask the question. 'We need to know what you want to do about Frank.'

Primrose tried to sit up, prompting Annie to rush forward and prop more pillows behind the girl who was still far from well.

'Ladies, you have done so much for me already, I can't ask any more of you.'

Mary's sudden anger spilled over when she said vehemently, 'Stop pervar... perv...'

'Prevaricating,' Violet said respectfully.

'Ar that,' said Mary, giving her a nod, 'just tell us what you want doin', wench!'

Primrose's tears fell as she sobbed, 'Look at what he did to me! He did this because I couldn't have his children... I'm glad I couldn't! I could never have love for a child gotten from rape!'

Seeing Violet flinch then physically stiffen, Primrose apologised, 'I'm sorry, Violet...' Not knowing of Violet's terrible time with John Sligo, Primrose thought she had offended her friend in some way.

Violet moved to hold the girl's hand saying, 'It's all right, Primrose, just tell us what you want.'

'Come on, wench,' Martha encouraged, 'tell us then you can leave everything to us while you get better.'

'Well,' Primrose said, composing herself, 'he'll do this again... not to me because I'm not going back there even if it means the workhouse! But if he takes up with another woman... we can't let that happen, please, don't let him do it to anyone else... please!'

'Fair enough,' Violet said, looking at each woman in turn, 'you all heard what Primrose said?' With nods from all that the only solution might possibly be another murder, she continued, 'Right. Primrose, you get yourself well again, everyone else... meeting tomorrow.'

Sitting up long into the night after Spencer had gone to bed, Violet pondered the situation of Frank Woolley. It was no secret that Primrose had been seen being carried to Annie's on a door; after all, half the townspeople had witnessed it. It was also no secret about the state she was in. Joshua Gittins had been sniffing around hoping for titbits of information, and surely he wasn't the only one. Whatever plan the Wednesbury Wives came up with, they had to tread very, very carefully. She shuddered as she realised Frank Woolley would have to meet his maker, 'accidentally'!

*

Ideas went back and forth across Kath Clancy's kitchen table the following day regarding Frank Woolley's 'accident'.

'We have to be very careful on this one,' Violet said, 'the whole town knows about Primrose!'

'Ar,' said Mary.

'True,' from Kath.

Joyce, having joined them as it was one of her days off from work, said excitedly, 'We could burn the 'ouse down... with him in it!'

Giving her a weak smile, trying not to burst her enthusiastic bubble, Violet said, 'We can't do that because Primrose will most likely have to live there after he's gone.'

With a click of her teeth, Joyce grinned, 'Oh ar, I forgot about that.'

Joyce could always lighten the mood of their meetings.

'Another concern is how Primrose will support herself. She could sell the house I suppose but it would make sense to stay there and find work. She's never had to do a day's toil, so she has no training in a trade of any sort, and we all know how scarce jobs are in this town,' Martha put in, 'and after all it's the Wives who will have brought Frank to bankruptcy.'

Violet said, 'Spencer said we could rely on his help if we needed it.'

'Bless,' said Mary, 'but he isn't going to want to be a hacksessory to murder!'

The ghost of a smile played on Violet's face at Mary's mispronunciation, but she was right, Spencer would not want to become an accessory to the disposal of Frank Woolley, not in the sense they planned.

A few moments of silence hung in the kitchen as each remembered once more the feelings of guilt and shame around the Ray Clews debacle. Now here they were again plotting and planning. Nervous glances passed between them, knowing all were feeling the same – they wished there was another way to get rid of Woolley, but there wasn't. Besides if they didn't deal with the man once and for all, Primrose was right – he would do this again to some other poor woman.

'Right then,' Violet said, using her fingers to rule out ways of ridding Primrose of her abusive husband, 'canal – out; gin pit – out; fire – out,' giving Joyce a wry look, 'so what's left to us?'

Mary muttered into her teacup, 'If you ask me, he should bloody well hang himself and save us the bother!'

As Mary looked around at their collective smiles, she realised she'd just provided the answer the Wednesbury Wives sought to the predicament of Frank Woolley.

Twenty-Three

It had been decided in their coterie that Violet should invite Joshua to dinner with Spencer, with Kath there too, to keep both men out of the way for the evening. Joshua could, if they weren't careful, become a thorn in the side of the Wednesbury Wives, but this way they knew he wouldn't pose a threat to their plan.

The others, Martha, Mary and Joyce, met at Annie's house at the end of Hobbins Street before they set off shrouded in darkness through the empty streets to Frank Woolley's house up on Church Hill. It was agreed Annie was to stay with Primrose.

With a long rope tied around Martha's middle, hidden by her long shawl, they walked in silence down Holyhead Road to the High Bullen. Walking up Church Steps, a small road that connected Trouse Lane with Church Hill, they kept to the shadows. With no street lighting and only the moon peeping around the clouds, they moved quietly through the dark streets. No one spoke as they trudged on, with ears and eyes straining to hear or see anyone who might be watching. But the streets were empty – it was too cold to venture out unless absolutely necessary. Turning right into the driveway of Rose Hill House, they scanned the house before stepping into the deeper shadows provided by the trees surrounding the lawns.

Mary had noticed a gas lamp burning through the living room window and alerted the others with a nudge. Staying off the gravel path, they quietly made their way to the back of the house, then entered by the back door. No one locked their doors in Wednesbury; there was no need, not many had anything worth stealing, and besides, Frank was probably too drunk to even consider it. Mary silently thanked God for that.

Making their way silently through the kitchen, their eyes already adjusted to the darkness, a few stone steps brought them up into the hallway. The light from the gas lamp filtered through the open living room door shedding an eerie glow over the body lying flat out on the hall floor.

Joyce heard Mary draw in a breath and clamped her hand over Mary's mouth. She removed it when Mary nodded her head. There was no sound except the ticking of the hall clock.

Why was Frank Woolley lying prostrate on his hall floor? Was he already dead? If that proved to be the case, how had it happened?

Taking a step forward, Martha's question was answered as the man let out a drunken snore. She mimicked drinking from a bottle to the others as they stood in the shadows. Nods confirmed their understanding. Fate could not have been kinder to them. Here was Frank Woolley right where they needed him, obviously too drunk to get himself to bed, he had passed out on the hall floor.

Martha unwound the rope from her waist, taking it up the sweeping staircase. On reaching the top, she tied one end securely to the hefty bannister rail. Mary stood beneath and caught the noose end as Martha let it go from the top. Mary brought the noose over as Joyce gently lifted Frank's head. Drunken murmurings sounded from his throat as Mary put the noose around his neck and tightened the knot. Lowering his head to the floor once more, Joyce jerked a thumb.

Following her lead, they joined Martha, who had taken up the slack of the long rope, at the top of the stairs. Loosening the knot around the bannister rail, each grabbed the rope and pulled, dragging Frank backwards a short way before he began to leave the ground. Working quickly, they heaved on the rope and, with his airway cut off, Frank roused and began to fight the rope now choking him. The three women pulled until his feet were clear of the ground. They struggled to hold onto the rope as Frank's weight bounced and jerked at the other end. With great effort, they managed to retie the rope in place and walking down the stairs they stood in a circle facing each other as Frank frantically tried to free himself from the rope strangling the life out of him. With eyes closed, unable to watch the final struggle, they held hands tightly and listened to the bannister creak. Each woman winced at the quiet gurgling coming from the man's throat, and prayed silently for the Lord to forgive them. Then all was quiet.

Held breath was released as eyes opened. Frank's legs had stopped jerking and his body stilled. Frank Woolley's life had ended.

Martha nodded then walked into the living room and picked up a foot stool. The others stared at the floor, unable to look at the dead man. Martha placed the stool on its side a few feet away from Frank's lifeless body, setting the scene of what was to be Frank Woolley's suicide.

Without looking back, they crept out the way they came in, leaving the crapulous Frank Woolley hanging from the bannister.

No words were spoken as they made their way home. The shivering taking over their bodies was not all down to the cold weather. They were all feeling the same – wretched – and were trying to come to terms with what they'd done. But even the picture of Primrose's battered body in their minds didn't help.

The meeting took place at Kath's house the following day. Kath and Violet had kept Joshua and Spencer out of the way and now were hearing what had taken place. Martha related the details as they sat at the kitchen table.

'Oh my God!' Violet gasped.

'It was terrible, Violet, hearing him gasping for breath,' Joyce said. Having finished work early, she had joined them.

'Serves him bloody well right!' Mary snapped. 'That aside though, wenches, I don't ever want to do anything like that again.' She shivered as she cast her eyes around at the others who nodded their agreement.

'God willing we won't have to,' Kath said. 'If we are to continue with our "club", we will have to find other solutions to the problems brought to us.'

'Definitely,' Martha said sternly. 'I can't sleep as it is.'

'This will hang over us for the rest of our lives,' Mary muttered. Seeing the others staring at her for her poor choice of words, she whispered, 'Sorry, I didn't mean it to come out that way.' There were no smiles at Mary's slip of the tongue this time, all were feeling too dreadful.

*

It was a week or so before the police found the body of Frank Woolley. The newspaper reported complaints of a very bad smell coming from the house which had alerted them. A messy business, by all accounts, the decomposing body having been cut down and carted away. The death was ruled as 'suicide' by the coroner; the police having no argument with that, after all, they had found him hanging from the balustrade with an upturned stool at his feet. It was obvious to everyone that Frank Woolley had taken his own life after his business had failed leaving him with nothing. The news of her husband's death was brought to Primrose's bedside by one of the constables. He was not surprised, seeing her still in bed from her injuries, when Primrose simply nodded at the news he imparted.

Primrose agreed to stay with Annie and Charlie until she was fully recovered, at which time she would try to find work. Having been left penniless by her brute of a husband all she had left was the house. If push came to shove she could sell it, but for now the prospect of finding work kept her mind focused while she continued to regain her health. She was however, very relieved Frank was no longer around to cause her, or any other woman, any more hurt.

None of the Wives attended the funeral of Frank Woolley when he was buried in a pauper's grave outside of the lychgate along the far wall of St Bartholomew's Church. 'Suicides' were forbidden to be laid to rest on consecrated ground. People passing by were not surprised to see only the vicar preside over the grave and the grave digger waiting quietly for his cue to begin filling in the hole.

*

A week later, a knock sounded at Kath's kitchen door and in walked Annie, trailed by Primrose.

'Oh it's so nice to see you both!' Kath exclaimed as hugs were given and tea was made.

Kath poured the freshly made tea as they sat at the scrubbed wooden table. The difference a few weeks of tender care had made to Primrose was astounding. She had filled out nicely thanks to Annie's good wholesome cooking and with head held high the sparkle was back in her eyes. All outward signs of injuries more or less gone; Kath knew it would take more than these short weeks to heal her mental wounds.

'I came to give you my heartfelt thanks, Kath,' Primrose said, 'we've been to see Mary and Martha, and I'll be seeing Violet and Joyce at some point too.'

The thin, frightened Primrose had disappeared, replaced by a healthy, confident young woman.

'What will you do now, wench?' Kath asked.

'Well,' she said, 'Annie's been teaching me how to bake, so I thought I might have a market stall selling my baking, you know pies and cakes…'

'Good idea,' Kath said enthusiastically, then tentatively asked, 'will you go back to the house?'

'Yes,' she nodded, no fear showing on her face, 'the house is mine now and it has a big kitchen, ideal to get a little business started. It was never the house I was afraid of, Kath.'

Casting a quick glance at Annie, Kath saw her nod, but she also caught the quick flick of regret that Primrose would be leaving. She suspected Annie had come to look on the girl as the daughter she'd never had.

When a knock sounded on the back door, fear froze the

three of them. Kath opened the door and a sonorous voice said, 'Hello Kath, I hope I'm not disturbing you.'

Leading Joshua Gittins into the kitchen, Kath saw the quick exchange between the other two women, her frown an answer to their puzzled looks.

'Arrrternoon ladies,' Joshua said jovially. The women greeted him before he went on, 'Nice to see you up and about again, Mrs Woolley.'

'Miss Berry,' Primrose replied confidently.

'Yes, of course, my apologies.' Joshua looked stung.

Primrose had reverted to her previous name, as Kath had, wanting in no way to be reminded of her hateful husband and miserable marriage. As the women stood to leave, Kath gave them a 'please don't go' look, but they left regardless, leaving her alone with Joshua Gittins who was tucking into a thick slice of home-made bread and jam she had placed before him.

'Good bread Kath,' he said, brushing crumbs from his mouth.

'Thank you... now what can I do for you ... and on a weekday too?'

'Always the lady you are, Kath,' he answered, looking her in the eye.

If only you knew, she thought.

Finishing his tea, he eyed her over his teacup. 'Shame about Frank Woolley,' he said finally pushing his plate away and nodding at the door through which Annie and Primrose had left.

Here we go! Joshua Gittins was going to spend time fishing for information.

'Indeed.' Short, sharp answers; he'd get nothing from her.

'Hmmm,' he went on, 'nice to see Primrose looking so well again...'

Kath nodded in confirmation.

'...I was wonderin'...'

Violet had told her mother about Joshua's 'wonderings' at one of the meetings previously and she was prepared for it. Setting the kettle to boil once more, Kath felt his eyes on her, and as she sat down opposite him, she said, 'Stop wonderin', Joshua Gittins, and spit it out. What is it you came here for?'

Taken by surprise, he became flustered before saying outright, 'I want to court you!'

Looking at her hands laid on the table, Kath shook her head, 'Thank you, Joshua, but the answer is no.'

'No? Why?' he said incredulously.

Raising her eyes to look into his, she said, 'I'm not ready for another man in my life; I'm not sure I ever will be.'

'I see,' he said, looking dejected, 'in that case...' Standing to leave, he kissed the back of her hand and strode from her kitchen, leaving Kath with mixed feelings; pleasure at being asked out to walk by Joshua, but disappointment knowing she couldn't. Her life was her own now and she wanted to keep it that way. With a sigh, Kath thought it would have been nice to have a man around the home again, but as her mind slipped back to John Sligo, she shuddered. No, she had made the right decision to refuse Joshua's offer, and with another sigh, Kath stood to boil the kettle yet again.

Twenty-Four

Sitting in his office at the nails works, Joshua felt again the flush of embarrassment that accompanied his thoughts of Kath Clancy. She'd refused his offer to walk out with him and become his social partner, politely... but it was still a refusal.

Casting a glance around, he turned his mind instead to how well the business was going. Orders for nails were flying in from all over the country now, so much so that Spencer's works had picked up the overload and both factories were working flat out. Following the thread of his thoughts led him to Frank Woolley and his hanging himself from the bannister in his home. *Poor bugger,* Joshua thought. It had not yet come to light exactly what had gone wrong at the factory. The women who had once worked at Woolley's Nails were now employed by Gittins' Nails, and they were turning out batch after batch of perfectly good nails. It was a mystery.

Crossing to the window overlooking the shop floor, Joshua gazed down at the women below as they worked the nails and chatted amongst themselves. Not one of them had spoken of Woolley's inferior nails, which he found strange to say the least. The women of Wednesbury, as in any other town, loved to gossip and yet...

Sitting again at his desk, his thoughts continued to wander. Something didn't sit right with him about all this, but he was damned if he knew what it was!

Unable to concentrate on work Joshua strode through the door; maybe Spencer could shed some light on the matter.

As he jumped down from his horse at Spencer's factory, a man nearby took the rein. Doffing his cap, he said, 'Arrrternoon gaffer, I'll take him for you.'

Making his way through the factory, Joshua was greeted by the workers with smiles and waves, each seemed happy enough, he thought, as he knocked on his son's office door before entering.

Spencer's face lit up as he saw his father and he leaned back in his seat. 'Father! Come in, have a seat.'

'Hello lad,' Joshua said, slumping into a nearby chair.

Another knock to the door followed almost immediately and a young woman brought in two cups of tea on a tray.

Thanking her, Joshua turned to Spencer, 'By God, son, you've got them well trained here!'

Laughing, he said, 'They don't miss much, Dad, be sure of it. They saw you coming in.'

'Ar well...' Joshua let the sentence hang.

'What's up dad?' Spencer asked.

'Aye? Oh nothing, lad...'

'Come on,' Spencer went on, 'two heads are better than one, isn't that what you always told me?'

'Ar lad, it is... well I went to visit Kath Clancy the other day and...' He began to feel foolish all over again and was not even sure why he was bringing it up now. He had come to ask about the nails, but had blurted out about his visit to Kath. Joshua felt he needed to talk to someone about it, and hoped his son would not stand in judgement of him regarding his feelings for Kath.

'And?' Spencer prompted.

'An' I asked her would she walk out with me?'

'You sly dog!' Spencer laughed, clapping his hands together.

'Ar well, she refused me,' Joshua managed quietly.

'Why?' his son asked.

'She said she wasn't ready for another man in her life.' There he'd said it!

'Oh, I see,' Spencer replied gently as he saw the hurt in his father's eyes.

'Damn it all son!' Joshua spat, feeling embarrassment, anger and disappointment fuse. 'I'm not that bad, am I? I mean to say, we've got the business, so I'm not short of a penny or two...'

'Dad, it's not about money,' Spencer said, trying his best to console his distressed father, 'it's about John Sligo.'

Looking at his son, Joshua asked, 'What about John Sligo?' He saw Spencer suddenly look very uncomfortable as he shifted in his chair. What was it he knew that Joshua didn't?

Spencer said without looking up, 'John Sligo was Kath's second husband and he...'

'He what?' Joshua asked, impatience getting the better of him.

Spencer fidgeted in his seat again before saying, 'He was a wrong one, Dad.'

In utter exasperation, Joshua said, 'I know he liked his drink, son, but that doesn't make a man a wrong one, does it?'

'No Dad.' Spencer was looking in more discomfort by the minute.

There was more to this and Joshua was determined to find out what it was. 'Look, lad, whatever you are hiding will come out sooner or later so...'

'I can't tell you, Dad!' Spencer snapped, 'I'm sworn to secrecy... so please... don't ask me again!'

'Oh I see! Can't even trust your old dad eh?' Joshua stood to leave and Spencer waved a hand for Joshua to sit down again.

'Dad, listen to me...' He steepled his fingers over his mouth as if trying to prevent any words leaving his lips. Drawing in a deep breath, he continued, 'Kath found out something terrible about John Sligo...'

Keeping his mouth shut, Joshua watched his son's face as the emotional battle raged in the young man's mind. Joshua wondered who had sworn him to secrecy – then it dawned on him. Kath! She had made him promise never to divulge whatever it was he was now hiding. Taking a deep breath himself, Joshua said, 'Son, don't tell me. Hold your tongue and keep your word to Kath.'

Letting out a big sigh, Spencer said, 'Thank you Dad. I'm sure if Kath wants you to know, she'll tell you herself.'

'Ar, maybe one day eh?' Standing and clapping Spencer on the back as he left the office, Joshua said over his shoulder, 'To work, lad, to work!'

Joshua trotted his horse down Hydes Lane in the cold winds. He began to shiver and he thought how quickly the seasons appeared to be passing. In the great scheme of things, life was very short.

Joshua looked out at the great expanse of heathland spanning either side of the road, and its long abandoned coal shafts. Bringing the horse to a walk he passed beneath the aqueduct bridge built over the Tame Valley Canal, before turning into Hall Green Road. Kicking the horse gently to a trot once more, he headed back to his factory in Stone Cross. Joshua's mind went over what had been said between him and his son. What had Kath discovered about John Sligo? Whatever had he done that was so terrible? Who else would know?

Suddenly another thought struck him. Joyce Clews was a gossip – she might possibly know. After all, she was the one who had known Woolley's nails were inferior and the contract with his buyer was up for grabs. Mrs Clews appeared to know an awful lot about what went on in Wednesbury; perhaps she'd know the secret surrounding John Sligo, particularly as she lodged with Kath. Joshua made up his mind: he would make sure to have a little chat with Joyce Clews.

Twenty-Five

Spencer arrived home late and he and Violet said little as they ate their meal. Sitting before the fire later, she asked, 'What is it, Spencer? Is there trouble at the factory?'

Shaking his head, he said, 'No, sweetheart...'

Enjoying the endearment she waited.

'It's just...' Trying to find the words, he thought a moment before he went on, 'Dad came to see me today and said he'd asked your mother to walk out with him.' Seeing the surprise on his wife's face, he continued, 'She refused him and in his tenacious way he questioned me as to why that was... in the end I said it was all to do with John Sligo.'

'Oh Spencer!' Violet gasped, her hands covering her mouth as she felt the blood drain from her face.

Rushing to her, he grasped her hands, saying, 'Violet... I didn't tell him I swear! I said if Kath wanted him to know, she would tell him herself.'

Violet released her held breath and began to relax a little, knowing her mother would keep her secret, taking it with her to the grave.

Spencer said, 'My concern is that he might get it out of

Joyce Clews; after all she did tell me after I was so relentless in my questioning.'

Again fear gripped Violet and she felt faint as she said, 'Oh my God, Spencer! I must go over to mother's house and warn them! I must go now!'

Rushing from the room, Spencer sent for the carriage as Violet snatched up her shawl.

The carriage was brought round by the stable boy and they set off at a pace.

Stepping into her mother's kitchen with Spencer behind her, Violet saw her sitting by the fire, Joyce taking the seat at the other side of the fireplace.

'Well now you two, this is a nice surprise,' Kath said as they sat at the table.

Joyce got the tea on and joined them. Kath brought out the cake and said, 'How's business Spencer?'

'Mum,' Violet said before he could answer, 'Joshua's been fishing again!'

'Oh bloody hell!' Kath retorted as she banged the knife down on a plate. 'What now? Sorry Spencer, but your father is getting to be a damned nuisance!'

Spencer, looking a little dejected, related the conversation with his father as they all listened carefully. 'My worry,' Spencer finished, 'is he'll try to get more information out of you, Joyce.'

Joyce shook her head, dropping her eyes to her teacup.

'Right,' Kath began, 'we all know what John Sligo did to Violet...' Casting a glance at her daughter she gave a grim smile, 'And we all know what happened to him.'

'He drowned in the canal while he was drunk, I believe,' Spencer added.

'He did,' Kath said. 'However, his disgusting behaviour

with my daughter has been held in secret these last years, and it *must* remain so!'

Violet looked at Joyce and saw the fear in her eyes.

'So,' Kath went on, 'if Joshua starts his... *I was wondering* with you, Joyce, you deny all knowledge of anything and everything. If he asks you about me, you tell him to ask *me*; if he asks about Violet, you tell him to ask *me also*; you know nothing about anything... understand?'

Joyce nodded, 'Ar Kath, I don't know nothin' about nothin'.'

'Good. Now, let's have some more tea.'

*

Violet fretted for days about Joshua's probing, knowing how tenacious he could be. She knew for certain he would question Joyce about her mother and herself. At least Spencer had proved he would not divulge her terrible secret, even to his own father. For that she was very grateful.

Sitting together in the parlour, Spencer yawned then said, 'I'm heading for bed, sweetheart.'

Violet replied as she stood, 'Me too.' Holding hands, they walked upstairs together and he kissed her gently at her bedroom door. As every night since their marriage, he turned towards his own room, whispering, 'Goodnight, my love.'

'Spencer...' she called after him quietly, 'won't you stay with me tonight?' Her voice quivered and she blushed. She was very nervous at the prospect but it was tinged with excitement.

Rushing to her, he held her close. 'Oh my love,' he said, 'are you sure? Are you absolutely certain?'

Nodding, she led him into her bedroom and closed the door.

Spencer was the perfect gentleman, turning his back while she undressed. No man had ever seen her naked, not even John Sligo. Climbing beneath the bedclothes, Violet watched as her husband undressed, shyly admiring his body as he stood before her. Coming to the bed, he asked again, 'Violet, are you sure this is what you want?' At her nod, he climbed in beside her.

His arm around her shoulder, her head on his chest, they lay together for a long time before Spencer moved to kiss her softly. With curtains drawn back and only the moon to light them, he whispered, 'I will be gentle, I promise, and if at any time you wish me to stop, just tell me and I will stop.'

Putting her lips to his told him of Violet's acceptance of both his words and his actions.

*

Another meeting of the Wives took place the following Sunday.

As they sat again around Kath's kitchen table, tea and cake served, she related to the others about Joshua asking questions.

Joyce took up, 'Ar, he had me in the office the other day and he started. What did I know about Kath? I said he should ask Kath. What did I know about Violet? I said he should again ask Kath. Well...' Drawing out the word as everyone listened eagerly, enjoying the drama, Joyce went on, 'He was quite amused and he said he'd heard I liked gossip. Me! Liked gossip!'

Everyone howled at Joyce's expression of incredulity.

'So, anyway,' she went on after the laughter died down, 'I said to him, "Look here, Mr Gittins, Kath helped me out of a tight spot a while back and she took me in off the street. As for Violet, she is my friend and that's all I know." So in a huff he tells me to get back to work, and that was the end of that!'

Slapping her hands on the table, she leaned back in her chair denoting the end of her contribution to the meeting. Everyone congratulated her on her dealings with Violet's father-in-law.

Mary turned to Violet and asked, 'He's not likely to make life difficult for you, wench, is he?'

Shaking her head, Violet said, 'Oh no, Spencer would have something to say if he did.'

All eyes turned to her and she felt the rush of blood to her face as a crimson blush caused her to lower her eyes.

'Well now…' Mary began, obviously detecting the change in the girl's demeanour.

'Mary!' Martha warned, giving her a frown. 'That's none of your business!'

Smiling her thanks to Martha, it dawned on Violet just how wily these women were.

*

Primrose Berry had already begun her business of selling pies and cakes on a stall in the marketplace and had made a small contribution to the money Kath was holding, when the purpose for it was explained to her. She considered it wise to have money in abeyance should anything happen to any of the Wives. She promised more as business picked up. Kath had also put in some of her own money and the Wednesbury

Wives fund was safely in Lloyds Banking Co. in Lower High Street in an account under Kath's name.

Violet walked to Primrose's stall on Monday morning to buy a pie big enough for Spencer and herself and she was pleased to see a queue had formed despite the nasty weather.

Suddenly the whole market went quiet as they watched a man dressed in ragged clothing walk past carrying a tiny coffin, the rest of the family walking slowly behind supporting a sobbing woman. Women crossed themselves and men held their caps at their chests as the cortège walked slowly through the market and up Church Street to St. Bartholomew's.

Eventually the mutterings of the market struck up again, and turning to Primrose, Violet said, 'No one should have to bury their own child, it's against the laws of nature.'

'Sickness took the child, I believe. That's the Carter family. Jean, the mother, gave birth a few weeks ago. They've got six kids – well, five now the baby's died. Joe Carter is out of work; they had no money for the doctor.'

Violet's hand flew to her mouth in horror. *No money for the doctor!* Paying for her pie, Violet hurried back to tell her mother the sad tale of the Carter family.

'It was so sad, Mum,' she said as she held a cup of hot tea in both hands. 'You should have seen it – Jean Carter was being held up by her other children. She could barely walk by herself. They were all dressed in rags. Joe Carter cried, Mum! In full view of the town... he cried as he carried the tiny coffin!'

'Don't upset yourself, Violet. I don't like it any more than you, but it happens, wench. There aren't many hereabouts have the money to pay for a doctor.'

'We have to do something, Mum!' Violet bawled. 'Anything!'

'What do you suggest?' Kath asked. She was not unfeeling on this, but she was a realist.

Looking down, Violet muttered, 'I don't know... yet!'

*

In bed that evening, Violet told Spencer about the small funeral cortège walking to the churchyard.

'I don't see what can be done about it,' he said after a while, 'but let me think on it a while.'

Spencer hugged his wife in their large feather bed, one they continued to share after that night she'd asked him to stay with her. Snuggling close to him, she whispered, 'What if that had been our child Spencer?'

Squeezing her body close to his, he said, 'Let me think on it, Violet, I feel sure something can be done. Now, sleep my sweet Violet, and leave this to me.'

She knew if she couldn't do something for that family herself, she could at least persuade Spencer to. Speaking quietly she said, 'Spencer... can't you find Joe Carter some work? What about putting him to work on the old cottage by the canal? Doesn't that belong to you? I remember you saying you'd bought it with the money left over from your inheritance. You did say it needs renovating... maybe he could do that for you. Please Spencer...'

Rolling his body towards hers, he kissed the tip of her nose and whispered back, 'That's a very good idea, Violet! I'll get on to it first thing tomorrow.'

Twenty-Six

Spencer had promised Violet he would think on the matter of the Carter family, and he did, but he knew the problem was spread further than one family. There were many people in Wednesbury who could not afford the doctor's fee, small though it might be. But he could at least help matters a little by getting Joe into work as Violet had suggested so now was as good a time as any.

Whistling across the factory, Jack Hesp, the foreman at Joshua's works, who had now taken over as Spencer's foreman, came running into the office, 'You whistled, gaffer?' he asked, catching his breath.

'Yes, thanks Jack. Tell me, do you know Joe Carter?'

'Ar,' he said, 'poor bugger... begging your pardon...' Waving his hand showed Spencer took no offence at his language, and Jack went on, 'He's just buried their youngest child.'

'So I believe,' Spencer said. 'He's not working, is that right?'

'Ar, been out of work for a while now,' the foreman shook his head, sorrow showing in his eyes.

'What was his work?'

'A miner, but the coal dust got in his lungs, and he can't dig the coal any more,' Jack said, shuffling his feet.

'Do you know where he lives?'

'Oh ar, the family lives in Wednesbury over by Bull Lane near Moorcroft Old Colliery...' Jack drew in a breath before continuing, 'on some waste ground under a tarpaulin.'

'What!'

'Ar,' he said, lowering his eyes with distaste, 'the pit chucked them out of their cottage when Joe finished working there, and with no money they couldn't find anywhere else to live.'

'How do they survive?' Spencer was appalled.

'Joe scavenges at the market. He walks the heath and traps rabbits and the like,' Jack answered a little sadly.

The shock of his words stabbed Spencer to the core. He had no idea people lived like that – *lived* – they didn't live, they merely existed. There was no way he could impart this discovery to Violet, it would be too distressing for her.

'Jack,' he said, cocking a finger so the man leaned in close to the desk, 'I want you to do me a favour if you would.'

'Ar anything, gaffer, you know that,' the foreman said feeling a little baffled.

'Right,' Spencer went on, 'get yourself over to Joe Carter and ask him to come to see me, get him to come back with you.'

'Yes sir!' Jack doffed his cap and was out of the office before Spencer could thank him.

*

A couple of hours later, Joe Carter stood before Spencer in

the office, his cap in his hand. Standing six feet, he had the look of a man tired of living. A head of dark hair already threaded through with grey hung over hunched shoulders, his eyes were lacklustre.

'I'm sorry to hear of your loss, Joe,' Spencer said, watching him carefully.

'Thank you kindly, sir,' he said as he shuffled his feet, unable to meet the other man's eyes.

'Joe, I have a favour to ask of you.'

'Sir?' he queried, at last looking up.

'Joe, take a seat.'

The man looked at Jack Hesp, who nodded, then glancing around the office, he dragged a chair forward and dusting the seat of his pants with his hands, he sat down.

'Joe, I have an old property over in Queen Place, just off Queen Street, do you know it?' The man nodded and Spencer continued, 'It needs a lot of work doing on it and I was wondering if you might be interested in doing that work for me, on a wage of course.'

'Yes indeed sir!' Joe brightened visibly.

'Good, well Jack here...' Spencer pointed to the fore-man who was standing by the office door watching the proceedings, 'Jack will tell you what needs doing, is that all right with you, Jack?'

The foreman grinned, his nod affirming his co-operation.

'Oh and Joe, you can move your family in there this afternoon. I know it's a mess, but I'd be a sight happier with the place being lived in while the work's being done.'

Joe shot across to his new boss and grasping his hand he pumped it up and down until Spencer thought it would fall off, then Joe said, 'I can't thank you enough, Mr Gittins sir, really, and the missis will be thrilled when I tell her.'

Jack Hesp nodded at his boss with a grin from ear to ear as he left the office with the new employee.

That evening Spencer explained about his meeting with Joe Carter.

Violet wrapped her arms around him, saying, 'Thank you, sweetheart, I knew you'd be able to help. I'm so pleased and I'm very proud of you.' She kissed him tenderly as they sat together on the couch.

*

Kath Clancy walked swiftly up to Gittins Manor one very cold evening and was led into the living room by the maid as Violet and Spencer settled by the roaring fire. After the customary cake and tea, she said, 'Spencer, that was a lovely thing you did the other day, I'm very proud of you.'

Violet looked from her mother to her husband with pride as Kath explained that she'd learned from the market people of Spencer's good deed regarding Joe Carter and his family.

Violet smiled widely at her husband as he said to her, 'It was you who gave me the idea if you remember.'

After an enjoyable evening, Kath, despite being offered a ride home in the carriage, elected to walk. The weather was cold but bracing and she felt the walk would do her good. It wasn't late but darkness had fallen. She smiled when she saw children kicking a ball on the cobbled road and heard their excited shouts. She nodded to the mothers who came to their garden gates to call the children in for bed.

Her mind again focused on Spencer and his good deed. He was such a good man and doted on Violet. She wondered if it was time he learned the truth about John Sligo. Should she tell him? What would be his reaction? Would he change towards Violet once he knew her mother was a killer? It was this that frightened her the most, that he might hold it against her daughter. Violet could not be held responsible in any way, after all it was Kath's doing. Would Spencer go to the police with the information?

Reaching home, Kath sat with a freshly made cup of tea to ponder the question again. Should she tell Spencer Gittins she had killed her husband? Yes, it had been an accident, but she was the one who had caused it.

She had more or less made up her mind to divulge her secret for better or worse. She just hoped that Spencer was the person she thought he was and that her secrets would not ruin her daughter's marriage.

*

The following day, Violet decided to call on her mother. Kath had been fairly quiet the previous night and Violet was worried something was wrong.

Dressed in a long dark coat, a felt hat sitting on her dark curls, she opened the umbrella as she stepped out into the rain. The cold was intense as she walked along. She heard the steam train's whistle as she hurried on.

Striding down the streets of tightly packed houses, her nose wrinkled at the smell of rotting rubbish thrown out onto the cobbles. She moved aside at the shout of a carter and as he passed he doffed his cap in thanks. The clopping of the horseshoes echoed loudly before growing fainter as the cart turned a corner.

Arriving in Hobbins Street, Violet walked up the entry collapsing her umbrella and shaking it free of excess rain. Stepping in through the back door, she called out, 'Mum?'

'I'm in here,' Kath replied from the living room where she sat crocheting squares for a blanket. 'Hello love, my but you look cold. Come and get warm by the fire.'

'Shall I put the kettle on?' Violet asked.

Kath nodded, 'I just want to get this square finished.'

Sitting together with tea, Violet asked, 'Is everything all right? I ask because you were so quiet last night.'

Kath set her finished crochet square aside.

'Come on, Mum, spit it out. What's riling you?'

Kath sighed loudly. 'I almost told Spencer about Sligo's death last night.'

'What!' Violet was aghast. 'Why?'

'He should know about me, Violet, about the family he's married into.'

'Mum, I don't think that's a very good idea,' Violet said quietly. 'I don't know how he'd take it. I mean, well, he might tell the police or never speak to you again – or me for that matter! Let's face it, how would you react if you were told something like that?'

'I know, love, and I've thought about all that, but I still come to the same conclusion – he needs to know.' Kath looked at her daughter and saw the angst written all over her face.

'Mum, are you planning to just tell him about Sligo, or about – everything else?' Violet asked tentatively.

'Maybe he should know about it all as Geordie, Jim and Charlie do. Well, they don't exactly know the details, but they are aware of our "club". They have been for years and they've never uttered a word. Maybe Spencer will be the same, and it could save us a lot of bother in the future.'

'How do you mean?' Violet asked

'Well, we had to keep him and his father out of the way when Frank...' Kath began.

'Yes, I know,' Violet agreed quickly.

'So, if he's with us, we won't have to worry about keeping him out of the way.'

Violet blew through pursed lips. 'There is that I suppose, but I'm still not sure. Oh Mum, what if he leaves me? What if he throws me out?' She began to get agitated just thinking about the consequences of Spencer finding out about them.

'He won't. My gut instinct tells me he wouldn't do that. Naturally he will be horrified, but when we explain everything properly I think he will understand what our motives were.' Kath was inwardly petrified of what Spencer's reaction would be but kept it hidden from her already distraught daughter.

Violet sat quietly mulling over their conversation. Then after a long time said, 'All right, if you think it best, but – we tell him together.'

Kath heaved a sigh, knowing the hardest part was yet to come.

*

Mother and daughter walked back to Gittins Manor together. The cold wind was exhausting to walk against and they felt like it was drawing the life out of them. They spoke little, their minds consumed with how to tell Spencer they were murderers. It's not as though they could say, 'Oh, by the way, we killed a man and were involved in arranging the murder of another!' This was going to be the hardest thing Violet had done in a very long time and she dreaded it, as did her mother.

Time dragged as they awaited Spencer's return from the nail works. Both women sighed a lot as their nerves jangled, and they prayed Spencer would understand how and why the past events had come about.

Spencer arrived home and was pleased to see Kath. The maid brought in tea and Violet asked they not be disturbed. She would ring if anything was needed.

'Spencer, Mum and I have something to tell you, and I'm not sure how you're going to take it,' Violet said and noted the frown form on her husband's face. 'All I ask is that you hear us out until we've finished.'

'Of course I will, darling, but surely it can't be anything that serious?' Spencer smiled at his wife.

Violet sat quietly watching her husband as Kath began. She spoke of the Wives club, and how it came to be. She told of the death of John Sligo and her part in it. She could see Spencer itching to speak but she held up her hands to prevent it. Then she related the incident with Ray Clews.

At this point, Spencer could hold his tongue no longer. He jumped up to stand by the fireplace and dragged his hands through his hair. 'You murdered this man?! Bloody hell Kath – Violet – I mean, how could you? I... I'm... Bloody hellfire and damnation!'

Violet shuddered as did her mother at his outburst. His reaction was not unexpected but it unnerved them nevertheless.

'Is that it – or is there more?' Spencer rasped.

'Spencer, sit down,' Kath said quietly.

'Christ Almighty! There is more!' He gasped as he dropped back into his armchair.

Kath continued and told him about Frank Woolley. She said they'd agreed the plan but had no hand in the doing of the deed, reminding him they were at dinner with himself and his father.

'Oh, so because you weren't actually there, then that makes it all right does it?' Sarcasm dripped from his words. Dragging his hands down his face, he muttered, 'God above! I don't believe this! Violet, whatever were you thinking? Kath, you too – how could you do it?'

Violet's temper flared high and fierce. 'I'll tell you why, Spencer! Frank Woolley beat and abused Primrose, and left her for dead, all because she couldn't conceive! As for Ray Clews, he kicked that unborn child from Joyce's body! The only thing she ever wanted, Spencer, was a baby to care for. So that's why, Spencer. That's why our club exists. To help the women of this town to right the wrongs done to them by men!' She watched her husband stare open-mouthed. 'And as for John Sligo, he raped and beat me! Mum killed him by accident, but if she hadn't I would have done it and it would have been no accident, I can assure you!' Violet burst into tears, her anger and frustration melting away into misery.

Tears had coursed down Kath's cheeks too as she listened to her daughter's diatribe.

Spencer looked at the two women sobbing and hugging each other. He was in total shock. What did he do now? He'd just learned his wife and mother-in-law were killers. He sat quietly, his mind in a whirl. Eventually his thoughts brought him to feeling that in a way it was retribution and, to a point, justifiable – but murder? Did anyone have the right to take another's life? He looked at Violet; his lovely wife was still sobbing. If anyone ever hurt her he would... the thought shot into his mind unbidden. What would he do? He let out a shuddering sigh. In his heart, he knew exactly what he would do.

Standing, he yanked on the bell pull at the side of the fireplace, summoning the maid.

Kath and Violet exchanged a frightened glance.

'Tea please, Betty!' Spencer barked as the maid opened the door.

Pacing the floor, Spencer's mind continued to swirl. The maid quietly brought in the tea tray and scurried away again aware of the heavy atmosphere.

Violet handed Spencer a cup and saucer as he retook his seat. No one said a word. All that could be heard was Spencer tapping the teaspoon on the rim of his saucer. The tension in the room was palpable as they waited for him to speak.

Eventually, he said, 'The next time there's a meeting of your "club", let me know. I wish to attend and speak with the others.'

Nodding, Kath swallowed hard and cast a glance at Violet who was biting her lower lip. Neither of them knew if this was a good or bad omen.

Twenty-Seven

With all in attendance at the meeting, Kath was the first to speak. 'Spencer Gittins will be joining us shortly.' Frowns showed on the faces of those sat at her kitchen table and she went on, 'He knows.'

Gasps sounded as the women looked at each other before glaring back at Kath. Violet kept her eyes on her mother.

'How?' Mary whispered.

'I told him,' Kath responded firmly.

'Why?' Annie asked, hardly able to believe her ears. 'Why would you do such a thing?'

'Because he needed to know what sort of family he'd married into.' Kath stood up, to give her courage to continue. 'He's had ample opportunity to go to the police but he hasn't.'

'Bloody hell, Kath!' Martha exploded as she shook her head in disbelief. 'After everything we said about secrecy and now you of all people have told an outsider! You've put us all in danger, don't you realise that? What about all the women who depend on us?'

'Martha, first of all Spencer is not an outsider! He's married to Violet so that makes him part of my family! We all shared the secret of the club with our husbands and this is no different. Now, let's see what Spencer has to say shall we? Then we can make an informed decision as to where we go from there.'

It was then that the knock came to the back door and in walked the young man they were discussing.

'Ladies,' he said as he took a chair squashed up to the table. He looked around. 'Will Primrose not be joining us?'

Violet said nervously, 'No, she's at her stall in the market.' After her mother had left last night, Spencer had said no more so Violet was still not sure what he was going to say now.

Spencer nodded. 'So...' he drew the word out, stretching the tension in the room even further. 'I am now aware of the existence of your "club" and what it has been up to these past years.'

The women drew in long breaths and exhaled quietly.

'Now you want to know what I'm going to do about it.' He glanced around at the frightened faces nodding back at him. 'Well I'll tell you... nothing.'

Mary gasped, 'Mary, Mother of God!'

'Oh shut up,' spat Martha, 'you ain't even Catholic!' To Spencer she asked pointedly, 'What's to stop you handing us over to the coppers?'

'My love of, and loyalty to, my wife, and my allegiance to you ladies.' Spencer spoke quietly but confidently as he sat relaxed with one leg crossed over the other, his arm draped on the table as he toyed with his cup on its saucer. He looked affectionately across at his wife. Both Violet and Kath felt the relief wash over them. 'Violet told me about your husband, Joyce,' Spencer went on, 'and I'm so very sorry.' A sob escaped her lips as she looked at the young man, his face serious. 'She also told me about Sligo and Woolley, both of whom, in my opinion, deserved to be punished. However, having said that I can't agree with the way you chose to deliver that punishment, but what's done is done.'

Martha's teeth clamped together in annoyance at this young chap coming in and spouting his opinions. She liked Spencer but she disliked the way he was lording it over all of them. 'Spencer, Frank Woolley left his wife in her bed to die while he drank himself stupid. Primrose weighed around six stone when we carried her home on that board. It was her decision as to what should happen to Woolley.'

Murmurs sounded quietly in the kitchen.

'I understand. Fortunately none of you have been caught, and I intend to make sure you never do. I want to be part of your group, ladies.'

Martha continued, her eyes screwed up in suspicion. 'What about the next time a problem pops up?'

'We all solve it together,' Spencer answered. 'Look, there must be countless ways of dealing with these problems without resorting to – murder.' Spencer saw the shudders take the women and they were all on the verge of tears. It was clear to him they carried a great weight on their shoulders, which was something they had to live with, but he could ensure that load didn't get any heavier.

'It could work,' Kath pleaded, 'it could help us all a great deal.'

The tension in the room was almost suffocating and Spencer felt he had to crack it wide open. 'I want to be included in the Wednesbury Wives,' he said, looking at Violet, 'but I draw the line at…' Pausing, he looked solemnly at each face before saying, 'Wearing a dress!'

Suddenly titters of laughter rippled in the tiny kitchen before Spencer laid a velvet bag on the table, explaining that there was twenty pounds inside to be added to the fund. Opening the bag, Violet spread out the money on the table for all to see before passing it to Kath to be put in the bank with the rest. Violet's affection for her husband shone brightly in her eyes. She loved him to distraction and was proud of the way he had dealt with all that had been laid before him. Kath nodded her thanks and gave her son-in-law a beaming smile. She had been right about Spencer, he was a diamond.

Thanks were given by each of the women with a curt nod of the head. Spencer accepted this and smiled back.

'Now then,' Annie went on, 'I hear that you helped the Carter family.'

Spencer gave his own curt nod and Martha barely contained her grin as she said, 'We give you our thanks for that, Spencer.'

'Ladies, it was Violet's idea, so the thanks should go to her. However, both she and I feel we need to do something to help more families,' he said, 'although I'm not sure, as yet, what that something could be.' Looking at Violet he went on, 'I'll come up with something.'

Violet gave him a beaming smile and for the briefest moment there was just the two of them in the room.

Twenty-Eight

Well, questioning Joyce Clews had been a waste of time; Joshua had gleaned nothing more than he already knew. She was loyal to Kath to a fault, and no one else was saying anything either.

Riding down Trouse Lane to have dinner with Spencer and Violet he looked at the well-to-do houses as he passed them. The wealthy people of the town lived in these houses, there was also an ironmonger, a tobacconist, a bedding manufacturer, a pork butcher as well as pawnbrokers and grocers that dotted the street. He counted himself fortunate to be living amongst them.

He was surprised to see the doctor's carriage stood by the front steps as he arrived at Gittins Manor. Joshua leapt from his horse and rushed in through the door held open by the maid. He was surprised to see Kath Clancy there.

'What's happened?' he shouted. 'Why's the doctor here?'

Violet said with a smile, 'He's come to dinner at Spencer's request.'

'Bloody hell!' Joshua said, rubbing a hand over his face. 'I thought...'

'So did I!' said Kath with a little laugh.

Spencer apologised for worrying them both as they took their seats around the dinner table. 'Dr Shaw has joined us for dinner as we have a proposal to put to you both. Violet and I have discussed this very thoroughly and now we'd like to hear your views on it.'

Glances passed between them and Joshua wondered what his son had in mind.

Spencer began, 'Dr Shaw charges a small fee to those seeking his services, and rightly so...' Spencer nodded respectfully at the doctor sat to his left. 'Unfortunately there are a good many families who cannot afford even this small amount. Therefore visiting the doctor is not an option for them.' Spencer cast a glance at the doctor who looked crestfallen. 'So what we want to suggest is this... the workers at father's factory as well as my own pay one halfpenny a month in order for them and their families to have access to the doctor at any time...' Joshua saw Spencer stay the doctor's interruption with a raise of his hand before continuing, 'Dr Shaw, if agreeable, would be paid a salary as a retainer for being available to our workers and their families; the halfpenny the workers pay a month supplementing this in the beginning. Now, Dr Shaw...' Looking at the doctor, Spencer spoke directly to him, 'this salary would be a regular monthly income for you, and more, if I may say, than you currently earn.'

The doctor now nodding was all ears, as were the others.

'There is however, one proviso...' They waited and Joshua thought, *What's he up to now?*

'Dr Shaw, one day every week will be given over to providing free medical care to the people of Wednesbury.'

'I wouldn't be able to afford that, and besides… where? Where could I treat them?'

'Spencer was thinking…' Violet said giving her father-in-law a smile, 'of that old building on the waste ground by the side of your factory, Joshua.'

'Well,' Joshua started, looking at the doctor, 'if your salary more than covers the free treatment, then you don't have a worry there.' Then looking at his son, he went on, 'You can have the building with pleasure, it's doing nothing at the moment, but it's a ruin.' Joshua was amazed at the scheme Spencer and his wife had come up with, but felt sure it would work out fine. He glowed with pride and beamed his smile to all.

'Thank you Father,' Spencer grinned. 'Now, Dr Shaw, what do you say to this proposal?'

'Well,' said the doctor, 'if the building is usable, I would need a nurse and medicines and the like…'

Joshua watched his son with pride as he said, 'If you don't mind, lad, I'd like to make sure Dr Shaw has everything he needs.'

'Thank you Father,' Spencer grinned.

'Then I accept your proposal, Mr and Mrs Gittins!'

*

Joshua watched through the window of his office as Spencer gave his orders regarding the old building. Jack Hesp had drawn workers from the 'bread line' in the town; men who waited every day in the hope of someone giving them some work. These men were work-worn and weary from their days in the coal pits. But a lot of them had been laid off from the closure of these collieries, which had meant losing their jobs and their homes. Some were lucky enough to find lodgings, but others lived in derelict houses or out on the heath.

Standing in the bread line at first was humiliating, they felt it was tantamount to begging and they were fiercely proud. However, soon desperation replaced their shame. They huddled together in small groups watching keenly for anyone who might give them work. Ragged clothes hung from their cadaverous frames and battered caps sat on unkempt hair. Boots lined with cardboard insoles covered bare feet. Lacklustre eyes stared from skeletal looking faces. Tiredness and depression weighed heavily and grew in intensity with each passing day.

Now, glad to be in work at last, they set to clearing the rubbish out of the building with gusto. As the men worked, they laughed and joked – it was a good sound.

Spencer came into Joshua's office with the sketches of the new building drawn up by W. Morgan, the architect in Pinfold Street. The accountant had advised Joshua and Spencer there was enough in the coffers to accomplish this task from the factory profits, provided they didn't overstretch themselves. Downstairs in the building there was to be a large waiting room, a consulting room too; out the back would be a lavatory. Upstairs would house the doctor's equipment and medicine stock and a cabinet for the patients' records. The doors would have sturdy locks and the keys given only to Dr Shaw. Houses hereabouts were never locked but this building was not a house; it would hold medicine to be kept safe and out of the hands of people who might decide to help themselves. As many in the town were illiterate and were unable to read the labels, the pilfering and use of medicines could turn out to be very dangerous.

Dr Shaw had been assigned the task of employing a nurse and a receptionist. Joshua and Spencer had agreed to cover the cost of their wages; a donation box was to be put in the waiting room for those able to contribute, until such time as the money from the workers would cover all the outgoings.

'Dad, it's good of you to help out with the building and all, but I do feel a bit guilty, after all this was our idea – Violet's and mine.'

'Look, son,' Joshua said, 'your mother was wealthy in her own right – old money – and she left you an inheritance, which you spent wisely. The rest she left to me. I know by rights it should have come to me when we married, but we agreed between us that wouldn't happen. I had no need of her money, you see, because I had the factory left to me by my father. He built it up from nothing and he made sure I'd want for nothing after he'd gone. As you know, I've worked bloody hard over the years to keep that money safe and to add to it as much as I could. In turn, it will all come to you when I'm gone, but for now I want to help in any way I can.'

'Thank you Dad, but I hope and pray that you will be around for a very long time into the future.' Spencer smiled, his eyes brimming with tears.

Joshua was amazed at the ingenuity of Spencer and Violet and clapped his son on the back as they stood together and looked through the window watching the men working happily below them.

*

Alone in his office again, Joshua's mind took him back to Kath Clancy. He had watched her over dinner at Spencer's and caught himself wishing she had agreed to his suggestion of a courtship.

Sighing heavily, he dreamed on. What was it about her that drew everyone to her? She was a kind soul and Joshua couldn't deny he found her a very handsome woman. There was a mystery around her he still had to fathom and he determined to discover what it was. Then again, if he discovered the mystery, would his attraction to her diminish?

For now, he turned his mind to work matters. Joshua walked the length of the factory before someone shouted, 'What's happening with the old building outside, gaffer?'

Not sure who had spoken, Joshua turned to see all eyes on him. 'It's to be a free medical clinic for the people of Wednesbury,' he said simply. 'Violet Gittins' idea, and a bloody good one I reckon.'

Calling his workforce together in the factory, Joshua related the plan regarding their halfpenny a month contribution to the wages of the doctor, nurse and receptionist. He explained that, if they agreed, this halfpenny would be deducted in the first week of each month before they received their wages for that week. Asking for their opinion on the idea, the applause, cheers and whistles gave him their answer. He was delighted with their response, and as the applause rang out again, he continued to walk back to his office hearing mutters of, 'God bless you Mrs Gittins, and you an' all gaffer!'

Before he realised it, Joshua found himself outside number four, Hobbins Street... Kath Clancy's house.

Christ! The woman was in his subconscious now too! Joshua scuttled away but not before Kath had caught sight of him.

Twenty-Nine

The cold of the winter months stung harshly as people walked the streets. Chilly and wet the mist rolled over the heathland like a huge wave, and hung in the streets like a grey veil.

Late skeins of honking geese flew over houses eager to be in warmer climes, and chimneys puffed out smoke adding to the thick pall covering the town.

Frowns replaced smiles as, heads down, the people hurried through the streets, feeling the cold seep into their bones.

Trees were deep in their winter slumber having shed their red and yellow leaves to lie in a multicoloured carpet on the ground long ago.

Annie Green had just finished pickling onions and shallots for the winter and, as she sat with a cup of tea, realised she was now in need of help from the others herself.

With 'Gittins' Medical Clinic' up and running, her husband Charlie had been the first to visit Dr Shaw on the 'free' treatment day. After a thorough examination, the doctor had said Charlie would be well advised to leave the pit. Coal dust was beginning to affect his lungs and although only in the early stages now, it would only get worse until he was laid up completely.

Charlie had told Annie over their evening meal, adding, 'It will mean we'll have to leave the house, the pit boss will want it for another pit worker and his family. Oh wench, I'm so sorry!'

Annie's concern sat squarely with Charlie's health and right now she didn't give a bugger about the house.

'Don't you worry about that, Charlie, you just give your notice in tomorrow morning and get yourself out of that pit.'

'But what about the house, Annie, we'll have nowhere to go!'

'Don't you fret none, we'll be all right. It's you I'm concerned about, so do as I say and get out of it now.'

Sitting in Kath's kitchen the following day, Annie listened to the news that the clinic was already doing well. Unable to concentrate, she hadn't realised she was tapping a spoon on the table until Martha relieved her of it.

Martha asked, 'What's wrong Annie?'

Tears threatening, Annie was about to answer when Spencer Gittins walked in. 'My apologies for my lateness, ladies,' he said as Violet gave him tea, 'did I miss anything important?'

Martha, looking at Annie, answered, 'We were just about to find out.'

Taking a deep breath, she lunged in, 'Charlie's been told by Dr Shaw he has to leave the pit – coal dust in his lungs – early stages but...' Drawing another breath, she resumed, 'He'll be all right if he gets out now. Charlie's putting his notice in today so I expect they'll want us out of the house by the end of the week, so I've got my work cut out packing everything up.' Her emotions burst their banks and the tears flowed.

Violet was at her side in an instant, wrapping her arms around the sobbing woman.

'Oh Annie! Don't cry, please, I can't bear it!'

After a minute or so Spencer spoke up, 'Annie, I'll send round some of the men who worked on the clinic to help you pack your things.'

Violet interrupted, 'Spencer, could I have a private minute with you please?'

The women exchanged puzzled looks as the two walked quietly outside and stood in the freezing back yard.

'Sweetheart, we have all those empty rooms at our house, would it be possible for Annie and Charlie to move in with us? I know it would mean sharing the house but they have nowhere else to go!'

Spencer sighed as he thought over what she said. Eventually he replied, 'It would make sense, I suppose, because they could end up on the street. Do you think they would go for it? What I mean is, will they see it as charity?'

'Oh Spencer! I think they would be so grateful. As long as you are happy enough with the situation?'

'I don't see another way out for them, my love,' Spencer said, enjoying the feel of her body against his as she flung her arms around his neck.

'Thank you my darling!' Violet stood on tiptoes to kiss his lips.

'Right, let's get in out of this cold and tell Annie.' He smiled.

'Annie, Spencer and I have agreed the men can bring your stuff to Gittins Manor.' She looked at her husband who smiled and nodded.

Faces with open mouths, Annie's included, stared at Violet as she asked Kath for another piece of her delicious cake.

'Violet... Spencer,' Annie said, 'I thank you both from the bottom of my heart, but we couldn't impose on you like that; with Charlie out of work we couldn't pay any rent.'

Spencer waved a hand, dismissing Annie's words, 'If it's all right with Violet...' he said, taking her hand, 'it's all right with me.'

Annie's tears fell again as she sobbed into the corner of her shawl.

Violet smiled her thanks to the man she loved beyond measure and now it was her turn to give him some good news.

'Besides which...' Violet said and waited as everyone looked her way, 'Spencer and I are going to need a nanny – fancy the job, Annie?'

Spencer jumped out of his seat and looked at her with a shocked expression on his face. Then he picked her up and danced her around the tiny kitchen in his excitement. Suddenly thinking she might be breakable, he sat her carefully back on her chair.

'Oh my God! I'm going to be a daddy! Oh Violet, thank you!' He kissed her tenderly then with both fists clenched he punched the air. Taking a deep breath, he added with a laugh, 'Violet, you really must refrain from dropping these surprises on me, I'm not sure my heart can take it!'

Kath's face was a picture; with her hands across her mouth she stared at her daughter.

*

True to his word, Spencer sent the men round with handcarts

to load everything the Greens owned and by the week's end they were settled in at Gittins Manor.

Each of the three rooms on the ground floor they were given sported a fireplace. They were big and square and all overlooked the gardens. These rooms had been built onto the music, sitting and living rooms and each had a door leading outside. They had been added before Spencer Gittins had bought the house and now were proving very useful. Annie turned one into a bedroom. Another she set her living room furniture in and the third she used as a makeshift kitchen. There was no range but the fireplace served her needs. Her kitchen table sat in the centre and her pots and pans were stacked neatly in the corner. There she could continue to experiment with herbs for the cosmetics and skin creams she loved so dearly. She spent many happy hours tinkering with herbs and spices seeing what would work and what didn't.

Not long after they had settled in, a knock came to their living room door and when Annie opened it she saw Spencer and Violet standing there.

'Oh,' she said, suddenly aware she was in their house but moving furniture around like it was her own. 'Erm... come in...'

The pair entered and Violet said, 'Oh Annie, you have your home looking beautiful!'

Your home, she had said. Annie smiled a little uncertainly as she looked at Spencer.

'She's right, Annie, your home is lovely.' There it was again... *your* home. Annie thought they were so good to her and Charlie and she beamed her pleasure at the young couple.

Charlie appeared, saying, 'Bloody hell, wench, shut your mouth and get the kettle on!' Realising only then he was speaking to her, Annie went into the room allocated as a kitchen-cum-beauty room.

Listening to the quiet voices in *their* living room, all around her Annie felt comfort, and relaxation at last began to settle on her. It had been a trying time, first worrying about Charlie's health and then about where they would live, but the Wednesbury Wives and Violet and Spencer in particular had come up trumps. For that she would be eternally grateful.

A moment later, Spencer walked in. Seeing the kettle on a bracket over the fire, he said quietly, 'Annie, please feel free to call the maid or, if you prefer, use the big kitchen downstairs.'

'Thank you kindly, Spencer, but I couldn't. It doesn't sit right with me.'

Spencer smiled then glanced at the pots and pans on the floor in the corner. 'You should tell Charlie to put some shelves up for those.' He grinned at her then rejoined the others.

Annie rattled around, setting cups on saucers while the kettle boiled. A warm glow surrounded her as she thought how lucky she was.

Joining the others, Annie listened to Spencer saying, 'Well Charlie, what do you think?'

'Ar well, it's a good idea, Spencer, but begging your pardon lad... are you able to afford it?'

'Yes,' Spencer nodded. 'The factory is making an incredibly good profit at the moment so I thought to invest and reap the benefits while the going is good.'

'Right then,' said Charlie, 'in that case I'm your man!'

Looking from one to the other, Annie said, 'Charlie Green, what exactly are you his man for?'

Laughing, Charlie said, 'The gaffer just gave me a job, overseeing the renovations of that string of cottages down

Cross Street. It seems…' Charlie looked at Violet, 'on Violet's suggestion, he's bought them to use as outworkers homes for the making of nails!'

'Bloody hell!' was all Annie managed to say, not knowing what she had done to deserve such good friends.

*

Spencer and Violet had, as a way of ensuring that this part of the house belonged to the Greens, given them a key to the front door of Gittins Manor. It was a symbolic gesture more than anything else to make them feel like they belonged; although they knew Annie and Charlie preferred to use the doors out onto the gardens. Spencer said to invite visitors as and when they liked; treat it as their own for that's exactly was it was – *theirs*.

Charlie hired some men from the bread line and took up his work at Cross Street and Violet and Annie set about sorting out a nursery for when the baby arrived. Kath went over frequently to help out and was in her element in the preparations for the birth of her first grandchild.

Joshua Gittins, it was said, was delighted at the prospect of a grandchild, wanting to invest immediately in a perambulator. Violet had begged him to wait until after the birth – the carriage before the baby invited bad luck. He finally gave in to her request and in his excitement he had given his workers at the factory a day off in celebration!

Everything was turning out fine when one day Charlie told Annie the help of the Wives was needed again.

Thirty

Sitting in their usual places around Kath's table, all the men out at work including Spencer, Annie repeated what Charlie had said.

'He was going about his business at the Cross Street cottages, and a woman rushed up to him asking if he had seen her young daughter. He told her he hadn't. The woman had wrung her hands, wailing that her five-year-old had gone missing. Charlie said for her to report it to the police while he and his men went on a quick search of the area. They didn't find the child.'

'Do you think she may have been taken off by somebody?' Violet asked, a sinking feeling in her stomach. The shaking of heads said they couldn't possibly guess. 'Right,' she began again, 'we need to meet with the woman; Annie, are you able to arrange it?'

'Yes,' Annie confirmed, 'I'll take some cake and scones down to the lads working with Charlie and see what I can find out.'

*

Later in the day, Kath answered Annie's shout of, 'It's only me,' with 'Come on in.' Annie walked in to greet the others with a woman dressed in rags. She was dirty from her head to her bare feet. Her desperately thin features made her teeth seem too big for her mouth, and her eyes bulged. Her arms were rail thin and they all wondered how she managed to stay standing on her stick like legs. Horror etched their faces as they looked on the woman, and they watched as she poured her tea from cup to saucer, blew on it once and slurped it down. The woman watched Kath cut thick slices of bread and put them with a chunk of cheese on a plate before her. Violet thought it impossible for her eyes to get any bigger – she found herself mistaken.

'I can't pay...' the woman began, and Kath waved her words aside. 'Ooh ta!' the woman said as she fell on the food.

'Take your time, wench, else it'll make you bad,' Martha said.

Nodding, the woman continued to chew, watching the bread in one hand and cheese in the other as though afraid it would disappear before she could eat it.

Everyone waited until she'd finished before Violet said, 'What's your name?'

Looking over another saucer of tea in her hand, she said, 'Hildy... Hildy Johnson.'

'Well Hildy, Annie here...' Violet said, pointing '...tells us your little girl has gone missing. Is that right?'

Head bowed, she said through the utter misery that engulfed her, 'Ar, I don't know where her could be.'

It was plain she had no more tears, she was completely cried out.

'What's your daughter's name?' Violet took up.

'Margy... Margaret, but we calls her Margy,' the woman said through a mouth full of cake.

Violet asked, 'Have you been to see the police, have you reported it to them?'

'Ar, they said as her's probably wandered off – her'll come home when her gets hungry.'

Mary put in, 'Bloody useless them coppers!'

Violet raised her hand and the assenting murmurs died down. 'Now, Hildy, think about it, would she do that – wander off on her own?'

'Nah,' the woman said, 'her don't go far, her's only five, her's still a babby. Her usually plays with daft Billy.'

'Who's daft Billy?' Kath asked, handing a piece of cake over.

'He's the lad up the road, he ain't all there,' Hildy said, tapping a finger to her temple.

Violet went on tentatively as she watched the woman cram the cake into her mouth, 'How old is daft Billy?'

'I don't know,' she said, trying to push the escaping cake back behind her teeth, 'about twelve I suppose, in his body, but his mind is about the same as Margy's.'

'Hildy,' Violet tried to broach her next question with care, 'do you think daft Billy could have taken Margy off somewhere?'

'Possible I suppose.'

Amazed Hildy was showing more interest in the cake than her daughter, Violet chastised herself when looking again at the woman's gaunt face.

Over the next few hours they learned that Hildy Johnson's husband had died in the pit cave-in that had taken Kath's first husband Harry, years before. Hildy had taken in washing to feed herself and her kids and on returning clean washing to a house one day had been raped by the man living there, the result of which was Margy. The older kids had been helping her with the laundry in order to continue to pay her rent, but the work was not to be had any more. People couldn't afford to pay to have their laundry washed.

Hildy had resorted to begging from the stalls in the marketplace as they closed up in the evenings, and searching the streets for any dropped coins. Eventually being turned out by the pit boss, Hildy and her children had moved into an empty house at the end of Cross Street.

'Right,' Martha said in her own inimitable way, 'this needs a deal o' thinkin' on.'

Violet watched as Kath packed a hamper of food for Hildy's kids and they agreed a sum to be given from the Wives' fund to help out with clothes and the like. Hildy had found the house at Cross Street empty so she'd just moved her children into it hoping no one would turn them out again.

Hildy left for home being told the women would do all they could to help find her daughter.

Mary looked at Violet, saying, 'Poor bugger, this one is a right bloody mess!'

It was decided that the Wednesbury grapevine would be needed again. The message being five-year-old Margy Johnson had gone missing from the bottom end of Cross Street. She was small for her age, with blonde hair, she may have been with an older boy known as daft Billy.

Kath and Violet would go to visit daft Billy's mother and see what, if anything, she could tell them.

*

Waving to Charlie and his men working on the cottages, Kath

and Violet walked down Cross Street which started halfway down Meeting Street and had cottages running the length of both sides before it met up with King's Place at the other end, then veered off to join Holyhead Road. There were around thirty cottages on one side of Cross Street and twenty or so on the other where daft Billy's mother lived. Hers was the last one in the row and, like the others, was covered in a layer of grime from the smoke constantly belched out by chimneys both domestic and industrial. Hildy Johnson lived directly opposite.

Banging on the door, they heard a voice shout, 'All right, I ain't deaf!' The door opened and looking the women up and down, the woman said, 'What do you two want?'

'Are you Billy's mother?' Violet asked quietly.

'What if I am?' The woman's tone was acerbic.

Violet went on, 'Is Billy here? We'd like a word with him.'

'What word? You can have it with me!' The woman became agitated.

'Mrs...?' Violet said.

'Miss...' the woman corrected, 'Cartwright... Patsy Cartwright.'

Violet persisted, 'Miss Cartwright, we really need to speak with Billy. Is he here?'

'No,' Patsy Cartwright said flatly.

Exasperation seeped into Violet and the frustration spilled over as she asked, 'Where is he?'

'I don't have to tell you nothin'. Who the hell are you to be asking after my Billy anyway?' The woman's hackles rose.

'I'll ask you one more time...' Violet said menacingly. 'Where is Billy?'

Bursting into tears, Patsy Cartwright sobbed, 'I don't

know, he took off a couple of days ago and I ain't seen him since!'

Looking at Kath, Violet saw the chagrin cross her face like a harbinger of doom. It seemed the Wives weren't looking for one missing child – but two.

Thirty-One

Violet had called everyone together including Joshua, although he had not been told about the club they felt his help would be needed. Later in the morning she relayed the tale of Margy Johnson and daft Billy. They needed to be found, and quickly. She said with a quiet confidence that, tomorrow, work all over Wednesbury would stop and the people would comb the town in search of the missing children; supposing they had not been found in the meantime.

Giving a desultory laugh, Joshua asked how Violet intended to get the message to all the people of Wednesbury in just one day, presupposing they would agree to it in the first place. 'Losing a day's pay to look for two missing kids will not go down well, so I tell you straight I think it's a foolish idea,' Joshua added.

'Getting the message out isn't the problem...' Violet said, eyeing Joshua over the table, 'but we need the backing of your good name. Spencer has agreed already but we need someone of stature to speak with the pit boss at Monway Colliery. I doubt the children would have strayed further than that, but you never know.'

Buttering him up in front of everyone, she'd put him in a position where to refuse would see his 'good name' go down in the estimation of all around the table.

Joshua gave a small shake of his head, then with a smile at his daughter-in-law said, 'All right, I'll give it a go but... don't be surprised if the pit boss says no. It won't be for the lack of trying on my part, but if he wants his workers in tomorrow... that will be it.'

'Thank you, Father,' Spencer said, 'just think, you can tell your grandchild of the part you played in the rescue of two missing children.'

'Let's get them found first!' Joshua said. A feeling of foreboding crept over him and he suppressed a shudder. He had doubts that they would find them at all, let alone alive and well.

*

'Hello Ezra,' Joshua yelled as he entered the pit boss's office half an hour later.

'Well damn my eyes!' Ezra Fielding said as he stood to shake the other man's hand. 'I ain't seen you in an age!' Sitting back down, Ezra looked at Joshua and then a grin spread across his face. 'I know that look Joshua Gittins, and I have a feeling it's gonna cost me. What is it you want?'

Over tea Joshua explained the situation.

'You are bloody joking of course!' Ezra said, his grin changing to surprise as he went on. 'No... I see you ain't!'

Shaking his head, Joshua began to appeal to the man again and Ezra held his hands up in mock surrender.

'I heard you...' Ezra said his exasperation evident, 'two kiddies gone missing, everybody stops work tomorrow to look for them... you know how much that's gonna cost me, Joshua?'

Taking a leaf out of Violet's book, he said quietly, 'Your good name would be added to the list of searchers, think of the prestige, Ezra; if those children are found alive and well people will say – that Ezra is a good man, giving his men the time off to search, it is down to him those kiddies were found.'

Allowing his words to sink in, Joshua casually finished his tea.

'Christ!' Ezra said... and Joshua knew he had him. 'All right, but... it's only for one day!'

Shaking his hand, Joshua left him to inform his workforce of the change of plans for the following day.

Joshua congratulated himself on a job well done as he returned to his factory to inform his own workforce of the plan. Although it would be a day off for them he felt sure all would turn out for the search of Margy Johnson and daft Billy.

*

It was early afternoon when Joshua heard a ruckus in the factory. Looking out of the window overseeing the workers, he spotted Violet at the heart of a gaggle of women.

Walking onto the factory floor, Joshua heard the oohs and aahs of the women as they enquired after her health and that of the baby. He stepped towards his daughter-in-law and ushered her upstairs.

Sitting Violet in his office with tea, Joshua told her about Ezra Fielding agreeing to the stoppage of work for one day.

'Oh Joshua,' Violet gushed, 'I knew if anyone could do it, you could. Thank you!'

Explaining she'd just come from the market, she said word was now out about the missing children, and she had every confidence people would turn out in droves. Kath had gone down to the canal basin to ask for the help of the 'cut-rats' too.

Each section of the town, she explained, were to form groups who would search a certain area. Violet appeared to have everything in hand.

'Don't you go tiring yourself with all this, you have to think about your own baby.'

'I'll rest when I feel the need, Joshua,' she said. 'I wouldn't endanger your first grandchild.'

Sharing a smile, he said, 'I like the sound of that... my first grandchild.'

*

The following day, the children still not having returned, the extensive search was being mounted. Joshua was overwhelmed at the number of people who turned out. Ezra organised his workers and stood ready for them to march off to the colliery area, to work above ground this time rather than below. Spencer's workers and Joshua's own were to set off in the direction of the marketplace and beyond, and other volunteers were ready to go off in the direction of King Street, Queen Street and the Holyhead Road. A big portion of Wednesbury was to be searched thoroughly in one day.

Violet stood on an upturned box and yelled across the crowd of people gathered outside Joshua's factory. Silence descended as she spoke. 'Thank you everyone for coming out today to help find Margy and Billy. I know it is a formidable task but I also know you will all do your best. We have one day... one day people, to find these children, so I suggest we make a start and... good luck everyone!'

Shouts rang out and boots sounded on the cobbles as the search began for Margy and daft Billy. As the people dispersed, Joshua saw Violet step down from the box and stand beside two other women, with Martha and Kath by her side.

As he approached, Violet said, 'These ladies are the mothers of the missing children.'

Joshua stared at the emaciated bodies hardly able to believe his eyes. 'Right, ladies, if you will come with me.' Taking an elbow of each of the women, he walked them over to the clinic where he passed them to Dr Shaw who was on hand with his nurse.

Nodding, the doctor took them inside for a complete check, knowing just by a glance that they were suffering from malnutrition.

Heading back to Violet, Joshua said, 'Something *has* to be done about that!' Waving his hand at the clinic door as the pitifully thin women disappeared through it.

Spencer had joined the women and said, 'Indeed, Father, let me think on it a while.'

Looking at all the people involved in the search, Joshua turned to Violet and asked how she had managed to accomplish such an amazing feat in the town.

She just smiled and said, 'The women of Wednesbury, Joshua, we all did it together.'

Thirty-Two

Violet and Annie, along with Kath, Joyce, Martha, Mary and Primrose set up trestle tables running the length of the street. Provisions had been brought by most people, whatever could be managed, and food was laid out for the return of the searchers. A dray cart pulled by two massive shire horses delivered half a dozen barrels of beer – no charge, the landlord from the Green Dragon Hotel had said before he joined the search, he wanted to do his bit to help. Home-made lemonade, pies, cakes, bread, chutneys, pickles, cheese... the list was endless, all lay in wait for the hungry searchers.

Each group of searchers had been instructed if the children were found to whistle. People that couldn't whistle through their teeth had their children's tin whistles to hand. The day wore on with no whistle heard through the eerie quiet which lay over the town. With no work being undertaken, Wednesbury seemed like a ghost town.

The heavy rain of the previous days made the search hard-going on the softer ground, but the people of Wednesbury trudged on. A line of women eventually came to the brook that cut across Hydes Lane down by the aqueduct of the Tame Valley Canal. The rains had swelled the brook considerably and forming a chain the women waded across the rushing freezing water which soaked their long skirts.

They called out as they made their way over the waste ground at the other side of the brook. On they went, cold wet skirts flapping around their legs, making them shiver. At the edge of the waste ground that butted up against the road stood an old ruined building and as the women approached it, soft sobbing was heard. As they rushed over, they saw Margy Johnson sitting in the dirt sobbing. Daft Billy was fast asleep near her.

Waking him gently, the women gathered the children and on the count of three they blew their tin whistles hard and long. Men appeared as if from nowhere and waded across the brook, one scooped up Margy and waded back with her, but daft Billy wouldn't budge. He was afraid and began to cry, calling out Margy's name thinking the men were taking his friend away from him. A big strapping miner waded over to daft Billy, saying, 'Come on Billy, I'll give you a piggy back ride if you climb on my back.'

Billy was on him before the miner could blink. Tucking his arms under Billy's knees, he crossed the brook at a gallop much to Billy's delight. When Billy's feet touched the ground again, he ran on to be with his little friend Margy, who was still in the miner's arms.

Whistles sounded all across the area to inform the searchers the children had been found. As everyone arrived back at the factory yard, the two mothers who had been seen by the doctor and given a tonic, rushed over and swamped their children with hugs and kisses; the children holding tight to their mothers' skirts.

Applause split the quiet of the town and backs were slapped and hands shaken before the people of Wednesbury tucked into the food and drink laid out before them.

Quiet descended as Spencer Gittins called out over the gentle mutterings.

'Thank you one and all for your hard labour today in the search for Margy and Billy. Thanks be to God they were found safe and well.' Cheers and applause rang out. Spencer continued, 'My wife would like to say a few words.'

Violet stood on the upturned box and shouted across the yard. 'Our thanks also to Joshua Gittins and Ezra Fielding for the part they played in this most amazing day.' More cheers went up aided by the free ale. 'However,' Violet said, throwing up her hands for quiet, 'without these women here...' her hand swept over to where her mother and her friends were standing, 'none of this would have been possible. So please join me in a toast to... the Wednesbury Wives.'

Violet knew the women of the town would understand the significance of her words, but she was certain the men were unaware of the club and they would remain in the dark concerning this. However, she felt happy all had been acknowledged for their part in finding the missing children.

Thirty-Three

Violet had noticed how, over the past months, the Wives had not been so active and mentioned this at the latest meeting.

'The requests for help have certainly been fewer,' said Kath.

'That ain't to say I wouldn't wade in and paste some bugger if the need arose,' Mary said and they all fell about laughing.

'It's all down to you, wench, you have the respect of the people of Wednesbury. Everybody knows how you feel about the giving and receiving of respect; of the treatment of women around here, and how you think it should be improved,' Martha smiled.

'Ar,' added Mary, 'and that husband of yours. The work on the cottages, the free clinic – it's fair bloody amazing what you've achieved, gel, and no mistake!'

'No,' Violet felt embarrassed, 'it's down to us all, *we* have made giant strides over the years to improve this town. But there's still more to be done.'

Casting their eyes her way, Violet went on in earnest, 'The

poverty in this town is appalling. I'm not sure what we can do about it, but there has to be something.'

'Well,' Martha took up, 'that man of yours is doing very well on that, especially with the cottages in Cross Street he bought from the pit boss. Hasn't he just set up them missing kids' mothers as outworkers on the nailing?'

Violet nodded feeling pride wash over her. 'Yes we had a little discussion on that score.' She looked at the others then continued, 'And Joshua Gittins is doing much the same down in Dale Street.'

Kath pointed out, 'Violet, your baby is due before long and you won't have time for any of this.'

'I understand that, Mum, that's why I have to do something now!'

Seeing Violet getting upset, Annie intervened, 'Now, wench, calm down because it ain't good for the baby you getting all riled up.'

'I know,' Violet said, feeling dejected, 'but what can we do? How can we improve life for the poor in this town?'

'Well now, that needs a deal o' thinkin' on,' Martha's stock phrase had them all crying with laughter, her look of 'What?' setting them off yet again.

*

The following day Dr Shaw arrived to see her on the pretext of checking on the pregnancy. After a quick examination, he pronounced everything to be progressing nicely.

Over tea he explained his real reason for the visit.

'I had a woman in the free clinic yesterday in a hell of a state,' he said, 'she'd had an abortion performed on the quiet by someone who obviously has no idea what they were doing!' He registered Violet's shock at his words, then continued, 'It would seem this is the normal practice for women who find themselves with the prospect of yet another mouth to feed.'

Feeling her baby move, Violet placed a hand on her belly gently massaging her little one back to sleep. Violet was so looking forward to welcoming her baby, and yet these women were so desperate they turned to charlatans to get rid of their babies. She was horrified as she compared her own situation with theirs.

Dr Shaw resumed, 'This is not the first time I have seen this, Violet, and my worry is, whoever is carrying out these abortions will eventually kill someone.'

'Who is doing it, do you know?' she asked, her shock still evident.

Shaking his head, 'No one will tell me, I'm a doctor, Violet, but... I'm also a man.'

Nodding at the meaning of his words, she asked, 'Would you like me to see if I can discover the identity of the person in question?'

'It would help, because once we know who it is, we can find out where they are, maybe then someone can do something about it. Perhaps you could have a quiet word with the Wives.' He winked. 'They do such good work in this town.' His smile broadened as Violet watched him finish his tea.

*

Waddling her way up Hobbins Street on her way to her mother's house, Violet pondered Dr Shaw's words. By doing 'such good work in this town' did he mean them pulling together to find the missing children? Or did he mean them dealing with the tyrants and bullies? No, he could not know about that... could he? If he did know... how did he know? Had he guessed something when she saluted the wives of Wednesbury in her toast to them? Surely this would only be significant to the women. Everyone who had given their time to find the missing children had been acknowledged. Her questioning thoughts gave her no answers; they just led to more questions.

Over tea with her mother Violet explained about Dr Shaw's worries.

'I guessed there was something,' Kath said. 'Joyce mentioned a few women going off sick from the nail works.' Violet tried to make the connection and Kath helped by adding, 'If they weren't off sick, we'd be seeing a lot more babies born!' Still Violet didn't seem to understand. 'The women aren't sick as in the flu, gel.'

'Oh my God! You mean...' Violet's hand flew to her mouth as the penny dropped.

'Yes,' Kath confirmed, 'and I'll bet Dr Shaw will be seeing a lot more women before long. Whoever is doing this is making the women very poorly.'

'Mother, we have to stop this!' Violet railed.

'What?' Kath said with resignation in her voice. 'The women taking dangerous steps to get rid of their unwanted babies, or them getting pregnant in the first place?'

Oh Lord! There in that last sentence lay the root of the problem. How to prevent unwanted pregnancies!

Seeing her daughter's dismay Kath went on, 'There are ways, Violet, I told you as you were growing up, but these women are ignorant. I'm being blunt, wench, because that's how it is... they can't or won't say no to their men!'

'Then they need to be educated!' Violet retorted.

'And who may I ask is going to teach them... you?'

'Yes,' she said firmly.

*

'Whatever are you thinking, girl!' Martha shouted at Violet over the table, her harsh voice causing heads to lower. 'What on earth makes you think the women of Wednesbury would tell you about who is responsible?' Slapping both hands on the table, a loud sigh left her lips.

Eyes but not heads lifted, awaiting Violet's reply.

Pacing the floor, she said, 'Well we have to find out who is performing these dreadful abortions! So, to me, it makes sense to ask. Then we have to stop them or drive them out! Then we have to start educating women in how to say no. Then...'

'All right!' Martha cut in. 'I can see you have a bee in your bonnet over this, and rightly so. First things first, we need to get the grapevine working, let's find this witch, for I'm sure it will be a woman!'

Throwing her arms around Martha, Violet hugged her, saying, 'I knew you'd help.'

And so it was that the grapevine threw up the name and address of the woman doing abortions, on the quiet, for an exorbitant fee.

Setting out, the women trudged over to the woman's little cottage at the end of Portway Lane. The cottage was the only one left standing in that area by the Monway Branch canal. It was surrounded on three sides by waste ground and disused mine shafts, the other side faced the canal which was busy in the daytime with barges moving up and down the waterway. At night it was eerily silent as the boats moored up in the Basin; navigation rules saying barge traffic should only travel in daylight.

Banging on the door with her fist, Violet waited. A small red-haired woman answered with, 'Ah now, who would be banging on my door with such force?' The smile on her fat face disappeared on seeing a quintet of women on her doorstep. Primrose was busy with her baking and Joyce elected to stay home. She had an idea forming in her mind that wouldn't go away. 'What would you fine ladies be wanting with me now?' The Irish lilt came through as she tried to force the smile back to her face.

Violet spoke. 'Are you the one they call Colleen?'

'To be sure,' she said, eyeing Violet's swollen belly.

'Well, we'd like a word, either inside or out here on the step I ain't fussed which,' Martha added.

Stepping aside, Colleen gave them entry and they piled in as she shut the door.

'Well now, what can I be doing for yourselves?' she asked.

'You can stop performing abortions!' Martha spat.

'And making people ill,' Violet added.

'And killing babies!' Annie's venom flared, and her rouged cheeks flushed a deeper shade.

'Otherwise...' Mary wagged a finger in the woman's face.

Kath said quietly, 'We just want you to stop what you're doing Colleen.'

Rolling her eyes, Martha said, 'Missis, you're a menace and if you don't stop being a menace you'll have us to deal with.'

'And just who would *you* be?' Colleen said derisively.

Boldly, Violet said, 'We are the Wednesbury Wives.'

'Bejaysus!' Colleen dropped into a chair, which groaned

under her weight, the colour draining from her face. Regaining her composure, she said, 'I heard about you so I did, but you must understand, I was only trying to earn a few bob!'

'So find a new profession,' Violet said with both hands covering her belly in a protective gesture.

'It's all right for you to be saying that,' Colleen snapped, 'but work's not easy to be found. What do you suppose I could do?'

'We don't really care what you do, Colleen, as long as it's not what you're doing now!' Martha rasped.

'And what about the women who depend on me?'

'Depend on you to do these dreadful things!' Annie's fury took everyone by surprise and they glanced at each other as she ranted on. 'I'd give my right arm to have a baby, and here you are... you are...' Annie couldn't continue she was so incensed. Reaching out she slapped Colleen soundly across the face. 'You are taking advantage of women in desperate situations; women who in other circumstances would not want to abort their babies. Women who, if they had the money to feed them, would keep them and watch them grow up!'

The woman pulled back, her hand going to her cheek as Violet dragged Annie away.

'There's no call for that!' Colleen whimpered.

'Oh yes there is!' Annie growled from where she had been pushed to stand behind Violet. 'There's every call for it, so heed this warning, Colleen!'

'You can be sure I will an' all,' Colleen muttered almost to herself as the women turned as one and left her house.

'Well,' said Mary, 'that was easy enough.'

As they walked away, Martha said, 'Annie, I've never seen you so angry – not even when we were kids.'

Annie looked at the hand that had slapped Colleen, inspecting her fingernails. 'My God, I could have done for her right then!'

'We saw that,' Violet said.

'Sorry ladies. Aww look here, I've broken a nail!'

Titters sounded as Annie tutted loudly.

In Violet's mind Mary's words sounded again. Yes, she thought, it did seem too easy, and she felt in her heart this would not be the last they would hear of the Irish woman named Colleen.

Thirty-Four

Being the eldest of the eight Slater children, Nancy was helping her mother get the others off to work and school. Her parents had worked hard over the years to make sure they all had an education; they wanted their children to do well in the world.

A shout from the kitchen door heralded Violet's arrival and in the quiet after the others had left, the three had tea and began to chat.

Violet had an idea and wanted some opinions on it. Laying her notion out in front of them, Martha said, 'Well now, that needs a deal o' thinkin' on.' Violet and Nancy both laughed at the phrase they'd come to know so well.

'So,' Nancy began, 'your idea would be for me and a few others to look after the children of the women of Wednesbury, until they are of an age to go to school, while their mothers work or try to find work. It might also stop them having to resort to having abortions too. The women would then pay a nominal sum a week which would give us a small wage, is that right so far?'

Violet nodded and Nancy continued, 'The question now is, where? We would need somewhere that we could watch over the children; we'd need to give them a bit of dinner an' all. It would be a long day so some might need a nap as well…'

'Our Nancy is right, wench,' Martha added.

Violet smiled, saying, 'If I could find a place, Nancy, could you find some helpers?'

'Yes, that would be easy enough. There's a lot of girls my age who don't have work to go to.'

Saying she would visit again soon, Violet set off for home in high spirits.

'Well, wench, what do you make of that?' Martha asked her daughter.

'I think our Violet has another bone to chew on and before long I'm going to find myself in work at last!'

Walking down Hobbins Street and along Holyhead Road to the market later that day, Nancy allowed her mind to wander. How many children would there be to take care of? How many helpers would be needed? Would the women be able to afford it? At least if their little ones were being looked after, the women could search for work. As her mind mulled it over, she began to think this idea of Violet's might actually work.

*

Friday came round and saw Violet, Kath, Mary and Annie in Martha's kitchen for a change, having tea. Joyce was at her work in the nail making factory.

Violet said, 'There's a building I want you to come and see,

Nancy – all of you – and tell me if it would be suitable for the caring of children. I want to start a nursery so the women of the town can hopefully find work.'

Looking at Martha, Nancy's eyes said, I knew it! She knew Violet wouldn't let this idea of hers fade away to nothing.

They all trudged up Crankhall Lane, passing the South Staffordshire Tube Works and the Allotment Gardens. Before coming to Brunswick Park they turned right and headed over a patch of waste ground leading to a huge derelict building. Had this been another part of the country Nancy would have said it had once been a mill, but the shudder that racked her body told her different.

'Tell me you are bloody joking!' Mary said as they all stared at the imposing structure.

Martha stopped her mid-sentence, 'Violet, it's the old epidemic hospital!'

The large building spread across the open heath and was situated right next to the South Staffordshire railway line. The three-storey structure with a high water tower at the centre was once used to house patients with diseases such as polio, diphtheria, tuberculosis, scarlet fever and many more besides. The entrance led to an administration block, a kitchen, stores, and a disinfecting station. The middle and upper floors were isolation wards, each of which would hold around twenty beds. In the grounds at the back of the hospital stood the nurses' home, a laundry, a sanitary wash house and the mortuary.

Only the people with money could afford to be admitted, the poor of the town relied on their own remedies. This hospital had been feared by the needy almost as much as the workhouse. However, with Florence Nightingale's 'miasma' theory proving that 'bad air' could cause disease; as well as the discovery of such things as cholera being a water-borne disease, cleanliness became paramount. Nevertheless, the building had been abandoned, being deemed too small, and the patients were moved to bigger and better hospitals in larger towns.

'I know what it was,' Violet enthused, 'but it's not been in use for many years!'

'I don't give a bugger!' said Mary. 'I ain't going in there!'

Nancy watched the light fade from Violet's eyes as her disappointment took hold.

Mary went on, 'It should have been fetched down years ago!'

Nancy saw again the instant spark in Violet's eyes and silently wished Mary would learn to hold her tongue.

*

In the market some days later a woman approached Martha and Nancy saying she wished a word with them.

Martha invited her home where their conversation could take place in privacy. As Nancy made tea, her mother settled the woman at the kitchen table.

'Now then, Jess Dower, what's on your mind?'

The woman looked at Nancy and then back to Martha before speaking. 'Well... I ain't sure I should say in front of the wench.' She jerked her thumb in Nancy's direction.

'Whatever you need to say,' Martha picked up, 'can be said in front of our Nancy.'

The woman cast another glance at the girl before she spoke again. 'Ar well... we ain't happy, Martha Slater.'

'And who, may I ask, is "we"?'

'Us women. It's on the grapevine that you and your friends

have sent Colleen packing. And the women in the town ain't happy about it... what's going to happen now she's out of business?'

'Now who's out of business?' Violet said as she walked in through the kitchen door.

Nancy said simply, 'Colleen.'

Martha explained to Violet what Jess Dower had said.

Full of fury, Violet interjected with, 'Maybe it's time for the women of Wednesbury to make a stand! To stop getting in the family way time after time with no money to feed the extra mouths! To start saying no to having one child after another!'

The others stared with open mouths, then Nancy said, 'I couldn't agree more!'

Rounding on Nancy, Jess countered with, 'It's all right for you wench – you don't have a husband to have to say no to!'

'If I had a husband and half a dozen children round my ankles, then I most certainly would say no! Sorry Mum, I wasn't referring to you.' Anger bubbled up inside Nancy as she glanced at Martha. 'There are ways to prevent this, Jess, we all know that! I'm not saying women shouldn't have children, I'm just saying why have such big families if the money isn't there to feed them?'

'Well said, wench,' said Martha.

Jess looked down as she said, 'Look here, I'm with you on this; I've got four little buggers myself and I ain't having any more, but there's other women who are not as strong as me. You know as well as I do, they're gonna keep having babies if there's no Colleen to stop it.'

Violet spat, 'Well, Colleen's gone, and anyone else thinking to be setting up doing what she was doing will get the same treatment!'

Jess stood to leave saying, 'Right then, I'll pass that back down the grapevine.'

After the woman had left Martha said, 'Our Violet, you've started something now and no mistake!'

Violet answered with, 'I know, but I'm about to start something else! I'm going to have a word with Dr Shaw. Maybe he can instruct the women who act as midwives to advise others against having so many children! It's all down to education, Martha.'

Thirty-Five

As Kath rolled out pastry on the kitchen table her thoughts were shattered as Annie flew in the door.

'Kath... come quick!'

Grabbing her shawl from the nail on the back door, her heart skipped a beat. As they ran down the road and on into Trouse Lane heading for Gittins Manor, Annie puffed, 'Violet's started!'

'Where's Dr Shaw?' Kath puffed back, suddenly feeling too old to be running.

'He is with her, I fetched him first, Kath.'

'Thank you, Annie,' she said, snatching breath into her lungs. 'How's Violet doing?'

Violet's time was very near and Kath worried for her. Many times women died in childbirth and although Dr Shaw was on hand, fear gripped her like a vice. She had watched her daughter's excitement as she had prepared for the birth of her child knowing all the time Violet had no idea what was to come. There was no way Kath could make it any easier for her and she silently prayed it would not be a difficult birth.

'She's all right just now.' Annie shot a glance at her

friend as they hurried on. Although she'd had none of her own, Annie had helped bring many children into the world safely, and she had witnessed the pain of the women during their labour.

Arriving at Gittins Manor, they dashed up the stairs and into Violet's bedroom, puffing and panting with the exertion.

Seeing the anguish in her daughter's eyes and the sweat on her brow, Kath rushed to the girl lying on the bed.

'I'm here bab, I'm here now.'

'Ooooh Mum!' Violet gasped as another spasm of pain racked her small body.

Looking at her, holding her hand, Violet didn't look more than a child herself. 'I know, wench,' Kath said as Violet gripped her hand, squeezing it tightly, 'you'll be all right, just try to relax between the pains, let Mother Nature do her work.'

Annie went off to get hot water and fetch clean towels and linen, and in a moment she was back. Kath watched Violet as another bout of pain rolled over her, her heart aching at her own child's suffering.

'Ooh Mum!' Violet called, the sweat beading on her forehead.

'You're doing well, Violet, I'm sure it won't be much longer,' Kath said, stealing a look at the doctor. She winced as she saw him shake his head.

Mopping away the sweat with a damp cloth, Kath talked quietly to her daughter giving her encouragement.

As another pain gripped her, Violet yelled out, 'Mum... why is it... taking so long?'

'Babies come when they're ready,' Kath said gently.

Violet closed her eyes in the brief respite from the agonising pains. Then she lifted her head and let out another howl.

Kath shot a look at the doctor who was at the end of the bed. 'Violet,' he said, 'just grit your teeth now for a couple of minutes.'

Alarm showed clearly on Kath's face as she saw him disappear below the sheet draped across Violet's knees before popping back up again. Something was terribly wrong; it was written clearly over the doctor's face. What was happening? Would the baby be stillborn? Would Violet die?

Agonising pains gripped the young woman again as she lay on the bed, her knees bent. She cried and gasped. She panted and cried some more. 'Mum, I'm scared,' she whimpered.

'I know, sweetheart, I know.' Kath felt sick with worry. She glanced again at the doctor and saw him dip down beneath the sheet once more. To her daughter she said, 'Come on, love, be brave.'

Violet screamed again as another bout of pain ripped through her.

'Right, Violet,' Dr Shaw said as he peeped through Violet's bent knees yet again, 'when I say, I want you to push down hard, we need to get this little one out.'

Violet let out an exhausted moan before catching her breath again.

'Now Violet, push wench...'

Violet let out a yell and then gritting her teeth she strained hard to no avail.

'What's wrong Dr Shaw?' Kath asked as she looked at him, 'Why isn't the baby coming?'

'It will,' he said, 'I just need to...'

Violet let out a shriek, lifting her head from the pillow; eyes wide with fear and pain.

'It's all right now,' the doctor said, 'the head's through. Now, Violet, one more push and your baby will be born.'

Dragging air into her lungs, Violet pushed down hard then fell back exhausted.

They heard a slap, then a tiny wail as Dr Shaw said, 'Violet, you have a fine healthy boy!'

Tears poured from Violet's eyes as the doctor finished his ministrations with her. The baby boy was passed to Kath and she quickly wrapped him in a warm towel and carried him to his mother. Kath swelled with love for the tiny bundle in her arms and kissed him gently on his forehead.

Violet held her child, gazing at him in wonderment, her face aglow with happiness. Kath watched her own child watching her child, and her heart swelled with pride.

Annie stood by with more towels and water for Dr Shaw and came to the bedside with tears rolling down her face.

'Annie,' Violet whispered, 'meet Harry Gittins.'

Annie clapped her hands in delight as Violet said to Kath, 'I named him after my dad.'

Putting her face in her hands, Kath wept uncontrollably then heard Dr Shaw say, 'Congratulations, Violet, he's a fine boy and you did so well bringing him into the world. Get some rest now, wench.' Turning to Kath, he said, 'She'll need you and Annie for a little while, and I'll be back tomorrow to check on her.'

The doctor left and they watched as Violet's eyes drooped. Lifting the baby from her arms, Kath passed him to Annie saying, 'You sleep, Violet, rest easy now.'

Annie washed and swaddled young Harry and cradled him while he slept, never taking her eyes from his little face.

Kath said quietly, 'I'll go fetch Spencer from the works.'

'Christ!' Whispered Annie. 'I forgot about him!'

Exchanging grins, Kath glanced at Violet sleeping peacefully before creeping out of the room.

*

Kath stayed overnight with Annie and Charlie and the following day she visited Violet. Spencer was like a cat who'd got the cream, a wide grin splitting his face.

Dr Shaw arrived and ushered Spencer out of the room so he could look over Violet and her baby. Satisfied all was well, Spencer was allowed back in.

As he moved to the door, the doctor flicked his head to Kath beckoning her to follow him.

'I'll see Dr Shaw out,' she said to the happy parents who were gazing at their newborn child lying peacefully in Violet's arms.

As they descended the stairs, Dr Shaw said, 'It was a close thing, Kath.' She shot a questioning look at him and he explained, 'The cord was round the baby's neck, if I hadn't released it when I did, it would have strangled him.'

'Dear God!' Kath stammered.

'Fortunately I was able to release it in time before Violet gave her last push. She's a strong wench, Kath, she'll do just fine and so will the baby.'

Thanking him, she watched his carriage pull away and then muttered her thanks to the Almighty. Kath walked round the gardens and heard the doctor's words again, *if I hadn't released it, it would have strangled him.*

Her thoughts immediately returned to Frank Woolley and she envisaged him hanging from the balustrade. As the picture formed in her mind her stomach lurched and she felt bile rise to her throat. She remembered how the others said Frank had struggled to free himself and how, as life left him, his eyes had bulged and his tongue lolled from his mouth.

Sitting on the bench by the lawn, Kath wept openly, partly

for the terrible things she had done in her life and partly in thanks for the safe delivery of her healthy grandchild.

It was as she sobbed into her shawl she heard hoof beats and looking up she saw Joshua Gittins jump down from his horse. Rushing to her, he said, 'Hey up Kath, whatever is the matter, wench?'

Drying her eyes, she related what Dr Shaw had told her.

'Bloody hell!' was Joshua's response. 'No wonder you're weeping, but it's all right now, mother and baby are doing fine aren't they?'

Nodding her head, the tears fell once more and before Kath knew what was happening she was in Joshua's arms. Holding her while she cried, she heard him whisper, 'It's all right wench, you're safe with me.'

Allowing herself to fold into him, Kath relished the feeling of his strong arms around her. It had been a long time since she had been held this way and she succumbed to the joy of it.

Thirty-Six

The feeling Spencer had each time he looked at his wife and child was so powerful it threatened to crush him. He was as proud as a peacock and revelled in the chorus of applause back at the factory as he walked to his office.

The foreman followed him in and Spencer said, 'Jack, I need you to watch over the works for a couple of days.' Seeing the man's nod, he continued, 'I wish to spend some time with my wife and son.'

'Yessir gaffer!' Jack Hesp doffed his cap. 'And congratulations to you and the missis.'

Thanking him, Spencer made his way out of the factory. As he rode home he thought about a gift for Violet for giving him such a beautiful child. He decided to call in on Martha; she would be the best person to ask about the ideal gift.

'Hello lad,' said Martha as Spencer knocked on the door and entered her kitchen, 'have a seat, tea's fresh made.'

Over tea and cake he said, 'Martha, I want to give Violet a gift as a thank you for giving me such a beautiful son, and I thought you might help me out with ideas.'

'Our Violet wouldn't want a gift as such, lad...' Seeing his puzzled expression, she laughed, saying, 'The only thing I can think of that Violet really wants is to find somewhere for my Nancy and a few of her friends to set up looking after the little ones so their mothers can try to find work.'

'Oh, her latest venture.' Spencer smirked.

'Ar lad, and the only place she'd found was the old epidemic hospital.' Spencer watched the shiver take Martha as she thought of it. 'Bloody awful place that is an' all. There's no way that place could be used.' Martha looked at him out of the corner of her eye, a grin slowly creeping across her face. 'Mary was right when she said it should have been fetched down years ago.'

'Martha Slater, you are a wily woman!' Spencer said as his grin joined hers.

'Well lad, you asked – I told. But it would take a lot of work and money...to pull it down and rebuild I mean...' Martha allowed the sentence to hang in the air.

'I would imagine so. Looks like I need to meet with the accountant...again!'

Giving her a hug, Spencer set off to see the accountant to check on the state of his finances. He was told, providing he was careful, it would be possible. Spencer worried about the amount of money he had spent recently trying to help the folk of the town. However, he set out for the Town Hall to make a bid for the derelict building with the powers that be. The old building had stood empty for some considerable time; no one had ever shown an interest in buying it, so in a matter of hours the deeds were in his hands, the council only too glad to be rid of it!

Riding to the bread line down by the marketplace, Spencer had decided to get the work underway immediately; he meant it to be a surprise for Violet.

The queue of men standing at the edge of the market seemed to grow longer every day and his heart swelled to think he might be able to help them. Sitting squarely on his saddle, Spencer shouted across to the men, 'I need workers!'

The scramble almost took him from his horse as shouts came back, 'Me gaffer,' 'I'm a hard worker.'

Holding up his hands, the men calmed before he spoke again. 'Anyone know the old epidemic hospital?'

Nods and mutters of 'Ar, we know it' sounded and Spencer saw heads lower in dreaded anticipation of working there... but work was work.

'I need workers to tear it down!' Spencer yelled.

Cheers sounded before one man shouted, 'About bloody time it was done away with, good on you gaffer!'

Spencer told the whole line of workers, about fifty men in all, to bring whatever tools they had and meet him at the hospital building.

An hour later every man was there with handcarts and tools. Spencer shouted over their heads, 'I want the building pulled down and the bricks to be reused if possible. The land is to be cleared ready to put up a new building. I will pay each of you a weekly wage until the building is completed. Any man found shirking his duties will find himself back on the bread line. Is that understood?'

Nods and shouts of 'Yes' filled the air.

'Now,' he went on, 'this work will take some time to complete, and if I'm satisfied with it, I may be able to find more work for you at the end of the project.' Cheers went up. 'Who was it shouted to me earlier?'

A man stepped forward, doffing his cap, 'Me gaffer, Fred Pincher is my name.'

'Right Fred, you'll be my foreman, it's up to you to set these men to work, and each Friday morning you come to me at Gittins' Nails to fetch the wages.'

'Yessir gaffer!' A murmur of approval ran around the men on hearing the mention of money.

'I will also want you to report on the progress of the work, Fred; I want it completed as soon as possible.'

'Be our pleasure, Mr Gittins sir,' he said as he turned to face the other men. 'All right, you heard the gaffer!'

As one, the men turned to face the old building and charged as if going into battle.

*

Dr Shaw had called and recommended at least ten days' bed rest after which Violet could get up for gentle exercise.

'While you're here, doctor, I wondered if I could ask a favour,' Violet said.

'You can ask,' Dr Shaw grinned.

'Well, I'm sure you know the women who act as midwives for their neighbours when they can't afford to come and see you...' The doctor nodded. 'There must be a way the women can encourage others to not have so many children. They struggle to feed the ones they have.'

'And you want me to speak with them about contraception so they can pass it along'

'Yes. Now I've experienced childbirth for myself, I don't understand how women would choose to have as many as they do! It's far too painful if you ask me.' Violet gave a nervous smile.

'Obviously I don't know what it's like, but I see the pain and, the deaths.' Dr Shaw shook his head sadly. 'I can't promise it will make any difference, but I will certainly give it a go.'

'Thank you doctor, we will wait and see.'

*

Spencer's son seemed to grow quickly as the winter finally came to an end. Work on the old hospital building was progressing rapidly. The building itself had been taken down and the men were busy clearing the land. Spencer had visited Mr Morgan, the architect in Pinfold Street, who had drawn up plans for the new building which promised to be exactly as he envisioned it. Another visit to the bread line had provided him with woodworkers given over to making toys for the youngsters to enjoy once the building was up and running.

Regular visits to Martha and her daughter Nancy allowed him to inform them of the work being done. Spencer had requested Violet not be told of his venture, he wanted it to be a surprise, but knowing the grapevine in Wednesbury as he did, he suspected news would leak out eventually. Martha had said Violet was far too busy with Harry to worry about that.

Spencer was on his way to Martha's once more and found her in the kitchen, hands flat on the table, staring into space.

'Martha?' he called quietly, afraid she was feeling ill. 'Are you all right?'

'Hey up lad,' she said. 'Ar, I'm fine.'

Taking the tea offered, he asked, 'What's going on, Martha?'

'Oh lad,' she began, 'I want Geordie to get out of the pit. I worry for his health in all that coal dust, but it's the only work he knows and he wouldn't give it up without something else to go to. Besides he won't listen to me.'

'What about if I asked him to leave the pit?' Spencer enquired.

'Surely lad, but what would we do without money coming in? We'd have to leave the house an' all. No, it ain't possible, but I thank you kindly for offering.'

Leaving it at that Spencer determined that he would think on it a while and discuss it with his wife. He wanted to find work for Geordie, but he wanted to be sure he could make the offer before mentioning it to Martha. He also thought that, with Martha confiding in him so readily, he really had been accepted as one of the Wives.

Thirty-Seven

Nancy had gone off to visit her friends who would join her in looking after the young children in the new building, and Martha was sat with her cup of tea thinking on the past months and her current predicament when Mary burst in through the kitchen door.

Slapping both hands on the table, she leaned forward catching her breath then, 'She's at it again!'

'Who's at what again?' Martha asked, pouring her visitor a cup of tea.

'That bloody baby killer!' Mary slumped into the chair with a curt nod as a thank you for the tea.

'Colleen?' Martha asked quite surprised.

'Ar, and this time she's gone too far!' Mary blew on the hot tea before taking a sip.

Martha waited for her friend to slake her thirst.

Mary went on, 'She's only gone and killed somebody!'

'Oh Christ! Damn the woman to hell!' Martha said venomously.

'I'm not quite sure who it is she's done in, but Dr Shaw is riled all to hell!'

'That's no surprise is it?' Martha asked, not really needing an answer.

'Martha...' Mary began.

Cutting her off, Martha said, 'Ar, this needs a deal o' thinkin' on.' This time the saying brought no smile with it.

*

Trudging up the road to Kath's house with Mary in tow, Martha's mind whirled. That Irish woman had killed a woman trying to rid her of an unwanted pregnancy. Anger boiled as they stamped their way to Kath's. Something must be done about this and the sooner the better.

Kath gasped as she heard the news of the dead woman. 'What can we do?' she asked. 'These women see her as their saviour!'

'Saviour my arse!' spat Mary.

'The time has come,' Martha expostulated. 'She was warned!'

'This calls for more tea,' said Kath, 'and ladies, I don't want Violet involved in this... After tea, we'll gather the wenches together and formulate a plan.'

All together later in Kath's kitchen, ideas were tossed back and forth. It was evening so Joyce and Primrose had joined them, along with Annie.

Joyce said, 'I knew this would happen, the doctor said the woman died of septa summat or other.'

'Septicaemia,' Martha put in helpfully, 'the blood was poisoned.'

A collective intake of breath showed the shock of all.

'So what are we going do about it?' asked Kath.

Quiet shakes of heads around the table, they sat in silence.

Looking around, Martha said, 'Does this Colleen know that woman has died? Because if she does, she'll take to her heels.'

Annie chimed in, 'If that is the case, we might never find her.' She patted her hair to ensure it was still in place.

'We'll know if we visit her,' added Kath.

'Not yet...' Martha said, 'we have to have a plan first, then we'll visit... by night.'

*

Going their separate ways, they decided to think about the matter and how they could put a stop to Colleen and her insalubrious business.

It wasn't until a few days later that Kath informed Martha that Joyce had taken it upon herself to visit Colleen as a potential 'patient'.

Joyce had been told by the Irish woman to go back in a couple of days with half a crown.

'Half a crown!' Martha said in disbelief. 'Where do the women get that sort of money from?'

Kath gave a weak smile, saying, 'Half a crown is nothing compared to the raising of yet another child.'

'Still an' all...' The sentence hung in the air as they stared at each other.

'You know if we took her to the police, she'd say the woman died of sickness, and we couldn't prove *that* sickness was caused by Colleen,' Kath said at last.

'Ar wench, I know that, then that Colleen would just carry on and we could have another death on our hands.'

Rubbing her hands over her face, Martha suddenly felt

very old. Weariness weighed heavily on her as she racked her brains for an answer to the latest problem facing them.

*

Geordie arrived home from the pit and while he washed down in the scullery sink, Martha laid out their meals of faggots and grey peas.

'Eeh lass, that looks good,' he said as he tucked in to his food. 'Eh, you'll never guess who came to see me the day,' he went on as he finished eating.

'Who?' Martha asked, her mind still on the problem of Colleen.

'Young Spencer Gittins. He came to the pit as I was coming out; asked me if I fancied a change of work.'

'What!' Martha said, all ears now.

'Aye, said he had need of a foreman at some new building of his.'

'I thought he had a foreman there already.'

'Aye well it seems he's taking on some new men like, and he wants me to oversee them.'

'So what did you tell him?' Martha asked, silently praying for a favourable answer.

Her prayer was answered when he said, 'Why aye, I told him, anything to get out the pit! Seems I'll be startin' a new job next week.'

'Thank God!' Martha said through her tears, and quietly through the rattle of gathering teacups, 'thank you an' all Spencer Gittins.' At least that was one of the problems solved, now she needed to work out what to do about Colleen.

Spencer sat with them all at Kath's table, Violet he said sent her apologies for not attending as she was still in her confinement. She had no doubt their son would be cooed over by the women workers.

'Well lad,' Martha said, 'first thing is, I want to thank you for taking on Geordie.'

All eyes went to the young man who gave a small smile and curt nod.

In explanation, Martha said, 'Our Spencer here has given Geordie a foreman's job on the new building so as to get him out of the pit.'

Spencer smiled again at the applause and stood to take a small bow. 'Martha, I know your house is tied to the pit.' Martha nodded only just then realising she would have to pack up and move. But to where? With her head down Martha nodded and Spencer spoke again. 'Violet asked me to give you this.' Taking a paper from his pocket, he passed it to Martha. Opening it, she looked at him with her mouth gaping as she passed the paper to the others. It was the deeds to the house. 'Violet bought it from Ezra Fielding. She wanted you to have it.'

'Where did she get the money?' Martha asked.

'From me, which I got from the bank,' he said with a grin. The loan he had taken out for this latest project was kept firmly to himself. It would be easily paid off once the nails made by the outworkers had been sold on. 'She bartered Ezra right down on the price. By the time Violet had finished, the poor man practically gave it away! I couldn't believe it when she told me.'

Tears flowed as Spencer received hugs and kisses from all the women in the small kitchen.

'I'll never be able to thank you both enough,' Martha sobbed.

The mood changed as the conversation turned to the remaining problem at hand. The tale of Colleen and the dead woman was related to Spencer who listened without interruption, nodding in the appropriate places.

'What we have to decide now is what to do with the bloody woman!' Acrimony spilling over, Martha felt her patience wearing thin.

Spencer put in, 'If she's already been warned by you ladies and has still carried on, it's my contention she will continue to do so.'

Nods of agreement confirmed they were thinking the same.

'Other women could die if she carries on Spencer, and that's what worries us all.' Martha said.

Mary muttered quietly, 'She should be sleeping with the fishes.'

As quiet descended on the room, Mary looked up to see them all watching her.

'Oh bloody hell,' she said as they all smiled at her.

*

The evening arrived for Joyce to take her half a crown to Colleen on the pretext of ridding herself of an unwanted baby. She'd related to them about the idea which wouldn't go away, and they had all agreed to Joyce's ruse to carry out their plan. The other four women, Kath, Mary, Martha and Annie – Violet was safely at home with Spencer unaware of what was taking place – trudged down the dark streets, each carrying a couple of heavy house bricks tied around their waists with rope hidden by their long shawls.

Mary puffed, 'One day I'll learn to keep my mouth shut!'

Titters came from the others as Martha responded, 'Never in a month of Sundays!'

Hiding on the lea side of the house in the dark shadows, they watched as Joyce tapped quietly on the door. Hearing the Irish woman say, 'Ah now, it be yourself,' they saw Joyce step into the house, and just as the door began to close, Martha and Kath pushed their way in, followed closely by Mary and Annie, taking Colleen by surprise.

With the door shut behind them, Colleen was pushed roughly into a chair by Kath.

'You were warned!' Martha said vehemently, 'But you didn't take heed. Now you will pay for what you've done!' She jabbed a finger towards the woman's face.

'I ain't done nothing,' wailed Colleen.

'You call murder doing nothing?' Martha asked, anger blazing.

'To be sure, I've done no murder!'

'That woman, Freda Watkins...' Martha jabbed the finger at her again, 'she died. You poisoned her with your dirty ways!'

The truth registered and Colleen drew a breath.

'You're a dirty witch,' said Mary savagely, 'now it's your time to meet your maker to explain yourself!'

Colleen jumped to her feet and tried to make for the door. Joyce leapt forward and grasped the woman's red hair, pulling her backwards. Colleen gave a strangled cry as she tottered, trying desperately to keep her footing.

Kath and Mary had been loosening the ropes around their

waists that were holding the house bricks. Seeing Colleen attempting to free her hair from Joyce's grasp, they dropped the bricks to the floor and shot forward to overpower her. Kath gave a swift kick to the back of the woman's legs and Colleen went down hard, leaving a handful of hair in Joyce's hand.

Instantly they were on her, pinning her to the floor. Mary pinched the woman's cheeks together and as Colleen gasped for air, her mouth open, a dirty rag was pushed into it. Arms and legs flailing, Colleen knew she was fighting for her life but against five of them, she stood little chance. They rolled her onto her back and Martha sat hard and heavy on her chest pushing the air from her lungs, almost expelling the improvised gag.

Joyce dashed for the bricks Kath and Mary had dropped and pulled them across to where Colleen lay desperately trying to drag air in through her nose. Tying her feet together with the ropes prevented Colleen from kicking out her legs. Struggling to hold her arms in place, Martha watched as Annie relieved herself of her own bricks.

Kath and Mary each grabbed an arm and pulled Colleen's wrists together as Martha bound them with the rope she had carried. With the woman now tied hand and foot and the gag firmly in place, Martha then scrambled to her feet. Watching Colleen struggle, she undid the rope around her middle, rubbing where the bricks had bruised her during the altercation. They lifted the Irish woman and set her on her feet before a rope and more bricks were tied round her waist.

Frightened eyes looked at Martha as she spoke, nose to nose, with the terrified Colleen, 'We warned you!'

Opening the back door, Joyce took a quick look outside

and crooked a finger as they dragged the Irish woman weighed down with house bricks out into the night.

In a few steps they were round the side of the cottage and at the edge of the canal.

Colleen's terrified eyes showed in the light of the moon before it slipped back behind the clouds.

They edged nearer to the black cold water and Colleen's eyes grew wider still at the prospect of sliding into its depths. Lifting her feet, they tilted the petrified woman towards the still water of the canal. Then abruptly they pulled her back to a prone position; the women carried the Irish woman back into her cottage. Kath pulled the gag from Colleen's mouth and they all watched as she dragged in great gulps of air. Still bound tightly, she was laid on the floor and it was Kath who spoke.

'Colleen, I hope this incident shows you we mean business.' Red hair bobbed as the woman nodded frantically. 'Now, we may not condone what you are doing but we recognise the necessity of it until women are educated enough in the ways of avoiding pregnancy.' Again Colleen nodded. 'So, we have come to this decision – *if* you seek help from a midwife or doctor in how to aid these women safely... and *if* you drastically improve the conditions you work in so the women don't get sick afterwards...'

'By all the Saints I swear I will!' Colleen interjected, the underlying threat being quite clear to her.

Kath went on, 'We understand the predicament of the women who come to you and we know they see you as their saviour, but – if you are to continue in your *business*, this place must be clean and sterile. Also, it is imperative you learn to administer to women safely. Do you understand what I'm saying to you?'

'To be sure, I'll be seeking that help on the morrow,' Colleen promised.

'I suggest you go and see Old Mother Johnson at Banks Farm first of all. She is more accustomed to bringing children into the world, I'm sure she may be able to assist you. Just mention that we sent you.'

Releasing her bonds, the women helped Colleen into a chair. Joyce made her a cup of tea while the others disposed of the ropes and bricks outside the cottage to serve as a reminder. Everyone sighed in relief that they had been able to take action without involving taking a life.

Each shook hands with a trembling Colleen to seal their pact before they left for home. As a parting shot, Kath said, 'Remember, Colleen, bad news travels fast.'

Thirty-Eight

The bond between Kath Clancy and Joshua Gittins had become stronger since the day he found her crying in the garden. The thread as grandparents was held together with young Harry Gittins being the knot.

Joshua had visited Kath often over the past months and they enjoyed each other's company over tea, although she had said many times that was not to be misconstrued as them being in a romantic relationship. She had to admit however, that she enjoyed his company. Nevertheless he found himself waiting eagerly for their next meeting and his heart warmed at the thought of Kath.

Sitting in his chair by the fire, Joshua allowed memories of her to flood his mind. Her sparkling eyes, shiny hair and her pleasing fragrance; her tinkling laugh like falling rain, her clear skin and her womanly figure – his mind was full to bursting with her. He had once been determined to solve the mystery that surrounded her, but now he realised this only added to her charm. He had also considered asking again if she would be his sweetheart, but decided against it – he would not jeopardise the friendship they had. If friendship was all she offered, he would accept that gladly and live in hope of more.

Joshua's thoughts shifted to his son and his family. He had not thought the match between Spencer and Violet a good one in the beginning, but that young wench had proved him wrong. Nothing of Violet's background ever came to light, and in time he had dismissed it from his mind. She had proved her worth time and again in Wednesbury, and along with Spencer had worked wonders in the small town, finding work for so many people, and increasing their wealth in the process. Joshua's own financial situation had improved considerably too since the demise of Frank Woolley. His young grandson, Harry Gittins, would be a wealthy man indeed one day.

Watching the dancing flames of the fire, Joshua luxuriated in the happiness that surrounded him. His only regret was that he may never have another wife to accompany him into old age.

*

The day eventually arrived for the opening of the new building and it seemed everyone in Wednesbury had turned out to see it. Despite Violet being in full health and active again, Spencer delighted in the knowledge it had managed to remain a secret from her.

With Spencer, Violet and young Harry in one carriage, Kath had accompanied Joshua in his. They drove up the long carriageway that separated what would be, in time, two vast lawns. The new building, although not very big, bore no resemblance to its predecessor and stood proud against the blue sky, being lit only by the sunshine of an early springtime.

Over the door hung a sign, 'Violet's Play House.'

As Violet stepped down from the carriage, Joshua saw her gasp with pleasure at the sight before her. Applause and cheers rang out as she walked up to the door. Nancy and her helpers were waiting and pushed open the door to allow her entry. Violet thought, *This must be what Queen Victoria feels like!*

They all walked around the inside which had been whitewashed; one room had a row of small beds, another a small kitchen, yet another housed the wooden toys, and outside a lavatory. It had everything needed to enable the caring of the children of Wednesbury.

Joshua had gleaned that the message had travelled the town grapevine, which was in fact just gossip that for a nominal sum, mothers could bring their children here, leaving themselves free to find work. The building had been erected in a very short time and he wondered if Spencer had employed every man in the town who had been out of work. He also wondered how his son had afforded it and made a mental reminder to ask him later.

Feeling a touch on his arm, Joshua turned to see Kath beaming. 'Well Granddad Josh, don't we have clever children?'

'Indeed we do, Grandma Kath,' he laughed, 'my question now is, what will they do next?'

Shaking her head gently, she walked with him back to his carriage; Joshua enjoyed the feeling when she slipped her arm through his. Was this walking out? Did people think it was? Did she even realise she'd done it? Pushing the thoughts away, he laid his hand on her arm that lay so comfortably along his own.

For all the world they looked like a courting couple and Joshua revelled in the idea.

*

Violet's Play House didn't take long to fill up with the youngsters of the town and every day women came to the factories looking for work. Some were in a position to take on outwork making nails, others were not so fortunate.

Riding across Stone Cross to Spencer's factory, Joshua wanted to hear any ideas his son may have regarding putting some of the many still unemployed to work.

'Hello Father!' Spencer said in greeting. 'I was about to have tea... join me?'

'Ar lad, never say no to a good cuppa.'

Spencer asked, 'What can I do for you Father?'

'Well lad, I was wondering about this here bread line. Every day women come looking for work on the nailing and men are standing by the marketplace waiting for any work that might be had.'

'Yes,' said Spencer as he steepled his fingers, 'I've had women here too, but what with the new building, I'm not in a financial position to take on more workers just now.'

'You are all right for money though, son?' Joshua asked, his concern evident.

'Oh yes Father, but I don't want to stretch what I have any thinner at present. In time maybe I can, but not right now. I need to take care of my own family first.'

'Good thinking lad, good thinking.'

Spencer smiled saying, 'I hear you've been seeing quite a lot of Kath Clancy lately.'

'Ar,' Joshua confirmed, 'and no, we ain't a couple, although I wish we were.'

'Ask Kath, Father.'

'Ask Kath what?' Joshua gave his son a wry smile.

'Ask her about any notions of helping Wednesbury people to find work. She's a wise woman, she and her friends may have some good ideas. Besides, you lose nothing by asking.'

'Good idea, lad,' Joshua said with a smile as he stood to leave, 'in fact I think I'll do that right now.'

Spencer watched him go. He smiled, shaking his head, his father hadn't even stayed long enough for that cup of tea!

*

Kath made Joshua welcome, as usual, with tea and cake. As they settled, he explained his feelings regarding the poor people of Wednesbury.

'It ain't right, Kath, these folk are as poor as church mice and every day they stand in that bloody bread line without a hope in hell of finding work!'

Laying her hand on his on the table, she said, 'Now, Joshua, don't get so het up, let's discuss this and see what we can come up with.'

'Maybe those friends of yours might have a few ideas an' all?' he asked.

'The ladies can usually find an answer if they think on the problem long enough,' she laughed.

Thirty-Nine

Once again the meeting of the Wives took place in Kath Clancy's kitchen, and after tea, cake and the usual oohs and aahs over Harry, they settled down to business. Although Violet had not been involved in the Colleen affair, Kath had told her about it and she'd felt it was justifiable retribution. Kath explained that Dr Shaw had seen no more 'sick' women in the past weeks, which was a blessing in itself. It also meant the message was getting through regarding pregnancy education.

The children filling the new building were faring well and Nancy and her helpers were enjoying their new-found work. This then brought them to the people still out of work and Joshua's visit.

'He asked,' Kath said to the women around her table, 'if we could think on the quandary, possibly come up with some ideas about getting people into work.'

Martha snorted, 'It ain't possible, wench, there is no work to be had. Geordie and Charlie still have a drink with the pit workers and they say there's nowt doing there.'

'There must be something, somewhere!' Violet spoke.

'No bab, there isn't,' Mary added. 'The pit is taking on no more, in fact there's talk of it closing down; your old man can't take on any more either...'

Grins appeared all round as Martha said, 'It's all he can do to keep Geordie and Charlie in work as it is, so this needs a deal o' thinkin' on.'

*

Before the week's end, Joshua Gittins was once again sitting in Kath's kitchen.

'So Kath,' he managed, after swallowing his cake, 'any of your girls have ideas regarding folk seeking work?'

'Not as yet, Joshua, but we're thinking about it.'

'Ar, righto. Erm... Kath, I was wondering...'

Smiling inwardly, she thought, *here it comes!* 'Yes?' she said.

'Well now, as we seem to be getting on so well lately, I was wondering if maybe...'

'Joshua,' Kath interjected, 'I have told you all along that I may never marry again – I take it this is what you're alluding to?'

'Well ar...' he said, looking shame-faced.

Kath went on, 'It would not be fair to start a romance with you, Joshua, knowing full well there would not be the prospect of marriage at the end.'

'I suppose you are right, Kath, but you know how I feel about you – I bloody love you wench!'

Feeling the blush rise to her cheeks, Kath looked at her hands folded in her lap. Emotions were running high in the small kitchen and she floundered looking for something to say.

'If you don't feel the same way, Kath, just tell me...'

Again Kath found herself at a loss for words, and she found the feeling most uncomfortable. 'Joshua, that's not the case...'

'I bloody knew it!' Slapping his hands on the table made her flinch, 'I bloody knew you felt the same all along!'

Holding her hands up as if in surrender, Kath said, 'Joshua, listen to me... I *am* very fond of you and enjoy your company...' Taking a breath to speak, her raised finger stayed his tongue. 'But I do not wish to put myself in the position – again – of being beholden to any man.'

'You don't have to be beholden to me, Kath, just be my wife!'

'As the law stands, Joshua, I *would* be beholden to you. All my "goods and chattels", as it were, would revert to you on our wedding day. I cannot – *I will not* – put myself in that position again!'

'Kath, you don't have to give me none of that, besides I have enough, I just want you to marry me.'

'It's not a matter of my giving you my money, Joshua, it's not even a matter of you not wanting it – it's the law!'

'Bloody stupid law if you ask me!'

His dejected look tore at her heart. If it had not been for this law, Kath knew she might well have agreed to his proposal, after all, she did love him.

'There is no way round this is there?' His voice was low and ready to break.

'It would seem not,' Kath said simply, trying to hide her sadness.

*

Bread and cheese was served followed by tea and cake in Kath's small kitchen and chatter abounded.

Watching Annie bouncing Harry on her knee, Mary suddenly spoke, 'Annie, what have you done to your hair?'

Sitting in Kath's small kitchen, everyone's eyes turned to look at Annie's hair shining in the sunlight streaming through the kitchen window.

'I just washed it,' she said.

'Ar, I know that, but washed it with what?' Mary's indignation was evident.

'Some herbs I found on the heath,' Annie replied. 'The ones I collect on my walks.' She rolled her eyes, 'You know, the ones I put in my creams and lotions.'

'Well it doesn't half look nice.' Mary smiled.

Kath felt Violet's eyes on her and when she returned the look, the girl winked.

All eyes now on Mary, she groaned, 'I've bloody well done it again haven't I?'

Laughter rang out as they all nodded.

Violet said, 'Yes Mary, you have. I vote we try making Annie's hair wash mixture and see if we can't sell it... maybe get a market stall. If we sell enough we could take on some workers!'

It looked as if Mary may well have come up with an idea for getting some unemployed women of Wednesbury into work after all.

Forty

Melting Castile soap over a low heat, Annie added water and a few drops of sweet basil oil which would make the hair shine. She had collected herbs and flowers from the heath over the different seasons, extracting the oil before drying the plants and storing them away. She had then accumulated pots of chamomile, rosemary, marigold, wild rose, and primrose... all giving the desired effect, but each with a different fragrance. Stirring the ingredients until they were well mixed, Annie then spooned it into pots to cool to a smooth, creamy consistency. A small amount used in the washing of hair gave a lustrous look and soft texture to even the driest hair.

When the women all met again, everyone had a head of shiny, soft hair, and so pleased were they with the results, it seemed they were about to go into business making and selling this wondrous 'new' creation!

With Harry in his perambulator and the weather so fine, Annie pushed him over the heath, a basket over her arm for the collection of the herbs and flowers she was gathering.

Violet had taken herself off to the glassworks in Lloyd

Street in an effort to strike a bargain for the making of tiny pots to contain the hair wash. Kath would write out the name on pieces of paper which would be stuck on the pots with flour and water paste.

It had been decided to make up a few pots and see how well they sold. If they sold it may be that they could employ some women to make up the mixture. Hopefully if the hair wash sold really well, it would cover a small wage for the workers as well as pay for the jars and having the labels printed professionally by Thomas Southern and Son, the printing firm based in Russell Street.

This, of course, was long-term thinking; they had to wait and see whether the initial batch sold first.

Annie reflected on the past years and how much had been achieved in the town by the Wednesbury Wives and how much had changed in their lives. Her husband Charlie and Geordie Slater were both out of the pit, working for Spencer Gittins out in the fresh air. Violet was settled and happy; Mary and Jim appeared to be doing well... and Kath? Kath Clancy seemed to have something on her mind, she was not ready to share yet, but she would – in her own time.

Annie was excited about what the future would bring.

Settling the little boy in his perambulator with a baby rattle, he shook it happily while Annie began her preparations of the herbs from the basket.

While she worked, Harry continued to shake the rattle – not sure how much longer she could take the noise, she removed the offending toy and began to sing softly. Rocking the pram she saw Harry drift into sleep fairly quickly.

Her thoughts turned again to the Wives and their families. Annie wished there was a way of Mary's husband, Jim Forbes, finding work outside of the colliery. She knew Mary also wished this and there was not a scintilla of doubt that Jim would want it too. Annie determined to have a quiet word with Spencer the next time she saw him.

On her return home and after putting a very tired Harry Gittins down for his second nap of the day, Annie continued her work and her thinking. What was it Kath had on her mind? Was it something she or they could help with? Annie had, now she thought of it, seen a change in Kath's demeanour when Joshua Gittins was mentioned. Was it something to do with him? Kath's jocularity wavered at times when she thought no one was watching, but Annie had eyes in the back of her head – she missed nothing. With a heavy sigh, she turned her attention back to the hair wash mixture. All would be revealed sooner or later she felt sure.

*

Later in the afternoon, whistling heralded the return of Spencer from his factory.

Annie's door standing open did not deter Spencer from knocking before walking in.

'Hello Annie, how's my little man today?'

'He's just waking up by the sounds of it, why don't you go and lift him while I brew the tea.' Annie watched as Spencer went to get his son; hearing the child's quiet complaint gave her a warm feeling.

'Spencer lad,' she said, pouring tea, 'I have a favour to ask of you – but just between the two of us mind.'

'Anything, Annie.'

'Ar well, we'll see about that in a minute...' Passing him the cake, she felt his eyes on her. 'I want to find a way of getting Jim Forbes out of the pit. I don't want him coming down with the lung disease from the coal dust. But then there's the matter of their house; it is still tied to the colliery as was ours.'

'Ah,' said Spencer, eyeing her over his cup, 'I see. Well, I'm not sure I have anything to offer him workwise and I know Father hasn't, but... let me think on it a while.'

Both laughing at the phrase she knew so well, Annie didn't see Violet walk in.

'Oh yes,' she said, 'I find my husband in another woman's kitchen and both laughing fit to burst! How are you, Annie?'

Watching her kiss Spencer, Annie said, 'I was just about to tell Spencer here how that little lad of yours nearly deafened me with that pea rattle of his.'

Smiling widely, Violet hugged Harry planting little kisses all over him making him snuffle.

'How did you get on at the glassworks?' Annie asked.

'Well,' Violet sat down at the table, 'at first, the manager wouldn't deal with me, didn't want to deal with a woman it seems. However, after I told him who my husband was...' she cast a glance at Spencer, 'he acquiesced. They can make what we're after but...'

Annie felt a sinking feeling in her stomach.

'...they will only make a batch of one hundred... keeps their costs down and, in turn I suppose, would keep ours down too. Otherwise we'd have to pay a fortune for, say... a dozen, and without knowing how well they would sell...'

'A hundred! We'll never sell that many, wench, people don't have enough money to be buying hair wash, it's a luxury not many can afford.'

'You don't know until you try,' Spencer put in.

'That's true enough,' Annie said still feeling sceptical, 'so what should we do about the jars then?'

'I ordered a hundred!' Violet said. 'We'll pay for them from the Wives fund, the money to be replaced when we sell them all! Mother was in agreement – I called in on the way home – and she thought you'd all feel the same.'

'Right then,' Annie said, wiping her hands down her apron, 'I'll be needing some help with this mixture if we have to fill a hundred jars.'

*

In the following weeks, Annie's small kitchen became a flurry of activity with the Wives preparing the mixture and spooning it into the tiny jars delivered from the glassworks. With a stopper in the top and a beautifully hand-written label, 'Annie's Hair Wash', the little pots were lined up on her kitchen table.

Standing with her hands on hips, Annie said, 'All we have to do now is sell them!'

Primrose had been happy for them to sell their little pots from her stall in the marketplace in the first instance, the manager of the market having no argument with the idea as an extra few coins were pushed into his hand by way of stall rent.

Kath had carried two baskets of pots to the market the following day. She had given her hair a thorough wash with the mixture and it shone brilliantly. She returned at the end of the day with empty baskets – forty pots sold in one day!

Martha stood in the market the following day and again another thirty pots were sold, leaving thirty for Mary to sell on the third day at the market.

Annie said to Mary as they packed the last of the jars into the baskets, 'What if we can't sell any more?'

'Of course we will,' Mary replied, 'you just get busy making more of that mixture!'

The end of the day saw Mary's words come true. In fact, there had been a disappointed queue of women turned away as the last pot sold.

Violet, on seeing the success of the sales, had ordered more jars from the glassworks and they all set once more to making the mixture to fill them, under Annie's keen eye.

And so it was that the business of 'Annie's Hair Wash' was founded.

Forty-One

Joshua was also aware of the little business the women had set up selling hair wash. He had arranged a visit to Gittins Manor to see young Harry and decided to have a little chat with the women who were probably up to their eyeballs in hair wash mixture.

Peeping into the perambulator Joshua tickled his belly, enjoying the baby murmurings. The women rushed out to ensure the baby was all right as they'd heard him wake, before tea was offered and Joshua was led into Annie's kitchen. The room was crowded and pots, labels and mixtures lay on every surface.

'How the bloody hell do you wenches work in here?' Joshua asked, looking around at the mess.

'It is hard an' no mistake,' answered Mary.

Annie ushered them into her living room with their tea.

Joshua said, 'Why don't you move your business?'

'To where, Joshua?' Kath put in. 'We couldn't find any-where we could afford.'

'Move it to my house!' He watched the glances exchange.

'Look, Gittins Lodge is a big house and there's only me in it! The kitchen is all yours to use if you've a mind to.'

'What about rent?' Martha asked, always the sensible one, never to be carried away with the excitement of a prospect.

'I don't want rent!' Joshua shot back, 'All I ask is that somebody cooks me a decent bloody meal now and then!'

Peals of laughter rang out and Kath said, 'We could do that, couldn't we ladies?'

In the next few days the hair wash business was moved over to Joshua's house and work began in earnest. He returned home from his work at the factory to the laughter of women filling the air, and the smell of home cooking filling his nose. He revelled in having time with his grandson while the women worked, and he loved the idea that he got to see Kath every day.

Joshua often walked the heath with Kath, picking plants and herbs to be dried and stored. His life was improved by her very presence and he couldn't imagine ever being without her. Each night she returned to her own house, his home and his heart felt empty. There had to be some way he could get her to marry him. Joshua thought long and hard on the matter but the answer eluded him. He wanted her – no, he needed her in his life!

*

One evening when the others had left Gittins Lodge after another busy day of working, Kath remained behind and shared dinner with Joshua.

'Kath,' he said, 'I have something I want to discuss with you.' Watching her take this in, Joshua continued, 'Why don't you be my housekeeper...?' Seeing the surprise register, he plunged on, 'You could have rooms at the other end of the house, like Annie and Charlie do at Gittins Manor; you could rent out your own house, which would provide a bit of extra income for you, then you wouldn't have to traipse home down the lanes every night.'

'Well,' she said, drawing the word out on a light sigh, 'this is a surprise! I'm not sure I want to take on another job though Joshua, and I certainly don't need the money were you to offer a salary. However, I have Joyce to think about too.'

'Bring her with you if you want Kath – just say yes.' Joshua was almost begging.

'I suppose it would make sense to move in here at Gittins Lodge, as I'm here most of the time with work anyway. I would insist on having the rooms you offer too but you do realise there would be talk in the town.'

'Ar well, there will always be talk no matter what, but if people are told you are running your business from here... gossip shouldn't be too bad.'

'Oh, the business side of things has already travelled the grapevine,' Kath gave a small tinkling laugh.

'Oh God Kath! I bloody love you wench, you have no idea!'

'Oh I think I do, Joshua.'

'Then marry me!' he pushed.

Tentatively Kath said, 'If I were to consider marriage to you, Joshua... there would have to be conditions.'

'Anything, anything...!' His excitement getting the better of him, he realised he was practically begging. Joshua watched as Kath composed herself.

'Firstly, I would not be giving my money over to you, because as you so rightly pointed out, you have enough of your own.'

'Fair enough,' Joshua replied as he fidgeted in his seat.

'Secondly, if we *were* to marry, it would have to be in total secrecy, and thirdly I would continue to use Clancy as my name for appearance's sake.'

'I agree!' he said, moving to her.

Throwing up her hands, she added, 'Promise me, Joshua, the only ones to know about this would be our children and my friends, the Wednesbury Wives.' He knew the collective name for her friends but he had no notion of their activities, and Kath wanted to keep it that way.

'I promise with all my heart, may the Lord strike me dead!'

'Then, Joshua Gittins, I accept your proposal,' Kath said with a beaming smile.

Forty-Two

K ath had told the little group of her plan to marry Joshua Gittins in secrecy, and although Violet worried for her in that she didn't want the marriage to turn out badly like the one to Sligo, she was also delighted that her mother had found happiness again. It seemed strange to her that her mother was to marry her husband's father... but love, like illness, didn't care where it struck.

Violet watched as her mother packed her belongings at Hobbins Street and stacked them on a handcart. A handful of men from the bread line had been paid to transport Kath's things to Joshua's house where the other women were waiting to store them ready for unpacking. The men were to carry the belongings into the other end of the house via the servants' entrance at the back which would ensure the grapevine had the facts correct about Kath using Joshua's house for her work.

A melange of feelings swamped Violet as she helped with the packing. She felt sad to see her mother leave the house, Violet, herself, had grown up in, but glad that Kath was moving into a whole new life. It was also a way for Kath to leave behind the negative associations with the house and put the memory of John Sligo far behind her.

With everything packed, they followed the last cartload of Kath's life along the cobbled streets to Joshua's house.

Passing tea to Kath when she came into the kitchen of Gittins Lodge, Mary said, 'Blimey Kath, you look fair worn out.'

Violet watched her mother give a wan smile as she sipped her hot tea.

'I have just the thing for that,' said Annie as she plunged into a shopping basket. Pulling out one of the pots used for the hair wash, she removed the stopper. 'Rub a bit of that on your face, wench.'

Holding the pot beneath her nose, Kath looked at Annie with a smile. 'It smells lovely, Annie, what is it?'

'Evening primrose,' said Annie.

'Where?' asked Mary, looking round for Primrose.

Annie rolled her eyes as she pointed to the pot in Kath's hand, 'In the jar...! Evening primrose cream!'

'Oh,' Mary said as everyone laughed.

Kath smoothed the cream over her face, saying it felt cool and refreshing.

'Ar,' said Annie, 'it's good for women who are past child-bearing years an' all.'

'In what way?' Kath asked.

'Well, make it into wine or a tonic and it beats off the sweats for anyone going through the change of life,' Annie said simply, 'and if you mix the oils from the flowers with castor oil, it helps hold the wrinkles at bay a while longer.'

'How's that then?' Violet asked.

'It holds the moisture, it seems,' Annie replied.

'Well I am *not* drinking castor oil!' Mary said, pulling a face.

'You don't drink it!' Annie said with a laugh. 'You rub it on your face!'

'Oh,' Mary replied as laughter rang out yet again.

'Annie!' Violet said suddenly, making everyone start.

'What?' Annie said, looking round immediately for Harry suspecting he had woken and she'd not heard him.

'This cream, couldn't we make it and sell it on the stall too?'

'Good idea,' said Kath.

'We are already working flat out with the hair wash,' said Mary with a frown.

'Well,' Violet added feeling excited now, 'we could take on more workers!'

*

The meetings of the Wives as such no longer took place as they all worked together on the hair wash and face cream, so anything of note was discussed then. Joyce had left her job at the nail-making factory to join them in their little business venture and Joshua had filled her position almost immediately. Yet another woman in work.

Joyce told of a tale she had picked up at the market as they worked. It appeared a woman, waiting for her husband to come home from the Green Dragon Hotel and seeing his dinner begin to spoil, had marched down to the public house to drag him home. The fact that women were not allowed in had not deterred her and pushing open the door she had stomped in. Silence immediately descended at the gumption of the woman as she had stood in front of her husband at the bar.

Everyone was listening carefully to Joyce, 'Well, she pokes a finger in his chest an' says to him, "you get yourself home right this minute before I set the Wednesbury Wives on you!" You'll never guess…' drawing the tale out a little more Joyce continued, 'but he run home like a scalded cat!'

Howls of laughter filled the kitchen and Violet said, 'It seems, ladies, we have acquired ourselves quite a reputation!'

*

Making her way to the glassworks to once more discuss an increase to the order of pots, Violet passed Phillips Carpenters, on Holyhead Road, the factory that made wooden packing crates as well as furniture and an idea formed.

That evening she brought it up with Spencer. 'If,' she began, 'we could hire a few carpenters to make small boxes, really nice ones, we could put a jar of cream and a pot of hair wash in the box and sell them as a specialty. We might even attract wealthier custom.'

'It sounds a grand idea, sweetheart. Would you like me to visit the bread line to acquire some woodworkers on your behalf?'

'That would be wonderful, Spencer, as I'm not sure anyone would take up the offer if I were to ask… I wonder how the carpenters would feel about having women as their managers.'

Spencer kept his word, finding four carpenters to work the small wooden boxes. Having drawn up a little sketch of what was needed and passing over two empty pots for sizing, the work had begun. The men worked from their homes, so Violet's surprise for presenting the finished article to the Wives was kept secret.

Violet asked Spencer how the men felt about working for women. 'They are actually being managed by a man,' he said with a smile, 'I asked Jim Forbes to oversee the workers, which got him out of the coal pit. Annie asked me to try and find him work outside of mining and I thought this would be the ideal opportunity. I hope you don't mind and... your little business can cover the wages!'

'Oh Spencer, thank you!'

'There is another difficulty though, their house is tied to the pit.' Spencer watched his wife frown as they sat thinking about how to remedy the problem of Mary and Jim having to find another home.

*

Mary came bustling in the next morning, 'Hey wenches...' she shouted, 'my Jim's got a new job, he isn't in the pit anymore!'

Applause rang out and when Martha asked about Jim's new work, Mary said, 'I'm buggered if I know, he's overseeing carpenters making something or other. I'm just glad he's out of the mining!'

They toasted Mary with cups of tea and Violet said, 'Have you noticed how the role of the Wives has changed? Although still a force to be reckoned with, we appear to be well known for our good works.'

Joyce piped up, 'Just as well we ain't known for our bad ones!'

Laughter rippled through the kitchen as work began once more on the hair wash and face creams.

'Mary,' Violet said quietly, 'with Jim no longer working in the colliery, won't you have to give up your house?'

Mary nodded, saying, 'Yes, we have to be out by Friday.'

'Bloody hell!' Martha gasped. 'I forgot about that!'

Kath said, 'That's not a problem, Mary, you and Jim can move into my house in Hobbins Street, it's only a few doors away anyway.'

Mary cast a glance at Joyce and said, 'What about Joyce? She lives there too.'

'I know, but Joshua said for you to move with me Joyce. There's more than enough room in that big house. All we need to do is move your belongings over there.'

'It wouldn't be fitting that I move into my old gaffer's house Kath,' Joyce smiled.

Kath returned the smile with, 'it would, if you became his housekeeper! Of course it would depend on how you feel about that.'

'I could do that I suppose,' Joyce said, 'it wouldn't take much to cook the odd meal and tidy round.'

Kath turned to Mary and said, 'So what do you say Mary?'

'Oh Kath,' Mary sobbed, 'I don't know what to say!'

'Say yes!' Violet gushed.

'Yes!' Mary said and applause rang out as everyone rushed to hug Mary and help dry her tears.

*

Jim Forbes arrived at Gittins Lodge one morning and Mary was thrown into a panic.

'I haven't come to see you woman,' he said, the love for her showing all over his face, 'I came to see Violet.'

Violet showed Jim into Joshua's living room and he produced their very first box. Holding it carefully, he passed it to her, saying, 'I hope this is all right.'

The small box had been planed smooth and polished with beeswax. On lifting the lid, Violet gasped, 'Oh Jim, it's perfect!' The inside had been lined with russet-coloured chenille, which she suspected once covered someone's dining table, and gave the box a luxurious look. The small pots snuggled inside making the whole thing look expensive. The cost of the box, pots, hair wash and cream were nothing compared to what they could charge in the right social circles. 'Well done Jim! Please give the men my congratulations on a job very well done. Now let's go and show the others.'

As they entered the kitchen, all hands stopped work.

'Jim and I have something to show you,' Violet said quietly before producing the box.

Glances of puzzlement passed between the women as she placed the box on the table and lifted the lid. Gasps of awe escaped lips that weren't covered by hands.

'Jim is overseer of four carpenters employed by us,' Violet said.

'You crafty bugger!' Mary aimed at her husband who grinned cheekily.

'It was to be a surprise,' he said, feigning innocence.

'Well, it certainly is that!' Annie added.

After discussion proving the business could stand on its own financially, Jim set off to instruct the carpenters that more boxes were needed. Speed was of the essence but not to the detriment of quality.

Giving Violet a hug, Kath said, 'Daughter of mine... I'm so proud of you.'

Forty-Three

The business was keeping all of the women very busy with exigent demands from the women of the town for their hair wash and face cream products.

Word had come through the grapevine of a fancy new shop recently opened in New Street, Birmingham, and Violet and Martha set their minds to visit in the hope that the shop might buy a stock of the new boxes. Spencer drove them there in his carriage and it was agreed he would be on hand for discussions, as male businessmen – no matter the business – would still not always deal with women.

Dressed in their Sunday best, they set off, the first of the boxes made tucked safely under Violet's arm.

As the carriage rumbled along the Birmingham streets, they saw the poverty in this town was as bad as in their own. People milled about as if having nothing better to do. Men hung around on street corners talking and smoking. Women with gaggles of small children around their legs stood gossiping, the odd errant child receiving a smack round the ear for some misdeed. Horse-drawn carts and wagons rolled along heading for Gas Street Basin where they would unload their goods. The buildings here were blackened too from the smoke from house and factory chimneys. The steam trains puffed out there smoke further adding to the smell in the town of burning coal.

Arriving at the shop, the manager, at first, refused to see the women until Spencer stepped in, saying, 'I suggest you hear what the Wednesbury Wives have to say before dismissing them out of hand!'

The mention of the name was an effective emollient on the manager, it seemed their reputation had made it even this far. The man listened patiently, an eye always on Spencer.

When the manager first saw the box, he was unable to contain his surprise.

'Well of course,' he said, quickly composing himself, 'I couldn't pay a lot for these, as I'm sure you are aware, I cannot guarantee they would sell from our *salon.*' Looking at Violet, his deprecating smile vanished.

'You'll pay what we are asking and will be wanting to order more before you know it!' she snapped. Salon indeed! It was a bloody shop, the same as all the others!

Regaining his composure, the man said with a sniff, 'I will take one dozen and see whether or not our clientele would be interested in such *trinkets.*'

Spencer shook hands with the manager in a gentleman's agreement and Violet huffed her way outside her indignation evident.

*

Martha was at home busy preparing an evening meal of sausage, mash and cabbage when Nancy came in sporting a swollen face.

'What happened to you?' Martha asked.

'A woman hit me in the face,' the girl said, bursting into tears.

'You what!' Martha demanded. 'What woman?'

'You know the family who live on the barge called The Margaret Rose?'

'Ar,' her mother said, moving to look at Nancy's swelling face.

'Well, they're moored up in the Basin and wanted me to have their kids for a week while they took some coal down to Worcester.'

'Bloody cheek!' Martha said putting a cold wet cloth to her daughter's face as Nancy winced.

'Well, when I said no because I only look after the kiddies in the daytime… the mother hit me and called me a spiteful mare!'

'Did she now… Right you're not going to work tomorrow, you are coming with me! The wenches can manage without you for one day. Now, get that cup of tea down you.'

Martha related the incident to the women the following morning in Joshua's kitchen.

'I am not having that woman strike my child!' she snapped.

Instantly shawls were grabbed as the Wives, with Nancy in tow, set off for the canal basin.

Marching down the towpath looking for all the world like a women's militia, they halted by the side of The Margaret Rose.

'Hello!' Martha yelled, her voice splitting the air. 'Anybody in?'

She watched as the canal folk climbed onto the decks of their barges. This particular issue was going to have to be settled out in the open. She didn't like public confrontation but she also knew they would not be getting an invitation to step aboard the boat.

A sallow-looking woman with dirty hair trying to escape the confines of a bun poked her head through the hatchway. 'What you want?' she yelled back.

Immediately seeing this was not going to go well, Martha's anger rose. 'You the one who smacked my daughter?' she shouted as she dragged Nancy into view.

'What of it?' the woman jeered.

Anger bubbled just below the surface as Martha said, 'Get your arse down off that boat!'

'I ain't doing no such thing,' the woman replied.

'Then I'll come up and bloody drag you down!' Martha exploded.

Kath and Joyce grabbed her arms, holding her back as the cheers of the canal people sounded loud and clear. Looking around, Martha saw a crowd gathering and someone from the next barge shouted, 'You go get her, missis, she's causing trouble on the cut all the while!'

The woman yelled at him, 'You shut yer mouth, this ain't nothing to do with you!'

Martha yelled again at the woman, 'Are you coming down here, or am I coming up there?'

'Bugger off!' the woman shouted, a nasty grin showing on her face.

Before anyone could stop her, Martha was on the boat having escaped the grasp of her friends. Quick as a wink, the woman's head disappeared into the belly of the boat, the hatch slammed shut and the bolt was heard sliding across, locking her safely inside.

To the accompaniment of shouts and applause from everyone watching, Martha hammered on the hatch with her fists. 'You haven't heard the last of this, lady!' Martha yelled. 'The Wednesbury Wives won't let this matter rest!'

'What are you going to do about this Martha?' Kath asked once Martha had climbed back onto the towpath.

'Buggered if I know,' she said, watching where she stepped.

'Well, if you ask me, I wish her boat would sink!' Mary grumbled; she carried on walking as the rest of them stopped.

Turning, Mary rolled her eyes, muttering, 'Oh Christ – not again!'

Forty-Four

Striding out once more for the canal basin the following day, the women knew they had limited time to sort out The Margaret Rose but had to ensure no one was aboard at the time.

The man who had shouted to Martha the previous day eyed them as they approached.

'She ain't in, nobody is there, missis.'

'Good,' Violet said as she stepped forward, 'I need a favour, one that will pay handsomely.'

'Oh ar, what you want then?' he asked.

'We want that boat a bit wet – inside!' Violet said quietly, tipping her head to the barge in question.

Nodding his head the man said, 'Well now, if you happened to be strolling past later in the day you might want to stop by again.' Giving her a wink, Violet replied with a smile and a nod and the women turned for home.

'What's he going to do, Martha?' asked Mary.

Martha's patience exhausted she snapped, 'Now how the hell would I know!'

Kath said, 'Maybe we'll find out later, Mary.'

Work finished for the day, the women again strolled towards the canal in the early evening sunshine.

At the edge of the canal towpath they saw a crowd of people gathered and, with an easy pace, made their way towards it.

A lot of shouting could be heard as they neared the crowd and the woman who had hit Nancy pointed, shouting, 'Them! They did it!'

The crowd turned and Violet asked her, 'We did what?'

Pointing to her barge, she spat, 'That!'

'I'm sorry, I don't understand!' Violet said unable as yet to see what the woman referred to.

'There's water everywhere!' the woman yelled.

'Yes, I can see that, and there are boats on it,' Violet replied, barely able to contain her grin.

'Oh ain't you funny?' The woman said sarcastically. 'There's water everywhere – inside! Look at this – it's sodden!' She held up a small rag rug which dripped dirty canal water.

Glancing at the man they had spoken with earlier in the day, who was sitting on his own barge, he doffed his cap and it was all Violet could do not to laugh. Instead she said, 'How do you suppose we did that?'

'I don't know how you did it, but you did!' the venomous reply came.

'I'm afraid you are mistaken,' Violet said with as much dignity as she could muster, 'my friends and I have been working all afternoon.'

Martha yelled, 'Just as well you didn't have the coal loaded else she might have gone down altogether!'

Howls of laughter erupted from the crowd.

'I'll have you for this, you see if I don't!' The woman, in a rage, was pacing back and forth on the towpath.

'That right?' shouted Martha in response, 'Word of warning, you don't want to be messing with us Wives. Still an' all, I expect you'll be too busy drying your stuff out!'

Cheers rang out as the woman spat on the ground and marched away.

The man jumped down from his boat and walking close to Violet said quietly, 'Job complete.'

Violet discreetly handed him a small bag of money, saying, 'Payment made.'

Strolling back the way they had come, they chatted about the woman and her wet boat. It would take time to dry out the things the man had drenched, but at least he hadn't sunk the boat thus leaving the woman and her children homeless.

'I wonder how he managed it.' Violet queried.

'A couple of buckets of water would be my guess, but then I'm not a "cut-rat" so what would I know?' Martha laughed.

'Blimey, Mum,' said Nancy when they told her of the event, 'it doesn't pay to get on the wrong side of you lot!'

It was considered justifiable retribution... yet again.

*

Later in the evening, Joshua and Kath sat on a bench in the garden of Gittins Lodge discussing their wedding plans. 'I saw the vicar today,' he said, 'and he assured me no one would know about the service other than those attending.'

'That's a relief,' Kath said, 'but how do we get everyone up to St Bartholomew's Church without people seeing?'

'We don't,' he answered with a smile, 'the vicar is coming here to us!'

'But, Joshua...' Kath started.

'It's all right wench, the vicar said something about blessing the house first, I'm not quite sure of the ins and outs of it, but he assures me it is all above board and legal.'

'Right, well we just need to set a date then.'

'What about the banns being read?' Alarm sounded in her voice. 'They have to be called in church!'

'We just ask the vicar to call them when there's nobody there!' Joshua said,

'But...'

'But nothing,' he went on, 'they'll be called, it won't be our fault nobody will be there to hear them!'

Laughing together, he said, 'I heard about an incident on the cut today.'

'Oh yes?' Fear gripped her as he continued.

'Ar, I also hear you were there...'

Kath's fear tightened in her chest. Joshua still had no idea about the Wives club and she wasn't sure he should – yet. So she answered with, 'And?'

'Well, the story goes you lot were blamed for a barge being sunk.'

Giving a little laugh, Kath said, 'Were we indeed?'

'All because some harridan slapped Martha's wench.'

'Firstly, Joshua, the woman was not a harridan – she was not nice, but she was not a harridan. She *hit* Martha's daughter, Nancy, not slapped her; we strolled the towpath after work, and yes... we were accused of sinking her boat.'

'And...?'

'No Joshua, *we* did not sink the barge – how on earth do you suppose we could have done that without being seen by countless people?'

'Ar, I suppose you're right,' he muttered, settling more

comfortably on the garden bench. 'Still an' all, she was a daft bugger to meddle with you lot!'

Exchanging a smile, Kath knew that he knew they had something to do with the dousing of The Margaret Rose, he just didn't know what, and she was not about to enlighten him.

Forty-Five

Riding into Birmingham to be fitted for a new outfit for his father's wedding, Spencer decided to call into the shop in New Street that had bought a dozen of Violet's boxes of hair wash and face cream. Having had Jim deliver them to the shop to a delighted manager, Spencer was now interested to know whether they had sold yet.

Seeing him enter the *salon*, the manager rushed up to him, gushing, 'I'm so glad to see you again, sir! Those little boxes you sold to me...'

Spencer corrected him, '*My wife* sold to you.'

'Yes, yes,' he flapped his hands in the air, 'they sold like hot cakes they did! I was wondering if...'

'How much did you sell them for?' Spencer asked nonchalantly glancing around him.

'Well, sir... I can't tell you that, it isn't good business practice!'

'Sir,' Spencer countered, 'it would be no problem for me to find out...' Leaving that to sink in, he went on, 'And of course, should you be wanting more...'

The manager reluctantly revealed the price the boxes had sold for and Spencer kept his surprise hidden.

'What I want...' the man said, '*is* some more! Can you... erm... your wife... send out three dozen?'

'I will pass on your request, sir, you can be assured.'

Spencer left the manager rubbing his hands together.

Riding home, Spencer considered what he had just learnt. The manager had sold Violet's boxes for three pennies more than he paid for them which had riled Spencer. Who had bought them? How could he find out? Should he suggest the prices at the shop be raised?

Calling in at Gittins Lodge, Spencer relayed the news of the sale of the boxes to the women.

'That's wonderful!' Violet was ecstatic.

'It is very good indeed,' he said.

'However wouldn't it be better to sell them directly to the women and cut out the shop making some of the profit?' Violet asked.

'She's right there,' said Martha, 'we do all the hard work, we should be getting all the profit.'

'Birmingham is a bloody long way to go to stand in the market every day,' said Mary.

'Very true, what you'd need is a shop of your own there,' Spencer said, which had been his thinking all along since leaving the shop. However, he knew all too well what the response would be.

Sarcastic laughter and comments filled his ears until he said, 'Let me think on it a while!'

*

Kath, Joshua, Violet and Spencer sat in the living room after everyone had gone home, discussing what to do about selling their boxes in Birmingham.

'Are there any buildings standing empty that way, son?' Joshua asked. Spencer shrugged and his father went on, 'Maybe you and I should take a ride out there tomorrow... have a look.'

Kath intervened, 'Even if there are any empty properties, Joshua, we couldn't afford to buy one. Our little business is doing well, but not that well!'

'Let's have us a look first; in fact, ladies... you should come with us, you know more about shops than us men!'

Violet elected to stay home and take care of little Harry but Kath took Joshua up on the offer and the following day Spencer, Joshua and Kath strolled the streets of Birmingham on the lookout for a building in which the women could set up shop.

Walking down Congreve Street, they passed the massive Corporation Art Gallery and moved on into Victoria Square. Looking around them, they saw the General Post Office on one side, the Town Hall on another; the Council House graced a third side and artists' galleries on the last. Further down New Street they passed Needless Alley, a narrow walkway leading up to St. Philip's Church. The whole area was packed tight with buildings either side of the network of streets and cobblestone roads. No trees or greenery was in evidence as they strolled along, there was no room for either.

The people they passed all appeared to be in a hurry, to where and for what, Kath had no idea. Most wore clothes that had seen better days and thin, pasty faces stared back at them as they sauntered along. It made Kath wonder just who had the money to buy their boxes. They heard the puffing of the steam trains at New Street Station and the occasional whistle blow. They smelled the smoke puffed out by the iron contraptions as they pulled away taking people on their journeys.

Kath pointed to a small building standing empty on the corner of New Street and Cannon Street; a hand-written sign attached to the door, FOR SALE… BARGAIN!

'Somebody wants to sell that place,' Kath said as they walked over to it.

'You want to buy it?' a voice over Spencer's shoulder sounded. Turning, he looked at the small man standing in front of him.

'Depends… on who's asking and… how much,' Spencer answered.

'A hundred pounds and it's yours,' said the man, putting out his hand for Spencer to shake, 'I'm the owner, James Cooke. I've been wanting rid of this place for a while, ain't got no use for it myself and the money would be more useful to me.'

Leading them inside, they took a good look around and Kath said quietly, 'This place would be ideal… but a hundred pounds is a lot of money!'

Kath and Joshua went outside to see the frontage again and Spencer pulled James Cooke to one side, saying, 'Fifty is all I will pay.'

Spitting on his hand, he held it out for Spencer to shake as he said, 'Done!'

Seeing the look of distaste on Spencer's face, James wiped his hand on his coat and then they shook hands.

'My name is Spencer Gittins.'

'Ar, Mr Gittins sir, I know who you are. Word travels with the "cut-rats" about you and your wife, about everything you've done for the people of Wednesbury.'

Taken aback slightly at this, Spencer said he would return the following day with the money as James shoved a document into his hand.

'The deeds,' James said simply, 'I trust you, Mr Gittins sir.'

Spencer walked out of the building and back to the others where he allowed himself a small smile. Once settled in the carriage for the drive home, he gave the paper to Kath, 'The deeds to your new shop... consider it a wedding present.'

'Oh Spencer, thank you!' Kath gushed as she held the paper to her chest.

The Wednesbury Wives now had their first shop!

Forty-Six

Leaving Harry with Annie, Violet and Kath, along with a handful of women looking for work who had been standing in the ever increasing bread line, arrived at the new shop in Birmingham. Jim had driven them to the town in the carriage, and after seeking out James Cooke and paying him the fifty pounds Spencer had entrusted to him, Jim made his way to the shop. Spencer had instructed the signwriter to hang the new name over the door – 'Violet's Luxuries'.

Opening the shop doors, the women set about cleaning the place from top to bottom. Scrubbing the existing fixtures and fittings allowed them to save money rather than buying new. A coat of whitewash would give the place a whole new look. With the sun shining in through the doors and windows they could now envisage how to display their products to their best advantage. Pots and boxes were set out with a till behind the counter for the money taken from the sales.

Annie had already selected two women to be in charge of the sales… women she'd known since a girl; trustworthy and hard-working. They lived nearby and so could be at the shop early to open up.

Jim, besides overseeing the making of the boxes, employed a couple of men from the bread line to transport the goods to the shop. He would also take the saleswomen's wages and bring back the takings.

The Wives had engaged Isaac Aston, an accountant from Wood Green in Wednesbury to keep their books. With so many now in their employ, money coming in and going out became difficult to keep track of.

The shop was ready in next to no time and, on the opening day, Violet travelled over to Birmingham with Jim Forbes, to spend the day there; Jim would collect her at closing time.

It was a busy first day, with women coming and going and the products selling quickly. Stacking new jars in the late afternoon, Violet turned as the shop door opened. Standing in the doorway was the man who had originally bought her boxes for his *salon*.

He had heard talk in the town of a new shop opening and had taken himself off to have a look. He wanted to know what would be on sale there and whether it might rival his own business.

'Decided to go into business for yourself then I see!' he said scornfully as he stepped forward.

'You see correctly.' Violet said, spreading her arms to encompass the room.

'Well, I think it's a bloody cheek!' he snapped.

'And why would that be?' she asked.

'You sold me your trinkets, then when I ask for more... you do this!' Sweeping his arm out, he knocked a few pots from the counter to the floor which Violet felt was a deliberate act on his part.

One of the saleswomen went into the back room to fetch

a broom to clean up the mess of broken jars that lay at Violet's feet.

Anger rising she glared at him, 'Mr...?'

'Potter!' he said confidently, returning her stare.

'Mr Potter, I would thank you not to come into my shop destroying my property!'

'Property...' he jeered, 'you won't stay in business long, lady... you can be sure of it!' With that another pot crashed to the floor as his arm swept out again. This time there was no question it was done deliberately.

'Are you threatening me, Mr Potter?' Violet asked full of fury.

'Women shouldn't be in business! You should be at home looking after your brats!'

'How dare you!' She took a step forward, but the woman cleaning up the broken jars put an arm across her front preventing her from going further.

'What I do, Mr Potter, has nothing whatsoever to do with you!'

'Oh but it does when you be tekin' my custom!' His slip into the vernacular revealed his roots as surely as if he wore a flat cap.

'I am taking nothing from you, Mr Potter. These products belong to me and I think you should be grateful I allowed you to sell them in the first place!' Violet said, trying to compose herself once more. 'Where women choose to shop is up to them. Obviously they prefer my shop to yours!' Smoothing her hands down her skirt, she pushed her nose in the air.

Stepping forward with hand raised ready to strike, he stopped as Jim Forbes stepped in the door saying, 'I wouldn't do that if I were you, mister.'

Breath she didn't realise she was holding escaped Violet's lips as her heart pounded. The man had been about to hit her...! The realisation sent shivers of fear coursing through her body.

'This be between me an' the wench,' said Potter, no longer trying to maintain his affected speech, 'so you stay out of it if you know what's good for you.'

Jim strode towards the man, who stepped back a pace. 'If *you* know what's good for *you*, you won't take on one of the Wives or their husbands!' Jim's voice was no more than a menacing whisper.

'Hah!' said Potter, stepping around Jim but continuing to face him. 'That don't frighten me...' Clearly it did, as he edged his way towards the door.

Jim cut him off and, as he neared Potter, he leaned his face close to the other man, saying quietly, 'Well it should!'

Potter backed out of the door with a sneer on his face. Turning on his heel, he marched away.

Jim, assuring himself the ladies were unhurt, waited while the shop was locked. On their own way home, he said, 'It's a good job I was there today; no telling what that bugger might have done.'

'Thank you Jim,' Violet said, still feeling very much shaken, 'you arrived at just the right time.'

'It's not safe for you ladies there, Violet.' Jim's face showed concern.

'Oh I don't think Mr Potter will be back, Jim,' she said, feeling very little confidence in her statement.

'Still an' all...'

No further words were spoken until Jim steered the carriage into the entrance to Gittins Manor, 'Here we are, you are safe home now.'

Thanking him, Violet went into the house, shaking again as she saw Potter's sneer in her mind's eye once more. Although there were three of them at the shop today, in future there would be only two defenceless women. Fear filled her as she thought of what could happen if Potter returned. Had they done the right thing opening the shop? Should they have stayed in Wednesbury? Violet decided to discuss it with her mother and the Wives the following day.

She heard the clatter of hooves on the gravel heralding Spencer's return from the factory as she was about to collect their son from Annie's care.

Rushing to her, Spencer said breathlessly, 'Violet! Are you all right? Jim told me what happened today at the shop!'

Jim must have gone straight from her to Spencer at his factory to tell him all about it. A quick thought flashed through Violet's mind that it wasn't only the Wives who were in cahoots, but that maybe the husbands had their own clan too.

'Yes, yes...' Violet assured him, 'but it did shake me up.'

'Dear God, Violet!' he said, holding her so tight she could barely breathe.

Pulling away slightly, Violet managed, 'It's all right Spencer, no one was hurt.'

*

It was around lunchtime a couple of days later when Jim came bursting into Joshua Gittins' kitchen where the business of making Annie's Hair Wash was bustling.

'Violet!' he gasped. 'Oh Violet wench!'

Mary pushed a cup of tea in front of him, saying,

'Bloody hell, Jim, you sit yourself down before you have a heart attack!'

Waving a dismissive hand at Mary, he looked at Violet, saying, 'It's the shop, Violet! The windows and most of the jars are smashed and... everything is broken!'

'What! How do you know?' Violet dropped into the nearest chair, her hands flying to her chest. She felt the colour drain from her face.

'I was taking the wages over and when I got there... My guess is it's Potter!' Jim said, only now taking up his teacup.

'Oh Christ!' Martha said, coming to Violet and laying a hand on her shoulder.

'We can't say that for sure,' Violet said, although she suspected Jim was right.

Having discussed the events of the previous incident with the Wives, all were aware of the despicable Mr Potter.

'It's a safe bet, if you ask me...' muttered Mary, setting the kettle to boil once more.

'Maybe so,' Violet said, 'but we can't accuse him without proof!'

'Then we'll bloody well get proof!' Kath said.

'How?' Violet asked, still feeling the shock waves roll over her.

Martha answered with, 'This needs a deal o' thinkin' on.' This time no one laughed, they were all too stunned to show any mirth.

Eventually it was decided that Martha and Kath should go into Birmingham immediately and ask a few discreet questions about the destruction of the shop; one of Jim's workers was summoned and drove them in the carriage.

Arriving in Birmingham a little later, the carriage waited along the street, and they went into the 'fancy' *salon* with spurious intentions of buying something. They asked the girl behind the counter about the damage at the shop on the corner of Cannon Street.

Overhearing the conversation, the curious Mr Potter had scuttled over and intervened, saying, 'Serves them right if you ask me.'

Martha asked, 'Why is that then?'

'Women don't have no place in business!' he said implacably.

Kath said quietly, 'I agree, sir, our place should be home looking after the babies.'

'Most definitely!' Potter saw his chance, 'The woman who opened the shop had no idea what she was doing. Trying to sell muck in cheap jars... well, I ask you... would you buy it?'

'I don't have the money to spend on such things,' Kath said, lulling him into a false sense of security, 'but who on earth would do that to the shop... and why?' Feigning ignorance and stupidity, she waited as she replaced a small vase she'd been looking at back on the counter.

'Well now,' said Potter, conspiratorially leaning in towards Kath and Martha, 'the "why" would be to put the woman out of business of course, and the "who"...' He let the sentence hang mid-air. Leaning back, he puffed out his chest.

'You don't mean...?' Martha asked in pretend shock.

Nodding his head, an evil grin spread across his face and he said, hunching his shoulders and spreading out his hands, 'That's business!'

*

'He said what?' Annie asked in pure disbelief after hearing what had occurred when the others returned from the town.

'Ar but...' Martha took up, 'that wasn't actually a confession. He didn't say it was him who did it.'

'Martha's right,' Kath added, 'so how do we find out for sure he's responsible?'

'Well,' Annie said, 'Violet asked Jim to get the glassworks to replace the windows and he's asking questions round and about. He's also finding a couple of men to stay in the shop overnight until we sort this problem out.'

'Good idea,' Kath breathed a sigh of relief, 'our profits can run to a couple of nightwatchmen's wages.' She looked at Violet who nodded in agreement.

It had been less than a week when the two night watchmen on guard at the shop reported to Jim about another attempted break in.

Jim had just returned from taking the men's wages and as he sat in the kitchen with the women, he related what the watchmen had told him.

Sitting quietly in the back room of the shop, the watchmen had been having their supper of cheese sandwiches when they heard the rattling of the front door handle. The door was locked, as usual, so the burglars had decided to try the door at the rear of the shop.

The guards, guessing the intention, quietly moved through the shop and slid back the bolt of the back door which would allow the burglars to enter without causing damage. After dousing the oil lamp, they had then hidden themselves in the shadows.

Jim watched the women's faces as he continued.

The back door handle had turned and the burglars' chuckles were heard, then the door was carefully pushed open. Two of them had stepped into the back room of the shop.

The watchmen jumped out from where they hid in the shadows and pushing the would-be burglars into the yard outside had 'pasted them both good and proper'.

The burglars had been persuaded to give up the name of the person who had paid them to steal the goods and wreck the shop a second time, the name they revealed was... Mr Potter!

'I guessed as much,' Violet said amid the gasps coming from around the kitchen table, 'now we have to decide what to do about it.'

Everyone then set to and hatched a plan to visit the said Mr Potter to, at the very least, ruin his day.

Annie, being busy with Harry and overseeing the making of the products, decided to stay behind; so it was that Martha, Kath, Mary, Joyce and Violet who took another trip into Birmingham, driven in Spencer's coach by Jim.

Mr Potter paled visibly as he saw the women enter his *salon*. He disappeared into a back room and they all marched across the shop after him.

'So, Mr Potter we meet again,' Violet said, looking him squarely in the eye, after throwing the door open wide.

'What you lot want? This is a private office. You shouldn't be in here!' He sat behind a desk where he considered himself safe from their wrath.

'The same as you shouldn't have had men in our shop the other night!' Violet boomed.

'I have no idea what you are referring to,' he replied confidently.

'Potter,' spat Joyce, 'the men gave you up! We know it was you who paid them to wreck our shop!'

His bravado melted away as he blustered, 'Then they are lying through their back teeth!'

Violet placed her hands flat on the desk, causing the man to lean back in his chair, before saying with quiet menace, 'Mr Potter, we now know for certain it was you who instigated the breaking of the windows and merchandise at our shop. The men responsible for doing your bidding have paid a heavy price for what they did – in fact...' She leaned in further, 'let's just say it will be quite a while before they'll be doing work of any sort.' Pausing, Violet watched the words sink in before resuming. 'Oh pardon my rudeness, let me introduce ourselves... we are the Wednesbury Wives!'

They watched him blanch as he absorbed the information then Violet spoke again. 'We did consider taking this to the police. However they would probably put it down to kids misbehaving, so I doubt they'd do anything about it, whereas we...' she spread her arm to encompass her friends '... well, I think you get the point. Now then, Mr Potter, just so you know, if anything... anything at all should happen to our shop again... we'll be coming for you!' She thrust a finger in his direction. 'Remember Mr Potter... if anything should happen... anything at all!'

They turned as one and left the room. Heads held high, they walked from the shop, leaving the open-mouthed shop girls in their wake. The door having been left open when they entered the office, the sales girls had heard every word; they had tried in vain to hide their smiles.

On their return to Gittins Lodge, Joyce said, 'Oooh Annie, you would have laughed your socks off if you had seen his face.'

'I'd be surprised if we hear anything more from Mr Potter again,' Violet said.

Little did she know those words would come back to haunt her.

Forty-Seven

Although Joshua knew Kath would have loved a lavish wedding, he also knew the secrecy was more important to her. It was a time when anything could be bought for enough money, and the clergy were no exception. The vicar had baulked at first about calling the banns to an empty church, but had soon changed his mind on sight of Joshua's wallet.

The Wives were to prepare the wedding breakfast in the kitchen at Gittins Lodge – all work on 'Violet's Luxuries' to be halted and cleared away for the day. Everything was planned down to the last detail; flowers from the garden, food from the kitchen, everyone would arrive as if to work but would change their clothes, which they had smuggled in, in the many bedrooms standing empty.

Joshua had kept his word to Kath regarding keeping to his part of the house at night until after the wedding. It was no loss, just knowing she was there with him in the evenings had been enough.

The house began to fill with people and excitement grew

as the vicar arrived – he was 'calling in on his rounds', so others of the town were led to believe.

With everyone in the living room save for Kath and Violet, fear swept over Joshua. Would she change her mind? What would he do if she did? How would he cope with the disappointment? The thought, however, dissolved as the door opened and Kath and her daughter entered the room.

Violet wore a blue brocade suit edged with navy blue piping, a hat of the same colour sat squarely on her head. The whole ensemble matched her eyes beautifully as she walked her mother over to stand beside Joshua. Looking divine in a pale cream lace dress reaching to the floor, one simple cream flower adorned Kath's hair. Her twinkling eyes met Joshua's and his fears of a moment before fled, replaced by a happiness he never thought he would feel again.

The vicar droned on, 'Will you, Joshua...?'

'I will – I do – Yes, oh get on with it, man!' His exasperation filled the air, causing ripples of laughter.

'Will you, Kath...?'

'Oh I will indeed!' said Kath; again more laughter sounded. Kath had sold her wedding ring given to her by John Sligo soon after his death and now she wore a shiny gold band Joshua had purchased at the jewellery shop in the town.

'Then I now pronounce you man and wife. You may kiss...' Watching Joshua lift Kath and swing her round, the vicar finished, '... the bride!'

Tears of joy ran freely from the eyes of Kath's friends as Joshua kissed his new wife over and over. The celebrations began, and the sight of money again secured the vicar's tongue into silence as he left to visit other people in the town.

He was unaware of the eyes that watched him from behind the trees in the garden.

Happiness prevailed in the mix of very special friends long into the night before tired people made their way back to their homes.

Kath and Joshua climbed the stairs and he said, 'Mrs Gittins... Miss Clancy...' Opening the bedroom door, he watched her face light up as she stepped into the room.

'Oh Joshua!' she said breathlessly, 'you have a four-poster bed!'

'No my dear, *we* have a four poster bed.' He said as they moved further into the bedroom. Closing the door quietly behind him, he at last was able to gather his wife into his arms and they shared their first passionate kiss.

*

Going about his business in the factory, Joshua had an extra spring in his step although he knew he had to keep his vow of secrecy. He felt whole again; Kath had filled the void in his life and he loved her to distraction. Having to curb his loving behaviour when in public with Kath had caused him a few problems to begin with; he wanted to touch her hand or give her a sweet kiss at every given opportunity. Eventually his mind would settle once more into married life albeit a secret one.

Bouncing into the kitchen one evening, Joshua asked the women where Kath was and was told she'd gone to the shop in Birmingham with Jim that morning and was not back as yet. Taking his grandson into the garden to play in the spring sunshine, Joshua waited for her return.

'Joshua! Joshua, come quick!' Annie railed. Grabbing

Harry, he rushed into the house to see what the commotion was about. Jim sat at the table surrounded by all the other women; he was shaking from head to foot.

'Jim,' he asked, 'what's up lad?'

'It's Kath, Joshua... she's gone missing!'

The words hit him like a thunderbolt and Joshua found himself asking, 'What do you mean Kath's gone missing?'

Exasperation evident, Jim said, 'She's gone missing as in... she ain't at the shop!'

'Wha—' Joshua began.

Cutting him off, Jim rushed on, 'I went to get her but when I pulled up the shop door was standing open and pots were strewn and smashed everywhere. It must have happened after the two serving girls had gone home. Kath's basket was there, but she wasn't. I searched everywhere but I couldn't find her!'

Joshua caught the look which passed between the women in the kitchen as they said in unison, 'Potter!'

'Oh Joshua, we have to go and look for mother, right NOW!' Violet wept, rushing to grab her shawl.

'Right, Jim lad, you go and fetch Spencer from the works, tell him what's happened. Annie, can you take Harry?' She nodded, sweeping the crying child into her arms. Joshua went on, 'The rest of us are going to Birmingham!'

Joshua drove Martha and Violet in one carriage and Mary and Joyce travelled in another driven by Jim on his return with Spencer.

On reaching the shop it was as Jim described. The door was still standing open, the pots inside were smashed to pieces.

Instantly Mary and Joyce set to cleaning up the mess, while Violet and Martha went to visit the women who worked there. They lived in Cherry Street which joined the other end of Cannon Street where Violet's Luxuries was located.

Spencer turned to Joshua, 'We'll find her, Father, don't worry.'

'I bloody hope so, lad! I knew we should have kept those night watchmen on at the shop.' Joshua replied.

'I know, Father, we'll ask them tomorrow if they would come back to guard the shop.'

Spencer, Jim and Joshua each went separate ways to look for Kath. After a long search of the nearby streets they still had not found her.

The women who worked in the shop had gone home at the usual time, they said, leaving Kath to wait for Jim before locking up for the night.

No one had seen where Kath had gone. No one had seen her leave. Joshua's wife was missing in Birmingham and as darkness fell, his fear for her safety began to build in him.

'We can't search in the darkness, Father, we have to go home and come back in the morning.'

Violet screeched, 'Spencer! We can't leave Mother out there alone, she could be hurt!'

'The lad is right, Violet wench,' Joshua said, trying to staunch the anger inside him, 'much as it pains me to say it – we have to leave it until the morning.' Locking the shop with a spare key kept in the till, they made their way home, each harbouring their fears quietly as the carriages rumbled over the cobbled streets.

*

Sitting in the living room of Gittins Manor with Violet and Spencer, the story of Mr Potter was retold to Joshua. He had known about the destruction of the property but until this moment was unaware of the visit undertaken by the Wives thereafter.

'This Mr Potter,' Joshua spat acerbically, 'surely he wouldn't be daft enough to have done this, especially after the visit made to him by the wenches?' he asked in disbelief.

Violet responded with, 'He was rather shaken when we left him that day.' Violet was tempted to reveal the true identity of the Wednesbury Wives at that moment, but fear of his reaction held her in check.

'Well he'll be more than bloody shaken when I get my hands on him!' Joshua said, anger swelling in him again as he stood and began to pace the room.

'Father,' Spencer said as he passed over a glass of brandy, 'we can't be sure he had anything to do with this, but we'll find out tomorrow. Mr Potter will be the first on the list for us to see.'

Violet sobbed, 'Maybe we women can ask around the area in an effort to find out about anything unusual happening around the shop. Someone must have seen or heard something! It's surrounded by buildings after all.'

*

The crack of dawn saw them all riding into Birmingham yet again. The shop had been opened by the saleswomen and they had set about restocking the shelves.

Whilst the Wives went in pairs, each taking a different street, to make enquiries, Spencer, Jim and Joshua went to see Mr Potter at the *salon*. The girl serving in Potter's shop said he wasn't in as yet which was unusual. Always first in and last out, she thought it strange he was not there this particular day. Maybe he was ill, she had queried, but showed no concern for her boss whom she obviously disliked immensely. Feigning concern for his health, the men had been told where Potter lived.

Striding out, they walked the drab streets lined with small shops and terraced houses before coming to Smallbrook Street where there was a marked difference in the housing. Large buildings stood in their own gardens with long gravel driveways. Behind them stood the imposing building of St Jude's Church. Coming to the place the shop assistant had indicated was Potter's house, they exchanged a glance of disbelief.

'How can he afford this?' Spencer asked.

'I was asking myself the same question, Spencer lad,' Jim muttered.

Walking straight up to the door, Joshua hammered on it and stood back. When no answer came, he hammered again. Still no one answered the door.

'Let's take a look around,' he said, gesturing Spencer to the left and Jim to the right. He stood back further looking at the upstairs windows. Nothing moved.

Spencer and Jim returned, shaking their heads – no one was there that they could see.

Making their way back to the shop, they arrived just as the women returned. Nothing – no one had seen anything. It was as if Kath had disappeared in a puff of smoke.

Spencer spotted a note pinned to the shop door and pulled it free.

'What's this?'

Joshua snatched the note from his son and tore it open. He gasped as he read the words.

Five hundred pounds if you want your wife back!

He dropped the note and it fluttered to the floor.

As fear for his wife consumed Joshua, he dropped to his knees in the shop, and throwing back his head in a silent howl, his shoulders heaved and he wept until he thought his heart would break.

Forty-Eight

'You won't get away with this!' Kath shouted, her gag removed to allow for easier breathing.

Potter struck her a glancing blow across her cheek.

'I already have!' he said. 'Now you shut yer mouth while I think about whether I should return yer safely.'

Tears stung her eyes as she tried to break the bonds tying her to the chair. 'My family will find me, and when they do...!'

'Oh ar, your family...' Potter looked at her through veiled eyes, 'you mean your new husband?' Yellow teeth grinned at her through thin lips, which hid beneath a beaky nose.

Shock took Kath's breath away and she stared open-mouthed at the man now sitting behind his desk. 'How did I know?' His grin widened. 'I make it my business to know, lady. How do you think I can afford all this?' Spreading his arms around the room, he grinned again. 'I find out stuff about people and then... they pay me to keep quiet about it.' He let out an evil-sounding laugh that would have been right at home in any musical hall.

Blackmail! So that was his game. Kath looked around the room at the top of the man's house, an attic he had converted into an office of sorts. She watched him as he stared back at her.

'I don't think five hundred was too much to ask, do you?' Potter gave a cackle before he went on, 'Yes, five hundred... this time!'

'What do you mean – this time?' Kath asked as panic began to take hold of her.

'You ain't very bright are you? But then you are only a woman, I knew you had no head for business,' he muttered, 'I've asked five hundred for you now but if I don't deliver you...'

'You can ask for more!' Kath said in absolute horror.

'Now you're getting the idea,' he gave her a feral smile.

'Joshua will bring the police,' she sobbed.

Leaning back in his chair, he studied her. 'Joshua... Ah yes, Joshua Gittins. Well he didn't find you an hour ago when he came calling now did he? I saw him standing outside... him and his two mates, then he just turned right round and went home.'

'He will come back!' Kath spat. 'And when he does and he finds me here like this,' she struggled again against the bonds restraining her, 'you'll be sorry – very sorry indeed!' Her diatribe left her feeling wretched.

'Oh, he won't be finding you here, but he might find you face down in the cut if you don't shut yer yap!'

Kath watched the anger in him rise and felt her own fear as she thought again of John Sligo found floating in the canal 'as dead as a doornail'. A cold shudder trickled down her spine as she tried to push the thought away.

'I'm going out a while now but I'll be back shortly. I have stuff to do.' With that he left her in the cold dark room with nothing for company except her fear.

*

Waking with a jolt from a sleep she had not realised she was in, Kath saw Potter standing in front of her, holding an oil lamp in his hand.

'I expect to be five hundred pounds richer by this time tomorrow,' he said, the evil grin back on his face.

'How did you know... about Joshua and me?' Kath croaked.

'Oh I watched it all happen,' he said, 'in fact I've been watching you since you opened that piddly little shop! Any woman who can open a shop must have had the backing of a man. Discreet enquiries led me to your house... and Joshua Gittins!'

The secrecy surrounding the family had been breached and Kath felt her stomach lurch.

Potter went on, 'It didn't take much to keep a watch on your house, taking the odd day off from the *salon*...' He sniggered. 'It ain't that far to ride over to Wednesbury. Then the Fates were kind to me and I was fortunate enough to see the vicar arrive one day. I was hiding in the trees, then I sneaked up and watched the whole proceedings through the windows. So *Mrs Gittins* the rest... is history.' He let out a laugh that made Kath shiver.

Lighting the lamp on the desk, he stepped towards her and traced a finger down her cheek to her throat and on to her décolletage, then he said quietly, 'You know, you are quite a handsome woman for your age.'

Kath felt bile rise as she shut her eyes tightly.

Dear God, she prayed silently, *don't let him do this... please don't let him do what I think he means to do!*

*

The light streaming in from the window woke her and Kath took in her surroundings once again. She breathed a sigh of relief when she remembered Potter leaving her last night. After his back-handed compliment he had turned and left the room, taking the lamp with him. Kath had cried into the darkness before eventually falling asleep.

Kath's body ached now from being tied to the chair for so long and her head throbbed with pain. She was thirsty, hungry and very afraid.

Bursting through the door, Potter glared at her. 'That bloody husband of yours...!' He spat the words into Kath's face. '...He just stood there! I told him in the note where to be with the five hundred pounds and he was there... oh yes he was there... with a load of blokes ready to bash my brains out! This is all your fault!' Another resounding slap sent her head sideways, leaving her cheek stinging and her eyes smarting. 'I stood in hiding round the back of the General Post Office watching him and his mates pace up and down so I took off.'

Kath sobbed, 'He would have paid you, had you gone to him.'

'I doubt that,' Potter snarled, 'he was waiting to give me a hiding, you idiot! I'll bet he didn't even have any money with him! Well Mrs Gittins, it don't look like you are worth anything to your husband, it don't look like he is willing to pay a penny to get you back!'

His words whirled in her brain. Surely Potter was wrong? Surely Joshua would pay him for her release? Surely he loved her enough…? Tears trailed down her cheeks as Kath listened to him laugh.

'It don't matter though,' he continued, 'I'll just chuck you in the cut tonight and find another daft bugger with money I can wheedle out of them.'

He left Kath to her misery. Joshua would come… she was sure he would. He would find her… but would he be in time? How long did she have left before she found herself sleeping with the fishes in the canal? Memories of a frightened Colleen flooded her mind.

Forty-Nine

Joshua, Jim and Spencer had waited at the designated spot for Kath to be handed over to them. Joshua held a bundle of newspaper wrapped neatly in brown paper tied with string. As they waited, their hearts hammered in their chests and they looked around them. The streets were busy with people coming and going; carts rumbled past and street hawkers touted their wares, keeping a keen eye out for a constable who would chase them away.

Spencer's eyes searched for the man who they suspected had taken Kath. He paced back and forth, anger and distress fusing together. They waited – and waited.

'I don't think he's coming,' Jim said quietly.

'He'd better bloody come!' Joshua growled. 'If I get my hands on him – I'll bloody kill him!'

'Calm down, Dad, you'll give yourself a heart attack.' Spencer laid a hand on his father's arm.

'I can't lad, I can't stop thinking he might have...' A sob caught in his throat.

'Kath will be all right, I'm sure of it. Let's just wait calmly.'

Unbeknown to his father, Spencer had been harbouring the same thoughts. What if the kidnapper had killed Kath?

＊

In the meantime, Violet had gathered the others around her in the shop. Harry was with Nancy at Violet's Play House so Annie had joined them.

Violet looked at each woman in turn. Martha, Annie, Mary, and Joyce watched her.

'I'm not waiting any longer,' she began, 'I'm off to find Potter, because it's my contention he has kidnapped my mother!'

'Right then,' Mary said, grabbing her shawl, 'let's get going!'

They walked to Smallbrook Street where Jim had said Potter lived. He had described the place, surprised the man could afford such a fine house. They stopped right outside.

'This must be it,' Violet said as she marched up the drive to the door. She hammered the knocker loudly. Receiving no answer, she signalled for the others to circle around the back of the house and to peep in windows for any sign of life. Coming back with heads shaking, Violet said, 'Right. We need to break that window!'

Joyce took it upon herself to do it and looking around for a boulder, she picked it up and flung it hard against the living room windowpane. There was a resounding crash as the glass gave way to the boulder. Wrapping her shawl around her arm, Joyce pushed out the rest of the glass. She scrambled through the empty window frame into the house and, finding the front door, she let the others inside.

'Spread out,' Violet said, 'let's find that bugger!'

Running around the ground floor, they searched frantically, and finding no one, they gathered at the bottom of the stairs. No longer worried about the noise, they ascended the stairs and, reaching the top, they heard a voice.

Looking up at the ceiling, Violet pointed, 'He's up there, the bugger's in the attic!'

Finding the attic stairs, they made their way up, all the time listening to Potter's voice raving. They stopped moving each time he drew breath, only continuing when he began to shout again. Who was he shouting at? Was there someone with him? If so, they would have to deal with the other person too. He had obviously not heard the windowpane shatter. Reaching the door, Violet turned to the women behind her; pointing at the door then pushing both hands forward, their nods reaffirmed the action she had indicated.

Each taking a deep breath, Violet threw the door back on its hinges and they all rushed in. Throwing themselves at Potter, they pinned him to the floor. Potter gasped as they set about him with clenched fists. Trying to throw them off him, he yelled and cursed, but still they held him down, their anger fuelling their efforts.

'Right Mary, find something to tie him up with,' Violet said through clenched teeth.

Mary cast a glance around the room. Seeing nothing suitable, she hitched up her skirt and rolled down her woollen stocking.

They managed to bind the struggling man's hands behind his back with the stocking.

'What the hell…!' Potter yelled.

Mary took off her other stocking. Dragging him up, they tied him to the chair by the desk.

'Where is my mother?' Violet demanded.

'How the hell should I know?' Potter answered with his own question.

'Tell me or I'll...' Violet was beside herself with worry, her fists clenching.

'You'll what? I have no idea what you're talking about,' Potter feigned innocence.

Martha intervened. 'We know it was you who kidnapped Kath, so tell us where she is and we'll let you go.'

'Kidnapped! Why would I kidnap someone? Who is this Kath? You're all mad!' Potter gave a nervous laugh.

'Five hundred pounds, Potter! That's why. We saw the note you left on our shop door. The money in exchange for Kath,' Martha spat venomously.

Violet pushed her face close to his, causing him to draw his head back so he could focus on her. 'Mr Potter,' she said with quiet menace, 'the mood I'm in right now does not bode well for you.' Leaning back, she studied him. 'Do you have children, Mr Potter?'

'Children? What's that got to do with anything?' His confusion caused him to frown.

'DO... YOU... HAVE... CHILDREN?' Violet yelled in his face.

'No – no, I don't,' he said, feeling fear creep over him as his eyes pleaded with the other women.

'That's a shame,' Violet said as her eyes roamed the small room. Seeing a letter opener on the desk, she picked it up and turned it gently in her hands. 'This is pretty.' Standing in front of him, she rasped, 'So you have no children.'

Potter shook his head.

The other women watched silently as Violet circled the man tied to the chair. As she came to face him again, her hand shot out towards his crotch, stopping short before the letter opener touched him. 'It may be that you will never have any offspring.'

Potter gasped, sweat forming on his forehead. 'What do you want from me?' he croaked.

Violet waggled the weapon, saying, 'I want to know where my mother is.'

'I... I don't know.'

Violet straightened up and turned to face her friends. 'What shall we do with this lying piece of rubbish?'

'We could stab him,' Mary offered up.

'Or we could cut off his baby-making equipment,' Annie suggested in her own inimitable way.

'Hmmm, I like that idea,' Violet mused, tapping the weapon against her lips.

'Ladies please...' begged Potter.

'Tell us what we want to know, or...' Violet brandished the weapon in front of his face.

'All right! All right, she's in the privy at the back of your shop. Now let me go!'

'Not so fast, Potter,' Martha said. 'You'll be coming with us, then we might hand you over to the coppers. However, what I want to know is how did you get her there without being seen?'

'At night! I took her at night when nobody was about! I threatened to kill her daughter if she made a sound – but I wouldn't have, I swear!'

Violet didn't hear all of Martha's words. She dropped the letter opener to the floor and rushed from the room, Annie close on her heels.

The others released Potter from the chair. As they did so,

he made a dash for the door, but Joyce stuck her leg out and tripped him. He crashed heavily to the floor, his bound hands unable to break his fall. He groaned as they tied the stocking around his throat like a leash. Helping him up, Martha tugged on the makeshift lead and Potter gagged.

'That'll do nicely,' she said. 'Right, let's get going.' She gave him a shove and he walked towards the stairs. Martha picked up the letter opener as she went.

Violet ran through the streets, her long skirt clutched in her hands. Her mind was in a whirl. The men were still waiting at the meeting point for Potter to arrive, but she would have to let them wait. She needed to get back to the shop – to the privy out the back. She prayed as she ran, *please God let my mother be there!*

Annie, behind her, had slowed her pace, but Violet couldn't wait for her. She began to sob as she rushed past people who stopped to stare. She dashed across the road, narrowly missing a carter who cursed loudly at her stupidity. Violet ignored him and thundered on, her boots rapping the cobbles in a steady rhythm. She felt a stitch in her side but ignored the pain. She *had* to find her mother!

Gasping for breath, Violet ran down the entry at the side of the shop. Yanking the privy door open, she saw her mother sitting on the thunderbox, her hands bound and a gag round her mouth.

'Mum! Oh thank God!' Violet tore off the gag as Kath stood up. Then she undid the restraints. Mother and daughter wept as they hugged each other tightly.

Annie came puffing up to them and wound her arms around them both. 'Thank the Lord you're safe!'

*

Joshua and Spencer arrived back at the shop, raging that Potter had not turned up at the rendezvous point.

Kath rushed up to her husband as he walked into the shop.

'Kath! Oh Kath, oh thank God you're safe!'

Clutching each other tightly, she said, 'The wenches saved me, Joshua.'

Looking at the women in turn, nods were exchanged in grateful thanks.

Speaking up, Violet said, 'However, we still have this to deal with!'

The line of standing women parted, revealing Mr Potter still bound and now gagged. The women had walked him through the streets without the leash, but he was well aware of Martha very close behind him with the letter opener occasionally digging him in the ribs. Joshua released Kath instantly and shot towards Potter with his fists clenched. The line of women closed again before Joshua reached his target.

'There are things you need to know first,' Violet said to Joshua, looking him directly in the eye. Kath shot her daughter a warning look and Violet said to her, 'It's time, Mother, time he knows everything.' The women exchanged a look before Kath nodded resignedly.

With everyone gathered in the shop area, Violet suggested they went home, taking Potter with them, where they could unravel the extensive tale of the Wednesbury Wives for Joshua.

Once back at Gittins Manor, Potter was pushed unceremoniously into the cellar to await his fate... a clear warning to remain silent being the last words he heard before the door was banged shut, leaving him in darkness.

Violet rang for tea and once the maid had left the room, the tale began.

The women watched as Joshua sat listening intently whilst the story unfolded before finally saying, 'Bloody hell!'

There was a long silence as everyone gave Joshua time to absorb what he'd been told. Nervous glances were exchanged as the women wondered what he would do about what he'd heard. Eventually he said, 'After all this damned nonsense with Kath, I can understand. I was ready to kill Potter myself!' Then using Violet's words of years before he added, 'Justifiable retribution for every one of them.' He was, of course, referring to the people the Wives had dealt out punishment to.

He had been holding Kath close throughout and now Joshua pulled her closer still, kissing her tenderly, a small but significant sign to them all they had done the right thing bringing him into their coterie.

*

The following morning saw them all meeting once more at Joshua's house, Gittins Lodge, to decide what should be done about Potter. Given breakfast, the man had once more been left alone to think on his plight.

'Joshua,' Kath said, 'he knows we are married, and I don't think money would keep his mouth closed. After all he was set to keep me in the privy at the back of the shop and continue to ask for more money!'

'Was he now?' said Joshua. 'Right then, ladies, what should we do with our Mr Potter?'

The women looked at each other at a loss for ideas when Mary muttered into her teacup, 'First of all, that bugger ought to lose all his money, if you ask me!'

Looking up into the silence of the room and seeing the

smiles on the faces surrounding her, Mary sighed heavily, 'Oh bloody hell!'

*

Later in the day, Joshua and Spencer returned to Spencer's house and went into the cellar.

'Where do you keep your money, Mr Potter?' Joshua asked as he walked around the man sitting on the floor.

'I ain't telling you!' Potter said indignantly.

'Tell us where your money is, and we'll let you go,' Joshua added.

'I don't believe you!' Potter's tongue dragged across his thin lips. 'The women said that and now look where I am!'

'Please yourself,' said Spencer as he and his father made to leave.

'You promise to let me go if I tell you?' said Potter pleadingly, as he turned his head to look at them.

Joshua turned around saying, 'Just tell us where the money is and we'll even take you home.'

Looking from one to the other with fear in his eyes, Potter made his decision. 'It's under the mattress,' he said resignedly.

Father and son walked from the cellar, leaving the man wondering what was to be done with him.

*

'Just like that? He told you just like that?' Violet asked.

'Ar wench, I think he preferred to deal with us rather than you lot.' Laughter erupted in the living room where everyone was gathered. 'So,' Joshua went on, 'I suggest we all take Mr Potter home, everyone agreed?'

Teacups saluted the air as nods came from them all.

Potter was marched up to the living room and he squinted as daylight assaulted his eyes. 'Now, Mr Potter,' Joshua began, once again taking a menacing walk around the man, 'we must have your assurance you will behave yourself on our journey to your house.'

Potter had swivelled his head in an effort to follow Joshua's movements and now it bobbed up and down on his neck.

Joshua went on, 'When we arrive you will show us where the money is.' Potter's head continued its bobbing. 'Good, then we have reached an agreement.' Taking hold of Potter's hand, Joshua shook it, smiling at the gentleman's agreement Potter had been forced into.

Potter and the women were packed into the carriage and Jim drove them to Potter's house; Joshua and Spencer riding beside it. He eyed them all warily on the journey but made no attempt at escape. Sitting so tightly together made the idea impossible anyway.

Potter faltered as he got out of the carriage, but led them into the house and up the stairs, albeit begrudgingly. Lifting the corner of the mattress, he revealed his money laid out all over the bedstead. Joshua and Spencer then tipped the mattress completely off the bed.

'Hey,' Potter said as he saw Spencer and Joshua gather up the money, 'that's mine!'

Joshua said, 'Oh we're not stealing it.' He placed the money on the dressing table which stood near the bed.

Heaving the mattress back in place, Joshua said as he picked up a pillow, 'I'm sure you are ready for a nice sleep now, eh Potter?'

'I'm all right for now,' the man returned, fear evident in his eyes as he looked from Joshua to Spencer.

Giving him a sturdy push, Violet said, 'I think the man is telling you to lie down.'

Dragging himself onto the bed, Potter lay down with his arms by his sides and only his head lifted. He did not know which of them to watch now, or indeed whether he should keep an eye on his money stacked on the dressing table.

'Now, Mr Potter,' Joshua said, standing over the prone man on the bed, pillow in hand, 'before we let you go... I think you owe Kath *Clancy* an apology.'

Violet watched the smile cross Kath's face at the emphatic use of her name.

'I'm sorry Miss Clancy,' Potter spluttered, 'I'm really sorry.'

Kath leaned down over the man on the bed and as she did so, he pulled away from her. 'Apology accepted,' she whispered. Then she moved away.

Violet picked up the money from the dresser. 'You have quite a bit saved here, Mr Potter.' She saw him nod and took twenty pounds, saying, 'This should cover the cost of the breakages at our shop – thank you.' She tucked the money down the bodice of her dress, then waving the remainder in his face, added, 'It's extremely kind of you to donate this to the poor. We know a lot of families who will be grateful to you, don't we ladies?' She saw the women grin.

Potter began to sit up, a scowl covering his face. 'You can't take that – it's stealing!' he protested.

Loud laughter echoed round the room.

'You've got balls, Potter, I'll say that for you.' Spencer laughed.

Kath spoke up. 'You blackmailed that money out of other people, I'm guessing. Besides, you "donated" it so how can it be stealing?'

Potter groaned. He knew when he was beaten. He nodded.

'Right, we'll give you a choice, Potter. You can stay here in Birmingham and face the police who will most definitely throw you in jail or...' Spencer paused.

'Or?' Potter asked, now very much afraid he was about to meet his maker.

'Or you can get as far away from here as possible and never come back!'

'I'll go!' Potter said quickly, then breathed a sigh of relief.

'Good choice,' Violet said, handing him five pounds of his own money. 'Your train fare. My husband and his father will escort you to the station. Don't bother to pack, you'll be leaving straight away.'

With the money in his hand, he rose from the bed and stalked from the room and down the stairs, followed closely by Joshua, who threw the pillow on the bed, and Spencer.

The two men watched Potter climb onto the steam train bound for London. They waved cheerfully as the great iron beast puffed its way out of the station, and laughed at the scowl on Potter's face showing through the window.

Jim had driven the women back to Wednesbury where they shared a congratulatory cup of tea.

The money taken from Potter was distributed to families known to be in dire straits and was accepted so gratefully no questions were asked.

The Wives felt they had scared Potter witless and knew his helping the poor with his 'donation' had galled him. Nevertheless, he had taken the choice given to him and left town.

*

Word around the marketplace told of a man in Birmingham

who had upped and left a good job and a big house. The girl serving in the *salon* had reported him missing to the police as she hadn't seen hide nor hair of him for some days. The police visited his property but could find no sign of the man in question. It was a mystery.

No one appeared to know why the man had gone just like that, and after reading out loud the article in the *Herald* newspaper to the women now sat before her, Violet said, 'Good riddance Potter!'

Fifty

Work and life in Wednesbury and in the shop in Birmingham went on as usual with profits soaring from the selling of Violet's Luxuries. The mystery surrounding the man who had left so suddenly and mysteriously had died down as everyday life had taken over.

Making her way to Annie's living room one day, Violet was surprised the door was still closed; Annie's door was always open. Knocking before she went in, she called out Annie's name. Receiving no answer, Violet thought she may have been out on the heath gathering wild flowers.

As she turned to leave she heard a sound from the bedroom. Walking to the bedroom door, Violet knocked before swinging it wide open and saw Annie still in bed. Rushing to her, Violet saw the pale face looking back at her.

'Ain't well,' Annie muttered.

'I'll get the doctor! Does Charlie know?'

Annie shook her head, 'I was in bed early last night because I was tired. Charlie went to work before I woke this morning.'

The stable lad was sent to fetch Dr Shaw and Violet went

back to Annie. 'Dr Shaw is coming, Annie,' she said. 'You just rest.'

Annie closed her eyes and Violet watched her breathe easier. Only now did she realise how much older her friend was, and the others too, including her mother. Why had she not seen this before? How is it she had missed everyone getting older?

Dr Shaw arrived and examined Annie. After giving her a spoonful of tonic, he came to Violet, sitting in Annie's living room. 'Annie's exhausted, Violet,' he said, 'she needs rest and lots of it. She should retire from working...' Holding up his hands to prevent her speaking, he continued with, 'I know she's young yet to retire, but if she doesn't stop working, this...' sweeping a hand towards the bedroom where Annie lay, '... will keep happening.'

'Thank you Dr Shaw,' Violet said, 'but I know Annie and I can't see her *not* working. However, if we put her in charge of the other workers, make sure she only supervises the work and rests often, she should stay well for years to come, is that right?'

'Good idea Violet, and yes, she needs to rest much more,' he replied.

Leaving the tonic with Violet to administer, the doctor left. Writing a note to the others regarding Annie, she sent the stable boy to deliver it to Gittins Lodge.

Within the hour they were all gathered in Annie's living room and Violet told them what Dr Shaw had said. They agreed to the last that Annie would collect no more flowers and herbs; she would make up no more creams or hair washes, she would only supervise the other workers. Her health had to come first.

Spencer and Violet had decided that Nancy would look

after Harry while she worked; the boy was faring well and was always excited to play with the other children at Violet's Play House.

Sitting with Annie after the other women had left, Violet thought of everything they had been faced with over the years. It was no wonder her friend was exhausted. The trials and tribulations, as well as the accomplishments, had taken their toll on them all, but more so on Annie it appeared.

Watching her sleep, Violet determined that she would take care of Annie and all the other Wives too from now on.

*

Good wholesome food along with the tonic the doctor brought saw Annie pick up quite quickly, until one day she said, 'I fancy a stroll over to see the wenches.'

Annie and Violet walked slowly down Trouse Lane and over to Joshua's house where she was greeted with tea and hugs. She watched as work continued around her, then said, 'I have something to say.' Work instantly stopped as everyone looked her way. 'I can't be working anymore.' Her statement was simple and held no regret. 'Dr Shaw says I mustn't... but it would be all right to supervise the wenches.' Nodding to the women taken on from Wednesbury to make the hair wash, she went on, 'Providing they don't mind having me as their boss.' Their answer was a round of applause and more hugs.

Sitting at the table with Annie, Violet addressed the others, 'If Annie supervises the ladies in their work... and if we took on more women to be trained... then we could all retire eventually!'

Kath said, 'Violet wench, that's a damned good idea!'

'Also...' Violet added, 'we could even think about setting up another shop... in Wednesbury.'

Cheers rang out and when they died down, Kath said, 'It would mean more work ladies, which would extend our retirement date, but if you're up for it, we would need to see how the money stands with the accountant first.' So, an appointment was planned for the following day.

Fifty-One

Sitting in his office, Joshua's thoughts swung to the events of the previous weeks. He had become one of the Wives, as Spencer had before him. He had married a murderer, as had his son. But he believed Potter had deserved more than being run out of town – taking his wife prisoner the way he had! A cold shiver ran down Joshua's spine as he thought about what could have happened to Kath, and again he thought, *justifiable retribution*!

A knock to the door lightened his mood considerably as Kath and Violet walked into the office.

'Hey up…' Joshua said, standing to find them each a seat, 'this is a nice surprise!'

Greetings, and tea brought in by a worker, over with, the purpose of their visit became evident.

'We just came from the accountant and we are now in such a good financial position we can open another shop!' Kath said, excitement exuding from every pore.

'That right?' Joshua asked tentatively.

'Yes,' Violet took up, 'but we want to open it here in Wednesbury.' Her excitement also began to bubble up.

'Ar well...'

Joshua was cut off by Kath saying, 'We need your help...' lowering her voice to a conspiratorial whisper, 'husband of mine.'

With smiles all round, he asked, 'What help can I give to you wenches?'

'We need your expertise on finding a suitable building in a suitable spot, to open our suitable business!' Kath's laugh tinkled, and his heart melted. She could ask for the moon and he'd find a way to get it for her.

'Right well,' Joshua began, 'I thought you were all "retired" now, but it seems I was wrong in that.' Smiles passed between the women. 'I would suggest you go and look at all the empty buildings, but...' he raised a finger in warning, 'you all go together!'

'Yes Joshua,' Kath lowered her head but not her eyes; the twinkle in them gave him a shudder of desire.

'You minx,' he said. 'Go on, the pair of you, bugger off and let me work!'

Laughing, they left and Joshua felt like a teenager again. Kath was as important to him as the air he breathed – he couldn't live without either.

*

Kath told Joshua over dinner that evening they had found a run-down building just off Lower High Street which was very near the marketplace. No one, it appeared, knew who it belonged to. Nobody laid claim to its ownership and she wondered whether they could stake their claim. It was a two-storey building and looked like an old school. With work it could be made into a shop downstairs and the making of the products could be done upstairs, so relieving the kitchen in Gittins Lodge of the women currently inhabiting it. Pressing her point, she said how nice it would be to have the house to themselves at last, save for Joyce who was now housekeeping and had taken over the whole of the servants' quarters at the top of the house. Joshua had to agree it had a certain appeal.

Their enquiries at the Town Hall came to nothing, they could find no documentation or information on who did, or had, owned the building, therefore Violet staked their claim with the powers that be and became co-owner of 'The Gift Shop'.

It didn't take the women long to lick the building into shape with Geordie Slater overseeing the renovations. Spencer had kept Geordie and his men busy with odd bits of work here and there and they were now making good headway on The Gift Shop.

Joshua was very aware of how close he had come to losing his wife and with his jaw set he rode towards the bread line near the marketplace. It was his intention to hire a handful of watchmen to guard the new building at night. Possibly not warranted in Wednesbury, but he was taking no chances after the last debacle.

Weeks came and went as spring turned into summer, which eventually gave way to autumn. Now winter was on its way as the cold air nipped noses. Fingers and toes tingled and people hurried along with heads shoved down into shawls and mufflers.

The nail factories and the shops were doing well and life couldn't be sweeter for Joshua who revelled in the happiness Kath brought him.

Fifty-Two

At three years old, Harry Gittins was growing into a fine lad. Violet was teaching him to read and write his letters and numbers and he was learning quickly. He kept everyone amused with his mischievous antics; they all adored him.

Violet collected him from nursery one bitterly cold day to be told by Nancy that she was closing down for a couple of weeks. Some of the children had gone down with a cold and she felt it best to shut up shop until they were well again.

'I'm trying to prevent it spreading,' Nancy said.

'Good idea,' Violet agreed as she placed a hand on Harry's forehead. 'He seems fine, maybe he's one of the lucky ones.'

Bundling him into his coat, hat, mittens and scarf, Violet and her son set off for home. They chatted on the walk back and Violet's concerns dissipated.

As the evening wore on, Harry's eyelids drooped so Spencer carried him up to bed.

'Some of the children at the nursery have been taken poorly so Nancy said to stay home for a while,' she told Spencer as he rejoined her in the living room.

'Sensible thinking,' he said, 'but Harry seems fine, he's just tired out, bless him.'

Violet nodded and continued to read her book while Spencer took up his newspaper.

The weather worsened over the following days and large snowflakes drifted silently from the sky. Harry wanted to go and play in the white wonderland forming outside the window, but Violet refused him, saying it was far too cold. Harry grizzled a little then Violet distracted him with a book on animals.

Looking up through the window, she saw Kath trudging up to the house. 'Grandma's here!' she said and smiled as Harry ran to meet his grandmother while Violet rang for tea.

'Blimey it's cold out there,' Kath said, nuzzling her grandson now wriggling in her arms.

'Hot tea is coming,' Violet laughed at Harry's giggling. 'Come and get warm.'

Sat by the fire, Harry playing happily on the floor, Kath said gravely, 'Violet, there's scarlet fever in the town.'

'Oh my God!' Violet's eyes shot to her son.

Kath went on, 'It doesn't look as though he has it, gel, so don't worry too much.'

'What if he has it and it's not showing yet!' Violet scooped up the boy, inspecting him for a rash. Harry snivelled, clearly disgruntled at being disturbed from his playing.

Allowing him his freedom once more, Violet said, 'There's nothing there, thank goodness. How many are affected?'

'Hard to say,' Kath answered, 'but I know Dr Shaw is run ragged, as well as all the other doctors in the town.'

'Oh those poor families,' Violet's heart went out to those suffering from the dreadful disease.

'Martha told me one of the canal children caught it in Birmingham and now it's here.'

Violet was shocked. 'So it's in Birmingham too. I wonder where else people are suffering?'

'It could be everywhere by now,' Kath sighed. 'The "cut-rats" travel all over the country so it might be widespread.'

'I do hope not,' Violet's eyes strayed once more to her son chatting away happily to himself.

Both Spencer and Violet watched Harry carefully over the next few days and thankfully he showed no signs of feeling ill.

Keeping to the house, Violet learned of the deaths of the children in the town on her mother's visits. It was terribly upsetting for Violet to hear that some of Harry's playmates had succumbed to the disease raging across Wednesbury. The newspapers were full of it and it appeared Birmingham was faring no better.

Towards the end of the second week, Violet became worried. Harry had refused his food and he was whiny. Lifting him onto her lap, she felt his forehead. He was hot and was snuffling as she carried him upstairs. Her heart hammered in her chest and fear gripped her throat as she changed him into his pyjamas. He grizzled again as she undressed him. Sucking in a breath, Violet stared at the rash covering his little body.

Oh dear God, no!

She settled him down and he fell asleep almost instantly. Rushing downstairs to the kitchen, she sent the cook home. To the maid she said, 'Please go to Dr Shaw and ask him to come quickly, then go home yourself. You and cook can return when this fever has completely gone from Wednesbury. Now go and hurry, please!'

The maid grabbed her coat and shot from the room.

Violet took the stairs two at a time to Harry's room where she checked on him. He was sweating, so she fetched a flannel and bowl of cool water.

Harry whimpered and shivered as Violet dabbed his forehead with the wet cloth.

'Oh my baby, please be all right, please!' she whispered tearfully.

Hearing the knock on the front door, she rushed downstairs. Dr Shaw stamped the snow from his boots and stepped inside.

Violet was shocked at the sight of him. His complexion was white and he had dark circles under his eyes. He looked exhausted.

'Where is he?' he asked.

Violet led the way and watched as Dr Shaw examined Harry.

'I'm sorry Violet, but it is scarlet fever. I'm run off my feet with it,' he said, reaching into his Gladstone bag. Passing over a ridged glass bottle with a cork stopper, he went on, 'One teaspoonful three times a day. I'm sorry but it's the best I can do. Ventilate the room. Sponge him down too, it will help reduce his temperature.' The doctor sighed as Violet thanked him. 'I wish I could do more.'

After seeing Dr Shaw on his way, Violet sat by Harry's bedside bathing his little body. She was so intent on her task she didn't hear Spencer until he walked into the room.

'Violet?'

'Oh Spencer! It's Harry, he has scarlet fever!' Only now did she allow her tears to fall freely.

'Oh Christ!' Spencer came to his son's side and looked down at the flushed little face.

'Dr Shaw has been, he left some medicine,' Violet croaked. 'Do the others know?'

Violet shook her head. 'I couldn't leave Harry, not even for a moment.'

Spencer wrapped her in his arms and Violet finally let go of her emotions. She burst into tears, the huge sobs heaving her shoulders. Then suddenly she realised Spencer was sobbing too. Holding tightly to each other, they cried out their fear into the quiet room.

Harry moaned and Violet quickly moved to bathe him down again. She saw Spencer wince as their little boy's body gave an involuntary shiver. His breathing was short and shallow, his eyes closed as he battled the disease that was ravaging him.

Violet trickled cool water on his lips and heard him swallow then he coughed. He opened his eyes and began to cry softly. She coaxed him to take his medicine then gave him a cool drink. He drank thirstily.

'That's a good boy, now you go back to sleep. Mummy and Daddy will stay right here with you.'

Closing his eyes again, Harry whimpered in his misery.

'Poor little thing,' Spencer said, his hand on Violet's shoulder as she sat by the bed. 'Violet, I'll go and let Annie know what's happening, then ask Charlie if he'd be good enough to tell the others.' He ended with a sniff.

Violet nodded. 'Tell them to stay away, Spencer – just in case.'

Spencer walked quietly from the room and across to the Greens' living room door. Tapping gently, he waited.

The door opened and immediately seeing his face, Annie asked, 'What's up?'

'Harry has scarlet fever, Annie! Violet says to stay away

until it's all clear as you know yourself adults can contract it too. Charlie, would you do me a favour? Would you go and tell the others. I know the weather is grim, but Kath, at least, should know. I can't leave Harry and Violet or I would go myself. Then I want you both to stay here, please.'

Charlie grabbed his coat. 'I'll be as quick as I can.' He then rushed out into the snowy night.

Spencer turned to leave and heard Annie's door close. He sighed but then saw Annie fly past him and bolt up the stairs. His heart swelled with love and respect for Annie as, despite his warning to stay put, she had put his wife and son before herself.

Annie tiptoed into Harry's room, followed shortly afterwards by Spencer, and heard Violet crying quietly.

'Oh my wench!' Annie whispered as she caught her friend up in her arms. She held Violet tightly as she wept, her own tears rolling unchecked down her face.

Letting go, Violet sniffed. She sat again by the bed. Spencer drew another chair next to her for Annie.

'Dr Shaw's been,' Violet whispered.

'I didn't see him come,' Annie said, 'I must have been in the other room. I've been working on my herb creams.' Violet nodded.

'I'll ring down for tea,' Spencer spoke quietly.

'Oh, I sent the cook and the maid home, sweetheart. I thought it best to stay isolated until Harry is well again.'

'That makes sense. I'll go and make the tea. We'll all feel better for a cup.'

A nod was the best Violet could manage. Without taking her eyes off Harry, she said, 'Annie, I'm so afraid!'

Grasping the girl's hand, Annie said, 'I know gel, but try to stay positive. That little lad is strong, he can beat this.'

Looking at her friend, Violet asked, 'Do you really think so?'

'Yes love, I do.' The older woman nodded. 'Look at him, he's fighting hard. He'll come through, you'll see.' Annie was not so sure her words would prove true, but she needed to bolster the child's mother.

Spencer brought in the tray and they sat in silence to drink their tea, all eyes on the little boy fighting for his life.

A little while later, Charlie arrived back with Kath and Joshua in tow. Regardless of the risk of catching the disease, their coming had showed their concern for Harry, Violet and Spencer rather than for themselves. They were frozen to the bone and it was Annie who went to make fresh tea; Charlie was right behind her.

Crying her heart out over the tea, Annie asked God how he could be so cruel as to let this happen to such good people. Charlie cradled her as she sobbed and for the first and only time in his life he was glad he had no children. He couldn't begin to imagine the heartbreak for them all if young Harry were to die.

Violet rushed into her mother's arms and they wept as they held each other tightly. 'How is he?' Kath asked at last as she peeped over at her grandson.

'No change,' Violet hiccupped.

Spencer brought another chair for Kath and stepped back to face his father. Joshua threw his arms around the young man, holding him in a tight bear hug. 'Oh Dad!' Spencer cried.

'I know lad, I know.' Joshua sniffed back his own tears.

Mother and grandmother sat either side of the bed watching over Harry. 'Mum,' Violet raised her eyes to Kath, 'he's so precious, what if...?'

'You stop that!' Kath snapped. 'Stop thinking like that, do you hear me?'

Violet's breath caught in a sob.

'Now then,' Kath went on, 'give him another wash down and we'll see how he goes through the night.'

Violet wet her child's lips again then sponged his body. She winced as he shivered when the cold cloth touched his skin and she wondered if it was hurting him.

After their tea, Annie suggested Kath and Joshua went to their quarters to get some rest. Reluctantly Kath agreed and they left to sit with their friends.

Violet watched the fever rage in her son and how he tossed his head from side to side as if trying to shake it off. He moaned quietly then whimpered like he was in pain. Her fear grew into panic when she couldn't rouse him to take his medicine.

'Leave him to sleep, sweetheart, it's the best thing for him at the moment,' Spencer tried to comfort his distraught wife.

It was in the early hours of the following morning that Harry opened his eyes.

Violet and Spencer both heaved a sigh of relief. Violet gave him a little drink of cool water.

'Mummy,' the child croaked.

'Hello little man,' Violet managed a weak smile.

'Love you Mummy, Daddy love you.' Harry whispered. Their little boy closed his eyes again before releasing his very last breath.

Violet began to pant. 'Harry…. Harry!' Then realisation struck and she screamed at the top of her voice. 'No! Oh God nooooooo!' The sound reverberated around the house like a howl from a wounded animal. Her bone-chilling wails rang out as she scooped up her son. Pushing his fringe gently off his brow, she cradled him close to her, rocking back and forth, her sobs loud in the quiet of the room.

Spencer dropped into a chair and yelled out his anguish, his face covered with his hands.

The screams and wails brought the others running. The sight that met them brought each to tears.

Violet was sobbing like her heart had broken, never to be mended. Spencer's sobs too were loud as he held his wife and son.

Kath made to rush to her daughter but Annie held her back. 'No Kath,' she said gently, 'come away wench, they need to say their goodbyes.' Annie's silent tears rolled down her cheeks and dropped off her chin.

Kath sobbed as she folded into Joshua's arms barely able to stand. Charlie lay an arm around Annie's shoulder and led the others back to their home before he set out once more along the snow-laden streets, buffeted by freezing winds, to fetch Dr Shaw, who would need to officially pronounce young Harry dead and issue a death certificate.

The exhausted doctor said he would be along shortly, so Charlie made his way to Martha and Mary's to impart the desperately sad news before returning home.

Dr Shaw arrived and bustled into the room. He shook Spencer's hand and moved to the bedside.

Violet looked up at him but her eyes were glazed over. She still cradled Harry in her arms gently.

'Come on, Violet, let me take a look at your boy,' the doctor coaxed. He had seen that look many times on other mothers' faces. She was not going to let him take her child.

The stricken young woman pulled her dead child closer to her in a protective gesture.

'Violet,' Dr Shaw went on, 'let me see the little one.'

She shook her head. The doctor sighed.

Spencer moved to his wife, 'Sweetheart, let me take him for a while.' He held out his arms and Violet allowed him to lift the boy away from her. Kissing his son's forehead, he laid him on the bed before putting his arms around his wife and moving her back a step.

The doctor moved in to examine the child. He shook his head, saying, 'I'm so very sorry.'

Violet began to wail again as if only now realising her son had died. She fought to get to him. 'Harry... no, no... Harry wake up! Oh God!'

Dr Shaw left a tonic on the bedside table. 'Give that to her, Spencer, it will help her sleep.'

Spencer nodded his thanks, his tears coming thick and fast.

Annie was waiting at the door to see the doctor out before she made tea and breakfast for all in the downstairs kitchen. No one ate, but everyone drank their tea.

Joshua left to inform the undertakers they would be needed while Spencer carried his wife to their bed and administered the tonic.

Kath and Annie held tight to each other as they sobbed their grief, before they would begin the laying out process. Silently they washed Harry's small body and patted him dry gently, before dressing him in his Sunday best clothes. Kath combed his hair then both stood looking down at the child who looked like he was sleeping.

The undertaker's cart rumbled up the snow-covered driveway; a small white coffin sat on the back. Joshua led him to Harry's room. He watched as the undertaker very gently lifted Harry and lay him in the wooden box. 'Sleep well Harry Gittins,' the undertaker whispered before placing the lid on the coffin.

Joshua sniffed back his tears and shook the man's hand. He had told them he wanted the best for his grandson and had paid well for it.

Joshua and the undertaker carried the coffin down to the parlour where it was laid on the table. Candles at the four corners were lit and the curtains remained closed.

The undertaker gave his condolences and left.

Joshua went back to his sobbing wife and their friends.

'Violet?' Kath asked.

'It's all quiet, she's probably sleeping.'

Annie had ensured the curtains in the whole house had stayed closed, announcing to the outside world there had been a death in the family.

Martha and Mary arrived and Annie brought them into her part of the house where Joyce had joined them. Violet and Spencer, she told them, were not up to seeing anyone.

Joshua and Charlie went to visit the vicar to arrange a time for Harry's interment.

The five women sobbed out their grief in Annie's living room.

*

Callers came from all over the town with condolences and flowers and the women thanked them all; Violet was too deep in despair to see anyone.

On the day of the funeral Joshua and Spencer carried the

small white coffin between them at the head of the funerary cortège to St Bartholomew's churchyard. People lined the streets, women sobbed and men doffed their caps as they walked slowly to Harry's final resting place. Kath and Annie held Violet up as she walked behind her husband and his father. No one noticed that the curtains of every house in the streets were closed as a sign of respect.

Standing around the grave, the vicar conducted the service amid sobs.

As the coffin was lowered into the ground, Violet collapsed onto the dirt, her arms outstretched to the tiny white box, and gave a desperate, heart-rending howl. 'Harry... noooooooooooooooo! My baby! Don't, please don't, he'll be all alone! Spencer stop them! Harry...!'

Everyone drew in a breath and held it for a moment as Violet threw back her head and screamed at the sky. 'Why? Why did you take my son from me?'

Spencer lifted her into his arms and swiftly carried her to the coach and sped away home.

Back at Gittins Manor, Annie reflected over the past few days. Everything had happened so fast, the disease hitting the town; Harry's death, other children dying all over Wednesbury. The grief of families spread far and wide and then... no more cases of scarlet fever were reported. The fever had gone as suddenly as it had appeared, leaving death and destruction in its wake.

Over the next few days, Kath and Annie stayed with Violet and Spencer; the other men throwing themselves into their work in an effort to deal with their grief in their own way.

Annie watched Violet as she sat and stared out of the

window of her living room. No words came from her, just an occasional dry sob.

Violet's heart had shattered like a pane of glass and Annie knew it would be something she would never fully recover from, but in time she would be able to cope with it in her own way. For now, she needed the love and support from her family, as well as the Wives, wrapped around her.

Fifty-Three

Grief lay over Wednesbury town like a death shroud, cloaking at least one family in three. Violet, as were other mothers, was deep in despair, and nothing seemed to lift her spirits. Work and the business forgotten, she sat day after day silently weeping for her lost son.

Spencer felt the waves of misery wash over him time after time. One minute he felt able to cope with Harry's death as much as it was possible, the next he sat crying his heart out. He felt he would drown in his misery. He had tried to talk to Violet, to encourage her to speak to him, but she remained in a dark world no one else could penetrate. Spencer was watching his wife waste away and there was nothing he could do to prevent it. The strain of this on top of his own grief was threatening his health too.

Violet stared out of her silent world. Snowflakes fell, adding to the pile already dumped overnight. The fire was lit but she didn't feel its warmth. There were quiet conversations going on, but she heard no words. Her mind only saw and heard Harry as he was growing up. The pictures played in her head but stopped just before he became ill, then began again from his birth. Over and over they played, like she was stuck in time, unable to break the loop.

Her life was conducted in a trance-like state. At night she would take herself to bed, only to lie awake. During the day, she sat staring out of the window. Even Kath could not snap her out of the stupor that held her tight in its grip.

At The Gift Shop work went on as usual, albeit in a sombre mood.

'Violet is worrying me,' Mary said to Martha one day, 'she's not eating much and she's not sleeping.'

'I know, wench. Christ it's hard – no parent should have to bury their child, it ain't right… it's against the laws of nature!'

Giving a nod, Mary went on, 'We have to do something, Martha… we have to!'

'She just needs time, wench, it'll get easier with time.'

'Martha!' Mary snapped without realising the sharpness of her tone until her friend looked at her. 'Sorry… but this grief is killing her!'

'I know, wench, I see it an' all, but there ain't nothing any of us can do. I wish she would come back to work with us, that might help.'

Settling back into the quiet, they continued working, each with their own thoughts about how to help Violet out of the blackness that surrounded her.

*

The snow continued to fall, adding bleakness to misery. The white landscape stood in stark contrast to the factory pall that always hung over Wednesbury.

Trudging to the marketplace, the cold bit to the bone and

Mary shivered as her skirts brushed the snow, soaking the hem, making the going harder with the added weight.

'Hello Mabel,' Mary said to the woman standing at their stall.

Returning the greeting, Mabel arranged the jars, saying, 'Bloody hell, it ain't half cold standing here today!'

'Ar wench, see how it goes, and in an hour if business is slack, get yourself off home.'

Smiling her thanks, Mabel turned to speak to a woman approaching the stall.

As Mary turned to leave, Mabel called, 'Mary... there's a woman here wants a word.' Retracing her steps, Mary looked at the woman Mabel indicated with a jerk of her thumb.

'Take a walk with me, it's too bloody cold to be standing. Mabel, never mind waiting, you just get yourself off home now,' Mary said, finding a handkerchief to wipe her cold nose. Mabel began to pack the stall up, grateful she could go home to a roaring fire.

They walked slowly through the market when the woman said, 'I need the help of the Wednesbury Wives.'

'What's your name wench?' Mary asked as they strolled along.

'Phyllis... Phyllis Brownlow.'

'Well Phyllis Brownlow... what can the wenches do for you?'

'You know them houses at Moore Street, over in Mesty Croft...?' Mary nodded her head, giving the woman leave to continue. 'Well there's a couple of young kids living in one of them. The mother died in childbirth with the littlest, and the scarlet fever took the father. The kids are living on their own but they ain't exactly living in the house.'

'How do you mean, Phyllis?' Mary asked perplexed.

Phyllis went on, 'Well the house belongs to the Burrs Colliery and the boss put another family in when the father passed, so the kids are living in the lavatory outside!'

'What!' Halting in her tracks, Mary looked at the woman by her side. 'How come they ain't been noticed by the family?'

'They go out in the day and then sleep in there at night.'

'How did you find out?' Mary asked.

'My kids told me, they saw them while they were out playing and I was shocked, I can tell you!' Phyllis said, shaking her head.

'Poor little buggers,' Mary said, blowing on her cold hands, 'they'll bloody freeze in there!'

'That's what I thought, but I can't take them in, I've got a house full myself.'

'Right,' Mary said, 'which house is it?'

'I'll show you if you have a minute?'

'Ar wench, come on!' Pushing her arm through Phyllis's in a show of unification, they strode out in an effort to combat the cold. They wound their way carefully down the snow-covered streets before Phyllis stopped and pointed. 'That one, there, on the end.'

'Right, Phyllis, I thank you for this; you can leave it with us now, wench. We'll sort something out for these babies.'

Waving as she left, Phyllis went on her way, leaving Mary staring at the house imprinting it on her mind.

Back in the warmth of The Gift Shop, Mary relayed to the others what Phyllis had told her and set off with Martha and Joyce for Gittins Manor to inform Kath and Annie.

Tea was given as they entered the living room and they saw Violet in her usual place by the window.

Spencer, still in no fit state to be at work, had been talking in low tones, and continued as the women sat by the warm fire. 'I'm at my wits' end,' he whispered. 'I love Violet with all my heart and soul as I do... did... Harry.' A sob caught in his throat as he corrected himself. 'I don't know what else to do! She won't speak to me, half the time she doesn't even know I'm here, and it's breaking my heart all over again!'

Kath sighed, 'I know lad. I see her every day and she's not improving.'

Mary shuffled in her seat, saying, 'I'm sorry Spencer, I can't imagine how both of you feel, and I understand how important this is to you but...'

Nodding, Spencer asked, 'You have something to tell us?'

'Yes... sorry.'

'Go ahead, Mary, let's hear what's worrying you.' Spencer inclined his head.

Mary began to explain about the two children she'd been told were living in an outside lavatory with no parents to care for them.

'Christ Almighty!' Kath exclaimed.

'Poor little buggers will freeze their arses off out there in this weather!' Joyce added.

Martha asked, 'Where are they, do you know?'

'Yes,' Mary acknowledged, 'I went over to take a look. They're in Moore Street over at Mesty Croft, just down from the infants' school.'

'Even if we rescue them, what will happen to them? Where will they go?' Spencer asked, anguish written all over his face.

'Probably the workhouse,' Kath said sadly.

'They won't get the chance if we don't hurry up and do something – them little uns will die of the cold!' Joyce said vehemently.

'Dear God, please don't take any more kids,' Martha prayed in a whisper.

Spencer burst into tears.

'Now look what you've done!' Mary admonished her friend.

'Spencer lad, I'm sorry, I didn't mean to upset you.' Martha patted his arm.

'No, Martha, you're right,' he said, drying his eyes. 'We cannot allow those children to perish.'

'Right then, what are we going to do about this?' Martha asked.

The silence that ensued was suddenly split by Violet's tiny voice, 'Bring them here to me.'

She was still staring out of the window as they all turned their heads as one to look at her.

'Sweetheart!' Spencer rushed to his wife and dropped to his knees by her chair. 'Oh sweetheart!' He laid his head in her lap and she stroked his hair. 'Oh Violet, I thought you were lost to me forever!' He gave a sob and looked up at his wife's pale face. The glazed look in her eyes had gone and they swam with tears.

'I want my baby back,' she said as her tears fell, 'but I know I can't have him. These children you speak of need help, they don't deserve the cards they've been dealt.'

The women who sat by the fire sniffed into their handkerchiefs.

'If you can find them, bring them here,' Violet reiterated.

Kath sobbed her relief that Violet was at last beginning to deal with the grief of losing her boy to scarlet fever. Mary knew she had a way to go, but this was the first step forward in what would take a lifetime in the mending.

As Martha said, 'Right, this needs a deal o' thinkin' on,' Mary could have sworn she saw the hint of a smile at the corners of Violet's mouth.

*

The temperature dropped severely at night and if they didn't act right away, someone could find those children frozen to death one morning.

As the day was pushed aside by darkness, it began to snow again. The snow glittered like millions of tiny diamonds in the light of the moon as Martha, Mary, Joyce and Kath made their way across the heath to Moore Street; their steps were silent as the snow cushioned their footfalls. The moon shone down reflecting off the snow bathing everywhere in a silvery light and Mary pointed to the end house. They swiftly made their way across to it keeping a keen eye out for anyone watching, it may look a little suspicious that four women were trudging about in the snow in the darkness. They then began to close their circle towards the lavatory in the backyard. Martha carefully opened the door as Kath lit a small lantern she carried, hiding it beneath her shawl to prevent prying eyes spotting them. If they were challenged, how could they explain why they were rooting around in someone else's lavvy block? They peered inside and sitting in a corner of the foul-smelling building sat two children, their eyes wide with fear and shivering with cold.

Moving in, Mary whispered, 'It's all right, we ladies are here to help you. We know about your mom and dad and we're going to look after you both.' The little girl began to sob and rushed to her. Scooping her up, Mary wrapped her in a warm shawl she'd brought with her. Watching the boy still cowering in the corner, Mary said quietly, 'There, there, you're all right, you are with the Wednesbury Wives now.' At the mention of the name, the boy rushed to her, hugging her skirts; he too began to cry.

Wrapping the lad in another woollen shawl, Joyce lifted him, saying, 'Come on bab, let's get out of this bloody cold.' The boy giggled at her language despite his misery.

Dousing the lantern before they left, they made their way back to Gittins Manor, talking quietly to the children as they went.

While the women had gone in search of the children, Spencer had drawn his wife to the fireside; he knew she loved to watch the dancing flames in the hearth, and thought it would help settle her nerves.

'Oh darling, it's so good to have you back, I missed you dreadfully.' Spencer held her hand as they sat side by side on the large sofa.

Tears escaped from eyes that seemed too big for her face as she answered, 'I don't know how we'll ever cope without... Harry!'

'Oh my love, my darling!' Spencer held out his arms and she leaned against him finally enjoying the warmth of his body once more. Kissing her hair, he whispered, 'We take things one day at a time – together.'

He felt her nod then she burst into tears. They sat and cried together for what seemed like an eternity before Violet eventually spoke. 'I hope the Wives find those children.'

'If anyone can, the Wednesbury Wives can.' Spencer answered with a smile.

Spencer was still holding his wife as the women bustled into the room carrying the two shivering children.

Joshua had arrived not long before and was busy building up the fire as they sat the trembling children before it. Eyes full of wonder they watched the dancing flames then turned to look at each of the people looking down on them.

Violet saw their dirty faces as they glanced around the

room. They sat very close, clearly afraid each might lose the other. Their ragged clothes hung from extremely thin bodies and their fingernails were chipped and broken. She gasped as she saw neither wore shoes or socks. Dropping to her knees, she began to rub the little girl's dirty feet in her warm hands. Kath did the same with the young boy, trying to get the blood flowing again.

Quietly Violet said, 'My name is Violet and this is my husband, Spencer.'

As Kath moved away, Spencer stepped forward and bending down he asked gently, 'What are your names?'

The little girl spoke, 'I'm Molly Fowler and he's James.' She poked a finger at her brother.

'I ain't James!' spat the boy. 'I'm Jim!' he added, puffing out his chest. For all they had endured, the boy's pride was still intact.

'Well,' Violet said, 'Mary's husband is called Jim as well, so if it's all right with yourself we shall call you Young Jim.'

'That's all right by me,' the lad said proudly.

'Well, children, a hot drink and some food is called for, what do you say?' Violet asked tenderly.

'Yes please!' they chorused.

Violet rang for the maid, who had returned along with the cook once the scarlet fever had left the town. She requested tea for all and hot chocolate for the children. She asked that some warm food be brought also.

It was not long when the cook and maid brought in a tray each for the two youngsters, containing a cup of hot chocolate, a bowl of re-heated stew and chunks of fresh bread. A small plate held a slice of cake.

Everyone watched with smiles as the children balanced

the trays on their knees expertly and tucked in like it would be the last food they would ever eat.

Violet stared and Spencer wrapped an arm around her waist. 'They were famished,' he said quietly. Violet nodded unable to drag her eyes away from the two small children. She thought them to be perhaps not much older than Harry. A dry sob escaped her lips at the thought.

As the children drank their drinks, Kath removed the trays.

More trays with hot tea for the adults were brought in and the empty ones set aside to be taken away, along with the now empty cups.

Suddenly Young Jim burped loudly and said, 'Compliments to the chef.'

The cook smiled as she and the maid left the room.

'Our Jim, you're such a pig!' Molly said, digging him in the ribs.

'I ain't! Our dad used to say it to our mum.'

Titters sounded as everyone watched the two orphans.

Violet's thoughts centred on the young children, thinking how they had appeared to have accepted their parents' demise. She wondered how it was they were so resilient, and dealt with things such as death so much better than adults. How had they come to terms with losing both parents? They had had to scavenge to survive; they had lived in a lavatory in mid-winter to avoid the worst of the weather. Maybe they hadn't had time to dwell on it, so great was their urge to live.

Violet watched as the boy wiped his mouth with the back of his dirty hand. Summoning the maid again, she waited a moment then said, 'I'm sorry to have you running around so much, Betty...' the maid smiled, '...but would you ask cook to see about heating some water for a bath for the children.'

The maid answered, 'Beggin' your pardon, ma'am, but cook thought as you might ask, so I brought in the tin baths from the scullery, and water is on to heat already.'

Violet nodded. 'Thank you – both.'

The maid disappeared and Annie said, 'Right you two, come along with me. You're going to have a nice warm bath.' She led the children down to the kitchen.

Martha asked, 'Now what? They have no more clothes to change into and no home.'

Kath and Joshua eyed each other across the room and Mary and Joyce shook their heads.

'Spencer,' Violet said at last, 'we can't bring our beloved Harry back, but we could offer those two children a good home.'

'We could and I think – we should!'

All had tears in their eyes as they saw Violet smile for the first time in a long while.

They all felt it was Molly and Young Jim who would be bringing Violet back from living in the twilight between life and death, and giving her life purpose once more.

Fifty-Four

Over the following weeks, the orphans settled well in the Gittins' household. Spencer returned to his work at the nail-making factory, and Violet spent her time getting to know her wards. They had accepted her readily as their unofficial guardian and enjoyed her attentions. Each having their own bedroom, they had also been kitted out with new clothes and boots.

Violet slowly came to realise they had brought vitality and laughter to the house, which, for a long time, had felt dark and foreboding. They bickered often, but deep down they were extremely close.

After the evening meal, Spencer would get down on the floor and play games with them. He laughed a lot, but she knew beneath that thin veneer he was terribly sad his own son was not there to play too. She knew this because she felt the same.

Only time would heal their wounds but it would leave behind scars that would forever remind them of their great loss.

Over the winter months, Violet realised she had come to

love the two little orphans as though they were her own. Molly and Young Jim never spoke of their past, only what the future held for them living at Gittins Manor with Violet and Spencer. The relationship between the four of them grew strong and Violet, although never forgetting her own boy, revelled in the love shown to her by the children.

*

Spring eventually pushed winter back a step, and with its arrival came the railway. The line had been laid to connect Wednesbury to Birmingham and there was great excitement surrounding it. The others flatly refused to board the 'great steaming beast', but Violet revelled in travelling on the steam train to New Street Station in Birmingham. The journey took less than half the time it took by horse and carriage and she was able to visit their shop in the town more often. Both of the shops were doing well and gave them a healthy profit. Life went on much as usual, until one day Constable George Micklewhite called in on Violet at Gittins Manor.

Over tea he said, 'It was a really decent thing you did taking those orphans in.'

'I couldn't leave them to starve,' she said as an uneasy feeling crept over her; she felt sure he had not visited just to tell her that.

'Ar... but it ain't that I came to see you about,' he said, as if reading her mind.

'I thought not,' Violet said as she watched the Constable search for the words to explain his visit.

'Last week Judge Stanhope let Ernie Pitt go from jail after he was accused of raping a wench on the heath...'

Violet's hand flew to her mouth and she gasped in horror.

'Ar, the Judge said that the wench had probably asked for it as she was on the heath by herself an' all.'

'What! So now us women can't cross the heath alone for fear of being attacked?' Violet was furious.

Bringing his hands up palms toward her, he went on, 'Hear me out, wench. Ernie Pitt denied the accusation, saying he was in the Three Swans Inn on the Holyhead Road all night drinking with his mates. Now, no one I spoke to saw him in there on the night in question... Obviously he don't have any mates...' The Constable grinned at his own wit.

Feeling all colour drain from her face, Violet watched the Constable shift in his chair. Keeping her counsel, Violet listened as he went on.

'Ernie Pitt insisted he was at the pub drinking and the Judge believed him.'

'And that proves what exactly?' Violet snapped.

'Well,' the Constable blustered, 'it doesn't *exactly* prove anything...'

'Who was the girl who accused Ernie Pitt of raping her?' Violet asked, her mind in a whirl.

'Phoebe Slater...' said the Constable as he looked down at the helmet lying in his lap.

'Phoebe Slater? Martha's daughter?' Violet asked incredulously as he nodded. 'Oh my God! Does Martha know of this?'

Shaking his head, he looked up. 'There is more to this than meets the eye,' the Constable said, 'young Phoebe isn't the sort to go accusing people... and, how come Judge Stanhope let Ernie Pitt go just like that?'

Constable Micklewhite was voicing the questions falling

over themselves in Violet's mind, then she asked, 'Tell me, Constable Micklewhite... why you have brought this to me?'

'Well, Phoebe is the daughter of your friend and...', his eyes met hers, 'you are one of the Wednesbury Wives.' A knowing smile crossed his lips before he brought his teacup to them to finish his tea. His eyebrows rose and wiggled.

*

Rallying the others in her kitchen at Gittins Manor, Violet explained about Constable Micklewhite's visit.

'Martha, I hate to tell you but it was your Phoebe who made the accusation against Ernie Pitt,' Violet said as gently as she could manage.

'What! Our Phoebe...? But she hasn't said anything to me... how come I am the last to bloody know?' Standing up, she growled, 'I'll bloody kill that man, you see if I don't... the bastard!'

Annie intervened, saying, 'This needs a deal o' thinkin' on.'

Despite the anger boiling inside her, Martha's mouth tilted upwards at Annie's use of her own stock phrase.

While the meeting continued, Joyce ran down to Hobbins Street to fetch Phoebe from Martha's house.

Violet said, 'It's that Judge that worries me.'

'Why?' Annie asked.

'Well, Annie, think about it. Young Phoebe accuses Ernie Pitt of... attacking... her on the heath; the Judge lets him go when Ernie says he was in the Three Swans. Now then, what is the Judge getting from Ernie Pitt that would secure his release so easily?'

Violet looked around the table at faces pondering her words before Kath asked, 'Where does Ernie Pitt work?'

Violet answered with, 'Constable Micklewhite said Ernie unloads cargo at the canal.'

'Hmmm,' said Annie, 'cargo such as brandy?'

The penny dropped with them all at the same time.

'Judge Stanhope likes his tipple an' no mistake,' said Martha, 'but would he let Ernie go for a bottle of brandy?'

'Not a bottle, Martha,' Violet said, 'but maybe for a case?'

Audible sighs filled the kitchen as Violet rang for the maid to bring some more tea.

Just then the door opened and Joyce walked in with Phoebe Slater trailing behind, her head bowed.

Martha rushed to her daughter, wrapping her arms around her sobbing, 'Oh wench, why didn't you tell me?'

'How could I?' Phoebe sobbed back. 'Besides I thought to go through the proper channels and report it to the police. I thought the Judge would deal with it!'

'Ar well, he didn't did he? But we will, be sure of it!' Martha added, leading Phoebe to a chair.

Amid tears from everyone, Phoebe told of how taking the short cut across the heath to the marketplace, Ernie Pitt had appeared. At her rebuff to his request that she be his sweetheart, he had attacked her.

'But the Constable said you accused him of rape!' Violet said.

'No Violet, I didn't! I told the police he'd attacked me and *tried* to rape me but I kicked him really hard in the... and when he fell down, I ran!'

'Thank God!' muttered Martha.

'This gets more complicated by the minute,' said Kath, 'perhaps we should speak with Joshua and Spencer about it?'

Everyone nodded their agreement.

*

Joshua, Kath, Spencer and Violet sat around the fire in the living room at Gittins Manor trying to decide what should be done about the situation of Ernie Pitt and Judge Stanhope.

'Maybe the Wednesbury Wives should make a visit to the Judge?' Violet suggested, not entirely convinced on this occasion it would work.

'No Violet wench,' Joshua pondered aloud, 'it's a man needed to deal with the Judge…' Seeing her wince, he went on, 'Now I'm not saying you can't deal with it, I am just saying he'll more likely talk to a man than a woman. Judge Stanhope has no time for women Violet, as I'm sure you know, so maybe us men should tackle him.'

Nodding, she saw the sense of his words.

He continued, 'As for Ernie Pitt…'

'We can take care of him!' Violet spat.

'Right then! Now, Spencer lad, we need to find out just what Judge Stanhope is up to.'

'How, Father?' Spencer asked.

'Well now… how would it be if we had a lavish dinner and invited the hoi polloi of Wednesbury? We could say we are raising money to… build a new courthouse!'

Clapping her hands together, Violet said, 'Joshua, you are so clever to think of that… of course the Judge would attend!'

'Ar, and with enough brandy inside him… many a slip betwixt cup and lip!'

Fifty-Five

The Judge's euphonious tones could be heard across the room as dinner was served the following Saturday night at Gittins Manor. The bosses of the collieries, factories and big businesses were all in attendance and ideas for raising the money for the new courthouse building were flowing as fast as copious amounts of wine were consumed. Slowly the guests drifted away as the evening wore on until only Joshua, Spencer and Judge Stanhope remained. The men took their brandy and cigars into the study.

'So Joshua,' said the Judge, holding out his brandy goblet for a refill as he sat sprawled in a leather armchair in Spencer's study, 'what made you decide to raise money for a new courthouse? Not that I ain't grateful of course!'

'Well Judge,' Joshua smiled, 'the one you are in now is falling down!'

'True enough,' Stanhope said as he drank greedily already showing signs of being tipsy.

'Judge,' Spencer said, 'you appear to be getting busier than ever in that old building, so a newer, bigger one makes much more sense.'

'I am fair rushed off my feet and no mistake,' again the Judge held out his glass.

Refilling it, Joshua placed the bottle on the table next to the Judge and his nod of appreciation showed he understood its meaning.

'Ar, just the other day I had Constable Micklewhite telling me how a wench cried rape on the heath. Bloody woman...' Judge Stanhope took a great swallow of his drink.

'Really?' probed Spencer.

'Ar really lad, she pointed the finger at young Ernie Pitt... nice young man that one.'

Exchanging a brief glance with Spencer who raised his eyebrows, Joshua went to the cupboard to fetch another bottle of brandy.

'Oh I think I know him, he works at the canal, doesn't he?' Spencer asked.

Joshua saw the Judge eye Spencer warily and he moved to empty the last of the brandy bottle into Stanhope's glass before removing the stopper from a fresh bottle.

The Judge's red nose from years of drinking couldn't catch the aroma of the brandy but his eyes lit up at the sight of the newly opened bottle. He was not a tall man, and good food and constant imbibing of alcohol took their toll on his body, making him almost as wide as he was tall.

'I believe he does,' he answered with yet another brandy in his hand, 'not quite sure what the wench hoped to get out of the accusation... unless it was a husband!' The Judge let out a guffaw at his own comment, and Spencer and Joshua pretended to laugh along with him.

'How come you never married, Judge?' Spencer asked, all innocence.

'Married? Me? Not bloody likely. I much prefer the

company of men. I'm not having a woman telling me what to do. I haven't got time for bossy women and their nonsense!'

'I can understand that,' Joshua added. He was finding it taxing to hold down his disdain for this man. 'A man in your position. So what happened with Ernie Pitt and the wench, Judge?'

'What? Oh yes…' Helping himself to more drink.

Joshua rolled his eyes at Spencer discreetly, not that the Judge would have noticed as his gaze was firmly fixed on the brandy bottle!

The Judge went on, 'Ar well, the lad didn't do it, did he? So I let him go.' The hand holding his cigar waved through the air in a dismissive gesture.

'Was there any proof of what the woman alleged had happened?' Spencer asked.

'Proof? It's a woman, lad! I don't need bloody proof!' the Judge's voice boomed across the room.

'Calm yourself, Judge, you just get another brandy down you,' Joshua said. 'The lad was only asking.'

'You listen to me, young Spencer,' the Judge said, calmer now his glass was full again, 'I am the law around these parts and what I says, goes. You understand me, boy?' The cigar hand pointed at Spencer as the Judge waited for an answer.

Spencer nodded with a quiet, 'Of course, my apologies Judge.'

Judge Stanhope harrumphed into his glass before saying, 'Bloody women are a menace to us men!' Getting unsteadily to his feet, he made his way through the door, 'I thank you both for your hospitality.'

Handing him an unopened bottle of brandy for his journey home, Joshua asked conspiratorially, 'Better than the stuff brought up the canal eh?'

Sniggering, the Judge winked, whispering, 'I told Ernie, the next time I want the good stuff!'

The driver flicked the horse's reins just as the Judge climbed onto the footplate of the carriage, causing him to fall inward onto the seat. The Judge began to harangue the driver for his stupidity then continued to mutter obscenities under his breath. With a cheeky smile and salute to the two men standing on the steps, the driver set off, taking a crapulous Judge Stanhope home.

*

The meeting of the Wives took place in Martha's living room the following day and Spencer and Joshua made it their business to attend. Relating the tale of Judge Stanhope and Ernie Pitt, they settled with tea as murmurs sounded around the table.

It was obvious to everyone that the Judge could not be allowed to continue to remain in his judicial position as things stood. Clearly he could not be trusted to judge anyone fairly. The question was, how could they oust him from that position? It was certain the Judge enjoyed the perks afforded him and therefore would definitely not consider retiring of his own free will. They had to find a way to besmirch his name; give him a good reason to relinquish his role of judge.

Martha said quietly as if to herself, 'If he doesn't like women...'

Joyce piped up, 'Maybe he prefers men!' All eyes turned to her as she said, 'What? It goes on!'

'It's a point to investigate,' Violet added, 'maybe we should find out.'

Martha said, 'My Geordie and Mary's Jim could watch

over him for a while, see where he goes, what he does and who he meets.'

'Good idea,' Violet smiled, 'that might provide us with enough information to confront him if nothing else.'

'He's already shot himself in the foot admitting about the brandy,' Kath responded.

'Right then, that just leaves what to do about Ernie Pitt,' Violet said.

'If he wants to have his evil way with women he should go to the brothel down Moorcroft Row!' Mary mumbled. As the talking ceased, she added, 'I know, I know... I've done it again!'

'How do you know about that place, Mary Forbes?' Martha asked sharply.

Mary sighed, 'Everybody knows about it; all of Wednesbury. I see you do as well.'

Martha harrumphed as the others smiled behind their teacups.

*

It was at the next meeting a few days later that the story unfolded. Violet and Martha had walked across the heath to Moorcroft Old Colliery, down Bull Lane and into Moorcroft Row amid the stares of women coming and going from the building at the end of the row of the only six terraced houses left standing. Martha banged on the door and it was opened by an older woman with rouge on her cheeks and lips. Dressed in a flimsy gown her eyes widened when she saw the two women standing before her.

Violet said, 'She was rather taken aback until Martha told her who we were.'

'Ar,' said Martha, 'she was a nice woman as it turned out, took us in for tea.'

Giggles sounded as Mary put in, 'Bloody hell, I never thought to see the day Martha Slater would go into a brothel!'

'Ar well, it was business...' The giggles turned to full laughter as Martha recognised the irony of her statement.

Violet explained how the woman had listened to the story of Ernie Pitt and Martha's daughter, Phoebe. The woman had asked why Ernie wasn't in jail and Martha told her how Judge Stanhope had dealt with the matter.

Kath asked, 'How did she respond to that?'

'She said we have to get Ernie Pitt to the brothel somehow and leave the rest to them!'

'What are they going to do?' Mary asked, pushing her head forward with interest.

'I don't bloody know!' Martha snapped before seeing the hurt look on Mary's face. 'Sorry wench, but I'm not sure what their plan is. They said we should be walking alongside the canal on Friday morning and be sure to bring Ernie's mother with us.'

Joshua added, 'Well Spencer and I can get Ernie to the brothel, can't we lad?' Watching Spencer and Violet exchange an embarrassed look, he said quickly, 'Don't worry, Violet, I promise to bring your man straight back home after we drop Ernie off!'

*

Geordie and Jim had discreetly followed the Judge for the rest of the week and reported back that Stanhope regularly visited a property in Paradise Street, Birmingham, a big house in its own grounds that stood near the Town Hall.

They had watched in the descending darkness of early evening as he had entered and then they quietly crept to the window to see inside. Listening carefully they had sat outside well into the night before hiding themselves in the bushes of the garden as the Judge emerged.

Glancing around him, the Judge had kissed his companion passionately before taking his leave. The Judge, it seemed, had found himself a lover... a male lover!

Fifty-Six

Martha sat now in the kitchen at Gittins Lodge surrounded by the other members of their select group.

Joshua had explained how he and Spencer had wandered along the canal towpath laughing about the house at the end of Moorcroft Row. Ernie Pitt, lounging on the canal side rather than working, overheard their conversation, and asked them about it. Imparting the knowledge to him, they had made it seem a place not to be missed, and said they would be willing to take him there if he wished to go. Ernie was all for it, and that very night had seen them visit the 'ladies of the night' at the house on Moorcroft Row. As soon as Ernie had disappeared with the lady of his choice, Joshua and Spencer had thanked the woman running the house and returned home to await the outcome.

Martha then related the events of Ernie Pitt and the canalside.

Martha had wound her way around the marketplace the following Friday morning looking for one person in particular, and then she had spotted the woman. Ernie Pitt's mother, Gladys, was arguing with a stallholder.

She heard Gladys screech as she approached, 'It's daylight bloody robbery! You can stick it up your arse!'

'Hello Gladys,' Martha had said, walking up to the woman.

'Oh hello Martha. The price he's asking for that scrag end of mutton!'

'I know wench, it's a disgrace.' Turning away from Gladys, Martha winked at the stallholder's smile. 'How's life with you then, Gladys?' Martha had asked as they strolled between the market stalls.

'Same as ever, Martha.'

'I've not seen much of that lad of yours lately wench, is he working?'

'Oh ar,' said Gladys, 'down at the cut unloading stuff.' Martha nodded, and Gladys went on, 'He's proper worn out, I don't know where he goes at night but he ain't at home with me and his father.'

'Got a sweetheart has he?' Martha had probed.

'I don't think so, he ain't mentioned anything to us about seeing a girl.'

'You don't think he's up to no good though, Gladys?'

Casting a glance at the woman by her side, Martha saw her planted seed of doubt instantly begin to grow.

'No,' Gladys had said swiftly, 'he's a good lad; he wouldn't shame us by doing something he shouldn't.'

'I'm sure you are right,' Martha had said, pouring more doubt into the woman's mind.

Parting ways at the end of the stalls, Martha had watched Gladys hurry away in the direction of the canal.

Kath and Violet had been casually strolling along by the

barges moored up in the Monway Basin glancing at the wares up for sale, all the time watching for Gladys Pitt. Spotting her at last they had walked slowly to within earshot of the woman.

Ernie Pitt was lounging in the weak sunshine as his mother approached him. Standing over him, she demanded answers. Why was he sitting on his arse and not working? Where did he go at night? What did he do when he got there? What time did he get in from wherever he'd been?

Ernie had begun to splutter, trying to find answers as the barrage of questions rained down on him.

Martha had arrived on the scene and moved towards Kath and Violet as Gladys grabbed her son's ear, dragging him to his feet.

Suddenly a voice shouted across to him, 'Ernie love, you coming to see me again tonight?'

All eyes turned to a woman from the brothel bedecked in flimsy dress, no underwear that could be ascertained, and over-exaggerated make-up. She rushed to Ernie, saying to the woman who had hold of him, 'You get your hands off my man, who the hell do you think you are?'

'His mother!' Gladys had snapped.

Ernie had visibly wilted as the two women screamed at each other and the crowds drew near, enjoying the spectacle. Jeers and taunts rang out as the women screeched insults and Ernie tried to slip away. His mother catching one arm and the prostitute catching the other, they pulled and Ernie cried out at the pain in his shoulders.

Kath, Violet and Martha had strolled away together, laughing as the insults and screaming faded behind them.

Looking at the others now, Martha said, 'I have a feeling that boy's heading for a pasting!'

Then discussions on how to deal with Judge Stanhope ensued.

'The thing is,' Violet said, 'how many more has he let loose? How many others got away with God knows what in exchange for a case of brandy?'

'He needs to be confronted, if he doesn't agree to our suggestions... maybe we should shame him, same as young Ernie,' Annie added.

Mary said, 'We can't shame the Judge in front of his mother – she's dead!'

Ripples of laughter filled the room.

'We need a plan,' Joshua said.

In unison they all chorused, 'This needs a deal o' thinkin' on!'

Violet cast her mind back to Mr Potter and how he had tried to blackmail Joshua out of five hundred pounds after kidnapping her mother. The idea began to form in her mind and suddenly she said, 'We could blackmail the Judge into retiring... threaten to expose his secret of having a boyfriend in Birmingham!' She screwed up her nose at the thought of the fat man who she disliked intensely. 'Spencer, could you and Joshua go and see him and let him know we're on to him?'

'Indeed, my love... we could indeed!'

*

Phoebe's mood was disconsolate as Martha had arrived home, until she relayed the events in the market.

'Oh Mother!' Phoebe giggled, 'Serves the bugger right!'

'He's been shamed in front of his mother and half the town, wench, and it's my guess his father will take the strap to him.'

'No more than he deserves,' Phoebe said as she poured tea.

'You want to leave it at that then?' Martha asked, sipping the hot tea.

'For Ernie Pitt, yes... but...' Phoebe looked at her mother unsure of how to continue.

'But...?' Martha asked tentatively.

'Well, that Judge let him go, Mother! After he attacked me on the heath – the Judge just let him go!'

'Ar well, you leave the Judge to us Wives, wench, we are sorting that one out.' Martha watched as her daughter accepted her words without question.

'Thank you, Mother, and the others too. I should have come to you in the first place.'

'Ar wench, you should,' Martha said as they smiled at each other.

Fifty-Seven

Joshua and Spencer trotted through Brunswick Park and down Walsall Road to the Judge's large house in Wood Green and they were invited in, being asked how well they were doing raising the money for the new courthouse.

'We are here on another matter, Judge,' Joshua said as they all sat down in the living room.

'I see,' Judge Stanhope stood to get himself a drink, holding the bottle out to his visitors. Joshua and Spencer shook their heads as the Judge shrugged his shoulders and returned to his seat with a full glass of brandy in his hand. 'What is this other matter I can help you with?'

'We need you to retire from office,' Spencer said simply.

Spluttering his drink, Stanhope brushed the brandy from his clothes as he barked, 'You what?'

'Retire, Judge... losing your hearing?' Spencer said his voice calm as he watched disbelief shadow the Judge's face.

'What the...? Now you listen to me...'

'No Judge. You listen to me!' Maintaining his calmness,

Spencer allowed an underlying hint of menace into his voice. Leaning forward, he went on, 'You are not fit to hold the office of judge. You proved that by what you said about the women of this town and by how you let a man out of jail for a case of brandy!'

'That was a gift!' the Judge shouted.

'It was a bribe!' Spencer spat back, anger lacing his words. 'How many others have bribed you to let them go free?'

'That is slander!' the Judge retorted, his jowls shaking with anger.

'You call it slander – I call it truth!'

'Call it what you will,' the Judge laughed, suddenly full of bravado, 'but you can't make me retire!' Emptying his glass in one swallow, he looked at Spencer with arrogant triumph in his eyes.

Trumping his triumph with his own, Spencer said, 'All right, have it your way, but we'll see what the people of the town have to say when they know you have a lover... a male lover!'

The light in the Judge's eyes instantly died and his mouth hung open. 'How did...?' Realising his mistake of almost admitting to this truth, Stanhope clamped his jaws shut.

'The Wednesbury Wives have been on your case, Judge Stanhope. Now, have we reached an agreement?'

They watched the thoughts of the impending shame, not to mention his breaking of the law, travel through the Judge's mind as he nodded, his jowls shaking again.

'Good man,' Spencer said as he and his father stood to leave, 'we'll expect to hear the news of your retirement in the next few days, if not... you and the man you are seeing will be exposed for all Wednesbury to see. Good evening *Judge* Stanhope.'

The two men left the Judge drinking brandy like it was the last he would ever taste.

*

Sure enough, the next couple of days saw Judge Stanhope announce his retirement and a younger man, reputedly as straight as a die, take his place.

The *Herald* made a big song and dance about Stanhope standing down from office and Joshua and Spencer watched the ceremony as the Mayor presented the Judge with a gold fob watch in honour of his past services to the town. The now retired Judge accepted the gift graciously, a forced smile on his face, which turned to a grimace as he saw Joshua and Spencer shake hands with each other.

'Another job well done, lad,' Joshua said amid the applause ringing out as the Judge smiled awkwardly.

'Indeed Father, but I can't help feeling he deserved much more. He's being given a hero's exit here.' Spencer said as his eyes turned once more to Stanhope. As their eyes locked, Spencer winked and the 'Judge' scowled.

'Aye lad, but at least he's out of our hair now.' Joshua said noting the Judge's bad tempered expression.

As the congratulatory noise died down, the Mayor spoke again. He explained that he was happy that his last act as Mayor was to have presented Stanhope with his gold watch. Holding his hands up to the gathered crowd, the Mayor announced he too was retiring from office. Glancing over at Joshua, he said a younger man was needed in the position of Mayor of Wednesbury.

The reporters dashed away from the Town Hall steps to write their columns for the next edition of the *Herald*.

*

Over tea in the kitchen of Gittins Lodge, Violet urged her father-in-law to stand for election of Mayor.

'I saw the look the Mayor gave you when he announced he was retiring,' Spencer said to his father, 'even *he* thinks you should stand.'

'What about the factory?' Joshua asked.

Giving her husband a smile, Kath said, 'Joshua, you could do both, run the factory and run for Mayor.'

'I think Violet or yourself is more deserving of this than me,' Joshua said.

'Oh goodness!' Kath exclaimed. 'A female Mayor? No Joshua, people are just coming round to the idea of women being in business so a woman standing for Mayor would be a step too far. We, I think, are more than happy with our roles in the Wednesbury Wives. It's you who should stand for Mayor, don't you agree Violet?'

Violet nodded, 'You would make a fine job of it Joshua.'

Candidates for the position of Mayor were submitted, Joshua being one of them, and in no time at all he found himself accepting the chain of office from his predecessor. Joshua Gittins had become the Mayor of Wednesbury.

At the ceremony in the Town Hall, everyone was present including Molly and Young Jim. Kath linked her arm through Spencer's as they watched the proceedings.

'Your mother would have been very proud of him... as we all are,' she whispered.

'It's nice that we know the new Mayor,' Young Jim said as he stood beside Spencer.

'Is he our granddad now?' Molly asked.

'In a way,' Spencer said, 'not legally but I'm sure he'd love it if you called him Granddad.'

Violet added quietly, 'And our new Mayor is to have another grandchild!'

Fifty-Eight

On a Saturday morning a few weeks after Joshua was sworn in as the new Town Mayor, Violet was sitting in the living room with Spencer, Molly and Young Jim.

'Spencer,' she said quietly, 'I think we should formally adopt Molly and Jim.'

The children, sitting playing with their toys on the floor by the fire, looked up at her. They didn't understand what 'adopt' meant, but they had heard their names mentioned and knew it either boded good or bad.

Spencer grinned from his place on the floor with the children, saying, 'I wholeheartedly agree!'

Joining the three on the carpet, Violet explained. 'Children, Spencer and I would like to adopt you into our family.' Seeing them look at each other in bewilderment, she went on, 'It means we have to go to the Judge and ask his permission for you both to live with us forever... or at least until you are old enough to have families of your own.'

The children rushed to Violet and threw their arms around her, tears coursing down their little faces.

'Steady now, remember Violet is to have a new baby too,' Spencer said, his smile lighting up his face.

Molly and Jim muttered their apologies as they sat close to Violet who draped an arm around each of them.

Young Jim asked, 'What if the Judge says no?'

'Oh, he won't say that,' Violet assured the worried child. 'However, it will mean you have to change your surname from Fowler to Gittins. How do you both feel about that?'

'That's all right with us, ain't it Molly?' Jim said. 'As long as we can stay with you.' Molly nodded her agreement.

'Good, then that's settled. We'll all go and visit the Judge first thing on Monday morning.'

Molly threw her arms around Violet and said, 'Thank you Mama.'

Violet looked over the child's head at her husband, seeing the surprised look on his face as they all began to play on the carpet once more.

*

Sitting in the Judge's chamber, Violet explained their intention of adopting Molly and Jim.

The Judge looked at the children, Molly sitting on Violet's lap and Jim sat in a chair next to Spencer, doing his best to look grown-up. 'So children, how do you feel about what is being proposed, would you like to live with Violet and Spencer forever?'

The children nodded their agreement and the Judge went on, 'And how do you feel about being called Molly and Jim Gittins?'

'Smashing!' Molly said and everyone laughed.

'Right then,' said the Judge, looking at Spencer then Violet, 'I'll get the paperwork drawn up for your signatures.'

Shaking hands first with the adults, the Judge bent down to shake hands with the children. 'It's very nice to meet you Molly Gittins, and you too Jim Gittins.'

Jim replied, 'Thank you sir.'

Violet glowed with pride and happiness as they left the Judge's chambers.

Back home, once again playing on the carpet of the living room, Spencer said, 'I think we should build a castle... Gittins Castle... it has a nice ring to it, don't you think?'

Jim said, 'This is our stronghold, no one will ever invade the Gittins fortification.'

Violet and Spencer exchanged a surprised smile before they all set to erecting the blocks of the wooden castle.

Every block set in place represented constructing and cementing their relationship together as a family; a relationship that would forever hold strong; a relationship they knew would remain warm and loving for the rest of their lives.

Violet watched the children playing with Spencer, delighting in their squeals of laughter, and she thought again of Harry taken by the fever. She thought of all that had passed over the years of her growing up and decided in an instant that there would only be good things in her life from now on.

The following day she requested a special meeting of the Wives; the meeting to take place on Friday. The women were intrigued but Violet would say no more on the matter, and as much as they asked, she would not be drawn. For the next few days, the mystery of a special meeting was uppermost in the women's minds.

Friday morning finally arrived and tea and cake was

served before Violet finally joined them in the living room at Gittins Manor.

'Ladies,' she began, 'we have, over the years, acquired ourselves quite a reputation.' Sniggers sounded and Violet held her hand up for silence. 'We now appear to have the police constable and the new Judge as our allies.' Seeing nods from the others, she went on, 'I now think it's time to concentrate solely on our business – the one that makes us money.' Glances passed between the women before Violet spoke again. 'I asked you here today to tell you I remain one of the Wednesbury Wives in name only. It is my suggestion that, in the future, we leave the punishment of the criminals of this town to the police. I now want to know how you all feel about this.'

Mary was the first to speak. 'Thank Christ for that! I've been wanting out for some time, I just didn't know how to say!'

'You open your mouth and the words come out!' Martha said sarcastically.

'Well I'll say this,' Mary went on, 'all this dealing with other folks' problems is turning me into an old woman!'

'I know the feeling, wench,' Martha agreed, 'it's been making me feel ill for a while now. I'll be glad to see the back of it.'

Each of the women in turn agreed with Violet and Mary, saying it was weighing heavily on them; each would be relieved to be free of the burden they had carried for so long.

Violet explained that the market grapevine would be informed that they were no longer in the business of dealing with wayward or violent husbands, but that the threat of being exposed to the Wives should help with their problems.

With more tea, Violet called for a toast. The women stood

and as they raised their cups in salute, she said, 'To the demise of the Wednesbury Wives.' Clinking cups was the solemn oath of every woman there that their violent behaviour of days gone by was at an end.

Turning the conversation back to the previous one, Violet wanted everyone's assurance that the women were all of the same mind. 'We have to promise each other we are finished with our old "business",' she said, 'ladies... promise me.'

Hands went to hearts and they gave their oath. Violet was satisfied. 'We can inform our men of our decision and the oath taken – I'm sure they will be delighted!'

Happy she could now turn her attention to her family, Violet watched the women she loved with all her heart. Although they would conduct no further 'business', she knew they would always be there for each other no matter what the future held in store for them.